Eleanor Coggins isn't exactly skilled in the art of cat burglary, but when she sneaks into the lavish West-field home to steal information about her best friend's death, she runs into an irresistible accomplice who gets her into a whole lot of trouble. . . .

"Get your hand off me, you perverted creep," she growled.

"Gladly, you homicidal thief. As soon as I get what I want."

She was about to spit a well-constructed string of profanities at him when the door opened forcefully and a dozen recessed lights flared on.

Eleanor tugged her dress down, but not fast enough to escape the scathing notice of the well-dressed woman standing in the doorway.

The woman's disdainful eyes shifted from Eleanor and rested on the man who'd just had his hand up her dress.

"Would you like to tell me what's going on here, or should I assume the usual?"

He stepped aside slightly, and Eleanor realized he'd made a vain attempt to shield her from view.

"Hello, Mother," he said, and Eleanor nearly did a double take. "I don't believe you've met my fiancée."

This title is also available as an eBook.

LIE
to
ME

STARR
AMBROSE

Pocket Books
New York   London   Toronto   Sydney

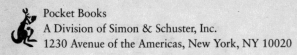

Pocket Books
A Division of Simon & Schuster, Inc.
1230 Avenue of the Americas, New York, NY 10020

This book is a work of fiction. Names, characters, places, and incidents either are products of the author's imagination or are used fictitiously. Any resemblance to actual events or locales or persons, living or dead, is entirely coincidental.

First Pocket Books paperback edition December 2008

POCKET and colophon are registered trademarks of Simon & Schuster, Inc.

For information about special discounts for bulk purchases, please contact Simon & Schuster Special Sales at 1-800-456-6798 or business@simonandschuster.com

Designed by Kate Moll
Cover photo by Plush Studios/Photodisc

Manufactured in the United States of America

10 9 8 7 6 5 4 3 2 1

ISBN-13: 978–1–4165–8664–7
ISBN-10:   1–4165–8664–4

To Jim, Stevie, and Ariana
for always believing

Acknowledgments

Much of novel writing is a solitary effort. But several special people deserve thanks for making this book what it is.

My critique partners, Philine Tucker, Patti Shenberger, and Diane Lutz, talented writers and amazing friends. I wouldn't be here without you.

Margie Carroll, author and friend, for insights into both my writing and the business of writing.

Kyria Joyner, brilliant sister-in-law, who said, "There's this contest you should enter . . ."

David Reynolds, who told me I should be writing romance; Adam Bernard, Linda Brender, Sally Wells, and Brad Field for insights and suggestions when I first followed that advice.

Eileen LaDuke, who saw my very first stories and still called me a writer.

My brother Andrew Cohoe for unquestioned faith, and my mother, Pauline Cohoe, who always encouraged my writing, but who thinks there aren't nearly enough dead bodies in my stories.

Chapter One

Eleanor Coggins paused before the three-foot-high hedge surrounding the dark patio. Scooting her tight dress up her thighs, she carefully hoisted a leg over the greenery. Midway across, a twig snagged her hose, her shoe heel caught in the hidden wrought-iron fence, and she fell in a sprawling heap onto the rough slate patio.

Eleanor grimaced and mentally added cat burglar to the long list of professions she sucked at.

Brushing off her palms, she stood cautiously. The nearby windows remained dark, and the secluded patio was blacker than the lawn she had just crossed, where she'd had to slink past streaks of yellow light from the large windows.

She hiked her skirt into place with a firm twist and brushed at her rear end to remove any grit she might have picked up from the flagstones. Not that the immaculate Westfield house and grounds would have a particle of dirt out of place this Friday evening. Even in exclusive Bloomfield Hills, Michigan, the grandiose Westfield mansion made its neighbors look shabby.

Eleanor tried to fluff some semblance of neatness into her long blond waves, then peered closely at her left leg. In the dark she couldn't see where the bush had torn her nylons. She could feel the hole, though, and the run that snaked up her inner thigh to the heavy leather strap of the holster. Damn. She pivoted her leg, checking to make sure the gun didn't show. If she had to make an appearance at the party, she needed to blend in. Firearms were probably frowned upon.

The strap was so tight her left leg was nearly white from the lack of circulation, and the weight of the gun made her feel so off-balance she nearly limped, but she felt confident that no one could see what she hid on her upper thigh. As long as she didn't cross her legs and shoot her toes off.

The tiny purse she'd slung over her neck had flopped onto her back during her fall. Eleanor repositioned the bag on her shoulder and removed two items. She switched on the little penlight, then held it between her teeth while she set to work with the lock pick on the French doors.

At least this part of the job went smoothly. The hours of diligent practice in the back room of her cousin's hardware store had paid off. After two minutes of concentration, studiously ignoring the laughter and music drifting from the front part of the house, she heard the lock click back. Eleanor softly turned the handle on the door, then slipped into the darkened library.

She was in the enemy's lair.

Her quick, nervous breaths sucked in the scent of leather and stale cigars. Shadowy rows of books rose beside her. Eleanor walked along them, running the tiny light over volumes of leather-bound classics, and snorted quietly. It had to be for show. A man could not have been exposed to such literary enrichment without absorbing a few virtues. And as far as Eleanor knew, Banner Westfield had none.

The penlight suddenly hit open space and slid over glistening blue scales. Eleanor jumped, then shone the light along the mounted body of a fish, mouth agape and dead eye unnaturally bright. Stepping back, she bumped into an expanse of leather large enough to be a cow, knocking the wheeled chair against a desk.

Cursing under her breath, she steadied the spinning chair, then stepped around it. The desk before her was a vast expanse of polished wood and inset leather, gleaming expensively even in the thin beam of her penlight. Her lips curved at the white frame of a computer monitor and the dull glint of brass locks on the side desk drawers. El Dorado. Right where it was supposed to be. Janet had been sitting at this desk when she found the information that got her killed. If Janet could find it, so could she. Only she wouldn't confront Banner with it like Janet had. She'd take it straight to the police.

At least that was the plan. If her answers weren't here, she might have to resort to the gun, an option she didn't want to think about.

She glanced at the dark bulk of double doors directly across the room. Still closed. And with the party at full tilt, they should stay that way. Unless someone felt the urgent need for a paper clip, or a quick dose of Tolstoy to go with their vodka, she should have a couple hours of undisturbed snooping and pilfering.

She snapped on the small brass desk lamp and blinked at the sudden glare. As her eyes adjusted, she glanced nervously at the hulking shadows of more bovine-sized chairs and sofas. Between the books, desk, and chairs, it was a wonder the room didn't smell like a cattle yard. Dismissing her prickling sense of unease, she bent to apply her lock pick to the lower desk drawer.

"I wouldn't do that."

Eleanor gasped and dropped the pick. The voice was low, menacing, and about ten feet to her right. She fumbled for the pick on the floor with trembling fingers while peering into the shadows. She didn't have to look closely. A tall man stepped forward and loomed over her. His body was visible in the dim desk light, but from the neck up he blended into the dark room behind him, a headless presence dressed in trousers, vest, white shirt, and tie.

Eleanor's fingers closed around the lock pick. From her crouched position she asked in an unsteady voice, "Who are you?" and immediately chastised herself for sounding so defensive. If she was going to bluff her way out of this, she had to be more assertive. And it better be a good bluff because she needed to be in this house.

She meant to stand with slow dignity, but she yelped in surprise as he wrapped one hand around her upper arm and hauled her to her feet.

"I think the appropriate question is who are *you*? And what are you doing here?"

He had her beat on assertiveness, with a good amount of anger thrown in. He didn't let go of her arm, and in fact pulled her closer to get a better look. She tilted her chin up and boldly met his gaze. His face was a grim visage in shades of gray, with dark, color-less eyes that drilled into her own from mere inches away, like a nearsighted predator zeroing in on its prey. A predator with a subtle woodsy smell.

Realization hit her like a fist. This was Banner West-field. The chiseled features were softened by the dark-ness, but he was the right height, about six foot two, with medium-length hair and the attitude of a pit bull. She had fallen into his hands, first time out.

This was not part of the plan.

Setting her lips in a firm line, Eleanor stared back. She had no bluff, so her only option was to remain stubbornly silent until she could figure something out.

He was not patient. Dissatisfied with either her silence or his inability to recognize her, he jerked on her arm and pulled her around the desk. She stumbled after him so closely that her foot tangled with his and she tripped, but his firm grasp kept her upright. The corner of the desk jabbed her hip before he thrust her against the front so roughly she was nearly sitting on the desktop. She uttered an offended, "Hey," then flinched and turned her head away from a sudden, blinding stab of light. His free right hand had turned the brass-shaded lamp upward, directing its beam at her face. He released it to grab her chin and force her face toward the light.

Eleanor blinked rapidly while her pupils tried to adjust, then managed an angry glare. He could look all he wanted; he wouldn't recognize her and she still wouldn't talk.

While he scowled and studied her face, she took her first close-up look at evil. In the yellow glare of the desk lamp, the sharply defined nose was more blunt than she'd expected, with a high bridge. The expected thin slash of mouth had a surprisingly sensual curve and more fullness than she'd noticed in photographs. The clenched jaw was certainly as firmly drawn as she'd known it would be, although the chin was flat and didn't show that model-perfect cleft she'd seen in the pictures. And the blue eyes . . . Eleanor frowned. The blue eyes were brown.

"You're not Banner Westfield."

Her chin moved against his cupped palm as she spoke. The accusation seemed to refocus his attention, and he dropped his hand. His eyes assessed hers for several long seconds.

"No, I'm not. Disappointed?"

She ignored his question and made another stab at a bold offense. "Then who are you?"

The attractive mouth flattened into a humorless smile. "My line again. We seem to be at an impasse."

"Right. Maybe we should just get back to the party."

She took one step forward, as though expecting her bluff to work. He put a hand on her shoulder and pushed her back against the desk. "Let's not."

He spread his feet apart and stood close to her, effectively blocking any escape. Arms folded, he studied her, his eyes moving slowly from head to toe. "I don't recall seeing you at the party."

She smiled. "Really? I saw you. You were talking to a pretty blond woman." It was a safe bet; the guy probably drew beautiful women like flies. "Perhaps you have a poor memory."

"Or perhaps you were never in the house until you came through those French doors."

At least his arrogant attitude was putting her in touch with some indignation of her own. "Well, you would know, since you were lurking here in the dark. I think that looks just as suspicious." She tilted her head and examined his attire in much the way he had looked her over. "Perhaps you came through those same doors."

"Nice try."

His sardonic look said she was wrong, but for a moment something had flickered across his face. A brief crack in that haughty confidence. Eleanor had watched the house for a long time before making her nerve-racking dash from the trees to the patio. No one had entered through those French doors before she had. No one had turned on the lights in the library, either, not even the little desk lamp. It didn't seem likely that he would have escaped the party to sulk in a pitch-dark library.

Eleanor lifted her head and gave him a knowing smile. He might have belonged at the party, but she would bet anything he didn't belong in this library. He might be running as big a bluff as she was, and that could be her way out.

He half closed one eye suspiciously. But before either of them could speak, a soft click sounded from the doors across the room. A crack of light appeared from whatever part of the house adjoined the library, and the faint background sounds of talking and music grew louder.

Eleanor stiffened. She had begun to feel a slight hope that she might wiggle out of a breaking-and-entering charge. But if someone else found her here, her chance of escaping plummeted. She had a brief, panicked thought of jumping behind the massive desk, but an arm had already appeared in the widening doorway. There was no time to hide.

"Trust me," he murmured.

Jerking her unceremoniously off the desk and into his arms, he lowered his lips to hers, wrapping her in a devouring kiss.

Eleanor's startled exclamation was muffled against his mouth and her breasts were mashed against his chest. She hadn't realized her arms were braced stiffly against his shoulders until his teeth moved against her lips and he muttered, "Hold me, damn it!"

She did. Her first instinct had been to resist anything he said, but in the next instant she knew what he was doing. It was a diversion, not an assault. Whoever was opening the door would see a couple in a passionate embrace and, if they were decently discreet, duck out again.

Eleanor threw her arms around his neck and kissed him back.

She meant to peek over his shoulder to see who was at the door and whether or not they left, but he surprised her again. His forceful kiss suddenly slowed, and his lips began moving lightly, sensuously over her own. A hand slid up her neck and cradled the back of her head. Eleanor's thoughts faltered, then took a sharp U-turn. Her entire attention was focused on what he was doing to her. She didn't care who was watching from the doorway, but whoever it was would be getting a good show.

She must have been kissed this passionately before, but not within recent memory, and not with this man's thorough attention to details. One hand pressed her body against his while the other strayed toward her face, caressing her cheek and smoothing back tendrils of hair. Meanwhile, his mouth nibbled and touched, and made long, slow explorations of her lips. When his tongue touched hers and she made a small sound of surprise, it seemed to inspire even more ardent kissing.

She was light-headed and flushed, and startled to find she was enjoying herself. This might all be for show, but the man was good looking and obviously knew what he was doing, and she ought to salvage at least one good memory from her cat-burglary debacle. What the hell, she told herself. You have to take what life gives you, and lately life had given Eleanor Coggins damn little. A passionate kiss with a handsome stranger might fall under partial compensation.

He pressed her backward and the desk came up against her butt again. If he thought she'd be intimidated by his dominant position, he could just think again. Her kisses never faltered. She laced her fingers through his hair, clung to his neck, and leaned backward, absorbed in every languorous touch of his lips. The guy was good, very good.

His body moved more intimately against hers, and he pressed one firm thigh between her legs. Operating on pure instinct, she bent her left leg and wrapped it possessively around his leg. By the time she remembered she shouldn't do that, it was too late. She knew he had felt the gun.

Eleanor froze. So did he. In the sudden silence, the library door clicked shut.

Inches apart, they stared at each other. His body still forced her backward, but she thought it best not to protest her position just now. He was breathing hard, but she suspected it was more from anger than passion. In the light of the desk lamp beside them, she watched his eyes go cold and stern.

When he finally spoke, it wasn't what she expected. "Who was it?" he asked in a low voice.

"What?" She glanced toward the door, then back to his face, hovering so close in front of her. "At the door? I have no idea."

"Describe him."

She stuck her chin out. "I can't, I had my eyes closed." She knew he'd take it as some sort of compliment, and from the arrogant twitch of his lip, it was obvious she was right. "Besides, I wouldn't recognize anyone. What difference does it make? They left."

"The difference is, if it was old George DeMarco trying to sneak some of Banner's imported cigars, he won't say anything. But if it was anyone with the last name of Westfield, we are going to be interrupted again very soon. I don't need any more problems with that dysfunctional, screwed-up family, and I don't think you want to be discovered in here."

She struck back with her only weapon. "I don't think you do, either." His irritated frown told her it was true.

"Look, sweetheart—"

"Don't call me sweetheart."

"I have no reason to trust your ethics, your motives, or your intentions. And I don't intend to be involved in your criminal life, including any plans for murder, so you'd better give me that gun."

"Sorry, can't do that. It matches my purse."

He looked more surprised than angry. For about

two seconds. "Yeah, you're a whiz at accessorizing. Hand it over."

She stiffened and tried to clasp her legs together, but his thigh was still between them. "No."

She could see his patience wearing thin with every second she delayed.

"This is not up for debate. Give it to me, or I'll take it," he demanded.

"Try it and I'll break your fingers."

It was a totally empty threat. He must have questioned her harmless nature, though, because he spent several long seconds looking into her eyes before his lip curved up.

"I believe I'll take the chance."

As fast as a darting snake, his hand reached up her dress and grasped the gun. Eleanor slapped her hand over his, clenching it through the slinky black material of her dress. He had a firm grip on the gun, but it was still holstered, and he couldn't release it as long as she held on to his hand. The leather holster was scraping her leg painfully, and his warm fingers touched her inner thigh alarmingly close to her panties.

"Get your hand off me, you perverted creep," she growled.

"Gladly, you homicidal thief. As soon as I get what I want."

She was about to spit a well-constructed string of profanities at him when the door opened forcefully, a hand hit a wall switch, and a dozen recessed lights flared on.

Eleanor jumped and felt his hand slip away as he whirled around to face the door. She tugged her dress down, but not fast enough to escape the scathing notice of the well-dressed woman standing in the door-way.

The woman's disdainful eyes shifted from Eleanor and rested with no more affection on the man who'd just had his hand up her dress. The woman's mouth pursed with undisguised contempt as she addressed him. "Would you like to tell me what's going on here, or should I assume the usual?"

He stepped aside slightly so Eleanor was able to see his relaxed smile, and she realized he'd made a vain attempt to shield her from view.

"Hello, Mother," he said, and Eleanor nearly did a double take. This stiff, unpleasant woman was his mother? "I'm sorry I didn't see you when we arrived. I don't believe you've met my fiancée."

He held out a hand to Eleanor. It took several seconds to understand that he was referring to her and not some woman he had abandoned at the party. She looked at his outstretched hand in stunned disbelief, then at him. Playing at kissing him was one thing, but now she was engaged to him? She was about to inform him that he could take his charade and stuff it when she noticed his tense stance and the silent plea in his eyes. He needed her to play along. Desperately.

Her mind rapidly sorted the available facts. Whatever reason he had for this absurd game, it could not hurt to have him indebted to her. More important, being engaged to him might give her access to this house, with more chances in the future to search for the evidence she needed.

Eleanor smiled graciously and took her new fiancé's hand, edging off the desk as smoothly as possible. Filling in the awkward hole in his introduction, she smiled and said, "How nice to meet you. I'm Eleanor Coggins."

The woman raised one eyebrow and repeated the name Coggins, apparently searching her memory for some respectable family of that name. She must not have found one, because her cold look said Eleanor had not risen perceptibly in her estimation. Eleanor was wondering what sort of woman would expend so much scorn on her own son and his future wife when her still-nameless fiancé completed the introduction.

"Eleanor, I'd like you to meet my mother, Elizabeth Payton Westfield."

Westfield?

Elizabeth tipped her head slightly at her, while Eleanor's mind raced. His mother was a Westfield. *He* must be a Westfield. She could have run through a mental family tree of cousins, but there was no point. She knew Elizabeth Payton Westfield was the name of Banner's mother. She had just become engaged to Banner's brother.

Eleanor flashed a look at her new fiancé that promised retribution. He smiled back with bared teeth, looking dangerously prepared for the confrontation, not to mention attractive as hell.

She really should find out his name.

Chapter Two

"John Michael Payton. But I've always gone by Jack."

"Payton?" Her voice nearly squeaked with surprise. "You're not a Westfield?"

"Shh, quiet!" He grabbed her elbow and moved them both two steps back. Silky drapes brushed her bare arm. They were standing unobtrusively where Elizabeth Westfield had left them, at the fringes of the crowd that mingled in the enormous Westfield living room. While the party buzzed around them, they did a fast background briefing on each other.

Eleanor obediently silenced her surprise with a sip from the glass of champagne he—Jack, she reminded herself—had thrust into her hands when they entered the room.

"Is Payton the name of your mother's first husband?" she murmured over the rim of the glass.

"It's her maiden name. She's one of *the* Paytons." Seeing her blank look, he rolled his eyes at her hopeless ignorance and went on. "She never married my father, and she didn't give me his name."

As Eleanor opened her mouth, he snapped, "Yes, I really am a bastard. That saves you the trouble of calling me one."

"I wasn't going to. This whole thing is beyond description, and I haven't yet decided what to call you."

She spared a sideways glance at the crowd. Most of the people were across the room, near the two-story-high windows that overlooked the floodlit lawn and pool. What seemed like an acre of carpet dotted with groupings of furniture separated them from the heart of the mob. Jack's mother moved elegantly among the sofas and chairs, offering occasional cheek kisses and overly bright smiles to a select few.

"So your mother lives here with Banner?"

"Oh, yes. She's very close to her golden boy. I'm the black sheep she didn't want around."

Eleanor suppressed a shudder and turned back to Jack. He was scanning the room with a jaded expression, apparently unimpressed and uninterested in the excess of wealth and power. In this light, she would never have mistaken him for his half brother. He looked older and lacked Banner's blandly perfect features. Jack's fuller mouth and dark eyes gave him a more intense look. Where Banner looked smooth and soulless, Jack had a dangerous sensuality. She could already testify to its effectiveness.

And the dangerous bastard was now her only access to this house and Banner's files.

"Come on," Jack prompted. "What else do you need to know before someone spots us?"

The odd thing was, they *had* been spotted, but no one had ventured near them. Eleanor had noticed several surreptitious glances and a few outright curious stares. She supposed it was only a matter of time before someone approached.

"Just give me the pertinent facts. Age?"

"Thirty-five. How about you?"

"Twenty-eight. Previous marriages?"

"None." He paused uncomfortably. "You may hear references to other women, but there weren't any serious relationships. I only dated. A lot."

"Oh, great, that just about guarantees I'll be a curiosity."

He grimaced, as if having this crowd think of Eleanor as someone special was truly painful. "What else do you need to know? My favorite color is blue, my favorite food—"

"No, no. No one cares about stuff like that. Do you play sports?"

"Baseball in high school, polo at college."

Her eyes widened. "Polo? You're kidding. Do people really do that?"

"Yes, they do. Get over it. What else?"

"What kind of car?"

"Jeep Wrangler."

Eleanor was expecting to hear something foreign and expensive. She shot him a questioning glance but left it alone for now. This conversation was going to need an in-depth follow-up later. "What kind of job?"

"I'm an accountant for Westfield-Benton."

She put a mental asterisk by that anomaly, too, and took another sip of champagne. Bubbly sweetness slipped down her throat. "You know, this really is good."

"Of course it is."

"I wonder what kind it is. I should buy this stuff."

He snatched her drink, swirled and sniffed, then took the tiniest sip possible. "Bollinger eighty-two. About a hundred and seventy-five dollars a bottle, if you're still interested."

He knew damn well she wasn't. He handed the drink back, and she noticed he hadn't taken one for himself. "Don't you drink?"

He gave her a long, hard look. "Not anymore."

That fairly screamed recovering alcoholic, another piece of pertinent information.

Jack had been furtively watching the room over her shoulder. He raised his hand to run fingers through his hair, and behind the cover of his arm he mumbled, "I think my aunt Grace and uncle Bill have spotted us. Hurry up."

She thought fast. "We'd better decide when and where we met."

He nodded. "How about at the park by Silver Lake? That's where I jog." He took another glance over her shoulder. "You're on in about twenty seconds."

She nodded and felt a sheen of nervous perspiration gather under her arms. The park was reasonable, neutral territory where the gentry might actually encounter common riffraff like her. She didn't bother to tell him that she wasn't likely to meet a jogger unless he ran over her while she was doing something sedentary, like lying on the grass reading a book.

"When was this fateful meeting?" she asked.

"Six weeks ago."

"That's all? That's hardly enough time—"

"I wasn't in town before then," he whispered harshly.

Oh God, one more piece of his recent history she didn't know. "Why? Were you working at another branch of the company?"

"I was in jail."

He flashed a smile at a spot half a foot over her left shoulder just as a large arm pulled her into a jarring hug. As Uncle Bill passed her over to Aunt Grace for a more sedate introduction, she aimed a poisonous stare at her ex-con fiancé. Their engagement had just become very rocky.

Enduring the next half hour was nothing short of heroic.

Uncle Bill gave her a wink and a leer that let her know he was the one who had walked in on their scorching kiss in the library. Knowing he had immediately tattled on his nephew made it difficult to keep her smile sincere and her tongue in check. Her new fiancé, however, seemed to have no problem sucking up to his relatives. It was hard to believe the man could be more infuriating. As she made polite conversation with Grace, she heard him cheerfully tell Bill Westfield, "We'd love to join you and Aunt Grace on Sunday. Ellie loves football."

It was amazing—two blunders in only three words. She took his arm and made sure he felt her fingernails. "Jack, don't we have that thing on Sunday. . . ."

"I changed it to next week," he told her, smiling broadly. "Wasn't that lucky? Almost like serendipity. I knew you'd love a private invitation to the Lions' preseason practice."

Eleanor seethed. When Bill and Grace left, she leaned close and hissed, "I detest football."

"Too bad. I love it."

She bit her lip and let it go, in favor of the more important issue. "And my name is *not* Ellie. If you don't like Eleanor, you can call me Nora. That's what most of my friends do."

She was staring him down when Aunt Grace's voice gushed behind her, "Come meet Jack's fiancée, Ellie Coggins."

Jack flashed a bland smile. "Whoops, too late."

Eleanor put her temper on simmer and reminded herself that this was a short-term engagement. As soon as she got access to Banner's files, they could have a nice, messy breakup. If the fates were kind, it would be before the Lions' practice on Sunday.

His jail time was what bothered her most. It was no wonder she'd never heard of him. She was certain Westfields didn't go to jail and imagined Paytons didn't, either. It seemed Jack was the bad boy of the family, and she was the lucky woman who had snagged him. Perhaps she would feel reassured if she knew what he'd been in for. Probably sexual assault, she mused as she waited for a free moment to question him.

It was worse.

"You *killed* someone?" she gasped.

"The charge was manslaughter," he said tersely. "I didn't mean to do it."

She stared at him, outraged. "Oh, that's all right, then."

Jack's jaw had developed a twitch. "I thought you'd be used to hanging around with the criminal class."

She opened her mouth to shoot an insult back at him, when she noticed two women talking and taking long, obvious glances their way. She'd seen them doing the same thing earlier. Her mouth closed into a speculative pout.

"Why have those two women been watching us?" she asked him. "Did you blackmail one of them into a compromising position, too?"

"What women?"

"Over there. The shiny silver pantsuit and the trashy red bandanna that's passing for a dress."

He looked quickly, then turned back to her. "I don't know the one in the shiny pants-thing. But you might say I compromised the other one. We dated a couple times."

"*That* sort of date?"

"Yes, *that* sort of date. Jealous, sweetheart?"

She ignored him and gazed thoughtfully at the little tramp in red. "I do believe they're wondering how serious we are." She gave him a sweet smile and lifted a hand to his hair. He flinched, then held still cautiously while she lightly traced his hairline around his ear and tilted her head coyly while she stroked the back of his neck.

"Bend close to me," she said in a low voice.

"Why?"

She lifted her eyes to his significantly. "Trust me."

He raised an eyebrow but bent close and whispered in her ear, "If you want me to kiss you again, you should just ask."

She remembered to keep her face pleasant. "You weren't that good," she told him, a huge lie that was still the least of her transgressions tonight. Then she laughed and pushed him playfully away, as though he'd just proposed something titillating and quite inappropriate. She watched with satisfaction as the women frosted over.

Jack glanced at them, then gave Eleanor a wry smile. "Having fun?"

Getting caught killed her smile. "You think it's fun pretending to be senselessly in love with you? Hardly. I'm doing my job, which you'd damn well better appreciate, because I'm going to expect similar cooperation from you."

"Oh, yes. You want me to cooperate in stealing from my family."

"I wasn't going to steal anything from your lovely family," she told him. "Just find some information. Nothing that would jeopardize your parole status, if that's what you're worried about."

She thought that was pretty darn considerate of her, but it seemed to annoy Jack. He put an arm around her shoulder and drew her close, so anyone watching might think he was whispering amorous suggestions in her ear. His voice was brusque and far from amorous.

"I suggest you forget about my past for a minute," he said, his breath warm on her cheek. "I wasn't the one caught in a criminal act less than an hour ago. And my parole status is already in jeopardy from this gun in my pocket."

"Well, that's your own fault, isn't it? You could give it back." She tried to turn away, but his arm held her firmly against him. He was probably one of those obsessively macho types who spent all their jail time pumping iron. He certainly had a strong grip.

He was also stubbornly persistent about that damn gun.

"At least I'm sure I'm not going to shoot anyone

here," he growled. "I can't say the same for you. If you only want information, why do you need a gun?"

"I told you I wasn't going to shoot anyone," she repeated, her voice terse and impatient. "It was just a scare tactic, in case I had to threaten him to get what I need." She might not know a thing about guns, but how hard could it be to pull a trigger?

"Threaten who?"

Eleanor clamped her mouth shut, seconds too late. If he had any affection for his half brother, he probably wouldn't appreciate the idea of her waving a loaded gun at him.

When she didn't answer, he drew his head back slightly and turned that intense stare on her. His dark eyes had a way of holding hers, making her feel like a bug pinned to a table, and she squirmed uncomfortably in his arms. It worked about as well for her as it would for the bug.

Unfortunately, the answer wasn't that difficult to figure out.

"You knew you were in Banner's library. You were going to hold a gun on Banner and demand information, weren't you?" He examined her closely, as if he had missed something earlier. "Are you insane?"

Maybe she was. Only a crazy person would break into the Westfield house, impulsively make out with a stranger who also happened to be a convicted killer, then betroth herself to him, all within one hour. Yes, she was definitely insane. Even worse, she had lied to Jack about only needing the gun to threaten his brother. If Banner wouldn't admit the truth, she knew she would have shot him. She owed it to Janet.

There wasn't enough time to tell Jack the whole

story. He probably hadn't even met Janet if he'd been in jail until six weeks ago. He would just have to accept the basics for now.

"You may not know it, but Banner committed a terrible crime. I intend to prove it."

His mouth opened in surprise. "You know about Banner?"

She stared back. "You mean *you* know about him, too?"

"Talking about me?"

They both jumped at the voice beside them.

Eleanor stiffened, and Jack was holding her so closely she knew he felt it. She wanted to believe it was some protective instinct that made him keep his arm around her as they turned to face Banner.

He was just as tall as Jack, but with lighter, almost blond hair, and sharp blue eyes that had the same intelligence behind them, plus something cold and calculating. That could be her own biased opinion, she admitted to herself. Janet hadn't seen anything cold in Banner. She'd paid dearly for that mistake.

Eleanor stood rigidly before him, thankful for Jack's reassuring arm around her shoulder. Jack might be an arrogant jerk, but she could deal with that. Banner's smooth evil left her weak with fear, and she appreciated the extra support.

Banner's look of amusement was as cool as his mother's. "Jack," he said tonelessly.

"Banner."

Jack's voice held an edge she hadn't heard before. Enough to make her wonder if Banner was actually in more danger with the gun in Jack's possession than hers.

"This party is to celebrate my promotion, but you

seem to have become the center of attention. Again."
His head tipped in a sort of ironic acknowledgment.

"This is my fiancée, Eleanor Coggins," Jack said,
ignoring the comment. She was glad he hadn't used his
preferred "Ellie." She had become resigned to it over
the past hour's introductions, but she didn't think she
could stand that sort of familiarity from Banner.

Her nemesis finally turned his eyes on her. She tried
for a pleasant expression and held out her hand. Banner turned the expected handshake into a kiss behind
her knuckles.

"Welcome to our family, Eleanor," he said, his eyes
quickly traveling over her from head to toe. "Congratulations, Jack. You've certainly made a good choice."

Jack offered a brief, "Yeah," seemingly unfazed
by a comment that made her feel more like a smartly
purchased piece of furniture than a future sister-in-law.
She pulled her hand back and resisted the urge to wipe
it against her dress.

Banner smiled at her, his handsome face reflecting
an undisguised curiosity. "I can see why Jack has been
keeping you to himself. I wouldn't want to share such
a beautiful creature with other men, either."

She smiled as if she thought it a compliment, trying
hard not to make it a snarl. Jack's grip on her shoulder
tightened, and she figured he'd expected the snarl.

"I'm afraid I have to spend time with my guests tonight. Business connections, you know," Banner said,
flashing a row of perfect teeth. "The two of you must
come back tomorrow for dinner with the family so we
can get to know you better."

"I don't think we—" Jack began.

"That would be lovely," Eleanor said, and felt Jack's

surprised glance. Taking a deep breath, she asked, "Will your wife be there, too?"

A sudden, uncomfortable silence fell between them. Eleanor glanced down at Banner's hand. "I noticed the ring," she said, offering a guileless smile.

"I'm sorry," Jack said quickly. "I didn't think to tell her. . . ."

Banner said solemnly, "My wife died a few months ago." The cold blue eyes met hers with no hint of emotion. Like the dead fish in his library, Eleanor thought, and wondered how Janet could ever have fallen in love with him.

"I'm so sorry," she said, and had no trouble looking sincerely regretful. Some of us actually do miss her, she thought.

From the corner of her eye, she could see Jack's suspicious look as Banner tilted his head in polite acceptance of her apology. "Seven o'clock tomorrow," he said with a glance at Jack. It was an order, not an invitation.

When Banner had blended back into the crowd, Jack turned on her. "What the hell was that?"

She wasn't going to pretend innocence. "Not subtle enough for you? I wanted to know what his official position is. I told you I was going to prove that Banner's guilty."

"Guilty of what?"

"What do you mean? You said you knew." They were staring at each other again, a standoff.

"Ellie, exactly what do you think Banner is guilty of?"

She hesitated. It obviously wasn't what *he* thought. Still, he might be willing to help her convict Banner.

After the stiff formality of their conversation, she had decided there was no love lost between the two brothers. And now that the whole blasted family had met her, she wasn't exactly anonymous. She was going to need his cooperation to search the house.

She looked him in the eyes. "He married my best friend, Janet, then killed her for the insurance money. And I don't think it, I know it." It was short and to the point, and he hadn't smirked or scoffed, an encouraging sign. "What do *you* think he's guilty of?"

Jack took a deep breath, then blew it out slowly. "Murder, huh?" He looked across the room, seeking out Banner among the crowd. "Interesting . . ."

She nearly turned purple in an effort to control her anger. *Interesting?* If Jack found Janet's death interesting, he was as cold and self-centered as the rest of his family. That wouldn't have been a surprise, except for the memory of those passionate kisses in the library. Which were not real, she reminded herself. Jack was as practiced at deceit as the rest of his family. If she forgot that, her fate might be the same as Janet's.

She poked him sharply in the ribs. "Hey, rich boy. Come on, reciprocate. What else did he do?"

The look Jack turned on her was one of unmistakable disgust. She made a mental note that he was sensitive about his family's wealth. Either that or he disliked being reminded that he had connected himself intimately with the lower class.

They were still in full view of the guests and he adjusted his expression before answering in a low voice. "The family's made a fortune since Banner took over Westfield-Benton, more than the financial reports account for."

She made the implied leap. "He's embezzling from the company?"

"No, nothing's missing. In fact, there's too much money. I think he's laundering it for some illegal operation. I just haven't figured out what it is."

It wasn't murder, but the results were the same: Banner got rich. The question was, why did Jack care? She didn't think an ex-con would quibble over a little dirty money, and she doubted he cared one bit about saving the reputation of his family. But he did have it in for the right Westfield, even if his reason turned out to be as unimaginative as "Mommy always liked him better."

She sized up his determined look and made the only deal that would work. "I'll help you if you help me."

Jack nodded curtly, apparently having come to the same decision. "We've got a lot of talking to do before tomorrow night."

"And planning." How did one dress for an intimate dinner with two killers.

After fawning all over Banner, meeting Ellie seemed to be everyone's goal, and Jack did his best to glue himself to her side. The woman had a way of saying the most unexpected things, and he'd become terrified of leaving her unsupervised.

He had to admit Ellie played her role well. She was an adept liar, using the few details she knew to appear intimately familiar with Jack's life. Even though he thought her invention of a mildly debilitating polo injury stretched credibility, the rest of her performance had been flawless. She had even fooled everyone into believing she was comfortable with vulgar displays of wealth.

That was her best lie. Jack had seen the way Ellie stopped and stared at the enormous chandeliers, dripping with crystal and gold, high above the entry hall. The living room had taken her aback, too, her eyes huge with amazement, taking in the intricate marble and woodwork above the fireplace, the soaring wall of mahogany-framed glass, and the carelessly strewn silk rugs, each worth as much as a new luxury car. That sort of affluence was obviously outside her experience.

He could use that to his advantage. That, and her ability to lie like a pro. He was going to need her services as a fake fiancée for longer than she knew. If he could tempt her into the Westfield world by dazzling her with wealth, it would be an easy sell. A jaded rich girl would have been far more difficult to sway. Ellie's middle-class background should make his proposition more attractive, and her talent for on-the-spot fabrication just might make it convincing. And despising him as she clearly did, he'd have no trouble getting rid of her later. All in all, he might have stumbled onto the perfect fiancée in Ellie Coggins.

"I never dated a convicted criminal before. It adds a certain spice to our relationship."

Jack jerked out of his reverie with a startled blink. Ellie was smiling serenely at an elderly matron whose blank expression spoke of a lifetime of social discipline. The lady's white-knuckled grip on her wineglass indicated that training was currently being strained to the limit.

He smiled and pulled on Ellie's arm. "Excuse me, Mrs. Ford. I need to speak to my fiancée a moment."

Ellie waved good-bye as she allowed him to draw her aside. As soon as they were out of range, he hissed in her ear, "What do you think you're doing? Do you have any idea who that was?"

"I don't know who she is, but I know who she wants to be: your future mother-in-law. God knows why, but she's checking out her daughter's competition before they convince you to trade up. You should thank me for scaring her off."

He gritted his teeth. "Thank you."

Her eyes crinkled with humor; she was obviously enjoying his frustration. It should have aroused his anger. Instead, he found himself distracted by the tiny dimple in her cheek and the way her lips curved with suppressed laughter, pressed into a sexy upturned bow. Jack remembered how those lips had kissed him with an eagerness and finesse that had sent heat tearing through his body. That unexpected armful of female lust had knocked him into a sensual response that had stayed with him all evening. He wasn't sure what to make of it.

Thank God she was a sarcastic bitch. If she'd offered him even half the enticement she'd shown in the library, he'd be tempted to throw her down right there on his mother's elegant Persian rug. One more scandalous incident for Jack Payton.

"Jack! We've been hoping to run into you!"

He smiled weakly. He'd been hoping to avoid them. Vivian Houston could worm information from the most skilled espionage agent, and Ellie seemed only too willing to oblige everyone's hunger for personal tidbits.

His fears were justified. Within minutes, Ellie was inventing an embarrassing story for Ed and Vivian about their first meeting in the park. Hands moving in a rolling circle, she said, "Then he tripped over my feet, flailed around like a scarecrow in a tornado, and pitched headfirst right into the duck pond."

Ed and Vivian laughed hysterically while Ellie gave Jack a mischievous wink, snuggled under his arm, and leaned into his side in a calculated display of affection.

Heat rushed through him as her body molded against his. As soon as they left the party, he was going to throttle her. Or make love to her. Or both.

He gritted his teeth and reminded himself to control his hormones. What made it more difficult was that she seemed to have no idea of the effect she had on him. She took his hand and entwined his fingers with hers while listening attentively to the Houstons. That casual touch meant nothing to her, but it had his palms as sweaty as a teenager's on a first date. Two years without a woman and he was a wreck. He wondered how priests did it for a lifetime.

He'd had all he could take. He spoke over Vivian's giggles. "I'm sorry, but Ellie and I have to leave. We have another engagement yet tonight. It was very nice to see both of you." He steered Ellie away before she could open her mouth in protest.

When they were far enough away that they couldn't be overheard, she brushed his hand off her arm and said, "What's wrong? Why are we leaving? I was just starting to have fun."

"You were having way too much fun."

She pouted. "I thought I was being perfectly charming." When she could see he wouldn't change his mind, her eyes did a critical scan of the room. "Everyone's keeping Banner occupied. Why don't we do a quick check in the library? You take the computer and I'll—"

"Not on your life. If we get caught in there again, the game's over. We need a plan next time. Come on."

He started toward the door, but she didn't move. "We can't go without saying good-bye to your mother."

Jack sighed heavily. She was right, but he'd spent the past six weeks avoiding advice and admonitions from his mother, and he didn't want to give her one more shot at him tonight. Ellie was either naive or far more fearless than he, because she had started across the room to meet his mother, who had already spotted them. They met and Ellie began talking, too far away for him to hear. Fine, let her handle it.

Content to let Ellie handle their good-byes, Jack waited impatiently. Then with concern. This was obviously more than nice-to-have-met-you. Elizabeth was tilting her head, asking something, and holding Ellie's hand. Jack frowned. He shouldn't have let Ellie talk to his mother without supervision. He started toward them, when the conversation ended and they came to meet him.

His mother's expression was one he'd learned to dread, a perfectly composed look with piercing, intelligent eyes that he just knew had seen right through whatever he was trying to get away with. It was the condescending Payton look, one he'd seen far too often. He braced himself.

"I'm sorry you have to leave so soon, Jack," she said. He nodded once but remained tense; her opening sentence was always deceptively casual. "I'll see you tomorrow at dinner. Perhaps Eleanor will have her engagement ring by then." Elizabeth smiled warmly at Ellie, then returned to the party.

Jack grimaced. "Ah, shit."

"What's wrong?"

"What did she say to you about a ring?"

"She asked if you were going to give me one, and I told her we hadn't had time for that yet, that you had just proposed at dinner earlier this evening." She looked pleased with her response. "I'm not enchanted with your mother, you know, but it was a perfectly innocent question."

"Nothing my mother says is ever perfectly innocent. I suppose you made up some cute story about me spilling vichyssoise all over you while I stumbled through a proposal."

Her delicate nose tilted further into the air. "I didn't describe the scene. But for your information, I would have made it very romantic. I'd have you get down on one knee in the restaurant, pledge your undying love, and beg me to marry you while everyone watched, and then have them all applaud when I tearfully accepted."

"Jesus," he groaned, "I'm glad no one had to hear that." They crossed the entry hall, his shoes squeaking and hers clicking on the glossy marble surface. "I have to give you a ring."

"What for? Just keep putting it off a few days, then we break up and you don't have to buy one."

He was right, she assumed this was going to be a brief partnership. God, she was going to be pissed.

He didn't want another confrontation with her tonight. He'd skip any mention of the plans he'd been formulating for now, but the ring was important.

"There's already a diamond ring, Ellie, and you have to wear it. I inherited it from my grandmother

Payton. If it's not on your finger by tomorrow, my mother and every other Payton and Westfield will know I'm not serious about you."

She shrugged. "Fine."

The doorman, part of the evening's hired staff, held the enormous front door open for them. Jack fished his keys out of his pocket and handed them to a red-jacketed valet.

"Green Jeep."

The man smirked. "Yes, sir. I remember it."

Jack glanced at Ellie as the valet trotted into the darkness. "Where are your keys?"

She bit her lip, then said in a low voice, "I'm afraid they'd never find my car. I didn't come in through the front door, remember?"

"Shit." He had an image of her tottering across the lawn in her heels and ducking into the rhododendrons. "I'll give you a ride. Where is it?"

"On a side street, back that way." She pointed east.

Jack looked across the dark lawn and raised an eyebrow. "You trespassed through Frank Hardenburg's backyard to get here?" He laughed once, loudly. "You must like to live dangerously. He's the most vicious criminal attorney in town."

She gave him a weary look. "No one saw me. Besides, I can look very innocent if I have to." She tilted her head and looked up at him, blinking her wide, blue eyes in demonstration.

He snorted. "I'll bet."

"Well, it's just trespassing. It's not like I killed someone."

He saw her mouth open as she realized seconds too late what she'd said. He turned away.

"I'm sorry, I—"

"Never mind." His expression hardened as the familiar anger washed over him. Anger at himself. She hadn't meant to offend him this time.

Ellie stood stiffly beside him, lips pursed and eyes downcast.

"Come on," he said in a gentler voice as the valet drove up in his Jeep. He opened the passenger door, as gentlemanly as any non-manslaughtering ex-convict would. She hesitated.

"What's wrong now?"

"Nothing." She moved forward and eyed the elevated floor and running board. Then, with a determined expression, she hiked her tight dress higher up her thighs. She gingerly extended one leg over the side and into the car, ducked in, then pulled the other leg after it. Jack watched with a new appreciation for his Jeep. That one moment would have lost so much appeal in a low-slung Jaguar.

The young valet was watching, too. Jack cleared his throat to get the man's attention, then handed him a folded bill. He wasn't sure if it was the denomination or Ellie's legs that put a more respectful look on the man's face.

They drove down curving streets where elegant homes were shrouded by trees and dense shrubbery. Her car was pulled to the side and nearly obscured by overgrown lilac bushes. It might have been taken for an abandoned car, except that no one ditched five-year-old Toyotas in Bloomfield Hills. He imagined the only reason it hadn't been towed was that the Hardenburgs were entertaining and the little silver Toyota near their driveway might have belonged to a servant.

He walked with her to the car. "We need someplace private to talk. We can go to my place, or yours, if it's closer. . . ."

She opened the car door and the dome light came on. Jack stared in disbelief at the cramped interior. An improvised clothing rack spanned the backseat, stuffed with clothes across the width of the car. A couple of suitcases were wedged behind it. Two bulging black trash bags and a laundry basket occupied the front passenger seat, and a small cooler balanced precariously on the center console. The car looked like a yard sale on wheels.

He said nothing for a moment, closing his eyes and running his hand over the faint stubble on his cheek, making sure his next question sounded very nonjudgmental. "Ellie, where do you live?" He hoped to hell she wouldn't say right here.

She gave him one of those defensive looks she was so damn good at. "Petoskey."

At least four hours north, on the other side of the state. Maybe she really was living out of the car.

Jack looked from the traveling yard sale to the exasperating owner of the mess and worried briefly about what sort of law-breaking vagrant he had become involved with. He thought his two-year stint in jail would have taught him to think before he acted.

"Follow me," he ordered, and walked back to the Jeep, reminding himself all the way that people who are too stupid to learn from their mistakes deserve whatever they get.

Chapter Three

Eleanor followed the Jeep along secluded side streets to a modest ranch house, possibly the least ostentatious in Bloomfield Hills. Either Jack didn't believe in flaunting his wealth, or there was a serious glitch in the line of inheritance.

She didn't bring any luggage in with her, and he didn't offer to carry anything for her. Wherever she stayed tonight, it obviously wouldn't be here.

She trailed him through the small entry area to a kitchen bare of everything but a table and chairs. She glanced around, trying to figure out what felt wrong. No magnets on the refrigerator, no canister set, no pictures on the wall. No stack of mail on the counter, no dishes in the sink. It reminded her of a model home, furnished to give the impression of people living where no one really did.

Curious, she peeked into the living room. Whatever she expected, it was not the perfect JC Penney exhibit that clustered in the center of the beige carpet, every item lifted from some showroom collection. A stage set, with no indication of personality, no sign of life.

This might be Jack's house, but no one was home.

Jack was opening kitchen cupboards, pulling out cups and jars. "Do you want coffee?"

"Do you have any herbal tea?"

From his look, she might have asked for poison. Eleanor sighed. "Nothing for me."

While the microwave heated his instant coffee, he leaned on the counter and studied her. She thought he was probably trying to decide whether to trust her, and just how much to tell her, since that was what she was trying to decide about him. She stared back.

When the machine dinged, he took his cup and wordlessly indicated the living room. She selected the large, overstuffed chair, slipping out of her shoes and curling her legs under her, prepared to listen to his story of jail and money laundering.

He took a sip of coffee and propped his feet on the coffee table, a move she instinctively knew would be forbidden in the Westfield house. "So tell me why you're so sure Banner murdered your friend."

"Me? Why do I have to go first?"

"You're the guest." He smiled. "Also, ladies first."

"Huh. Who'd have thought you'd have good manners?" He wasn't even perturbed. "First tell me what you know about Janet. I know you never met her, because she didn't mention a brother. I'm guessing they never told her about you."

His mouth flattened into a grim smile. "That's not surprising. For two years I didn't exist for the Westfields, except for monthly letters from my mother."

She blinked in disbelief. "She didn't even visit you?"

"You've met my mother. Can you imagine her going through jail security, or waiting in a common room with the families of other prisoners?"

She couldn't. But neither could she imagine her own parents deserting her so thoroughly. She felt an unexpected twinge of sympathy for Jack.

He swirled his coffee as he recalled what he knew. "I heard they met at some big dinner after the Port Huron–to-Mackinaw yacht race. They hadn't known each other long when they surprised everyone and got married. Surprised me, too, when I heard about it. I never thought Banner would miss a chance to make a big social splash, and that wedding would have done it."

She nodded. "They eloped. Just took off for Europe one weekend and came back married. I thought it sounded romantic. Anyway, there was no big wedding and I never met Banner. That's why he didn't recognize me tonight."

"No, you don't strike me as being in the same social circles."

That took care of any feelings of sympathy. "Nice of you to point that out," she said, irritated that his opinion would matter to her.

He raised an eyebrow. "That wasn't an insult, Ellie."

"Oh." Recalling how disdainfully he had looked at the crowd in his mother's living room, she believed him.

"Get to the murder part," he prompted.

She nodded and gave him the condensed version. "They were only married three months. At first her calls and e-mails were all happy. The last two weeks she was more subdued. She'd say things were okay and change the subject. Then just before they left on their trip to Colombia, she e-mailed me that she'd learned something from Banner's files, and she needed to talk to me. 'I've made a big mistake,' that's what she said." Eleanor still had a hard time saying the last part. She took a deep breath to steady her voice. "I never heard from her again. Her parents got a call from Banner and a faxed copy of the death certificate."

"Uh-huh." He took a long drink of coffee. "And why does that mean he murdered her?"

"Well, don't you think that's pretty cold, just a phone call and a fax? It's not like he sobbed through the whole explanation, either. It was sort of a 'Sorry about that' call."

Jack nodded. "That sounds like Banner—inhuman, no emotions. Doesn't prove a thing. Did he tell them how she died?"

"Yeah, kidnapped by terrorists. How likely is that?"

"Pretty likely, actually. Before I royally screwed up my life, I was in charge of South American operations for Westfield-Benton. We always had to guard against kidnapping attempts on Americans. Large ransoms are a source of income for rebel groups."

"Then why did they kill Janet?"

He shrugged. "I heard it was an accident. Maybe she fought them."

She shook her head. "Janet wouldn't have resisted armed men. Fainted maybe, but not resisted."

"You don't think that's how she died?"

"I don't know. But I don't think terrorists did it. The funeral home advised us not to look at her body.

They said her face was"—she paused and drew a shaky breath—"that she was nearly unrecognizable. I don't believe she could have been shot so brutally by mistake. Also, Banner insured her life for a million dollars when they got married. Three months later, he collected it, plus her trust fund."

"Ellie, a million dollars may sound like a lot to you, but I assure you, it isn't to Banner. At least, not enough to risk a murder charge."

"What risk? He got away with it."

"I see. You think he knew he had a foolproof plan to make a million, so he married a rich girl, took her to Colombia, killed her, and collected his prize?" He shook his head. "Sorry, as little as I think of Banner, I'm not convinced. By the way, just how did you get to be best friends with this Janet? I heard she was from a wealthy family." He held up a hand to forestall an outburst. "I'm not trying to imply that you don't fit in with the filthy-rich aristocracy, but you have to admit—"

"I don't fit in. You're right." She'd known she couldn't pretend at elegance and sophistication for long and get away with it. She bit her lip. He might as well know just how far astray he had gone to get a fiancée.

"Janet's family had a summer home in Petoskey. They were members of the country club, and I hung out there all the time. My father is the groundskeeper and my mother runs the banquet service."

She watched to see how he reacted to that financial news. They were not only solidly in the lower middle class, they were practically servants. She imagined Banner would have been brushing off the cooties if he found out he'd been in a recent lip-lock with one of the common folk. But Jack didn't blink. Maybe he'd developed an immunity to the lower classes in jail. Or maybe, like some of the young country club studs she'd fended off, he hadn't been averse to an occasional frolic with the hired help.

"We hung out together every summer, became best friends, and it stuck. That's all. She was a wonderful, funny, nice person, until she had the misfortune to meet your slimy brother—"

"Half brother."

"—half brother, and get murdered in the friggin' jungles of Colombia."

She was too tense, the way she always got when she discussed Janet's death. Forcing herself to relax, she unfolded her legs and stretched them out on the coffee table, her nylon-clad toes almost touching Jack's shoes. Massaging a cramp out of her calf, she pretended not to notice her toes curling sensuously onto his ankle under the hem of his slacks. He quickly shifted his leg away. Yup, cooties.

Jack cleared his throat. "So what is it you expect to find in Banner's study that will prove he's a murderer? Some private notes? 'Dear Diary, today I killed my wife'?"

She stopped rubbing her leg and gave him a hard look. "I expect to find whatever Janet found. She lived in that house with him, and she discovered something that worried her. Something that got her killed." She plopped back in the chair. "I'll know it when I see it."

"Ah." He set the empty coffee cup down.

"Your turn." When he looked blankly at her, she said, "Your turn to tell me why you think Banner is doing whatever bad thing it is you think he's doing. And don't leave out the part about jail."

He pulled his legs off the table and leaned forward with his elbows on his legs, hands clasped in front of him. He looked like he was searching for the right words. Eleanor realized the wound was only beginning to heal, and he didn't want to reopen it. Too bad. She waited patiently.

He finally spoke in a carefully controlled, emotionless voice, staring straight ahead at nothing.

"Three years ago I had a couple drinks at the club, was stupid enough to get behind the wheel, and I killed a man standing at the side of the road. The man happened to be Joe Benton, the president of Westfield-Benton. I was convicted of vehicular manslaughter. I could have gotten twenty years, but Leonard, my stepfather, used his money and his connections, and I got three years and probation. I served just over two and got out six weeks ago."

He looked at her. "The party tonight was the end result of the chaos Benton's death caused in the company. My stepfather also died while I was in jail. He'd been CEO, and Benton was president. Joe's son Allen became president, and Banner got booted up into my former position, vice president of South American operations. This week he became senior VP."

She lifted her eyebrows, remembering what he'd told her at the party. "You were a VP and now you're an *accountant*?"

He smiled tightly. "My name isn't Westfield or Benton, and after my accident the Paytons weren't too fond of me, either. They stuck me in Finance and said they'd move me up after people got over looking at me like I had a disease and I was socially acceptable again. I don't intend to stay that long."

She skipped commenting on his family's shallow loyalty. "Why work there at all? I mean, it's none of my business, but I don't think I'd take a token position in a company where I wasn't wanted."

She saw a flash of genuine amusement this time. "No, I don't believe you would. But good jobs for ex-cons are hard to come by, and they do pay me well. Believe me, I'd rather work at a car wash than for Banner Westfield, perfect son, corporate whiz kid, and major asshole, but it's absolutely vital that I have a good, steady income for now. They have something that belongs to me, and as soon as I get it back, I'll leave."

"What is it?" she asked a bit breathlessly, picturing heirloom jewelry held hostage or a fortune in company stock.

"My daughter."

"Your *daughter*." She repeated it, trying to make this new piece of information fit into the picture that was forming of Jack Payton's life. He leaned back and waited, now that the hard part of his speech was over.

"Your daughter," she said again. "I thought you said you hadn't been married."

He looked at her sideways, waiting for her stupidity to clear up.

She nodded. "Oh, right. So how and when?"

"How was in the usual way, and when was thirteen years ago, although I didn't know about it until three months ago."

"Thirteen years? Your daughter is thirteen?"

"Twelve, actually." For a moment, he looked almost as surprised as she felt. "I'm still trying to get used to it. Her mother was a, uh, brief friend, and she never told me about Libby. The lawyers said she kept her for two years, then dumped her with her parents and disappeared. The grandparents were in and out of poverty, depending on the old man's gambling fortunes, but they raised her until three months ago, when they both became ill and the girl became too much for them to handle." He raised one sardonic eyebrow. "I think that last part is the real reason I got her. Or, I should say, the reason my mother got her, because I was still in jail. But if I can establish that I'm a decent, responsible father, I can get permanent custody."

Eleanor looked at him with growing comprehension. "A decent, responsible father with a good income and a potential fiancée-slash-mother."

"That last part was rather fortunate, wasn't it?"

She narrowed her eyes. "You son of a bitch." He winced slightly, as if he had been expecting that response yet was disappointed to hear it. "You want to take a twelve-year-old girl from the nicest home she's ever had, to live with an ex-con, then dangle a potential mother in front of her, before you discard the new mommy and say, 'Whoops, sorry, honey, but don't worry, *I* won't leave you'? You lousy, thoughtless . . ." She groped for words.

"Son of a bitch, I know," he finished for her, frowning. "It's not that bad."

"It's exactly that bad. You don't even know this girl."

"Libby. Her name is Libby. And none of us know her, but I have to get her out of that house. You tell me, after knowing my mother for all of ten minutes:

Do you think Elizabeth Payton Westfield should raise another kid after the way Banner and I turned out?"

Eleanor hesitated, picturing a bewildered twelve-year-old girl cowering before that tower of icy authority. "You may have a point."

"Damn right." He ran a hand through his hair, looking as harried as any new dad who wasn't sure he was ready for fatherhood. "I spend as much time with her as I can, but it's hard to make up for twelve years in just six weeks. We both need to adjust. I don't know anything about adolescent girls, and she never heard of me until three months ago, so it's going to take some time. . . ."

His voice drifted off, but Eleanor was able to deduce the rest of it. "She hates you."

He sighed. "Yeah, pretty much."

His voice was miserable, but his jaw was rigid, as if he was controlling an impulse to give in to the helplessness he must feel. She didn't want to make him feel worse, but she had to let him know where she stood.

"I refuse to have any part in tricking this innocent young girl into thinking I'm going to be her mother."

He leaned forward again and looked directly at her, his eyes rapidly going cold. He might feel sympathy for his newly found daughter, but she knew he wasn't going to spare any for her.

"You don't have any choice, Ellie. It's part of the deal, if you want to get back inside that house. And you and I both know you need to do that. Besides, I may be able to help you more than you know."

She watched him like she'd watch a snake that might strike at any moment. She didn't trust him for a second, but she couldn't pass up any chance to expose

Janet's murder. Between angrily clenched teeth she asked, "What do you know?"

"I know what you're looking for, which is more than you know. I think we are both looking for the same thing, and I think it's possible your friend Janet found it. I know there are discrepancies in the company accounts. If Janet found the reason for them, and if it's as illegal as I suspect, it could be enough to get her killed. I'm not saying I'm convinced that Banner killed her, but I will help you prove there's something there worth killing to keep hidden."

His eyes held hers while she considered it, doing that penetrating trick they performed on her, which did nothing to help her clarity of thought.

Their phony engagement was far more than she'd bargained for, and that wasn't even considering the cocktail parties and flaming hot kisses that went with it. With Jack, she would not merely have access to the house. She would have a partner, one who already had half the information she needed and was motivated to get the rest.

She'd also have a young girl whose feelings and expectations might get trampled in their attempt to catch Banner.

Eleanor recited a string of bad words under her breath. Where did she go wrong? This mission was supposed to be clear-cut—expose Janet's murder, see that Banner spends eternity in hell. Simple. But the world kept throwing in complications. An unnervingly sexy man who kissed like it was an art form, a house full of rich socialites thinking she's engaged to him, and a young girl with God knows what problems, expecting to call her Mom.

Reject that, and she lost any chance to avenge Janet.

She gave Jack a stern look. "Okay, I'll play the future stepmom. But I will also be looking out for this girl's interests, so don't think I'll let you traumatize her, even if that means"—she couldn't believe she was saying this—"leaving her with your mother."

Jack looked at the polished fingernail jabbing him in the chest, then up at her, his eyebrows drawn into a bemused expression. "Good, then we have the same priorities."

"Fine." She withdrew her finger and folded her arms. With that settled, she was unsure what to do next.

He stood. "I don't suppose you were planning to stay with a friend?"

That must be his friendly way of saying that the night was over. She stood also. "Um, no, I thought I'd find a motel." A lie, but it felt more respectable than the truth.

He uttered a sharp laugh, a concise comment on her naïveté. "It's not exactly the right neighborhood for a Holiday Inn. Come on, show me what you need from that mess in your car and I'll help carry it." He grabbed his empty coffee cup and headed toward the kitchen, muttering, "I can't have my fiancée sleeping in her damn car."

She snapped her mouth shut, then said to his back, "How gracious. I accept."

Chapter Four

E leanor woke up to the same showroom perfection she'd seen in the living room, but in a bedroom suitable for a young girl. Rich wood and pastel shades of blue, green, and yellow fabric glowed in the sunlight that filtered through slatted blinds. She would have killed for this room when she was twelve.

There was only one problem with Libby's bedroom—it felt utterly empty. The closet and dresser drawers were bare, and the computer on the desk still had factory stickers on it. The lifeless showroom feeling wasn't even relieved by the lacy comforter and decorative throw pillows. The only source of brightness and personality came from a large stained-glass dragonfly clinging to the window, filtering beautiful colors across every surface. Eleanor touched it gently and wondered why this one bold expression of individuality had been chosen. Stroking a multicolored glass wing, she pictured Jack anxiously shopping for anything featuring dragonflies based on some casual, offhand remark by his daughter. She guessed that, despite an eagerness to make her happy, he had no idea who Libby was and what she liked.

Eleanor found the room sadly touching. It could almost make her forget what a manipulative bastard Jack was.

The house was silent when she emerged in shorts and T-shirt. No dishes clattering, no radio, no running water to indicate another sign of life, even though it was eight thirty in the morning. Maybe he liked to sleep late.

Down the short hallway on the other side of the living room, a bedroom door stood open. She hesitated, then walked toward it as noisily as bare feet on carpet would allow.

"Jack?" She peeked inside. The room was empty and the bed made. The same showroom designer had been at work in here, artfully arranging bed, linens, mahogany dressers, and upholstered chair in a masterpiece of style, complete with casually draped afghan. For the sake of the unknown salesperson, she hoped he worked on commission, because he had certainly cleaned up when Jack walked into the store.

She was struck by one major difference between her room and Jack's: His was much smaller. No adjoining bath meant he had to use the one down the hall. It took a few seconds for the realization to hit. He had given Libby the master bedroom.

"Big, dumb softy," she mumbled to herself, backing out of the room. The kid wasn't even here yet and she had the best of everything. Eleanor left before she could mar her low opinion of Jack with any mushy sentimentality.

Jack wasn't in the kitchen, and his car wasn't in the

driveway. If he'd gone to the Westfield-Benton office on a Saturday morning, she thought he would have at least left a note.

An empty bowl and spoon awaited her on the kitchen table, next to a box of cereal. Bagels and cream cheese were on the counter. At least the man believed in keeping food in the house, which was more than she expected after the barren decor. She found orange juice in the refrigerator and helped herself to a bagel. Halfway through it a car door slammed and Jack walked in.

"Hey, good morning," she greeted him, wiping the corner of her lips in case she'd missed some cream cheese. "Where've you been?"

"The bank. My safe-deposit box, to be exact."

His tan knit shirt, dark blue slacks, and polished loafers looked far nicer than her khaki shorts. Perhaps one never got too casual in Bloomfield Hills. She shifted her legs farther under the table.

"Are they open on Saturday morning?" she asked brightly, trying to keep his eyes from spotting her bare feet. "Mine just opens the drive-through."

"They are if you know the right people. Here." He pulled a hand from his pocket and dropped a small black box in front of her.

"What's this?" she asked, then, "Oh," as she recognized the velvet covering. It had to be his grandmother's ring, the one she was supposed to wear.

She set the uneaten half of her bagel down, wiped her fingers against her shorts, and picked up the box. Jack stood watching her, hands in his pockets, no doubt trying to look as disinterested as possible during this engagement ritual.

Eleanor snapped the lid open and stared.

"Oh, my," she whispered, and gingerly picked up a white gold band with the most enormous diamond she'd ever seen. She tipped the ring slowly back and forth, letting the marquis-cut stone catch tiny rainbows of light. She finally dragged her eyes off the ring and looked at Jack. "Is it real?"

"Of course it's real. It was my grandmother Payton's twenty-fifth anniversary present. See if it fits."

Her mouth dropped open at the very thought. "I can't wear this!"

He frowned. "Yes, you can. What's more, you *have to*. Put it on."

She swallowed. She had seen expensive jewelry before, even tried on Janet's mother's ten-thousand-dollar sapphire necklace once just so she could say she had, but she'd never seen a gemstone as large and brilliant as this one. It made her nervous just to hold it.

"It must be worth thousands of dollars," she said.

"About two hundred thousand. And I'm probably stupid as hell for handing it over to a known burglar, but I'm a little stuck here. So let's assume you're too smart to try making off with it, and just put the damn thing on."

"Wow." She batted her eyes. "That was so romantic."

As staggered as she was by the price, his surly attitude was making her feel a little less frightened of the ring. Carefully, she eased it over the knuckle, pushing gently, then let it sit comfortably atop her left hand. It fit perfectly. The diamond winked and flashed at her from its new home.

Jack didn't say anything, so she assumed he was

satisfied. Eleanor held her hand out and admired the sparkles from a distance. The diamond was intimidating, but she decided that getting used to it might not be too much of a sacrifice. Without taking her eyes off the ring, she said, "Do you know what I'd think if I saw someone wearing a rock like this at home?"

"That they're filthy rich?"

"Nope. That it was fake."

"Not in this town. Here it's the stone that's real and the woman who's a fake."

"Ooh, how cynical."

Jack pulled out a chair and sat down. "Yeah, jail will do that to you. Maybe I'm misrepresenting some decent people. It's just my family and their friends who are such hypocritical—" He stopped, a puzzled expression on his face. "Ellie, what are you doing?"

She was holding the empty cereal bowl in her left hand, extending it toward the chair across the table. "I'm practicing," she told him. "For tonight, at your mother's house." She offered him the bowl, making sure she angled the ring toward his face, and wiggled her hand unsteadily. In a lofty tone, she said, "Please pass the gravy. Oh, excuse me! The glare from my diamond blinded me for a second. I do hope that comes out." She wiped at an imaginary spot on the table, again shamelessly flashing the ring.

Jack grunted. "Just make sure my mother sees it."

"Are you kidding? How could she miss it? If I stood on your porch and caught the sun just right, I'll bet she could see it from here."

He looked at it warily, as if diamond rings made him nervous. "I guess it *is* pretty big."

Big? It was so ostentatious it was embarrassing,

but since it was *the* Payton diamond, she didn't say so. She settled back in the chair and rested her hand on the kitchen table, contemplating the ring. If this was the Payton idea of jewelry, she wondered just how far out of touch with reality the family was. Glancing at Jack, she said, "You do know this little bauble represents more than the average family makes in three years, don't you?"

"Yes, I do," he said, sounding a bit touchy. "And if you're going to tell me how decadent it is, I agree. I didn't buy it. My grandparents worked hard and thought treating themselves to a few luxuries wasn't out of line."

"Your grandmother wore this thing every day?"

He nodded. "For the rest of her life."

"So why do you have it? Why didn't she give it to her daughter instead of her grandson?"

"Didn't you notice? My mother has her own embarrassingly large diamond ring. So this went to the first grandchild."

"And your wife, whoever that turns out to be," she added quickly, "is supposed to wear this thing for the rest of her life, too?" She tried to imagine selecting hot dogs at the grocery store or typing on a keyboard at work with that enormous twinkling stone on her hand, and failed. But then, his wife probably wouldn't do those things. Eleanor would wear it for the duration of their charade, but she didn't think she'd ever get used to it.

To stop herself from staring at the thing, she dropped her hand to her lap, which happened to be her bare leg. The elegant ring was glaringly out of place next to her shorts and T-shirt. It made her feel she should be in formal attire, or at least in a dress and heels like last night. The ring would have looked great last night with her black dress, silver earrings, and . . . She frowned.

"Hey, I want my gun back."

Jack gave her a stern look. "No guns in my house. It's in my safety deposit box, and by the way, I didn't care for the feeling of walking into the bank with a gun in my pocket." His brows frowned with a sudden thought. "Is it really yours, or am I hiding a stolen gun?"

"Of course it's mine. I bought it especially to shoot Banner."

His look said he was trying to decide how psychotic that statement was.

Eleanor picked up her half-eaten bagel, intending to ignore him. Before she could bite into it, he said, "Do we have to take you shopping before our dinner tonight?"

She lowered the bagel. He was looking her over from head to bare foot, taking in the shorts and T-shirt. He might have reason to wonder, but she bristled, anyway.

"No, we don't have to take me shopping. I have several suitable outfits I can wear." Actually, she could think of only one possibility, but she was pretty sure it would work.

He arched one eyebrow in the condescending look he was so good at. "Yes, I'm sure your garbage bags are full of haute couture."

She knew her fair skin was blushing but couldn't help it. "I may be a little short on luggage, but I have some very nice clothes in my two suitcases." He

looked doubtful, which only made her more defensive. "Wasn't I properly dressed for the occasion last
night?"

"For breaking and entering, no," he said with an
amused twitch of his lip, and she knew he'd seen her
less-than-graceful arrival on the patio. "But for the
party, yes. Your dress was very . . . appropriate."

Appropriate was about as flattering as if he'd said
adequate.

Remembering last night seemed to make him uncomfortable, because he stood and jammed his hands
back into his pockets, jingling his car keys and pacing
around the kitchen. She wondered if he was beginning
to regret their spontaneous engagement.

"When can we search Banner's library?" she asked.

"I don't know."

She shot him a suspicious look. "What do you
mean, you don't know?"

"I mean I don't know when the opportunity will
present itself. I doubt that we can slip away from a
family dinner tonight and search his personal files."

"Why wait until tonight? I'm not busy now."

"In case you haven't noticed, I don't exactly have
free access to that house anymore. That's where my
daughter lives, and I don't have custody. I have to be
invited over, and we aren't invited until tonight."

That was not good news, but it seemed to be a
touchy subject. She kept her voice casual, as if getting
in the house weren't the most important thing in her
life right now. "Don't you have visitation rights? We
could go see her earlier."

"She's not available earlier," he said in a snooty
voice that was an obvious imitation of his mother.

"They've got her enrolled in every sort of enrichment program they could find. She's at tennis lessons about now. Piano is after that. Afternoons are golf, I think, or maybe the community theater group." He ran a hand through his hair in frustration. "I can't keep it straight."

"What, no polo?"

He shot her a hard look. "Riding lessons are on Sunday."

"Oh."

The poor kid. Maybe Libby enjoyed immersing herself in her new elite social circle. Eleanor hoped so, for the girl's sake.

Jack leaned against the counter and said bitterly, "Libby's the new Payton-Westfield protégée. Since I was such a disappointment, they're concentrating their efforts on turning her into a polished and well-rounded little socialite. I've become an embarrassment, and if it weren't for my daughter, they probably wouldn't invite me back there at all. I'm not the reason you'll get into that house, Ellie. Libby is."

Eleanor stood. "I told you I wouldn't be part of tricking your daughter into believing I'm going to be anyone significant in her life. It sounds like enough people are manipulating her already."

"Damn right they are. That's why I want to manipulate her the hell out of there."

"And what does Libby want?"

His jaw tightened. "I don't know. I don't think she knows."

She opened the cupboard door and threw the last hardened piece of bagel in the small garbage can. "Well, you and Libby figure it out. And until you do, figure out a way to get us into the house, and into Banner's library. Because that's what I'm here for, not to be the stepmom who helps rescue Libby from culture shock and a life of extreme privilege."

"We already had this discussion, Ellie. You don't have any choice."

She stood toe to toe with him. "Neither do you, unless you want to find another woman to play your fiancée. Of course, I don't know how well a game of musical fiancées will go over with your mother."

His silent look told her better than any words how much he hated her. "I'll take care of Libby. If you want an opportunity to get into that library, just make sure you're charming as hell tonight, and get us invited back."

She tilted her head and looked directly into his eyes. "I can do that," she told him, and walked out of the room.

Chapter Five

J ack had spent the whole day thinking about it, and there was no other solution: He needed to get laid.

Two years of jail had done strange things to his libido. He thought he'd mastered his sexual urges, but it seemed he had only diverted them. He could resist all the old temptations, the elegant and cultured women who filled his world, but he had no defense against an amateur burglar with a defiant attitude and a distinctly unrefined tendency toward blackmail. Every time she pursed her lips and glared, he found himself distracted by the shiny pink swell of her lower lip. When she had massaged those long, perfectly curved legs last night, he'd been so mesmerized that the touch of her foot had jolted him like an electric shock. And when she'd sat stunned by the sight of his grandmother's ring, for one fleeting moment he'd let the fantasy suck him in, and he'd actually felt a thrill of pride at being the reason for that ring on her finger.

That one had scared the shit out of him.

He knew what had happened. Living with criminals

had inured him to the lawless, unconventional type. And now, just when he most needed to avoid any appearance of impropriety, this contrary, sexy handful of trouble was stirring up dangerous thoughts. He had to deflect that desire. His relationship with Ellie was purely business. The only solution he could see was to choose one of those other, more acceptable women and get himself laid.

The problem was he didn't *want* any of them. He wanted the woman he couldn't have, and that was a new and frustrating experience for him.

He'd probably fixated on Ellie because she was the first woman he had kissed in two years. He could take care of that. Tomorrow he would look up one of those women who had dropped such suggestive hints at his mother's party and have a night that would be exhaustive enough to put ex-convicts on the lady's permanent sexual shopping list.

He just had to get through tonight.

Ellie wasn't making it easy. He was waiting in the living room when she walked down the hallway in the outfit she had chosen for dinner and turned a full circle in front of him.

"Well? Is it appropriate?" she asked.

She was perfect, from head to toe. The creamy pants clung to her hips before falling in demure straight lines to her feet. The matching sleeveless top had a scooped back that exposed a sensuous curve of spine behind the casually upswept hair. Something woven through the material glittered when she moved, competing with the sparkle on her left hand. It was informal and elegant at the same time, perfect for his mother's dinners.

"It's fine," he conceded. "Looks expensive."

"It probably is. Janet gave it to me for my birthday."

He walked behind her to the Jeep just so he could enjoy the way the silken material moved over her rear end without actually defining it. Anyone but Ellie, he reminded himself firmly, and deliberately walked around the Jeep without opening the passenger door for her. They were only business partners.

She didn't seem to notice his lapse in manners. In fact, she looked preoccupied as he drove through the tree-shaded streets.

"Nervous?" he asked.

"Maybe. Should I be?"

Hell, yes, he thought. He was. His future with Libby was in the hands of this woman he hadn't even known twenty-four hours ago. He tried to look comfortable. "You'll do fine."

"Uh-huh," she said, not entirely convinced. "Your mother doesn't strike me as stupid."

"Not in the least."

"Then don't you think she'll suspect that I'm exactly what I am, a temporary ruse?"

"It's your job to convince her otherwise."

She wasn't happy with the answer. Remembering the unexpected, and wholly fabricated, things that had come out of her mouth last night, he thought some guidelines might be a good idea. Libby was touchy, and he didn't entirely trust Ellie.

"When you talk to Libby, don't bring up her other grandparents. I think she's a bit defensive about their lack of money."

"Okay."

"And you'd better not ask about school. Her grades

were just average and she had some behavior problems."

She looked at him. "Fine."

"And she hasn't had enough time to make friends, with so many kids away at summer camp, so you probably shouldn't mention that, either."

"Is it okay if I say hello, or would that be too personal?"

Who knows? he thought. It might be. He glanced at her irritated stare and shut up.

The circular drive in front of the house was empty. Jack drove past it and parked in front of the four-car garage. Next to them, a middle-aged man paused as he opened the door of a black sedan. Their eyes met, and Jack got the odd feeling he always had when he met Ben Thatcher. He had never been able to figure out whether the man was his friend or his adversary.

Jack stepped out of the Jeep and spoke over the roof of the black car. "Hello, Ben."

"Jack." The man's eyes stayed on him for several seconds, making the usual wordless assessment, then strayed to his left, where Ellie was coming around the back of the Jeep, and lit up with interest. Damn, he should have opened her door. He always felt like he'd done something wrong when he was in Ben Thatcher's presence.

"This must be Eleanor," Ben said, and stepped around the car, smiling. "I've just been hearing about you."

Ellie looked puzzled but took the offered hand. Jack watched her go through the usual female response to Ben. She couldn't help smiling back. Even in his mid-fifties, with hair that was more gray than brown, the man seemed to always get that same long, appreciative look from women that Ellie was giving him now. He'd witnessed the phenomenon many times over the years. The fact that Ben never seemed interested in any of his female admirers was curious, but none of his business.

He cleared his throat. "Ellie, this is Police Chief Ben Thatcher. He's a family friend." Jack thought that was the best description, since the man had come to the house so often during Jack's delinquent years. Make that his delinquent decade.

"Hello." She was smiling shyly, already charmed by that boyish smile and intense gaze. Jack shook his head. What a shame to waste that sort of animal magnetism.

He interrupted the mutual admiration and cut to the usual reason for Ben's visits. "Your reports to my mother must be pretty boring these days. I sold the Maserati, and I haven't thrown one party since I got out."

"I know." The unperturbed smile said the police chief had been keeping tabs on him. "You're not the reason I'm here. I came to tell your mother about a prowler in the area. The Hardenburgs reported someone sneaking across their lawn last night."

Ellie's eyes darted to his, and he was careful to look nonchalant. It was best to say as little as possible to Ben Thatcher; the man had too many years of experience reading him.

"What happened?" Jack asked.

"Not much. No break-in attempts at the Hardenburgs' or any of the neighbors. Banner said the alarms were turned off here because some of the guests were in and out, wandering around the pool area, but the security patrol didn't see anyone. The detectives found tire treads from a parked car and prints from high heels. Doesn't sound like a prowler. Probably some woman out searching for her stray poodle."

"Yeah, probably," Jack agreed.

"There was a security patrol?" Ellie asked weakly. Jack nudged her in the ribs, but Ben didn't seem to find the question odd.

"Just a couple guys with dogs, walking the perimeter. You wouldn't have noticed them."

From the look on Ellie's face, he was certain she hadn't. Either the security guards had been slacking off, or Ellie was a better burglar than either of them had thought.

"I heard about your engagement. Congratulations, Jack." Ben's smile for Ellie became noticeably tighter. "Good luck."

They watched him get in the black unmarked car and leave. Ellie said, "'Good luck' isn't exactly like 'best wishes,' is it?"

"No."

"Are you sure he's a friend?"

"No. Come on."

He took her hand as they walked up the wide front stairs and pressed the button next to the carved double doors. Jack fidgeted. He hated the formality of this house. He'd grown up in an older home, with quiet, understated luxury. This house was new, glaringly expensive, and had Banner's prints all over it.

Ellie was twisting to take in every extravagance she hadn't been able to see in the dark last night. He tugged her back around just as the door opened on a black-suited butler.

"Good evening, Mr. Payton."

"Hello, Peters." Jack stepped through the doorway, with Ellie still attached to his hand. "Ellie, this is Peters." He nodded briefly at Ellie, completing the introduction. "My fiancée, Eleanor Coggins."

The man dipped his head in a formal gesture probably practiced by no one in America except his mother's high-priced butlers. "A pleasure, Miss Coggins."

Ellie stuck her hand out. "It's nice to meet you, Mr. Peters."

Jack squeezed his eyes shut in momentary pain. He hadn't thought to rehearse elementary etiquette, and knowing his mother, he was going to regret it. Ellie had already managed to make the damn butler uncomfortable with that handshake.

"It's just Peters, Ellie," Jack told her.

"Nonsense. If you're Mr. Payton and I'm Miss Coggins, then this is Mr. Peters. That is your last name, isn't it?"

The man had recovered quickly and took the offered hand. Jack could have sworn he was pleased behind that bland expression. "Yes, ma'am, it is."

In a flash of insight, he decided it was some sort of class thing. Her parents' jobs at that country club probably made her sensitive about giving servants equal respect. Judging by the secret delight in Peters's eyes, he conceded that it might be a fortuitous blunder. At least one person in this house liked her, and that was one more than he could claim.

"They're expecting you in the solarium, sir."

"Thanks, um, Mr. Peters."

Ellie took his hand again as they crossed the marble floor past the long curve of staircase, to the solarium that jutted off the kitchen at the back of the house. Its southern exposure through the tall windows and skylights captured enough light to sustain a small jungle. A few lucky ferns and small, leafy trees enjoyed the sunbath. The impression of foliage came mostly from the brightly patterned cushions on the cane and wicker chairs that somehow managed to look uncomfortable in their perfectly positioned arrangement on the imported rugs. It was his mother's most informal decorating effort, and he thought it reflected her personality perfectly—a studied casualness completely overcome by stiff formality.

Elizabeth Westfield was waiting for them. She stood in the center of the room and watched their approach with the regal air of a queen receiving her subjects. Only when they stood before her and Jack said, "Hello, Mother," did her features soften.

"How nice to see you, Jack," she said, sounding sincere and kissing his cheek, an elaborate display of affection. In an expansive gesture, she kissed Ellie's cheek also, not simply pecking the air next to her face, but actually landing a polite kiss.

He was impressed. He was also suspicious. He'd been sure Ellie would receive a more reserved welcome. He watched his mother take Ellie's right hand in both of her own, saying how pleased she was at their engagement. He knew she hoped for both of Ellie's hands in turn, that she was burning with curiosity over that left ring finger. Jack rather enjoyed seeing her cope with the suspense. He kept a firm grip on Ellie's left hand.

"Where's Libby?" he asked.

"Dressing. She'll be down soon. We were just having a drink before dinner."

Before he could ask who "we" meant, Banner stepped out from the small bar tucked behind a clump of fig trees. A woman followed, each of them holding two drinks. Apparently Banner had brought a date to the "family" dinner, a conspicuously improper move a mere two months after his wife's death. The woman moved from behind Banner, raised her head, and flashed a brilliant smile at Jack.

He stopped breathing. Now he knew the reason for his mother's easy acceptance of Ellie.

The sleek black hair was shorter, but the deliciously curved body and the natural ability to command attention were the same. Christina. He had been set up.

The unsteady lurch in his stomach wasn't desire. It was the sudden memory of his wild past and the daring girlfriend who'd had the same unbridled appetite for adventure.

Elizabeth Payton Westfield was dangling Christina before him like forbidden fruit. It was cynical and manipulative, exactly his mother's style. He should have expected it.

"Here's your drink, Mother," Banner said, handing a glass to Elizabeth and ignoring Jack's tense stare.

Christina held out her extra glass. "I brought one for you, Jack. Scotch and rocks, right?"

"I don't drink anymore," he muttered. Of course, she would already know that.

"But I do."

Ellie's hand reached across him and took the glass. Her left hand, which she had pulled from his clenched grip. She grasped the drink, the Payton diamond sparkling brilliantly in the sunlight pouring down from the skylights above. The finger wiggled slightly in the same move she had practiced at his kitchen table. She smiled beatifically and sipped, seeming not to notice the three pairs of eyes staring at her left ring finger.

Jack bit his cheek to keep from grinning. The way the smile had slipped from Christina's face was priceless.

Not commenting on the obvious would have been rude. "What a lovely ring," Christina managed.

Ellie actually looked self-conscious. "Thank you. It's larger than I wanted, but Jack insisted. You don't think it's too much?"

God, she was good. Christina murmured assurances that the ring was fine, no doubt choking on bile. Jack decided he might enjoy this evening after all.

Just to increase Christina's fury, he put his arm around Ellie while Banner stumbled through introducing the two women. A movement caught the corner of his eye, and he looked over Ellie's shoulder to see Libby standing in the doorway, watching. His arm dropped quickly enough to draw a curious look from Ellie, and she turned, too, when a small but composed voice said, "Hi, Jack."

He had the same feeling he always got when he looked at Libby, a profound amazement that he'd had some part in creating this little girl. This intimidating, intelligent little girl. Her hair was dark like his, but thick and straight like her mother's, and the eyes had a slight tilt that he couldn't recall no matter how hard he searched his memory of Libby's mother. But the chocolate-brown irises, straight nose, and wide mouth were definitely his, the Payton genetic stamp, and it gave him a strange thrill every time he saw her.

The child was the sudden focus of attention for five adults, but it didn't seem to bother her. Libby's head tilted and the gaze that rested on Ellie was as coolly assessing as Christina's.

He cleared his throat. "Libby, this is Ellie Coggins."

"Grandmother said you'd be bringing your girl-friend."

"Did she?" He darted a look at his mother's care-fully blank face. "She must have wanted to save the big news for me. Ellie is my fiancée, Libby. We're engaged."

The dark eyebrows lifted, but she didn't say any-thing.

Ellie stepped forward with a gentle smile and out-stretched hand. "Hello, Libby. It's nice to finally meet you. Jack talks about you all the time."

Libby looked as surprised at that comment as Jack, but she politely took the offered hand. If there was one thing his mother could teach, it was manners, and Libby had quickly learned the futility of resisting her grandmother.

"He didn't tell me how pretty you are, though."

"He has a picture of me." Libby was unmoved. Jack mentally kicked himself for not having shown Ellie the wallet photo.

"It doesn't do you justice."

Jack thought Ellie's flattery was sincere and spon-taneous, but Libby was as guarded as they came. He suspected any other twelve-year-old girl would have been pleased by the comment.

He was suddenly nervous, realizing the viper pit he had tossed Ellie into with Christina, Libby, and his mother. The female friction was almost palpable. She'd been doing fine, great even, but it would be better if he could at least even the odds a little.

"Libby, Ellie hasn't seen much of the house. Maybe you could give us a tour before dinner."

His daughter's eyes shifted to her grandmother briefly. She must have received the regal permission he would not have stooped to ask for. "Okay." It was dutiful, uninterested. But who cared, as long as it got them away from the scheming little trio in the solarium.

Libby started off without another word. Relieved, he took Ellie's hand and followed.

Eleanor tried not to gawk like a peasant visiting the palace, but since the analogy was accurate, it was difficult. She couldn't help counting ovens in the huge kitchen (six! Who needed that many?), noticing the large displays of fresh flowers in every room, and walking gingerly over the gleaming hardwood.

Libby appeared uninterested in each room they passed, and Jack kept his eyes on his daughter. Ellie couldn't blame him. The thick, dark hair, even features, and exotic eyes were pretty, and in a few short years she would be drop-dead gorgeous. It was a mesmerizing combination, and it was having a hypnotic effect on the father who had already been knocked off-balance by the simple fact of her existence.

Ellie recognized the rear hallway just before Libby stopped at the open double doors to the library.

"This is Banner's library. I'm not supposed to go in there."

Eleanor yearned to cross the threshold and snoop for just a minute, but Jack took her hand again, as if he'd read her mind.

"No problem," he told Libby.

They took a rear stairway, only slightly less elegant

than the one in the entrance hall, and toured the upper floor of bedrooms and sitting rooms, a blur of floor-to-ceiling windows, huge canopied beds, and small furnished alcoves that would have passed for living rooms in her parents' neighborhood.

"This is my room."

Eleanor stared. A vision in puffy, flowery pink flowed into leafy green where French doors opened onto a treetop-level balcony. She thought that perhaps Jack's daughter wouldn't be impressed by the bedroom he had waiting for her after all.

She turned to Libby, who finally looked less blasé about her luxury accommodations. As much as Libby tried to act nonchalant about her sudden wealth, a small part of her had to be jumping up and down with excitement at the recent Cinderella twist her life had taken.

"Wow," Eleanor said sincerely.

Libby made a happy sound that was almost a giggle. "Yeah. My favorite thing is the computer." She pointed to a sleek screen and keyboard on a writing desk. "It's got a DVD drive, CD burner, and more gigs than the one Banner has in the library. It's so cool."

Momentarily, she lit up like a kid with a puppy. Jack watched intensely, and Eleanor suspected he was alert for the next addition to his daughter's room. He was hopeless.

Libby sat at the computer, which awakened at her touch, and flashed through several screens as she showed off her favorite programs. Her comfort with the machinery impressed Eleanor, who could fake only just enough computer skills to land a receptionist job. Keeping the job was another story.

"I have some games, but mostly I talk online with my friends. See, Tanya and Rashid are on right now, and if I IM them, they'll answer me. That's instant message. Do you know how to do that?"

Eleanor shook her head, fascinated by Libby's knowledge and her sudden animation.

"It's easy. See, I send out a message like this, and if they want to talk to me, they send one back. There! That's my user name up there, Dragonfly."

Aha, the window decoration. If they gave points for good intentions, Jack would be in the running for father of the year. Either Libby was unaware of his efforts or unmoved by them. She felt sorry for both of them.

Libby's hands flew over the keys as she answered her friends. "See? You type in this box and press *Send*, here. Easy."

Eleanor nodded. "Like talking on the phone."

"Yeah, I guess." Her tone said Eleanor had done as well as her limited intellect allowed. "I just told them my dad's girlfriend was here." With a quick sideways glance, she explained, "I didn't know how to spell *fiancée*."

"That's okay." Eleanor looked at the answer that popped up on the screen: "You'll have a stepmother. Good luck!" It was followed by a string of letters. She squinted. "What's ROTFLMAO?"

Libby smiled self-consciously. "'Rolling on the floor, laughing my ass off.' That's Tanya. Usually I just say LOL, for 'laughing out loud.'" Her gaze darted to Jack. "But *ass* isn't really a swear word."

"No," he agreed. "Just not polite."

"Duh. I wouldn't say it in front of Grandmother."

Eleanor smiled at Jack. They'd been included in the cool group, not the one that included stuffy grandmothers, which was probably the most progress Jack had made with his daughter to date.

Libby's reserve returned as she led them back to the main floor, then down to the lower level. Eleanor hated to see the happy smile disappear and searched for ways to bring it back. Spotting a baby grand in one corner, she said, "I heard you're taking piano lessons, Libby. Do you like it?"

"Not much." The girl shrugged as she led them through a room decorated with enough silk tapestries and carved Oriental figurines to fill an import shop. "This is the Japan Room. Mrs. Stevens comes here to give me piano lessons."

Jack laughed. "No kidding? Mrs. Stevens with the thick glasses and fuzzy hair? She must be ancient. She gave me lessons, too. I didn't like them, either."

Libby looked at him with open curiosity. "Did you have tennis lessons, too?"

"Sure. I liked those."

She lit up. "Me too. And swimming." Perhaps not wanting to share too much happiness with her father, she turned her sudden excitement on Eleanor. "Grandmother said I need to be well-rounded, so I get to do all kinds of neat stuff. In the fall I'll get to take dance lessons. And I take riding lessons, and I can take them for as long as I want to. She even bought me *my own horse*. He's speckly gray and his name is Tango. I can show you a picture of him."

This was apparently the most amazing thing that had ever happened to Libby, so Eleanor gushed, "I'd love to see him." One horse looked exactly like another to her, but she'd be sure to act like Tango was the most beautiful thing on four hooves.

Libby looked suddenly awkward at her burst of enthusiasm, as if enjoying her privileged life meant she'd somehow sold out. With her former composure back in place, she continued the tour. "This is the gym. I don't think anyone uses it. And that part is Banner's private rec room."

"Really," Jack said in a flat tone.

By now Eleanor was jaded enough not to be surprised that the gym had more exercise equipment than her fitness club, with private showers and dressing rooms. The adjoining bar had the feel of Banner's library, wood paneled, expensive, and very male. The odor of cigars lingered around the poker and pool tables.

Eleanor pointed at two heavy oak panels set in the stone wall beside the imposing arch of a fireplace. "Those things look like they should have a function, like doors or something."

Libby shrugged. "They don't open. I tried."

Jack looked at them both in turn. "Can you keep a secret?"

"Sure," Eleanor said.

Libby looked suspicious. "Yeah, I guess."

He reached high on the right panel with one hand, caused something to click twice, then pushed. "Banner loves hidden mechanisms," he said as the panel became a thick door and swung open to darkness. He flipped a switch.

Recessed overhead lights lit brick corridors lined with wine racks. Eleanor stepped onto a red-tiled floor and counted eight rows, like book stacks in a cool, dim library.

"You couldn't drink this much in a lifetime," she said, awed.

"Don't underestimate my family's parties."

Libby's mind had been working in other directions. "You weren't supposed to know how to open the door, were you?"

"No. And you're supposed to keep my secret."

"Why doesn't he trust you?" she persisted. "Is it because you drove drunk and killed someone?"

Jack's molars ground together audibly. "No. It's because he doesn't trust anyone. Nothing personal."

Libby absorbed that with a nod, then walked back through the bar. Eleanor said softly to Jack, "That's one tough little nut."

He nodded grimly.

"That's a good thing, you know. She has to deal with some pretty tough people."

"Yeah, I guess," he said, unconsciously echoing his daughter's favorite phrase.

Libby waited for them to catch up, then led them to a media room that featured a theater-sized screen and enough CDs, DVDs, and fast food to survive a nuclear winter.

"This is incredible, Libby."

"I know. I've watched twenty-four movies so far."

"Twenty-four?" She tried not to look as amazed as she felt. Between the media room and the computer upstairs, this kid was spending an awful lot of time alone. Unless she was watching movies with friends. Ignoring Jack, she deliberately crossed into the territory he'd told her to stay away from. "I'll bet your friends like to watch movies with you. This is a great place for a party."

Libby turned those calculating eyes on her, looking far too much like her father. "I don't have any friends here. I have trouble bonding, and my emotional state is very fragile."

"Oh." There were obviously a few therapy sessions on the weekly calendar, too.

Libby bit her lip. "Maybe sometime you could—"

Light poured in as the door opened and Mr. Peters stepped in. "Excuse me, sir. They're ready to serve dinner now."

Eleanor wished she could shove him back out the door for one more minute, but whatever window had opened in Libby was now closed again. At least she'd seen a tiny crack in the kid's reserve. Maybe she could work on it later. With an emotionally remote grandmother and uncle, and a father who rarely got to see her, the girl was obviously in need of a friend.

A temporary friend, she reminded herself.

In the dining room, Libby faded into the background with practiced ease. Eleanor had hoped to draw her out but quickly decided the girl was better off being ignored. Between the intense focus of Banner and Elizabeth Westfield and the predatory scrutiny of Christina, Eleanor felt like a canary cornered by three cats. She hardly noticed what she ate, concentrating on an appearance of ease while desperately trying to catch the underlying meanings and motivations in every question.

Christina watched her closely from across the table. "I'm surprised no one has seen the two of you around town before this," she said. "Where have you been spending all your time?"

The little barracuda was still suspicious. Jack

deliberately took a large bite of food and looked pointedly at Eleanor to supply the answer. As if she was the expert at fabricating stories. He could have helped out a little, she thought. In fact, he might wish he had.

"We spend most evenings at home, alone. Sometimes we talk for hours. Jack is the only man I know who can quote Emily Dickinson." She smiled sweetly.

Three surprised pairs of eyes swung toward Jack, and he managed not to choke while he swallowed.

"I read a lot in jail," he managed weakly.

Christina's eyebrow lifted, and she turned back to Eleanor. "Really? He used to be a bit more . . . stimulating. I dated Jack for several years, you know."

"Oh? Did you go to school together?"

Jack hastily shoved a forkful of something into his mouth, smothering his laugh.

Eleanor knew she'd hit dead center when Christina's smile disappeared. The woman had to be at least five years younger than Jack and was not at all pleased to be taken for thirty-five.

Banner spoke up as if his date weren't turning purple. "I don't believe Jack mentioned what sort of work you do, Ellie."

Eleanor paused with her fork halfway to her mouth. Next to her, Jack stopped eating and listened with frank curiosity. They hadn't covered this.

Her mind scrambled for a respectable answer. She couldn't tell them that her typing sucked, that she had limited computer skills, and that her own cousin had fired her for incompetence when she talked his customers out of as many sales as she made. There must be some vague position she could name to fend him off.

"Well, I . . ."

"Ellie's in the security business," Jack said smoothly. "You know, breaking and entering, robberies, that sort of thing." He flashed a grin at her startled look. "Preventing them, that is. She could probably tell you where your own security system is lacking. Couldn't you, sweetheart?"

She shot him a dangerous look, but fortunately Banner was incapable of admitting to any inadequacies.

"I'm sure our security is quite adequate." He smiled tolerantly at her.

"I'm sure it is." She smiled back.

"Is your business here in Bloomfield Hills?" Elizabeth asked politely.

"No, I don't live here. I'm from Petoskey." Thank God. They wouldn't expect to recognize the name of a business so far up north.

Elizabeth Westfield slowly set her water glass down. "Do you mean you are staying at Jack's house?"

Eleanor hesitated, wondering if the woman was really concerned about her son sleeping with his fiancée.

"Yes, he has that extra bedroom. . . ."

"That just won't do. We have plenty of room here, and it would be lovely if we could spend more time together. Jack can help you settle in tomorrow morning."

It was another regal decree. She looked at Jack. He must have been thinking the same thing she was: She had just won a twenty-four-hour-a-day pass into the fortress he himself couldn't breach. She couldn't have hoped for a better shot at checking out the library.

"That would be wonderful. Thank you."

"I'll bring her over before lunch tomorrow," Jack promised.

Christina took a vicious stab at her poached salmon.

Libby spoke up from the end of the table. "Ellie, if you're going to be here in the afternoon, you could come to my riding lesson with me. I mean, if you want to."

Everyone paused at the shift in conversation.

Eleanor had little desire to spend an hour watching a horse circle a dusty arena, but she couldn't reject the slightest offer of friendship from Jack's daughter. Libby had asked her directly, leaving her grandmother no polite way to counter her suggestion. Also, it was better than Jack's threat to drag her to a football practice. She smiled at Libby. "I'd love to."

"You can bring Jack if you want to."

Jack slowly lowered his fork to his plate. Eleanor watched him uncomfortably, wondering how he would solve the dilemma. She knew that his uncle's invitation to the Lions' practice was meant to get him back into the men's social circle, an opportunity he'd probably been waiting for. A social outsider wouldn't look like a good parental prospect to children's services.

She came to his rescue. "I'm afraid Jack already promised to—"

"I can go. The other thing isn't important."

"Okay." Libby went back to eating, studiously avoiding her father's eyes.

Jack leaned back and glanced at Eleanor gratefully, and she knew nothing else she'd accomplished this evening was as important as that invitation.

Dessert was a wonderful confection filled with chocolate and brandy that didn't even pretend to be nutritious. Jack ate part of his, to be polite, but Eleanor devoured every sticky, cholesterol-packed morsel.

By the time they were sipping port in the living room, she was feeling full and very content. Also a little tipsy.

Libby had been excused, quickly disappearing upstairs. The conversation turned to Banner's boring promotion and tediously exclusive social events. Eleanor had relaxed her guard when she noticed Christina slink up to Jack while he returned her glass to the tray across the room. Narrowing her eyes, she watched Christina bend forward far more than necessary to set her glass down, nearly spilling her ample feminine charms right out of her low-cut dress. Jack ignored the display, but he wasn't happy when he returned to sit beside her.

He leaned close so the others couldn't hear. "We still haven't convinced Christina that I am no longer available."

"I noticed."

"I want this to end tonight. If we can convince her to stop chasing me, it'll be a good indication that our engagement is legitimate."

"Hey, I'm doing my best. Were you really such a hot commodity?"

"She's just doing her job. My family is pulling her strings, and I intend to cut them for good. Come on, we're taking a walk." He pulled her to her feet and addressed the others. "We're going out by the pool. Ellie hasn't seen the grounds yet."

It was easiest to follow complacently, but she told him as they opened one of the French doors, "I don't see how going for a walk will convince Christina of your unavailability." She said the last word slowly, befuddled enough by the evening's liquor that she didn't trust herself to handle more than three syllables at a time.

"We're going to tempt her out here by looking like we're taking a break from our little display of affection," he said, putting both hands in his pockets and keeping a few feet between them.

"We are?"

"Yes. And we will try not to look happy."

"Okay." She obediently frowned at him in imitation of his solemn look.

"Then when she follows us to overhear our conversation, I'm going to kiss you."

"You are?"

"Yes, and she's going to catch us in a private moment and know that we aren't faking it."

"Even though we are."

"Yes."

"Is this an unimaginative variation on your move in the library, only without the hand up my dress?"

"Exactly. It worked before, it'll work again."

"I'm not so sure your mother bought it, or we wouldn't be putting on this little show tonight."

"Shh." He took her arm and guided her around the corner of the pool house, stopping by a rose-covered trellis. The low yard lights lit the walkway, and even though it was nearly ten o'clock, the summer sky was not completely dark. If he was right about her following them, Christina would have a good view.

Jack put a hand on a piece of trellis behind her, angling himself so his back was to the house and leaving a clear view for Eleanor over his shoulder.

"Don't push me into the flowers," she told him. "These things have thorns."

"Then lean into me. This is supposed to be a romantic moment."

"Are all your romantic moments this staged?"

"Quiet, I hear something."

"How can you? That waterfall makes so much noise." She looked over his shoulder, past the man-made waterfall that fed the nearby koi pond. "I don't see anyone."

He leaned in closer, his mouth whispering right next to her ear. "Keep looking over my shoulder. Tell me when you see her."

"You're so sure you know what she'll do, but—" She broke off as a figure rounded the corner of the pool house. "I'll be darned. There she is."

"Is she watching?"

"Yes."

His mouth shifted suddenly and caught the corner of hers as she blinked at the shape over his shoulder.

"Is she still watching?" he murmured against her lips.

Eleanor giggled at the flutter of his mouth against hers. "Yes. Is that what you call a romantic kiss? Because—"

His free hand found her back and pulled her against him as his mouth landed fully on hers. This time he kissed her the way she remembered from the library, soft lips pushing gently against hers in a long, slow merging that effectively narrowed her attention to the interesting things happening to her mouth. The hell with Christina.

"Is she still there?"

Breathing rapidly, Eleanor blinked and made herself focus on the lawn over his shoulder. The figure was gone.

"Yes."

Her arms slid around his neck and into his hair as he met her mouth again, lips moving with more firmness and intent. She kissed him back just as passionately, her languor from the wine slipping into a light-headed heat that removed any inhibitions. You're just doing your job, she told herself as she flicked her tongue across his, prompting him to pull her even closer. And doing it pretty damn well, too.

He kissed her with deliberate care, each part of his mouth caressing each part of hers. She tasted chocolate and port wine and a heady, foreign flavor that was purely Jack. His kisses weren't the quick, frantic kind but had a way of pushing and softly sucking at the same time. She fell into his rhythm, letting him pull on her lip, then pulling gently on his. When his tongue explored inside her lips, she eagerly returned the intimacy. He was becoming as aroused as she was by the increasing pressure of their lips and the depth of their kisses. He seemed to want more from each kiss, which was fine, because so did she. Boldly, she moaned and opened her lips on his. Jack obligingly plunged his tongue into her mouth, and God help her, she closed her lips around it and sucked as it slowly slid from her mouth.

She hadn't meant to do it, couldn't recall ever having done it before in her life, but she couldn't take it back.

Lips parted and eyes fluttered open. She couldn't blame him for the stunned look on his face, since she was sure she wore the exact same expression. He hadn't missed the blatant sexual innuendo in what she'd done, and his eyes burned into hers.

He looked at her for several long seconds while her chest rose and fell noticeably, his face so close his breath mingled with hers. There was no mistaking the thought behind that intense, feverish expression.

She closed her eyes. She could not let this happen. Don't even think about sex, she told herself. It was absolutely, unquestionably a mistake and would complicate things enormously. It simply could not happen. Never, ever, ever.

"I think we should go home," he said, his voice husky.

And her traitorously slutty mouth said, "Okay."

Chapter Six

"You're going to change your mind, aren't you?" He started the Jeep and glanced at her as he threw the floor shift into reverse.

Damn right, she was going to change her mind. Temporary insanity was no reason to jump into bed with her phony fiancé, no matter how incredibly sexy he was or how many cardiac arrhythmias his kisses induced. And he was getting too good at reading her mind.

"What makes you say that?"

"You don't like losing control to me." He turned onto the street and shifted through the gears. "You're used to being in charge of your life, and it makes you nervous when I get around your defenses so easily."

She fluttered her eyes at him. "My, what a big ego you have."

He took his gaze off the road long enough to meet hers, a penetrating look that started little fairies dancing in her chest. "You don't always have to be the aggressor, Ellie. Stop listening to your head and follow your instincts. They seem to be right on target."

She swallowed. Having met her just twenty-four hours ago, he couldn't possibly know what he was talking about, so it was probably best to just ignore him.

"You can let the other person take control and still enjoy it. Especially since I know exactly what you want."

Some things she couldn't ignore. "You do?"

"Oh, yes." His eyes narrowed thoughtfully and a tiny smile caught his mouth. "You're a bright girl, Ellie. But sometimes it's good to stop thinking for a while. Let something—someone—overwhelm your senses. Someone who can stimulate every part of you and take his time doing it. Fortunately, I'm the perfect man for the job."

"Really." Her mouth had gone dry.

"Absolutely. After two years without a woman, I want to savor every second, every nuance of lovemaking."

"Yes, a newly released prisoner would have been my first choice."

His grin made her belly do little flip-flops. "I'm glad you have a sense of humor about it. I don't know your story, but it's obvious that you and I are both in need of a slow and exhaustive sexual workout. That's what I have to offer. I would want to kiss more than your mouth and touch more than your breasts. To make love to your whole body, slowly and thoroughly."

She had to admit, he had her interest. Eleanor bit her lip to keep from agreeing that it sounded like a wonderful idea. If she kept her big mouth shut, she had a chance of hanging on to her principles.

Jack kept his eyes on the road, his head cocked to the side as he considered how best to execute his idea.

"I would start by taking your hair down and running my hands through it, because I think it would feel just as silky as it looks. It smells good, too, which I noticed back there by the pool house. Or was that your skin? I'd enjoy caressing its softness again. Running a finger along your cheek, maybe on that spot under the ear where it's so sensitive." He paused for a moment, as if enjoying that very thing. "I might even kiss those freckles on the bridge of your nose, because I think they're cute and you shouldn't try to hide them with makeup. Then I'd have another intimate session with your mouth, because I don't think I could ever have enough of that. You certainly do know how to kiss." He smiled appreciatively. "Which only makes me want more. That top has a zipper, doesn't it?"

He was looking at the little gold top speculatively. Oh, God, he was making this difficult. She kept her back pressed firmly against the seat, nervously shifting her eyes forward.

Jack smiled. "I'm sure it does. And I would unzip it slowly, to relish the anticipation. I know you're wearing a bra, because don't think I haven't noticed the way that material shimmers where it rises across your breasts, and if they weren't confined, it would have been flashing every time you moved. Too crude to be tempting, and that's not your style. I wouldn't unhook it right away, though, because first I'd want to touch you with gentle little circles and see if I could make your nipples hard enough to feel through the material. I'll bet I could. And I'll bet they're light pink with a nice, rosy center."

God, he was good. She knew she was flushed and hoped the car was dark enough that he couldn't see it. His words were causing a reaction that her last boyfriend couldn't achieve using both his hands and mouth. To think she'd ever appreciated old what's-his-name—oh yeah, Richard.

Jack downshifted for a turn, then went on with his narrative, which he seemed to be enjoying tremendously. He was driving slowly, below the residential speed limit, unconsciously matching the leisurely pace of his fantasy.

"I hope you'd have my shirt unbuttoned at this point, Ellie, because when I have your breasts fully exposed, I'd want to know how warm and soft they felt pressed up against my skin. Christ, that sounds nice. Of course, I'd have to touch them all over again, pressing, and cupping, and teasing the nipples."

She shivered and clenched her fists at her sides. She couldn't help glancing at his long fingers where they curled around the gearshift. Long, and sensitive, and entirely capable of sending her out of her mind with desire. She pressed her eyes shut.

"And I'd want my mouth all over them. Licking, sucking, kissing—you know what I mean."

In his direct gaze she felt completely naked and had to consciously keep from crossing her arms in front of her chest. Thank God they were turning onto his street. She didn't think she could take much more of this.

"I know I'd be pretty aroused by this point, but I wouldn't hurry, no matter how hard it was. Sorry, that was an inadvertent pun. I meant to say that I've had a lot of practice being patient, and some things are better if you don't rush them."

She gritted her teeth. His house was only half a block away.

"A woman's hips are sexy, especially in those little lacy under-things. I'm betting you wear the kind with lace trim, because you don't look like the plain, ordinary cotton type to me. There's *nothing* ordinary about you, Ellie," he added with a chuckle. "I would pull them off slowly so I'd appreciate every curve of those hips and legs." He took a deep breath. "Then I'd kiss you, and stroke you, and touch you deep inside, just to watch you enjoy it before . . ." He stopped in the driveway and put the Jeep in park. "Well, you know what comes next. Let's just say the second orgasm would be as good as the first."

The second? What had she missed?

"That's how I'd make love to you. It's what I think you want, and it's what I want to do." He turned off the ignition and looked at her. "Whether we do it or not is up to you."

She hadn't moved. She stared straight ahead as he got out and walked around to her side. Her heart was pounding, her breasts were tingling, and her panties were damp. And she was certain he knew it. She didn't know if he'd ever practiced this type of verbal seduction before, but it was the best foreplay she'd ever experienced. He probably knew that, too. And this time, before mentally damning him for knowing her so well, why shouldn't she just take advantage of it? Why not accept a gift when it's handed to you?

Jack opened her door. "Ellie?"

She took his hand and stepped out. She met his eyes briefly but didn't say anything. He might have been curious, but he didn't ask. Wisely, he kept quiet and followed her into the house, through the living room, and into his bedroom. She stopped in the middle of the room and turned to face him. She was trembling, but it was anticipation, not fear.

"Show me."

He did. His seduction was every bit as unhurried and sensual as promised, beginning with kissing her senseless. By the time the shimmery gold top lay on the floor, she was breathing deeply and fumbling through a fog of desire to open his shirt, ready for that promised embrace. Thanks to his narration, she knew each move before he got to it, and her desire for the next one made her impatient. She had his shirt off and was tugging at his belt and zipper when he locked his hands around her wrists.

"Hey, slow down." His eyes smoldered and his chest rose and fell quickly. It was a great chest, as well made as the rest of him promised to be. She would stroke those lovely contours if he'd just release her hands.

"I want to touch you."

"And I want you to, but this is going to be over too fast if you don't keep your hands out of my pants."

She bit her lip. "I don't think I can stick to the script."

"No? Then we'll ad-lib. But I lead and you follow."

"Lead faster."

"God, I've never told a woman to keep her hands off me before, but there's a first time for everything." He took two steps forward, backing her up to the thick post at the foot of his bed. She felt the pineapple-carved top bump between her shoulder blades. "Here, hold on to this and don't move." He placed her hands behind her back, on the post, and turned his attention to her bare chest.

"That's no fair, I can't . . . mmm . . . I mean, I want to touch . . . Oh, yes . . . If you'd let me . . . Ooh, that's nice, but I . . . Oh, God, Jack, do that again . . ." She gave up her protests and let her mind go stupidly blank. She couldn't think when he touched and licked and sucked like that, his mouth following his hands down her body.

"See what you'd miss if you rushed me? Ah, small and lacy. Very sexy panties, Ellie. Who'd have suspected?"

"You did. I don't see why I have to keep my hands on this post."

"Because you're going to need the support."

"Why would I—" A finger slid inside her and another one knew exactly where to touch outside. Her knees went weak and she clutched the post behind her.

"Oh my God. I can't . . ." She panted and fought to order her thoughts. "My legs are shaking."

"Ellie, just shut up and hold on."

"But . . ." Her voice became weak and squeaky. "Is that your tongue?" Then she couldn't talk anymore, and seconds later her mind and body exploded together.

She went limp, slumping against the bed. Jack lifted under her arms and set her on the edge while she got her breath back.

"Here, hold this."

She looked down and found a condom in her hand. He was stripping off the rest of his clothes.

"More?"

"Don't you want more?"

She was sure she was grinning foolishly, but she didn't care. "Oh, yes. Please."

She would have bet she couldn't come again, and she would have been wrong. He took his time, and when he was finally moving inside her, she went over the edge so quickly it took her breath away. He was right about the second orgasm being as good as the first. He was right about knowing exactly what she wanted. He was right about everything when it came to sex.

So she couldn't understand why something felt wrong. Lying beside Jack in the messy afterglow of tangled sheets and sweaty bodies, with every part of her body blissfully content after the best sex of her life, she realized that her mind wasn't in agreement with her body. It was stuck on the fact that she didn't love Jack, that she'd only known him one day, and that she had no intention of having anything resembling a real relationship with him. She'd always needed to feel an emotional bond before climbing into bed with a man. The only emotions she'd felt so far for Jack Payton were anger and annoyance. And pure lust.

Eleanor threw her arm over her forehead and groaned.

"What's wrong?" Jack mumbled sleepily beside her.

She turned her head to look at the handsome face half buried in the pillow, the tousled hair, the beautifully firm butt, and the arm that was flung possessively over her stomach.

"I've never done this before."

A laugh was muffled by the pillow. "Liar."

"No, I mean with someone I don't know. I don't really know you."

He didn't open his eyes. "Yes, you do. We're engaged."

"Yes, I was already a rotten person for lying to your mother and daughter about that, but this clinched it. I'm officially a bad girl."

He frowned and propped himself up on one elbow. "You can't be serious. You think what we did was wrong?"

"No, but I think it's a bad idea to do it with someone you don't care for. And we don't care for each other, Jack."

"I wouldn't say that. I'm beginning to see some good qualities in you, Ellie. In fact, I'm looking at a couple right now."

She tugged at the sheet that was crumpled beneath them to cover herself, but he pushed her hand away, saying, "Don't do that," and began tracing invisible lines over the contours of her breasts. Because she was a bad girl, it felt good and she let him.

"I like your breasts, Ellie," he whispered, and kissed one lightly.

She shivered. "Why do you call me Ellie?"

"I like it, it's who you are. Eleanor is someone's sexually repressed spinster aunt." He grinned at her. "You aren't sexually repressed."

She flushed slightly, recalling the past half hour. "I guess I'm not."

"For which I'm extremely grateful. Two years is a long time to go without sex, and I couldn't have found a better woman to end my abstinence with."

Somehow that didn't sound like a compliment. "You mean I was convenient and, luckily for you, I was easy?"

"No, luckily for me, you were uninhibited."

"I was convenient and uninhibited."

He hesitated, as if suspecting a trap. "Yes?"

She rolled out of bed and picked up her clothes, holding them in front of her.

"Hey, come back, I didn't mean—"

"Thanks for reminding me why I shouldn't sleep with someone I don't care about. They don't mind insulting you."

"Ellie, I wasn't trying to insult you."

"I know, you were just stating the facts. Thank you, but I don't want to be in someone's bed because I'm convenient, Jack. Good night."

She turned her bare back on him and marched out with as much dignity as she could muster naked. Before closing the door behind her, she heard him fall back on the bed and mutter, "Hell."

They stood in the east upstairs hallway of his mother's house, just outside the bedroom where Mr. Peters was depositing the last of Eleanor's bags. Jack leaned close enough that their conversation would appear lovingly intimate.

"Don't you dare try anything stupid," he hissed. "Wait until I'm with you."

"Not if the opportunity presents itself," she whispered back stubbornly. "I didn't come to play house with you, I came to search that library, and that's what I intend to do."

"Ellie, I'm warning you, if he catches you in there he'll get suspicious. How much checking would it take to find out that Eleanor Coggins was Janet's best friend, Nora?"

"He won't catch me."

"Oh yeah, I forgot, you're so good at sneaking past security systems."

"Don't get nasty with me, you manipulative, lying—"

"Lying! You have no—"

They broke off as footsteps rounded the corner and Elizabeth Payton Westfield walked toward them.

"Has Peters brought your bags up, Eleanor?" She looked through the doorway at the stack of expensive luggage, most of it hastily borrowed from Jack. "Good. Thank you, Peters. Teresa will be up soon to unpack. Come join us in the solarium for mimosas, Eleanor. Jack has promised to pick up Libby's new saddle before her lesson, so he can meet us at the stable."

Jack's jaw clenched at the dismissal, but he gritted his teeth and smiled at her. "That's right. I'll catch up with you later, sweetheart," he said, and reaching out with unexpected quickness, he pulled her into a firm kiss.

He'd done it just to piss her off. She flashed a venomous smile with lips that smarted from holding them stiffly against his while he mashed them into her teeth. "Bye, honey," she said cheerfully. Idly touching the open collar of her blouse where she knew her hand was plainly visible to Jack but out of his mother's line of sight, she raised her middle finger.

He grinned, then whistled as he walked toward the wide front staircase.

She took a deep breath, willed her face into a pleasant expression, and turned toward Elizabeth Westfield. "I'd like to freshen up a bit before I join you, if that's all right."

"That's fine, dear. We'll be waiting for you."

In other words, *Hurry up so we can commence with the morning debriefing.* Eleanor watched the older woman walk away before turning toward her room.

Her parents' whole house could have fit in the suite she'd been given. The bathroom alone was as large as their living room and nearly as inviting, with a silk-upholstered vanity chair and a window seat strewn with cushions. A tiny refrigerator was stocked with fruit juices and cream cheese, and the bagels on the granite countertop were soft and fresh. She wouldn't even need to appear downstairs before lunch if she didn't care to.

She'd intended to set out her own toiletries but found the bathroom fully stocked with far more expensive and unfamiliar brands. At least she could unpack her own underwear before Teresa went through her luggage. She wasn't used to having strangers handle her clothes and would die of embarrassment if any of her bras were frayed or her socks had holes. She shoved the underwear in a small dresser drawer. She was testing the firmness of the unusually high king-sized bed, another of the four-postered, canopied monstrosities the Westfields were so fond of, when she heard Banner's voice speaking from the wall.

"Is everything all right, Ellie?"

She found the intercom and answered, "Yes, fine, I'm on my way down." If they kept such close tabs on her all the time, it was going to be difficult to sneak into that library.

Banner was pacing when she entered the room, but soon relaxed. She didn't know if it was the orange juice and champagne that calmed him, or the fact that she was no longer roaming the house unchaperoned.

She sipped at her mimosa and watched him warily. This was the first time she'd been near Banner without Jack beside her, and she found that she missed the security of that buffer. She couldn't read Banner. He seemed watchful and secretive, as if he was always holding something back. Not at all like his older brother. Jack had no problem letting her know his feelings, whether he was irritated or pleased. Or aroused, her brain happily reminded her. He'd been very good at sharing that information.

"I've reconsidered, Ellie." Banner pulled her attention back. "I would like you to review our security systems, as Jack suggested."

She swallowed her drink carefully while her mind desperately tried to figure out what Banner was planning behind that blank stare. Stall him, she thought.

"Why?" Oh, brilliant.

"We've had a prowler in the area. I think it would be wise to get a second opinion on our system, don't you? We'd pay you, of course."

"That won't be necessary." She hoped she looked confident and professional. "I'm in the process of moving my business from Petoskey, and I'm not really equipped to handle clients yet."

"That's why it would only be a consultation. If you have recommendations, we could have our original firm make the changes. If Jack trusts your expertise, that's good enough for me. I would feel reassured to have your opinion, and it would keep things in the family." He smiled smoothly. "So to speak."

She smiled back, trapped. "Okay. I'll look into it." If he hoped to expose her ignorance, he couldn't have picked a better place to start. Apart from picking his library door lock, she was clueless about security systems. She desperately hoped Jack could help her bluff this one out.

She had an hour to worry about it. As soon as they met at the stable, she drew him aside.

"Why does he suddenly want me to look at his security system?" she asked in a low voice.

Jack frowned. "I don't know, but he's up to something."

"I figured that much. He had that flat stare, like a snake ready to strike. I don't think Banner ever blinks."

"I'll give it some thought. Don't worry about it," he said, distracted.

She followed his gaze down the concrete aisle to where Libby was grooming her horse. The gelding, huge to Eleanor's untrained eye, was cross-tied in the center of the aisle, and Jack's eyes followed every motion as she brushed first one side, then the other.

"Yeah, well, think fast, because he might expect me to do it soon."

He looked down at her. "If we need to stall, we'll just tell him we're going out. Whenever you need to get away from Banner, use me as an excuse. I'll be a very demanding fiancé."

"Oh, swell," she muttered.

"I have to help Libby tack up now," he said, shifting the small English saddle that he held under one arm. "You can go watch from the observation room with my mother."

"Aren't you coming up, too?"

"I think I'll stay down here beside the ring. It's dusty, so you'll probably want to be upstairs."

Smelly, too. She had no desire to let eau de horse cancel out the flowery, light cologne she'd discovered in her impressive bathroom.

Eleanor found Jack's mother sitting at a table next to a wall of glass that overlooked the arena. She took a chair across from her. For several minutes they watched in silence as Libby and her horse made boring circles around the arena below, following directions from a woman in the center of the ring.

Without taking her eyes off the ring, Jack's mother finally asked, "Do you ride?"

"No."

"Jack is an accomplished rider."

"I know."

"Libby takes after him. She's very athletic."

Ellie looked out at the dark ponytail hanging below the riding helmet, the familiar features, and the determined expression. "She takes after him in a lot of ways."

Elizabeth Westfield turned and raised an eyebrow in the same manner Jack had, and Eleanor knew she was waiting for an elaboration.

"She's a tough little girl, already hardened by life. She closes out what she doesn't like around her and focuses only on what she's interested in, like her horse. Jack does that."

The eyes narrowed a tiny bit and she nodded. "You're very perceptive, Eleanor."

Not knowing how to respond to that, she looked back at the arena. But Elizabeth was no longer watching the lesson below.

"You were a bit of a surprise to us, you know."

"Yes, I imagine I was." Since the older woman

seemed to expect an explanation, Eleanor blithely added to the fictional history of their relationship. "Jack said he didn't want to introduce me to his family until he was sure we were going to make it permanent." All these lies were going to come back and bite her in the ass, she just knew it.

She thought that had ended the conversation, because Elizabeth Westfield turned back to the window and was silent for another minute.

Jack's mother fingered her diamond solitaire necklace thoughtfully. "Christina thinks you want Jack for his money," she said, keeping her eyes on the horse and rider, who were trotting now.

Eleanor glanced at the older woman, then looked back at the arena. It seemed they were going to take off the gloves. She could play that game.

"I'm not used to money, at least not in your terms, Mrs. Westfield."

"Call me Elizabeth."

"Elizabeth. I'm not sure I care to be rich. It seems to make people superficial, even downright mean. Like Christina," she added, so Elizabeth could pretend she hadn't been insulted.

"That's good, Eleanor, because Jack doesn't have much money. I have control of his trust fund, you know. When he went to jail I rescinded his monthly allowance, so he only has what he earns as an accountant."

That explained the Jeep. "I said it didn't matter."

The other woman watched her closely. "Then why *do* you want Jack?"

Eleanor should have been able to righteously claim that she loved him, but that lie didn't want to come out of her mouth. Instead, she went for the brutal truth, just to see how Elizabeth would react.

"I'd have to say it's his body."

The older woman was unperturbed. "Some parts more than others?" she asked dryly.

Eleanor started. She had to give the woman credit for coolness. "Oh, yes." After one night with Jack she had no trouble being sincere on that point. She glanced at Jack where he leaned on a rail fence that separated him from the riding space in the arena. He was grinning and calling out occasionally to Libby, complimenting her, from the look on the girl's face. "Jack can be very . . . passionate."

"If you're lucky, he takes after his father. He was a very *passionate* man, too."

Eleanor turned with unconcealed surprise, then gradually allowed a large smile to show. The creased ends of Elizabeth's mouth turned the slightest bit upward in response. "Even the rich know there is more to life than money, Eleanor," she said blandly.

Eleanor laughed. She'd forgotten that a young Elizabeth Payton had had a secret romance with a man whose identity she'd never revealed. A man who had evidently been as skilled a lover as his son was. It delighted her to imagine the stiff, formal Elizabeth being as sexually undone as Jack had left her.

Elizabeth allowed a quick, ironic smile. "I married for social position instead of passion. At times I wish I had chosen differently. If you thought to shock me, Eleanor, I am sorry to disappoint you."

"I'm not disappointed."

She was dying of curiosity, though. If Jack's father had been unable to provide the desired social status, exactly how far astray had Elizabeth gone when she'd succumbed to passion? Did she have a fling with the gardener? The chauffeur? Was his status as far off the *Social Register* as Eleanor's own? Couldn't she have married him anyway?

"If you thought your marriage was a mistake," she began carefully, "then why didn't you, um . . ." She faltered, realizing the question sounded intrusive, no matter how she worded it.

"Why didn't I dump Leonard Westfield and go back to Jack's father?"

Eleanor blushed. "I'm sorry, it's none of my business."

"No, it isn't. But I'll tell you anyway, since you seem to have evoked the same feelings in my son. Oh yes," she insisted, when Eleanor tried to object, "I've seen the way he looks at you, the hunger in his eyes that has nothing to do with love and everything to do with sex."

Eleanor shifted uncomfortably.

"I soon had another son, and I put my children's welfare ahead of my own. The Paytons have wealth, but no amount of money can buy the social acceptance, the heritage, that an old name brings. An unwed mother and a bastard son would need that. Leonard Westfield had it, and Jack's father did not. It was that easy. I thought it would be better for my sons if I sacrificed my own private pleasure to guarantee their social standing." She paused long enough to ensure the impact of her next words. "So perhaps you can understand why I would like to see Jack salvage whatever he can of that social position."

"Yes, I—"

"And why I expect him to make the same sacrifices for his child when he chooses a wife."

Eleanor closed her mouth. She could feel the heat rise in her face, but she couldn't think of any response to such a reasonably stated insult. It was okay for Jack to use her for a fling, but she wasn't wife material. It wouldn't even have surprised her if the older woman had flatly stated her disapproval. But she had warmed her up with shared sexual confidences, then slapped her across the face with the hard facts. Eleanor was like Jack's father, the memorable lover who had to be relegated to the past.

Even while she blushed with anger and humiliation, she could appreciate the artistry of the insult. Only someone convinced of her superiority could have so calmly dismissed her as unworthy. She should respond in kind. She should just as calmly retort that social status wasn't the most important thing in life, that Jack might have been better off if his mother had chosen a man she loved over one with a prominent name, and that Eleanor and Jack would make that decision without her influence, thank you very much. That's what she should have said. But Libby had dismounted her horse, and Elizabeth was doing a stately glide out of the observation room. She'd missed her chance.

"Did you watch me?" Libby asked, her serious eyes flashing an excitement she couldn't quite conceal.

"Yes, you're very good," Eleanor told her warmly. "I never could get the hang of posting, myself. I need one of those Western saddles with the horn to hang on to."

"Tango makes it easy. He's a talented horse, and Grandmother said he moves well," Libby said seriously. She glanced shyly at her father. "Jack thinks I'll be ready to jump soon. That's only for advanced riders."

"That's great." She wasn't eager to watch Libby cling to Tango while the huge beast threw itself over jumps. Thank goodness she'd be gone by then.

"Who's up for ice cream?" Jack asked. "My treat."

"Me," Eleanor said decisively. "I'm an advanced-level ice cream eater. How about you, Libby?"

The girl bit her lip thoughtfully. She seemed to be weighing the temptation of ice cream against the obvious pleasure her company would give her father. Whether she intended to punish Jack or simply guard herself against emotional involvement, making her father happy was obviously against her wishes. Jack kept his expression as casual as he could, even though Eleanor knew he wanted to beg his daughter to come with him. Elizabeth said nothing.

All eyes were on Libby as she considered her reply. Eleanor had no doubt the girl knew how much power she wielded.

Libby's face became expressionless, and her eyes grew remote. "No, thank you."

She didn't offer any explanation. Elizabeth touched the girl's shoulder and said, "Come along, then."

Jack forced a smile that stabbed at Eleanor's heart. "Okay, see you later." His eyes followed Libby as she walked off. She moved stiffly, without the usual careless kid-slouch, as distant and composed as her grandmother.

He looked so forlorn, Eleanor felt she had to say

something positive. "She needs to go slowly, Jack. I think she enjoyed having you here today."

"Yeah."

She sighed. She refused to play family counselor to these people, no matter how desperately they needed it. Jack was sane enough to work it out on his own.

"Come on, buy me that ice cream."

He blinked. "Oh. You really want some?"

"Well, duh."

A wry smile touched his mouth. "You have a way with words, Ellie."

He ushered her to the Jeep. Pulling out behind Elizabeth's Jaguar, he asked, "How are you getting along with my mother?"

"Dandy. She thinks I'm social trash, good enough for your bed but not for this diamond ring. I'll be expected to give it back, so our breakup isn't going to come as a disappointment."

He frowned. "She said that?"

"Pretty much. I told her I was hot for your body, and she's fine with that."

"What?"

"But she thinks your daughter needs a mother with a better pedigree."

He couldn't seem to get past the first part. "I don't believe you discussed my body with my mother."

"Not your whole body, just parts." At his horrified look, she said, "Oh, relax. It was really about me, and how I'm good enough for a fling, but not to marry."

"I thought that thing with Christina would convince her that I was serious about you."

"It may have, but it doesn't matter, Jack. You're

expected to sacrifice your feelings for Libby's social betterment, the way she did for you."

"What do you mean, the way she did for me?"

"She told me how she didn't marry your father because she wanted you to have a more socially prominent name."

"Son of a bitch," he said softly.

"What, you didn't know?"

"She has never said a word to me about him, just clams up and says she hardly knew him and to forget it. I actually wondered if she'd been raped and didn't want to tell me." He bit his lip much the way Libby had. "Did she say anything else?"

Like his name? Eleanor could almost hear it, tacked hopefully on the end of that question. "No, not about who he was. But they had a passionate affair." She paused, then decided the rest was worth saying. "I think she was in love with him."

Jack looked at her, then back at the road, and said again, "Son of a bitch."

She let him drive in silence for a while, but some things couldn't wait for his mood to improve. Like her safety in the Westfield house. "How are you going to keep Banner from pestering me for a security assessment?"

"I have an idea about that, but I need some time. Meanwhile, we'll keep you out of his way." He thought for a moment. "We can kill some time at the club, have lunch and let you flash that ring around some more. It's not my favorite place, but my mother spends time there. It'd probably look good for me if she thought I was trying to fit into that social circle again."

"Lunching with the elite; this gig is such a pain. Do they have a good crab salad?"

"You're just in this for the food, aren't you?"

She tried not to look smug. "It's a perk."

As perks went, it was on a par with Banner's party—an elegant atmosphere, delicious food, and lots of people trying to be inconspicuous while watching every move they made. The crab salad was a good distraction, but once she was finished, each glance around the room caught someone looking away quickly.

"I get the feeling these people all know you," she said. "It's like being with a celebrity, only creepier."

"It's like being with a killer."

She could sense the hurt beneath the bitterness and touched his hand. "Come on, Jack, they aren't treating you like that." Not quite. More like he had a contagious disease. Curiosity couldn't quite overcome caution, and no one had approached them, despite the stares.

"I can't believe my mother wants to drag Libby into this world," he muttered.

"I can."

He gave her a hard look. She didn't blame him; she didn't believe she was about to defend Elizabeth Westfield's actions, but he'd hit her hot button.

"She's giving her every possible advantage, Jack. Social contacts others would kill for, the ability to feel comfortable in every situation, and the skills to play their games, whether it's on the tennis court or at the dinner table. It will change her life."

His eyebrows went up as he studied her. "Coming from a girl who was raised without those advantages? Because from what I've seen, Ellie, you can handle any situation. I can't believe you'd be afraid to stand up to anyone who got between you and what you want."

She had to ignore the warm feeling that spread through her in order to respond seriously. Leaning across the table, she kept her voice low. "I may have been an outsider, but I was on the fringes, and I watched. And learned. And once I knew Janet, I was included in whatever she did. If it weren't for that, these people would intimidate the hell out of me. You don't want your daughter to grow up like that."

"Huh."

"So don't knock what your mother is doing for Libby. And if she wants to include her less-well-off friends, let her."

If he watched her more closely, he'd be looking through her. "Okay."

She must have sounded preachy, judging by his odd look. Avoiding his gaze, she scanned the other diners. "That still doesn't excuse how these people treat you. What's wrong with them?"

"My fault. I crossed the line by coming here."

"How?"

"This is the scene of the crime." He nodded toward the adjoining room. "The bar over there, anyway. It's where I was drinking the night I got behind the wheel and killed Joe Benton. Who was, by the way, a prominent member of this club. I'm not exactly welcome here."

"Excuse me. Mr. Payton?"

Jack looked up at their waiter. "Hi, Ryan."

"Mr. Fulton asked me to give you a message. He invited you and your lady friend to join him in the Tap Room, if you have time."

"Trip's here?" He looked at Ellie. "Trip Fulton went to high school with me. He runs his dad's contracting business now. If he's brave enough to be seen with me, I should say hello. Do you mind?"

"Of course not."

Handing Ryan a credit card, he said, "We'll be in the bar."

"Yes, sir. And it's nice to see you back here, Mr. Payton."

Jack grinned at the young man. "Thanks. It's nice to see a friendly face." As he led her toward the Tap Room, he said, "Nice kid. He's going to Wayne State on a scholarship from the club. Premed."

Ryan wasn't the only one who had been nice to Jack; a couple other staff members had greeted him warmly. Maybe they were all soft on drinking and driving. Or maybe they'd hated Joe Benton. At any rate, Jack's jail term hadn't shaken their loyalty, and that meant something. The club in Petoskey that employed Ellie's parents might not have been as grand as this one, but she was certain one thing was the same: Employees always knew the inside scoop on members. They knew who fudged their golf scores, who tipped well and who didn't, and who would blame the tennis pro for missing equipment. They knew the dirty secrets and the secret benefactors. And these employees liked Jack. As far as she was concerned, their opinion counted for more than that of the stuffy membership.

Trip Fulton shared a table with two other men in business suits who rose when she and Jack approached. She knew a boring business lunch when she saw one, even if food wasn't involved. She said hello, then excused herself to order an iced tea at the bar, leaving Jack to reestablish himself in the business network.

The woman behind the bar brought her drink but seemed in no hurry to leave. "You with Jack Payton?"

Ellie nodded. She wouldn't have been the first or even the fiftieth to answer yes to that question. She wondered if the bartender had been one of that number. She was cute, about Ellie's age, with short blond hair and too much eye makeup, which somehow worked with the pixie look.

"I heard he was engaged," the pixie said.

"That's me."

They exchanged smiles while Ellie got as much of an up-and-down assessment as the view from behind the bar offered. "I'm Pam."

"Nice to meet you. Are you a friend of Jack's?"

Pam laughed. "Who isn't?"

Ellie tipped her head toward the dining room. "Most of the people out there, for starters."

"Hmm." It was as noncommittal as possible. "Our Sunday lunch crowd is kind of conservative. You know any of them?"

She knew what that meant. "No. I'm from up north, no connections down here." And no possibility of taking offense at remarks that were a little too honest, if Pam cared to offer any.

"That's the heart of the old contingent out there, the backbone of the club. Also the ones least likely to know Jack."

"And to know him is to love him?"

"Sure." Pam's eyes sparked with amusement. "Ah, you mean to *know* him."

She hadn't, but was suddenly curious.

"He got his share of love." Pam chuckled and Ellie felt a surprising twist of jealousy knot her stomach. "But I meant to know him is to know he'd never do what he was accused of doing."

This was new. "The manslaughter conviction? You mean someone else ran into that man and killed him?" She wasn't even sure how that could happen.

Pam shrugged. "I don't know what happened. All I know is Jack Payton wouldn't drive drunk. And he didn't. I tended bar that night. When he left here, Jack was sober."

Ellie frowned. "The police must have done a blood alcohol test."

"Yeah. I don't know how it registered so high. He'd had a couple drinks, but that was more than an hour before he left. My theory is he hit Mr. Benton by accident and was so upset he took a few drinks from a bottle he found in the car. Who could blame him? All I know is he was dead sober when he got behind the wheel."

She'd love to believe it. But Ellie doubted Jack would have gone quietly to jail on false charges. She knew Jack well enough to be sure he wouldn't stand for being unjustly accused. With his family's resources, the legal fight would have been epic. Pam's loyalty was sweet, if misplaced. But it did say something about Jack's character.

"You got a good one," Pam assured her.

He wasn't hers. But she had to admit he was beginning to look a little better than the sneaky, manipulative ex-con she'd thought he was.

It was late afternoon when Jack and Ellie returned to the Westfield mansion. In front of the garage, a man was bent over a dark blue Mercedes, polishing the glossy surface.

"Damn," Jack muttered, "Banner's home." He got out of the Jeep with her. "Look, I'll hang around here for a while to make sure he doesn't bother you about that security check. Then I'll—"

A ringing sound interrupted him, and he pulled a cell phone off his belt, looking at the readout before answering. He smiled. "Ah, finally." Holding up a finger to indicate that she should wait a moment, he switched on the phone and said, "Rocky! Where the hell have you been, buddy?"

Guy talk. Eleanor leaned against one of the cement lions at the foot of the front steps and waited while Jack did some good-old-boy bantering and arranged to meet this Rocky person at some address he inked on the back of his hand. As soon as he clicked off the phone, he was in motion, taking her elbow and hustling her up the front steps.

"I have to go see this guy, Ellie. I think he can help us. Will you be all right here? Stall Banner if you have to. Can you fake it if he asks any questions?"

She gave him a withering look. "Everything I've done the past two days has been faked. Just don't leave me with him for too long."

"Right. Call my cell if you need me. Here." He grabbed her hand and used his pen to write the number on her palm.

She rolled her eyes at his sudden haste. "I have paper in my purse."

"No time. This guy might disappear on me. I'll see you in a couple hours."

He left her at the front door, dashing down the wide

concrete stairway. At the foot of the steps he stopped, turned, and flashed a grin at her. "Ellie."

"What?"

"You haven't faked *everything* the past two days."

He didn't see her blush only because he was jogging toward the Jeep.

"Arrogant bastard," she muttered, opening the huge front door. Across the gleaming marble floor, Banner stopped in his tracks. A slow smile thinned his lips, revealing white teeth.

"Hello, Ellie. I've been looking for you."

Chapter Seven

"What did you say the name of your company was?"

She closed the door and took one step forward, preferring to keep her distance. "I don't believe I said."

"My mistake." He dipped his head in a sort of apology and politely asked, "What is the name of your company?"

"Are you checking on me?"

The smile was disarming, a neat trick for a snake in a three-piece suit. She wondered if the suit indicated a Westfield practice of formal Sunday dinners.

"I'm a businessman, Ellie, and I'd like to know that I'm entrusting the security of my home to a professional."

"Very practical."

"Thank you. The name?"

She flipped her hair back nervously, letting her eyes dart around the foyer, hoping for inspiration. They took in the velvet-covered chair, the dramatic curve of staircase, and the ubiquitous bouquet of fresh flowers on an ornate table. Red and white roses mixed with baby's breath. Her mind raced, then desperately grabbed at an image.

"Red Rose Security," she said. Inside, she winced at her lack of imagination. How lame! It wasn't even a good lie, the one skill she'd been able to fall back on.

Banner's eyebrows lifted. "An unusual name."

"It had sentimental meaning. I'll probably use a different name when I set up business here."

"I don't recall seeing it in the yellow pages."

It was her turn to look surprised. Amazed, in fact. "You have a Petoskey phone book?"

"Online." The lips thinned again in a smile that said, *Gotcha.* "I think I would have remembered such a"—his eyes shifted briefly to the bouquet on the side table—"flowery name."

At her sides, her hands clenched into fists. She let the nails dig into her palms, hoping the pain would distract her from the profanities she wanted to hurl at him and let her think of a plausible excuse for having an unlisted company with no phone number.

Making sure her voice was steady, she said stiffly, "It was a new company. I did private consulting while I was working at my cousin's hardware store. Perhaps you'd like the name of the store, or some of my clients?" Her mind frantically sorted through any possible people who would cover for her: Aunt Pat and Uncle Bill, her cousin Frank, Pastor Ferguson . . .

"That won't be necessary, I trust you."

The man was a bigger liar than she was.

She started toward the staircase, speaking confidently in her best business voice. "Unfortunately, I have some calls to make right now, but perhaps I can look at your system after dinner." *Please, please be back by then, Jack.*

She stopped politely at the first stair, and his eyes pinned her for several seconds. Then his posture relaxed and he said, "My mother and I are having dinner at the club. Perhaps later this evening?"

"Fine." She smiled, sure Jack would be back by then. She only hoped he was not relying on her to bluff her way through the Westfield home security system.

She stayed in her room until the blue Mercedes left an hour later. She was briefly annoyed that they would leave a twelve-year-old at home unsupervised, since she had no idea where Libby was, until she realized Mr. Peters and the other servants were probably in the house.

The thought made her pause. She should do a quick tour of the house to determine exactly who was there before she made her next move. When she closed herself in Banner's library, she wanted to know she wouldn't be interrupted.

The house was as eerily silent as a museum after hours. Faint music from Libby's bedroom made her conclude that the girl had isolated herself with her own entertainment, most likely on her computer. Eleanor left the upper floor without bothering her.

The main floor was as deserted as the lower level. Mr. Peters was reading on the patio outside the kitchen, where she left him undisturbed. Creeping softly down the hall, she opened the library doors a crack, slipped in, and closed them behind her.

Eleanor had already decided to scan the papers in the drawers first, then search the computer files. Settling into the big black leather chair, she pulled at the lower right drawer. Locked. So was the one above it. Good plan.

She was about to search for a key when she noticed the drawers had no keyholes and remembered what Jack had said about Banner loving hidden mechanisms. She felt along the inner sides of the desk, even getting on her knees to see the wood better, until she gave an exasperated tug at the top drawer and nearly pulled it off its track, it opened so quickly.

Brilliant; she hadn't even thought to try it first. Further proof that security was not her line of work.

She sat down. The drawer held only writing paper, pens, and stamps, all totally innocuous. But it had opened. She pushed aside the paper and felt along the seams of the drawer. In the back, her fingers hit a protruding peg. She couldn't depress it, but it pulled up easily. She eagerly tried the second drawer; it was stuck fast. But the bottom drawer slid out with barely a touch.

File folders. She flipped hopefully through several folders labeled "Westfield-Benton" that contained what appeared to be background checks on employees. She pulled one out. William B. Crandall had the usual list of previous employers and college degrees. He also had an ex-wife, a shaky marriage, a son with a chronic illness not covered by insurance, and maxed-out credit cards.

There was no good reason for an employer to have that information. Certainly no legal reason. Eleanor held the paper gingerly as if the dirt might rub off.

Banner got creepier by the minute. *My God, Janet, what were you thinking?*

In the very back was a fat, unlabeled folder bulging with laminated pages. She tugged the drawer out as far as it would go, spread the folder apart, and lifted out two laminated eight-by-ten photographs. The first showed two naked women in an embarrassingly intimate embrace; the other showed a nude woman standing before a mirror, one hand fondling her more-than-generous breasts.

Eleanor made a face and returned them to the folder.

It took several minutes to find the trip peg for the middle drawer, and the effort was unrewarding. She wasted time flipping through papers before reluctantly conceding the possibility that not everything Banner touched was necessarily illegal or immoral.

So far the search had been productive, but only in confirming what she'd already guessed: Banner was slime. Nothing she'd found seemed to apply to Janet. Taking a deep breath, Eleanor prepared to locate the same hidden mechanisms on the locked drawers to her left.

They weren't there. Ten minutes later, she accepted defeat. She'd already been in the library over an hour, and she hadn't even touched the computer. If she hurried, she could still check the files before Banner got home. Dinner and the mandatory before, during, and after drinks would surely take more than two hours.

And speaking of two hours, where the hell was Jack?

Eleanor reached for the phone on the desk. Checking the smeared numbers on her palm, she dialed Jack's cell phone.

"What?"

His phone's display must have told him the call was from Banner's phone. "Hi, Jack. Where are you?"

"Oh, hi. I'm in Detroit. We're on our way back there. Is something wrong?"

She supposed "we" meant Rocky was coming, too. "No, but I've been going through Banner's files and I could use some help before he gets home."

"What? I told you to wait until I was with you. If he catches you—"

"He's having dinner at the club with your mother. It's perfectly safe. By the way, did you know your brother is a scum-sucking, porn-addicted blackmailer?"

"Damn it, Ellie, get out of there!" She heard a car horn blare and a growled profanity from Jack before he got his voice under control. "Listen to me. If Banner really has something to hide, he could be dangerous. You ever think of that?"

"Of course I thought of it, that's why I want you here. But I'm not going to sit in the sunroom, wasting my best opportunity and leafing through copies of *Architectural Digest*, until you show up."

"I'll be there in half an hour. Meanwhile, just get your sweet ass—"

"What's that? Sorry, Jack, you're breaking up. I'll see you soon." This was getting tedious. She hoped he was as worried as he sounded; maybe he'd get back in time to be of some use.

She ended the connection and booted up the computer. Banner might have kept files on disks, but she didn't know where he stored them. Probably in one of those locked drawers. Document files on the hard drive were all she could hope for, and she wasn't disappointed. There they were, thirty-two files all arranged in neat alphabetical order.

And all, she soon found, required a password.

She was defeated before she started. If there was a way to get around passwords, she had no clue what it might be. How could Banner even remember thirty-two passwords?

He couldn't. She smiled triumphantly as she spotted a file called "Passwords" and clicked it. It asked for a password.

She was screwed. She could sit here all night guessing passwords and never find one that worked. But she couldn't give up; she had to find a logical way to narrow her guesses.

What did people use for passwords? Names of pets? If Banner ever had any, she'd never heard about them. Janet had said he loved his boat, so she typed in the name *Fortunate*. No luck. People he admired? She had no idea who that might be, but typed in *Darth Vader* just in case. Nothing.

Think. What had Janet told her about Banner? Very little. They'd eloped to Paris and visited several major European cities; the computer didn't like any of them. Nor did it like family names, including Janet's. Quickly, she ran through things that might have meaning for a shallow, self-centered rich man—*Mercedes, Jaguar*—and, remembering the wine cellar, the name of every prominent winery she could think of, including the outrageously expensive Bollinger she'd had at his party. Still nothing.

This was taking too much time. It had to be something simple, because if he kept a list of passwords, he obviously didn't depend on his memory. Absently, she typed in the word *password* as she thought. The box on the screen disappeared. With a brief flicker, a list of files and passwords appeared. She blinked. She was in!

For a lying, murdering creep, Banner wasn't all that clever.

She scanned the list. Which file to open first? Her eyes ran down the list, then halted abruptly at the file name "Jack." The simple fact that Banner had a file on his half brother disturbed her. She quickly called it up and opened it with Banner's childishly mean password, "Bad."

Eleanor frowned at the screen. She was looking at a brief list of three names, all men, with numbers after them. Dale Messner, 10,230; Ralph Lundburg, 46,500; Robert Tull, 27,250.

She couldn't make sense of the numbers. Twenty-seven thousand what? Dollars? Employees? Frequent-flyer miles? They could refer to jelly beans for all she knew. She moved the mouse to close the file, then impulsively chose the printer icon instead. What the heck, maybe Jack would understand it.

The paper was out of the printer in seconds. Eleanor had just stood to slip the folded sheet into the front pocket of her khakis when she heard a distinct click. She glanced at her watch—a bit early, but it could be Jack. She waited, but after a full minute of silence she decided it must have been Mr. Peters. She clicked the "Jack" file closed and looked for something that might relate to Janet.

The library door swung open abruptly, and Banner stepped inside. Eleanor gasped and drew her hand back from the mouse. Her heart pounded in her chest and a flood of ice water rushed through her veins, but she drew a deep breath and smiled nervously.

"Banner! You startled me. I didn't hear you come

in." Her eyes widened with a fear that she hoped would pass for innocent surprise.

"I'm sure you didn't." From the dead calm in his voice, it was obvious that the innocent act had little effect. He strode to the desk. "What are you doing on my computer?"

"Nothing. I—"

He grabbed the thin screen and turned it toward himself. Relief mingled with fear. She had closed the "Jack" file in time; all he would see was a blank page.

His eyes flashed angrily, waiting for her explanation.

"I wanted to write a, uh, a . . ." Damn it, she should have been prepared with an explanation, and now she couldn't think with him staring at her like that.

"A what?" he demanded impatiently.

Elizabeth Westfield's voice came from the hallway. "Banner, to whom are you raising your voice?" She flung open the other side of the French doors and paused at the threshold, gazing imperiously into the room in a pose much the same as the first time Eleanor had seen her. "What is going on here?"

"That's what I'm trying to find out."

Eleanor gathered as much dignity as she could, which wasn't much, considering that her knees were shaking with fear. "I simply wanted to use the computer."

Banner enunciated each word with ill-concealed anger. "What for?"

What for? Good question. She wasn't sure what lie was going to come out of her mouth, when footsteps pounded in the hallway, and they all turned toward the sound. Elizabeth backed several steps into the library as Jack barged through the door, followed by . . . Rocky?

Three pairs of eyes gaped at the man with Jack.

He removed his sunglasses and baseball cap. A shaggy, black mop of hair promptly flopped over dark Hispanic eyes. The Hawaiian shirt in paradise blue and brilliant orange was a strong focal point, topping cutoff jeans and flip-flops. Gold glinted from chains around his sun-browned wrist and neck. The young owner of this ensemble turned a boyish grin on Eleanor and said happily, "Hi, boss."

She hesitated. "Rocky?"

"Sorry I'm late. Car trouble again. You know how that old Chevy of mine is."

Eleanor nodded, dazed.

"Your fiancé here intercepted my message and was nice enough to pick me up. Hey, he's a pretty cool guy, Ellie."

She bit the inside of her cheek, helpless to do anything but play along and hoping she could follow the script. "Yes, he is."

"So, is this the place we're supposed to do the security assessment on? 'Cause if it is, I can tell you right now you need more light fixtures near the front door. Those little sparkly things are decorative, but they don't throw off enough watts to scare prowlers out of the shrubbery."

Eleanor smiled at him. "I'll make a note of that, Rocky. I was just about to type up one of our assessment forms, since I didn't bring any with me from Petoskey." She looked at Banner, her confidence soaring now that she'd found the right lie. "That is, if I'm permitted to use the computer."

Banner turned his dead-fish stare on her, then curled his lip distastefully at Rocky. "Who is this person?"

Jack said, "Mother, Banner, this is Rocky Hernandez, Ellie's assistant."

"Partner," Rocky corrected, deftly promoting himself after ten seconds on the job. "Pleased to meet you, ma'am. You have a lovely house."

Elizabeth's hand fluttered to her neck, and she swallowed visibly. "Thank you, Mr. Hernandez."

Rocky grinned. "Call me Rocky." He held his hand out to the older woman, and Elizabeth, operating on decades of breeding and good manners, automatically took it, shaking hands gingerly.

Banner spread his glare over Rocky and Jack, then let it settle on Eleanor. "You can skip the printed form. A verbal summary will do."

She shrugged. "Whatever you say."

He ground his teeth with ill-concealed tension. "I have work to do. Will you all excuse me now?"

"Sure, go ahead," Eleanor said. At least she got out of doing the security assessment tonight. When Banner's frozen stare didn't waver, she said, "Oh. You mean you have work to do here. No problem."

Except there was a problem. If Banner opened a file, the computer would show him the last four files that had been opened. He would know she had opened the file titled "Jack." She grabbed the mouse.

"Just let me close up what I was doing here first. Oops, wrong heading. I'm not very good with these things." She was clicking frantically, opening and closing random document files. She had just opened the fourth one when Banner grew impatient and stomped around the desk, knocking her hand aside.

"Here, let me do it." He shut the file with one fast click.

She smiled sweetly at him. "Thank you."

She felt his suspicious glare piercing her back all the way out of the room.

Elizabeth seemed relieved to go in the opposite direction when they headed for the living room. As soon as they were safely away from the foyer and anyone who could overhear them, Eleanor threw herself into Jack's surprised embrace.

"You saved me! God, I thought Banner was going to eat me alive."

"You probably deserved it," he said, but without conviction. His arms tightened around her and she felt his breath in her hair. It felt nice.

A little too nice. She turned quickly in his arms, forcing him to drop them, although she noticed that he stayed close against her back.

She smiled at Rocky. "You must be the solution Jack told me he'd find. Are you faking it like me, or are you really in the security business?"

"Faking?" He looked from her to Jack, then smiled at her, scratching his head. "I'm not sure Jack gave me the full explanation on that. But no, I am not faking. I'm very good at what I do. Never thought of it as the security business, though."

"Rocky and I were roommates for a year," Jack told her.

"In college?" That couldn't be right, because Rocky looked younger than Jack, closer to her twenty-eight years.

"In jail," Rocky corrected, grinning.

"Oh."

"That's where I got my nickname. Rocks are my weakness." He saw her confusion and said, "You know, gemstones? Rocks." He nodded at her left hand. "Like that one."

She held up the huge engagement ring and looked at it. "Oh," she said again. Such scintillating conversation; Rocky was going to question his boss's intelligence any moment now.

"May I?" Rocky looked at the ring eagerly.

Eleanor glanced back at Jack, who seemed unconcerned, then held her left hand out to Rocky. He took it in his own, drew a jeweler's loupe from the end of a dangling neck chain, and peered closely at the ring, turning her hand to make the diamond flash in all directions.

He gave a low whistle. "Excellent. A truly colorless D?"

Jack shrugged. "I think so."

Rocky sighed and lifted her hand higher to catch more light. He looked rapturous, like a man in love. "Magnificent. Two hundred fifty thousand, easily. Probably more."

"You think so? Maybe I should increase the insurance."

"Do it," Rocky said seriously.

Eleanor frowned and pulled her hand away. The increased value wasn't comforting, and she found the admiration of a professional thief slightly disturbing. If the diamond had to be attached to her hand, she'd like to feel she wasn't a target for every "Rocky" out there.

Her new partner gave her that easy grin again. "Don't worry, Ellie. I never steal from a friend.

Besides, I prefer emeralds." He finally pulled his attention away from the ring and took a good look around the vast Westfield living room. "Hey, man, did you grow up here? We all knew you were high society, but I never imagined this." He strolled past a seating arrangement, pausing to run an appreciative hand over a Chinese vase.

"It's my mother's house, not mine," Jack corrected firmly. "I never lived here. It's a little big for my taste."

Rocky smiled broadly. "I'd have managed."

Eleanor watched him look for alarms along the two-story-high windows and remembered the first time she'd been in this room, on the night of the party. She'd gotten in the house far too easily, even if it had been dumb luck. It had been a gap in their security. She would dearly love to point out flaws in the system, if only because Banner seemed to think she would be incompetent. Raising her voice so it would carry to Rocky, she said, "You know, if we're really going to do a full security assessment, don't you think we should have more information? Like who installed the system, and what service they use for added security during big parties. Caterers and valets, too."

Rocky turned, surprised. "Not a bad idea."

Eleanor nodded. "I'll ask Elizabeth tomorrow morning." She wasn't going to speak with Banner any more than she had to. He didn't seem too fond of her after the incident with his computer.

"Oh, I nearly forgot." She pulled the folded paper from her pocket and handed it to Jack. "I printed this off Banner's computer. It was in a file named 'Jack.' Does it mean anything to you?"

He examined the paper with a furrowed brow, even flipping it over as if he expected there to be more to it. "I'm not sure. The middle name, Lundburg, is our family lawyer. There could be any number of reasons each month for Banner to have dealings with him. Messner seems familiar, but I can't place it. What are the numbers supposed to mean?"

"I don't know, that's all there was."

He looked at it a few seconds longer, then refolded it. "I'll hang on to it. If Banner had a file on me, it can't be anything good."

"That's what I thought."

"And that's why you need to stay out of that library unless I'm here." His voice was stern, but he looked more concerned than angry. "I know he's not above doing something illegal. And if he's as bad as you say he is, I don't want you anywhere near him."

"Oh, he's bad, all right."

"Ellie, I mean it." He took her chin in his hand and made her look into his eyes. "Promise me you won't do that again."

She felt pinned again, but this time she didn't want to squirm and get away. This time that penetrating gaze stirred something warm and familiar inside her. She took a quivering breath. "I promise."

"Okay." He didn't release her, and his eyes didn't leave hers.

"Hey, Jack. I gotta pick up my car if you want me back here tomorrow morning," Rocky interrupted.

The gaze flickered and his hand dropped. "Yeah, okay."

He looked back at her and hesitated. He wanted to kiss her, she was certain of it. She should have stepped away, but she kept looking at him, caught in the moment. He was really a very good kisser, and what would it hurt to try it one more time?

She could have sworn he started to move toward her, when they both became aware of Rocky standing near them and watching expectantly. Jack cleared his throat and took a step back.

"I'll call you from work tomorrow."

She nodded, suddenly relaxing muscles she hadn't realized were tense. "Okay."

"Lock your bedroom door."

It was an unpleasant reminder of Banner sleeping in the same house. "I will."

"Bye, boss," Rocky told her with a wink. "Looking forward to my new job."

She watched from the front door until the Jeep's headlights disappeared.

Rocky settled contentedly into the Jeep, pulling the cap back over his shaggy hair and sticking the sunglasses in his shirt pocket. "I like her," he said. "She thinks on her feet."

Jack shifted gears viciously. "She has to. She keeps doing these goddamn stupid things."

"Like getting involved with you?"

He took his eyes off the road long enough to scowl at Rocky. "I told you, that's all pretense. I'm using her, she's using me."

Rocky smacked his forehead. "Oh yeah, I forgot for a minute there." Jack's warning look only amused him. "She's got guts, too, breaking into that house like you said. In the middle of a party—that's style, man."

Jack grunted. "Like I said, it's stupid."

"And checking out the rent-a-cops and caterers is a smart idea. I think your Ellie would have made a great partner in my former profession."

"Just swear to me that it *is* your former profession."

"Word of honor," Rocky said. "I'm not crazy enough to risk going back to jail. Besides, I only stole from other thieves, not the innocent public. But I gotta find an honest way to make a living. I can't live off my savings forever."

Jack knew the feeling. He was still mulling over how he might find a job at Westfield-Benton that was suited to Rocky's peculiar skills when he reached the parking structure. He pulled in next to the new silver Lexus Rocky indicated and looked it over.

"Looks pretty good for a broken-down old Chevy."

"Hey, the Chevy was a good excuse. They believed it."

"This is how you live off your savings?"

"What can I say? I had a good retirement plan. Diamonds, emeralds—they make for a pretty fat 401(k)." He got out of the Jeep, then leaned on the open window. "Hey, Jack. You sure there's nothing going on with you and Ellie?"

"I told you, it's an act."

"So, since Ellie doesn't mind hanging out with ex-cons, you think she'd go out with me?"

For some reason, he found that irritating. "She's kind of busy being my fiancée right now. Besides, don't you have about five girlfriends?"

"There's always room for more lovin'."

Jack couldn't tell if he was kidding. He'd hung out with Rocky before, and despite his tendency to dress like an out-of-work handyman, women unaccountably succumbed to his tall, dark, and boyish charm. "Ellie has style, remember? She's not your type."

"I'm trying to upgrade. I think she's adventurous enough to go for a younger, wilder guy."

Ellie was adventurous, all right, and she didn't need someone who would encourage her to be more daring. She needed a more steadying influence. "Just do the job and don't mess around with the boss, Rocky. She's not available."

"If she's not with you, she is."

"Leave her alone."

"Leave that cute little ass alone? I don't think so. That sweet body is just begging me to do bad things to it."

Jack felt something snap. "Damn it, Rocky, keep your fucking hands off—"

Rocky pointed at Jack while pulling an imaginary trigger. "Gotcha," he said, gloating.

Raw anger slowly faded and was replaced by an irritated embarrassment. He wasn't happy about the feeling that had just surged through him. He was even less happy to know that his friend had seen it before he did. Jack looked at Rocky's smug face and growled, "Oh, shut up."

He got a laugh in return. "I like her," Rocky repeated. "You, on the other hand, have something entirely different going on."

Jack refused to think about it and deliberately shoved Ellie out of his mind as he drove home. He focused instead on the piece of paper she had given him.

The name Messner kept nagging at him. He was sure he'd heard it before, had some connection with it, but couldn't place it in any familiar context. The name didn't belong to anyone he knew at Westfield-Benton, didn't fit with the social roster at the club, didn't even belong to anyone he'd met in jail. He tried placing the name with less obvious groups—his college fraternity, the polo team, even his family's household staff—without success. He was beginning to think he'd only imagined a connection.

Tomorrow at the office he would check through the company's employee directory, just to make sure, even the South American division. Tonight he would put the name out of his mind. He would also put Ellie Coggins firmly out of his mind. He would not think about how panicked he'd been when he thought she might be in danger, or how nice she'd felt snuggled against his chest. And he definitely wouldn't think about how easily she stirred a sexual urge that had been completely under control until she'd slid under his defenses and cuddled up to his libido.

It wasn't going to be easy.

Banner was gone by the time Eleanor joined a silent Elizabeth and Libby in the breakfast room the next morning. She had gone to the dining room first, before recalling that the Westfields had a room dedicated, incredibly, to one meal. The room was sunny, filled with the light of what already promised to be a hot day, but the woman and girl seemed unnaturally quiet. She hoped talking at the table was not frowned upon, because she had business to take care of.

"Elizabeth, I intend to do a thorough analysis of your security for Banner. I'll need the names of any catering companies, valet services, and professional security companies you use. I should check the background of anyone who is given access to the house."

She expected questions, but Elizabeth simply nodded and said, "I'll ask Peters to give you a list of names."

"Thank you."

She started on the pancakes someone had placed before her. For the next couple minutes the only sounds were of silverware scraping on china, and it was beginning to make her uncomfortable. It seemed especially unnatural for a twelve-year-old to be so quiet.

"What are your plans for the day, Libby?" Eleanor asked.

The girl stopped eating and looked up, as if the question surprised her. "I have tutors in math and English every Monday and Wednesday morning. Social Services says I'm behind my grade level in those subjects."

She listed her failings as if they were the clinical diagnosis for some other kid. What was more troubling was the robotic way Libby jumped through every hoop placed in front of her. The girl wasn't having any fun.

"Maybe we could do something together this afternoon."

A tiny spark of interest flared, then died. "Social Services says I have to visit my grandma and grandpa in Wyandotte this afternoon."

"Oh. You *have to* visit them?"

"I'm supposed to stay in touch with them. I have separation anxiety." She pronounced the words carefully, as if they were well rehearsed.

"I see." The kid's life was as regimented as a new

recruits in boot camp. She was bright, obedient, and gradually getting sucked into a culturally enriched vacuum.

"Libby has many obligations to meet," Elizabeth told her. Then she surprised both Eleanor and Libby by adding, "But she is free tomorrow."

Libby stopped eating. Her cage door had been unexpectedly opened. She looked at Eleanor.

"We'll definitely plan something," she told Libby, jumping at the opportunity. "You think about it today, and so will I, okay? I'll talk to you this evening."

Libby nodded and looked far less like a zombie as she finished breakfast.

Rocky rang the bell at nine thirty, and Eleanor rushed to the door ahead of Mr. Peters. She found her assistant leaning over the cement balustrade, examining the shrubbery five feet below. He straightened when she said hello.

"Is something wrong with the bushes?"

"Nope. Looking for basement windows behind them to break into."

Cautiously, she asked, "Related to our security analysis, right?"

"Ellie, you wound me." He grabbed his chest dramatically. "I am a reformed and honest citizen."

At least his clothes were more normal today. He wore jeans and a T-shirt, just as she did. Since they were apparently going to be checking behind every bush, Eleanor decided she had dressed appropriately.

"Come on in. Mr. Peters is going to show us the cameras, monitors, and alarm pads, then we're on our own. Or rather, you're on your own. I'll just be following you and pretending to understand."

"Pay attention, boss. By the time we're done, you'll be an expert."

She wasn't, but she learned an amazing amount, the most significant thing being that she had been incredibly stupid to try breaking into the Westfield house and incredibly lucky to have succeeded. Rocky thought so, too. When she led him to the secluded patio and showed him how she'd done it, he shook his head.

"It's enough to make me reconsider my old profession. They've got great electronics but lousy guards. No wonder you wanted to check out that part."

"That's what we do next. But you'll have to give me time to change clothes."

"Dress for success?"

"Right. What makes a woman look more authoritative? I figured a business suit and medium heels. No open toes or sling-backs. I have to look serious."

Rocky looked her over thoughtfully. "Put your hair into some sort of bun. It's too sexy when it's loose like that."

"Okay. Anything else?" She tried to envision the completed look and realized what was missing. "A briefcase! We'll have to find an office supply store. Do you know this town? I'm totally lost here."

"Sure. Professionally speaking, this area was always one of my favorites."

"Good. Here." She reached into her pocket and pulled out the list of companies Mr. Peters had written out for her. "While I'm getting changed, you figure out the most logical order to do this in, so we aren't running back and forth all over the place."

Twenty minutes later she pulled him away from the

young kitchen maid and led the way to the Lexus. He followed reluctantly.

"You've got the whole corporate image goin' on there, Ellie, all slick and smart. Are you sure you need me for this part? I'm the blue-collar partner. I'll just detract from the perfection. I could wait here for you."

"Save the bullshit for the maid. You're my assistant, and I need the moral support."

He shrugged, having given it a shot. "You're the boss. But this is where I watch while you run the show."

That thought was suddenly troublesome. She'd never held a position of authority in her life and wondered what had possessed her to add one more fabrication to her phony résumé. If her cousin Frank could see her now, he'd collapse in fits of laughter. He'd fired her from his hardware store when she kept convincing customers that they didn't need what they'd come in for. If she couldn't cut it as a salesclerk, how did she expect anyone to believe she ran her own company?

By the time she stood outside Premier Catering, sticky and hot in the humid summer air, doubt had completely taken hold.

Rocky saw her hesitation. "What's wrong?"

"I'm getting used to playing parts," she told him, "but I'm not sure I'm qualified for this role. I've never had a job I didn't screw up. If I can't cut it as a store clerk, how can I make someone believe I own my own company?"

"The same way you pass as Jack's fiancée. If you act confident, they'll buy it."

"And if I sound like an idiot, they won't."

"Hey, you're the one who stood up to Jack's badass

brother and lied like a pro. Besides, this isn't General Motors. These people make fancy meatballs on a stick."

It sounded ridiculous enough to calm some of the quivering in her stomach.

"So, what do you think?" Rocky asked. "Shades on or off?" He put his sunglasses on, then off, so she could decide.

She smiled. "On. You're more intimidating that way."

"You got it." He put the wraparound glasses on, slicked back his hair, and assumed a serious expression. He looked more like a hit man than a business associate, but what the hell, an implied threat might help.

Inside, they waited for the receptionist to fetch the manager, who seemed to be the only other person in the store. Eleanor smiled and held out her hand as the woman approached.

"I'm Eleanor Coggins of Red Rose Security." The name sounded slightly less frivolous when she said it with a business suit on. "We're doing a security analysis for the Westfields. My records show they've used your services several times."

The woman frowned and looked confused. "Is there a problem?"

"Not at all. But for security reasons, we recommend a background check on any people who have access to their home. You probably have many wealthy clients, so I'm sure you understand."

"Not really. I check out my employees myself, when I hire them."

"Then I won't find a problem, will I?"

She placed her slender new faux-leather briefcase on the receptionist's desk to emphasize her professional look, the way a gunslinger might throw back his coat to expose his guns. *Watch out, lady, I know what I'm doing.*

"It's your job to provide catering, and it's my job to provide security. To do that, I need the background and qualifications of everyone who has access to the Westfield home. I can only recommend the companies I'm able to approve."

She watched the woman consider the threat of losing a major account. "I'll have to clear this with the Westfields."

"Of course. We'll wait while you make the call."

Eleanor relaxed. While the woman talked to Mr. Peters, Rocky gave her a wink. Her first assignment as president of Red Rose Security was going well.

After half an hour of looking at employment applications and references, Premier Catering passed their inspection. Eleanor celebrated her first executive success with a B.K. Broiler and fries.

"This is fun," she admitted to Rocky between bites. "I must like bossing people around. Where can I find a job doing that?"

"Management. You've got such a natural line of bullshit—even I believed it."

She smiled. "I think I'll take that as a compliment."

Rocky squinted as if trying to figure out how it could be taken as anything else. Her phone rang and she opened the thin briefcase to retrieve it.

"Jack?" Her high spirits spilled over into an eagerness to tell him about her first business success. "You should see me! I've morphed into a small-business owner today. Rocky says I lie well enough to be in management."

"Then maybe I can get you a job at Westfield-Benton. That seems to be a requirement around here." His voice was cynical and not nearly as happy as hers.

"What do you mean?"

"The accounts for the South American division have disappeared from my office. Those are the ones where I found discrepancies. So I went looking for them. They're gone."

"Gone?"

"Disappeared. I was told that Spencer in Billing had them, then Spencer tells me Steinberg has them, but Steinberg says he hasn't seen them, maybe Kelly has them . . . the wild-goose chase goes on and on. The end result is someone doesn't want me to see them."

"Banner."

"Exactly. And I don't know which employees are his lying minions and which are just kept in the dark. So I spent the rest of the morning talking with people in Colombia I can trust to tell me the truth. I've learned some interesting things."

Eleanor listened while she chewed, prompting when necessary. "Like what?"

"Like the accounting office down there was eliminated and all operations transferred up here. Very suspicious. And they switched shipping firms. This is the part that might interest you, Ellie."

There was only one thing that interested her. Eleanor put her burger down, her hunger forgotten. "You found out something about Janet?"

"For starters, I found out her last name was Aims."

"That's right, Janet Aims. I could have told you that."

"As in Aims Air Freight?"

"That's her dad's company. Janet worked in the Latin American Operations department for a while."

His voice became even more dry. "That's the company my stepfather was trying to buy for the three or four years before his death. Aims wouldn't sell. Then Banner marries his daughter, and the next thing you know, Westfield-Benton owns Aims Air Freight."

She didn't want to believe the glaring implication that Janet had been duped into marriage just so Banner and his father could acquire her father's company. "Why would Leonard Westfield want to own an airline company?"

"To get better rates on shipping, or so he claimed. But they don't ship enough to make it worthwhile. Or they didn't when I ran the division, which is why I argued against it. Apparently, that's changed, because Banner is raking in huge profits from the air freight division."

The line of reasoning wasn't too hard to follow. "You think something illegal is going on with Aims Air Freight, and Janet found out."

"I'd bet on it."

And just like that, a piece fell into place in her mind with an almost audible click. It was so obvious she didn't know why she hadn't seen it before.

"Jack, I think I may know where some information is on the Aims account. When I was searching Banner's computer files, I saw one titled 'AAF.' That must mean Aims Air Freight, but at the time it didn't mean anything special. And then I saw that file with your name and I got distracted. But now I'm sure it has something to do with that shipping account. Damn it, Jack, we need to get into that computer again. Before tomorrow would be good, because I'm spending Tuesday with Libby." There was a prolonged silence on the other end. "Jack? Don't you agree?"

"Sorry, I was momentarily stunned. I'm enjoying the notion that my name distracted you from looking for evidence about Janet."

Now she was the one who was flustered. "Don't let it go to your head. Just because I was nice enough to put aside my concerns to do you a favor—"

"No, you weren't nice, you were distracted. You said it."

She could picture his smug face, and it only infuriated her. "I'm not discussing this with you. But I strongly suggest you get into that computer and open that file."

"Tonight." His voice was as unconcerned as if he'd arranged a time to play tennis. "I want you there."

It was entirely his fault that her mind got stuck on the "I want you" part. His playful mood had encouraged an erotic flashback to Saturday night, when she'd received a detailed lesson in exactly what "I want you" meant.

She didn't think she could respond without giving him another reason to take her words out of context. She settled for a strangled, "Bye."

"Problems?" Rocky asked.

Oh yes. Big, huge, enormous problems. Jack had apparently flipped some sexual switch in her body, and she didn't know how to turn it off. No matter how she resisted, some primal part of her responded to him. Her wanton little body kept lusting after his, and very sensitive parts of her flushed and tingled when he showed the slightest interest. Even over the damn phone! The worst part was, her formerly rational brain was starting to wonder why she was denying herself so much fun. She had a problem, all right.

"Nothing I can't handle," she told Rocky, and firmly refused to think about various pleasurable ways of handling Jack.

She hadn't realized that checking out the security and valet companies would take the rest of the day. It was nearly six o'clock when she and Rocky returned to the Westfield house.

She felt slightly uncomfortable opening the big front doors and walking in, but it didn't seem proper for a houseguest to knock. They walked into the living room as she handed Rocky a list of notes she'd taken on the security company Banner had used for his party. Distracted by a sound, she looked up. Across the expanse of carpet, wood, and silk rugs, five people rose from their chairs.

Eleanor stopped. Elizabeth and Banner had stood immediately, the three women with them rising belatedly, like guests at a church service attempting to follow the unfamiliar rituals. At least the women looked genuinely curious and could not see Banner frowning behind them. Elizabeth stared at Rocky warily, apparently even less captivated by his hit-man look than she had been by yesterday's surfer dude outfit.

"I'm sorry," Eleanor said. "I didn't realize you had company."

"Please come in," Elizabeth replied, surprising both Eleanor and Banner. "I'd like to introduce you to the advisory committee for the Arts Council."

Tucking a stray wisp back into her no-nonsense businesswoman bun, Eleanor crossed the room to shake hands with the older women. She noticed Rocky hastily run a hand through his hair before he followed.

Elizabeth recited three names that Eleanor promptly forgot, except that they all sounded like British towns, ending with *cliff* and *shire*, each properly suffused with money. She stood aside when Elizabeth reluctantly introduced "Eleanor's business associate, Mr. Hernandez," and Rocky stepped forward to briskly pump each wrinkled white hand.

The women were intrigued. Eyes alight with unasked questions darted between the pale blue business suit and the slick Hispanic Mafia look. The conversational possibilities tempted Eleanor, but Banner's impatience put her off. No need to annoy him any further than she already had.

"I don't want to interrupt your discussion. We've just completed your security assessment, Banner, so I'll put a summary together and go over it with you later."

She had turned to leave when Banner's voice cut across the group. "That won't be necessary, just tell me now."

She hesitated. "Here?"

"Yes, here. Is our security adequate or not?"

What a jerk. He seemed to enjoy treating her like the hired help in front of guests. She exchanged glances with Rocky, who smiled and lifted an eyebrow. If it was a dare, they accepted.

"It's more than adequate. You have an excellent system."

"I thought so. Thank you," he added in dismissal.

"The hardware, that is. The human aspect, however, is seriously flawed. It's a wonder you haven't been robbed."

It had the hoped-for effect. All five of them stared, the Anglo-Saxon contingent with open interest, Elizabeth with concern, and Banner with annoyance. He growled, "What are you talking about?"

"I'm talking about Armed Alert, the company you use for added security during social gatherings when your house is filled with people and your alarm system is off."

"It's a highly regarded, professional company," he said, emphasizing the words, implying that she was neither highly regarded nor professional. "Their guards are retired police officers. I think they know what they're doing."

All eyes shifted back to her. She met Banner's gaze unflinchingly. *Okay, buddy, you asked for it.*

"Yes, and they have shiny new patrol cars and spiffy uniforms. I'll bet that impressed you. Do you know how many retired cops you get when you ask for four security men? One. Do you know what qualifications those other three men have? Two hours of instruction and a permit to carry a gun. I'd like to say they require a high school diploma, but they don't. Their background check consists of a phone call to determine if there are any current warrants out on them. I could give you a profile on the three men who accompanied the retired officer the night of your most recent party, if you're interested."

Elizabeth appeared keenly interested, but Banner didn't. His lips were pressed together and a muscle beside his eye had developed a pulsing tic.

"Perhaps later," she told him. "I'm glad to say that your catering service and valet company are staffed with excellent, well-paid people. If this had been a more thorough check, I would have examined hiring procedures and qualifications at the search company you use for hiring household staff." She smiled at Elizabeth, who was listening intently. "Although I'm sure Mr. Peters does an excellent job of screening all applicants." From the slight nod that she received, she had guessed correctly.

Turning an innocent gaze back to Banner, she said, "Mr. Hernandez is an expert in the field and knows the reputations of several local security companies. He could recommend an alternative to Armed Alert, if you're interested."

"Also a lawn service to remove a few bushes by your front porch," Rocky said. "Too many opportunities for concealment close to the front door."

The three guests appeared impressed with Rocky's expertise, and he favored them with a small, confident smile. When he did, the stern Mafioso transformed into a suave gigolo. Eleanor wasn't sure but thought it must be the slicked-back hair.

The group was watching her. She faced four impressed women and one very pissed-off man. Her job was done.

"It was nice to have met you." She smiled warmly at the members of the Arts Council before she and Rocky turned and made a dignified exit.

Back in the foyer, and out of sight of the living

room, Rocky grinned and raised a hand in front of her. "Slap me five, boss."

She slapped her hand against his and laughed. "We looked good, didn't we?"

"You were cool. I'm glad you didn't let that bastard intimidate you."

"He makes me nervous," she confessed. "But then he makes me so mad I forget to be scared. It helped that you were there with me."

"I was very cool, too," he agreed. "We make a kick-ass team, lady."

She let the feeling of success wash over her. She didn't get to experience it that often. "We are good, aren't we? I can't wait to tell Jack—"

Heels clicked on the marble floor and she turned to see one of the Arts Council trio determinedly heading toward them. Eleanor couldn't recall her name but knew it was something-shire. She mentally sorted through the possibilities. Yorkshire? Cheshire? Staffordshire? There were too many possibilities—those Brits really stuck with a suffix when they liked it.

"I'm glad I caught you, dear." The woman looked pleased with herself at this accomplishment. "I had to tell you how impressed I was with your work."

"Thank you."

"And I would like to arrange a similar analysis for my home. There is no substitute for a good security system, and I am not at all certain I am getting what I paid for. I'm not good at these technical things, you know. Mr. Hampshire used to make all those decisions."

Hampshire! "That's very flattering, Mrs. Hampshire, but I don't have my business set up here yet."

"So it may take a few days before we can do it," Rocky finished smoothly. "But we'd be happy to make you our first customer as soon as Ellie opens the office."

What office? Eleanor was about to interrupt him, but Mrs. Hampshire was beaming with satisfaction.

"Thank you. I will feel so much safer if you do. Please call me soon. Elizabeth has my number, dear." She directed the last comment at Eleanor before pivoting smartly and heading back toward the living room. Eleanor watched, speechless.

"Nice going, boss. I think this little business just might work out."

"You shouldn't have done that, Rocky."

"Why not?"

"Because I don't know how to run a business. And I have other things to do."

"Like what? Sit around by the pool, flashing that ring and distracting passing airplanes? You have something pressing to get back to up north?"

"No, but I came here for another reason."

"I know, I heard all about it, but you'll still have plenty of time on your hands. And don't tell me you can't run a business, 'cause you've been doing it all day. Like I said, you're a natural, Ellie."

She looked skeptically at Rocky, then back toward the living room. "You really think we should do it?"

"We're good at it." He watched her waver. "And you'll be keeping me legal, putting an ex-con on the path to honest employment."

She gave him a warning look. "Don't try to appeal to my sense of social responsibility, because I'm not your parole officer. I'm trusting you because Jack does. Tell me that's not a mistake."

"I promise." He sketched a cross over his chest.

She was silent for a moment, then bit her lip thoughtfully. "I suppose I could help you get the business started, then hire someone to run the office when I leave."

He nodded. "Sure."

"You'd have to come up with the front money."

"Got it covered."

She couldn't help it—ideas started to prioritize themselves in her mind. Renting office space, buying a computer and printer, and ordering shirts with the company logo, whenever they decided what the hell it would be. "We'll need business cards," she said aloud.

"Something simple but classy. What's our company's name again?"

"Red Rose Security."

Rocky's brow furrowed momentarily as he silently mouthed the name, then he shrugged. "I can live with it."

Chapter Eight

When Jack arrived he asked to see Libby. To his surprise, Mr. Peters directed him to his daughter's bedroom. Even before he reached the door he could hear Ellie's voice, light and playful, followed by the lower sound of his mother's response, then, drowning out both of them, the surprising sound of Libby's laughter. He stopped in the doorway, curious.

They had their backs to him. Libby sat at her computer with Ellie leaning over her shoulder, both of them excited about something on the screen. He took a moment to appreciate the long, bare legs below Ellie's sundress, acutely missing the feel of them entwined with his own. His mother sat nearby on an upholstered chair, paging through a magazine, listening and offering occasional comments that seemed to relate to fashion. As he stood there, she said something in a dry tone that elicited giggles from Libby and Ellie. Watching, he couldn't help smiling himself.

"Hi, what are you ladies doing?"

Ellie turned and exclaimed, "Jack!" with what

appeared to be sincere joy. At the same moment, Libby looked over her shoulder, her smile became tighter, and she turned back to her computer without comment.

Conflicting emotions tore at him. The stranger who was his daughter was, as usual, annoyed by his presence, while the stranger pretending to be his fiancée had, in the moment before regaining her composure, seemed truly delighted to see him. And the most confusing part was, for that brief moment of Ellie's delight, a warm glow had wrapped around him and deluded him into feeling a similar joy.

What a sap.

Stupid, too, because he knew what a good liar Ellie was, and that she was only pretending to be thrilled for the benefit of his daughter and his mother.

His mother. At least there was a dependable presence. She looked up from her magazine and said, "Hello, Jack, I'm glad you could make it. You've kept us waiting quite a while."

He smiled, not the least bit disturbed by her passive-aggressive greeting. It was safe and familiar; no emotional surprises there. "Hello, Mother."

"Jack, come look at this." Ellie grabbed his hand and pulled him toward the computer. As he stepped forward she seemed to recall her role and paused to give him a dutiful kiss, just off center enough to miss his mouth and catch his cheek. It was over before he could pucker, a properly chaste kiss performed for the benefit of his mother and daughter. Still, in the highly charged state that possessed him whenever he was near Ellie, it awakened every male instinct in his body. He had a sudden vision of tugging her back against him, entwining his fingers in her hair, and holding her head steady while his tongue played slow, erotic games with her mouth. He knew exactly how she would react. She would relax into him and make those little moans that drove him crazy and sent blood surging to parts of his body that—

"Libby designed a business card for me." Ellie's words penetrated his fantasy and he struggled to concentrate. "She can do just about anything on this computer, but I want to keep the design simple. What do you think?"

He must have missed something. "Business card?"

"You know, for Red Rose Security." She was giving him a piercing look, and he got the feeling he was supposed to shut up and pay attention. "I know we said I wouldn't open the office right away, that we'd wait until after we're married, but Mrs. Hampshire asked us to do a security analysis for her, and Rocky wants to get started soon."

"Rocky said that?" Rocky was supposed to have been doing him a simple favor. The guy must be more serious about finding employment than he'd realized.

"I'd like to order a sample business card tomorrow when we go out shopping."

"I can make one, Ellie," Libby offered.

"We're going shopping?" Jack asked.

She rolled her eyes. "Not you and me. *We're* going," she said, circling her hand to include Libby and Elizabeth. "Girls' day out."

"It's going to rain tomorrow," Libby explained logically, "so we have to plan something indoors."

He remembered Ellie telling him about her promise to spend Tuesday with Libby. "What are you shopping for?"

It was evidently a stupid question. All three of them looked at him with the sort of pity reserved for the simple-minded.

"For whatever we find that we decide we want," Ellie said slowly so his feeble male brain could comprehend.

He filed away a woman's propensity to shop with other great mysteries of life he would never understand. He pulled out his wallet. "Here, take my credit card."

Ellie looked at the card in surprise, but it was his mother who spoke first. "For heaven's sake, Jack, I have plenty of credit cards."

"Fine, use them. But Ellie and Libby will use mine."

"That's not necessary," Elizabeth insisted. "The shopping trip was our idea, and I can certainly buy things for my granddaughter. And Eleanor," she added.

"I will be the one to pay for my daughter and my fiancée," he said firmly. He shoved the credit card into Ellie's hand and commanded, "Here, take it."

She looked at the card. "I have my own," she said hesitantly.

Judging from the car she drove and her Hefty Cinch Sack luggage, it already carried a large balance. His voice was gentler but just as determined. "Use mine, Ellie."

She shrugged and slipped it into her pocket.

What the hell was he thinking? For all he knew, she would run directly to Saks Fifth Avenue and merrily restock her closets. His mother couldn't be depended upon to stop her; she wouldn't blink at thousands of dollars in charges. He might have just plunged himself into debt, and after the way he'd insisted, he couldn't take it back. He would have to trust her. That was a whole different thing from lusting after her. He felt slightly ill.

While they argued about who should have the privilege of spending money on Libby, his daughter had ignored them and inserted a CD into the computer. Music with a pounding bass beat came from the speakers as she printed out Ellie's business card.

"This song is by the Junkyard Dogs. Do you know them?"

He perked up. Random conversation with Libby—this was a nice change. "Never heard of them."

"They're from Detroit. They're going to be famous someday."

From the clashing sounds coming from the speakers, it was hard to believe, but he tried to look impressed. "Good for them."

"They're going to be in concert at Freedom Hill next weekend."

Uh-oh.

"Some of my friends from Detroit are going. They want me to come, too, but Grandmother won't let me."

He made a noncommittal sound.

"She thinks I'm too young."

She was watching closely, expecting some sort of comment. "I'm afraid Banner and I broke enough rules when we were your age to make her cautious with you."

"So if you got to decide, you'd let me go?"

Go to a concert with thousands of strangers, most

of them unsupervised teenagers? Visions of drug dealers and child molesters targeting his twelve-year-old daughter flashed through his mind. "No." As her face turned stormy, he added, "Besides, you know I don't get to decide. Your grandmother has custody."

"But you could tell her to let me go."

He didn't want to tell Libby that in his mother's opinion he was barely more responsible than his daughter, and taking Libby's side against her would not be especially persuasive. Ellie was watching silently to see how he would handle this.

"Sorry, Libby, I agree with your grandmother on this. But if you really want to go, I'll volunteer to go with you. That means you can sit with your friends, but I'm right there beside you every minute. Maybe your grandmother will agree to that."

"I will," Elizabeth confirmed.

Libby weighed the pleasure of attending the concert against the horror of showing up with her father. She sulked and considered the offer, then finally returned to the computer. "I'll get back to you," she said. He was dismissed.

There was no doubt about it. She was calculating and manipulative—definitely his daughter. She'd zeroed right in on his desire to make her happy and used it. That's what he got for being pathetically needy. He would have to change that.

"Okay, kiddo, you let me know. But don't wait too long, or I might have other plans." There, that sounded better than "I'll do anything to please you." Ellie gave him a sympathetic smile, so he must have handled it okay.

It wasn't until they went downstairs for dinner that

he hung back and had a couple minutes alone with Ellie.

"Banner's home, and he's planning to spend the whole evening here," she whispered, walking close beside him.

"I know." He kept his voice so low she had to brush against him as they walked in order to hear what he said. This intrigue stuff had its advantages.

"I thought you said we'd get into his computer."

"We will, don't worry." He wiggled his eyebrows at her. "I have a plan."

"What kind of plan?"

They were approaching the dining room. "Tell you later. But I promise he's going to have to leave the house." He grinned and said the words guaranteed to make her suspicious: "Trust me." He hoped it would remind her of the first time he'd said that, followed by that first, all-consuming kiss. He was not done pursuing more of those kisses, and she might as well have fair warning.

Dinner passed uneventfully, with the exception of Libby's talkative mood. Tomorrow's shopping trip had her hyped.

The phone rang during dessert, and Jack tensed. So did Libby. Mr. Peters appeared just as he noticed his daughter's odd reaction.

"A Steven Beyer calling for Miss Payton."

It took them all a moment to realize he meant Libby. She stood so fast her chair nearly tipped over. "I'm finished with dessert. I'll take it upstairs."

Elizabeth's firm voice halted her escape. "Libby."

"What? Oh, sorry. May I be excused?" She rushed off without waiting for an answer.

Jack looked at his mother. "Who the hell is Steven Beyer?"

"I believe he's a boy in her golf class at the club, the twelve- to fifteen-year-old group."

He couldn't believe how quickly he had learned to think like a parent. "Twelve to *fifteen*? How old is this Steven kid?"

Elizabeth's tone was tolerant but condescending. "He's from a good family."

Good meant rich. What difference did that make? So was he, and he didn't want to remember the kind of thoughts he'd had at fourteen and fifteen, not to mention what he'd done about them. "Christina's from a good family," he reminded her pointedly, and was gratified to see a look of concern grow on her face.

He was still grumbling about Steven when a cell phone rang in Banner's jacket pocket. A second phone call during dinner was annoying enough to his mother. When Banner took the call at the table, she set her fork down with a deliberate clang.

Jack pretended disinterest. Only an emergency would make someone call Banner during dinner, and from the growing look of concern on his half brother's face, this was the emergency Jack had been expecting. Right on time.

Banner's chair rocked back as fast as Libby's had. "There's a fire at the main office. I have to go."

Elizabeth looked at Banner with concern. "A fire?"

Ellie looked at Jack in alarm. She mouthed the word, "Fire?"

Jack was the only one who remained calm. "Do you want me to come along?"

"No, they think it's under control. I'll take care of things myself."

Of course he would. Jack had been counting on it.

His mother stood as Banner rushed out, calling after him, "Keep us informed."

Dinner was abruptly over. For an uncomfortably long while Jack wondered how to discreetly slip away to the library, but then the police chief was ushered in the front door. His mother seemed relieved to have Ben's up-to-date information on the fire, and he and Ellie left the two of them in the living room, slipping down the hall to the library.

He opened the library doors and paused. Memories of pressing Ellie against that desk hit his mind, not to mention other interested parts of his body. He was going to have a fondness for this room for the rest of his life.

"Stay here. Leave the doors open a crack and listen for anyone coming down the hall."

She pouted stubbornly, her pretty lower lip thrust forward. "I want to see what's on the computer, too."

"I'm not going to keep it secret. I'm going to get in, print out as much as I can, and get out." And then find someplace private to try talking her into his arms and out of that dress. But one thing at a time.

He crossed to the desk, instructing over his shoulder, "Stand guard."

She stayed beside the partially open door but kept her eyes on him.

"Did you cause that fire?"

"It was just a minor trash-barrel fire set with a timer. It should have set off the alarms and the sprinklers, though. The administrative wing is probably a mess." He opened Word as he talked and went straight to the documents. Calling up the AAF file, he asked, "Where was that list of code names?"

"Under 'Personal.' Stupid," she added, that last bit apparently for Banner, not him.

He printed out the password file for easy reference. As he tapped keys, he said, "I'll agree with you there. Banner was never exceptionally bright. That's why I was so amazed when the South American division became more profitable after he took over. His organizational and management skills are lousy." He paused. "This is interesting."

"What?" She came away from the door, eager to see.

"Stay there, I'm printing it. It's a list of flight dates for Aims, followed by two columns of figures. I'm guessing one is amounts delivered and the other is the value in dollars."

"Amounts of what?"

He looked through the file as he talked. Five pages of numbers—damn, that boy had been busy. "Guess. What's the number one export of Colombia?"

"Petroleum." At his irritated look, she said, "What? It is. I did a report on Colombia in eighth grade. Most people think it's coffee, but that's just the largest agricultural— Oh, you mean cocaine?" Once she got it, her voice lowered, full of trepidation. "Is that how he's making his money?"

"That would be my first guess." He was moving on to the file named for him and stopped suddenly when he looked at the password. "Oh, shit."

Her response was quick and worried. "What is it?"

"Damn. The password for my file is 'Bad.' "

"I know. I thought it was childish."

The name that had been nagging at him suddenly made sense. "Goddamn it," he said. "Ellie, 'Bad' refers to my car. I had a Maserati with a vanity plate that said 'Bad.' And now I know why Messner sounded familiar. That was the name of the arresting officer. Damn it, why does Banner have a file on my accident?"

"And that other name was your lawyer?"

"Yeah, Lundburg. But who is Tull?" He had a very bad feeling about that file.

Jack forced himself to move on. He could figure it out later. The next four files were collections of porn, lists of porn Web sites, and lists that looked like a log of gambling wins and losses on sports teams. The fifth file, named "Bogotá," looked like the jackpot. Lists of names, some grouped under Westfield-Benton, some under Aims, and all with numbers. Payoffs at the Colombian end, he guessed, his fingers working quickly to send the file to the printer. He could read it later. One thing was still missing and he needed to find it—if Aims was delivering smuggled drugs, who was on the receiving end? Banner was certainly not dealing himself.

Jack searched each file, but nothing seemed to relate to the Aims operation, and nothing mentioned Janet. Ellie wouldn't be pleased with that. He had eliminated all but the most pedestrian-sounding files, like "Taxes" and "Household Staff," when Ellie hissed at him, "Jack! Someone just came in the front door."

He closed the files and grabbed the papers in the printer. They were heading toward the front of the house when Banner's voice stopped them. His brother was heading their way. Jack turned sharply, pushing

Ellie ahead of him, back into the library. From there, only one avenue of escape was possible; they went out the French doors to the patio moments before Banner entered the room.

Eleanor followed Jack through a break in the hedge, wishing she'd seen that passage the night she'd performed her crash landing on the patio. Damp grass tickled above her sandals as they dashed across the lawn and rounded the corner of the house. They stopped near the pool, with a view across the night-time lawn.

Low yard lights made circles of green in the dark grass. In the pool, water shone with a yellow luminescence from submerged lights, with barely a ripple disturbing the surface. Beyond lay the perfect illusion of countryside, complete with the chirping of crickets and the distant splash of the man-made stream and waterfall.

Eleanor hugged her bare arms. The air was warm and heavy with approaching rain, but their race from the library moments ahead of Banner's entrance sent goose bumps creeping across her skin in spite of the heat. She was scared and exhilarated at the same time, and gripped by an undeniable thrill at sharing the experience with Jack. The sense of danger gave their partnership a heady, almost sexual edge. She wondered if he felt it, too.

"What now?" she whispered.

"Now we find someplace where we can read these printouts and not be disturbed. Someplace with a light." Eleanor looked doubtfully around the dark lawn with its decorative lights that stood no more than two feet high. She tried to imagine crouching close to one of them, when Jack said, "There. The pool house."

She'd never been inside it, but she shouldn't have been surprised by the facilities after having seen the house. Shelves of fresh towels and bathing suits awaited guests, and two large changing rooms looked like the ladies' lounges in department stores, with carpet and chairs. Toilet stalls and showers were in the area to her left. She'd seen vacation cabins smaller than this and was surprised there wasn't a small refrigerator for refreshments to complete the accommodations. But then, fetching drinks would be Mr. Peters's job.

Jack turned on the lights in the changing area and pulled her by the hand into one of the small rooms, plopping them both onto a wicker love seat so they could look at the pages together. Shoulder to shoulder, her bare arm rubbed against the hair of his forearm, and her thigh was crammed against his. Tiny electric shocks of awareness accompanied the familiar feel of his body pressed against hers. Since they'd been naked in his bed the last time her bare skin had rubbed against his, she flushed and momentarily forgot to breathe.

He looked at her. "Are you all right?"

She nodded.

"Okay, look at this list of Aims cargo runs. Those are flight numbers, and here are the dates for the past two years. Aims makes the trip between Colombia and Michigan once a week, carrying shipments for Westfield-Benton and other companies, but Banner was only interested in one shipment a month, the one on the second Thursday. The cargo he tracked always went to a company called Michigan Janitorial Products."

It seemed simple enough to follow, even with Jack's thigh radiating heat onto hers right through the material of his trousers and her dress. "You think he's shipping drugs up here once a month?"

"He's tracking these for some reason. I think someone in Colombia is adding them to the manifest as a cleaning compound or something similar, and sending them to a dealer at this MJP company. There's only one problem with that—we can't pin it on Banner."

"Why not?"

"Because if the drugs are found at customs, Aims gets the blame, or someone back in Colombia. If they're found here, MJP takes the heat. Either way, Banner's hands are clean."

"I don't get it. How is Banner making money if there's no connection to him?"

"I suspect the money is paid to Aims in extravagant freight charges. Banner makes the Aims operation look highly profitable and is rewarded with a fat yearly bonus. It's simple money laundering, giving him a clean source of profit and making him look like a capable executive at the same time." He smiled wryly. "Pretty clever. I only wish it were more than conjecture."

Recalling her original concern, she asked, "You think Janet figured this out?"

He shrugged. "She could have, if she saw this file. Or maybe she actually saw something she shouldn't have when she was in Colombia."

"No, whatever got her killed, she found here. This must be it, but it doesn't help us connect him to her death."

"No, I'm sorry, it doesn't." He did look genuinely regretful. "I'd love to pin that on him, Ellie, but I don't see how we can. In fact, all of this"—he slapped a hand at the pages in his lap—"just gives us theories, not evidence."

She wanted to make some sarcastic remark about him focusing more on Banner's money laundering than on Janet's murder, but she knew he was right. They'd searched the computer and hadn't found anything that led to Janet. She bit her lip and mentally reviewed what they'd learned. "What do you think the file on your accident means?"

His brow furrowed. "I'm not sure. Knowing Banner, and knowing he wanted me out of the way of his drug-smuggling scheme, I'd suspect payoffs. That accident sure got me out of his way at Westfield-Benton. But I don't see how anything could have been fixed. I *was* driving under the influence, as much as I hate to admit it."

"Are you sure? I talked to the bartender at the club, and she said you weren't drunk that night."

"Ellie, they did a sobriety test right at the scene. I failed. And I know I hit Benton. He was standing beside the road one minute, and dead the next. How could Banner have anything to do with that?"

"I don't know," she murmured, still unconvinced. The Jack she knew was sober and responsible, and she had a difficult time reconciling that image with the man he was talking about. Banner couldn't be trusted, but Jack wasn't as bad as she'd first believed. In fact, she thought, with a sidelong glance at him, Jack had some very good qualities.

"What are you thinking?"

She smiled. She was thinking that she could smell a subtle bayberry scent from his soap or shampoo, and she wanted to bury her nose in his neck and inhale deeply. She was also thinking that she needed a break from stalking killers and drug smugglers. A hedonistic and entirely selfish feeling was growing inside her. She decided to go with it.

She said, "I was thinking of you."

That surprised him. She could see him search for the right response before he settled for, "Really?"

"Yes, really." For once he looked a little off balance, and that suited her mood. She stood, and his eyes followed her curiously as she stretched and looked around the small room. Walking the length of it and back, she aimlessly trailed her hand along the wall, assessing the feasibility of what she had in mind.

"Is this about my drunk-driving conviction?"

She smiled tolerantly. "No." A growing feeling of power was making her brave. "This is actually about me. About the fact that I had a very good day playing business executive and getting to inform Banner that his little nobody houseguest found a flaw in his precious security network. I'm not used to that feeling of success. It's a high, you know?"

"Yes, I know. And you're not a nobody, Ellie."

She stopped to face him, her head tilted thoughtfully. "No, I'm not. I'm Ellie, aren't I? I used to be Eleanor, or Nora, but I've gotten used to Ellie, and I think I like it. Ellie is a different person." He looked confused but was smiling back now, which only encouraged her more. "I'm not really the passive type, Jack."

He nearly laughed. "I never thought you were."

"Hmm. Well, I did. At least Eleanor was passive. But it turns out that Ellie isn't." She looked at the top of the wall, which was lined with windows. "Do you suppose they can see this light from the house?" Without waiting for an answer, she moved a step and flicked the wall switch.

In the sudden darkness, she could see his eyes shining from the faint glow of the yard lights filtering through the windows. Still sitting in the shadows, he watched her with rapt attention. She stood close before him so he could see her better.

She was leading this time, and all he had to do was follow. He looked quite willing to do that.

A row of buttons ran down the front of her dress, and she began opening them. He watched wordlessly as she made her way down, until the whole dress fell open. Keeping her eyes on him, she pulled the thin straps off her shoulders and let the dress drop to the floor. It puddled at her feet, and she kicked it aside. As she stood before him in only her panties and strapless bra, a part of her was amazed at how boldly the new Ellie met his gaze. She watched as his eyes ran down her body.

"I do love your taste in underwear."

She grabbed his shirt and pulled him to his feet. She wanted to tell him that he needed to kiss her now, but all she got out was, "You need to—" when his lips came down firmly on hers and he pulled her against his chest. Smart man, she thought with satisfaction.

It took only a few moments before her hands left his shoulders and began fumbling with his belt. As she rapidly unhooked it and searched for a snap, he stopped kissing her and chuckled.

"Are you in a hurry?"

"Yes." She looked down to find the snap, then met his eyes. "*Eager* would be a better word."

"You're not kidding."

"I've had sex on my mind all day, and I'm a little impatient. Here." She reached into her bra and handed him the condom she'd stashed there.

Jack took it, surprised. "You came prepared." She saw his eyebrows rise as that thought led to the next. "My God, you planned this seduction," he said, amused.

"It's not a seduction when you declare your intentions beforehand and drop your clothes. It's a proposition." She got the snap open and the zipper down. With a mischievous grin, she tugged on the waist and dropped his pants. "I'm making you a proposition, Jack. What's your answer?"

He pulled her closer so she could feel his answer poking against her stomach. "You know, you could have selected a more comfortable location for your proposition." His voice was low and intimate as he nibbled at her neck. Her skin quivered pleasantly. "This is a hard floor."

"Good point."

Which was why he was the one who ended up on his back. He didn't look at all uncomfortable and took full advantage of having his hands free, playing with her breasts while she rocked atop him, until she collapsed onto his chest, heart pounding, skin damp, and nerve endings happily numb.

He held her while she caught her breath, one hand running over her hips where they were still joined. "All better?" he asked, amusement in his voice.

"Mmm," she answered into his shoulder, then raised her head to look at him. With her eyes used to the darkness, his playful expression was easy to see. "It's a good start." She kissed him lightly. "Do I have to stop now?"

"I'm glad you asked, because I wasn't done with you." She knew he hadn't climaxed yet and was not at all displeased when he rolled over and reversed their positions. He reached for his pants on the floor beside them. "Here, put this under your lower back."

"Such a gentleman," she said, arching so he could jam the crumpled slacks beneath her.

"Is that what you're looking for, a gentleman?"

"No. Get down here." She reached for his shoulders.

"Patience," he admonished as he reached to guide himself into her. But instead she felt him rub himself against her, wet and slippery against her pleasantly swollen crotch. The nerve endings that had been numb were suddenly awake and interested, and she closed her eyes and groaned her appreciation.

She seemed to be an endless source of amusement for him tonight. "Ellie, are you sure you were ever inhibited?"

She wasn't sure. Sex had never been this good, but she suspected it had more to do with her past lovers than with her inhibitions. Jack touched all the right places at all the right times, and his skill made her respond without reservation. What else could it be? He turned her on so easily, it had to be due to experience. Like now, when her body was responding to his faster than she would have expected.

"Jack, get inside me," she whispered hoarsely, and

he did. She clutched his back and uttered a satisfied, "Oh," then let him do most of the work. He did, proficiently, and minutes later she hooked her heels behind his thighs and arched hard against him, as he took them both to a climax.

They stayed together for a minute longer before he rolled off and lay beside her. The warm, humid night air wafting through the window screens touched her hot body and felt wonderfully cool. She could stay like this forever.

Jack's fingers found hers and curled around them in a way that was friendly but not possessive. It was really sort of sweet, until he ruined it.

"If I were to use a crude term, I'd say you were a good lay."

She rolled her head to scowl at him. "If that's your idea of flattery, then you've been dating the wrong kind of women."

"Probably. Are you the right kind?"

"Yes. I mean, no. I don't know." What in the hell was he asking her?

He laughed. "Well that's perfectly clear. Ellie, whatever happened to your aversion to sex with someone who's simply convenient? It seems to me I was pretty darn convenient. That's not a complaint," he added. "I'm just curious about how we got here."

He was right. Had she simply chosen a likely partner because she wanted one and he was willing? That's exactly what she'd accused him of doing.

She felt Jack's hand on hers and the heat of his body close beside her, and knew her contentment had to do with more than sexual release. She hadn't wanted sex tonight, she'd wanted sex with Jack. That revelation hit her with surprising force. Disturbed, she sat up beside him and hugged her knees while she tried to figure out exactly what he was, if not convenient. She'd never had this sort of relationship with a man before, one based on the physical rather than the emotional. There must be a term for how she felt about him. He had invaded several aspects of her life, and she'd begun to feel comfortable with him. Strange as it sounded, she could only think of one answer to his question.

"I guess I think of you as . . . a friend." Her own statement left her bemused. When had that happened?

He considered it, then gave her a cocky grin. "A close friend, I'd say. Well, that's a new one for me, but I think I like it." He got to his feet and pulled her up beside him. "Come on. There are showers in the next room, and plenty of towels."

The pool house turned out to be an ideal place for surreptitious sex. Small recessed lights above the shower shone directly down, leaving the corners and high windows in shadows. They kept the shower blissfully cool and stood under the spray far longer than necessary, soaping each other, rinsing, and lathering again just for the enjoyment of touching each other. Ellie decided it was nice to have a friend you could both shower and have sex with. The relationship was easy, and you didn't have to wonder if he cared as much as you did, or if he'd call you the next day. Neither of them considered it a commitment, just a good time. It was liberating.

She smiled thoughtfully at her insights and turned her face upward into the spray. Water streamed deliciously over her chest and poured off her slicked-back hair in a cleansing stream. For several long seconds, she enjoyed the soaking massage. Blinking water from her eyes, she saw Jack through the curtain of water, drenched and dripping and smiling enigmatically at her.

"What?" she asked.

He reached toward her and she assumed he meant to brush a strand of hair aside, but he cupped his hand around the side of her head, ducked into the spray, and pulled her into a kiss. She stood on tiptoes, expecting a friendly peck, the sort of affection she supposed friends might share. But his other arm pulled her against him, and she stumbled into his wet embrace and a long, soulful kiss. Their naked bodies stuck together while jets of water pounded her hair and Jack's mouth slowly made love to hers. Amazingly, she felt an eager heat grow between her thighs where she thought she must surely be numb with exhaustion, and a corresponding hardness against her lower stomach where his renewed erection pressed against her.

He released her suddenly and she nearly staggered. Her mind was as bewildered as her feet, spinning with confusion. And every place their bodies had pressed together, from her chest to her thighs, was shivering from the sudden loss of his body heat.

Jack's clouded gaze cleared and he blinked. "I'll go get us some towels," he said gruffly, and disappeared quickly around the corner. She was left standing under the pouring water, wondering what had just happened. His kiss had felt more intimate than the sex, seductively drawing emotions to the surface with that concentrated and thorough way he had. And those emotions felt frighteningly vulnerable and needy.

Her simple, friendly relationship with Jack was already becoming complicated.

What the hell happened?

Jack tried to replay what had seemed unreal even then. She'd been standing there like some centerfold fantasy, water coursing over her, glowing from the light above, lost in thought and looking more like a dream than reality. Except he could reach out and touch her, so he did. And the ability to touch the fantasy, and the knowledge that he might be responsible for that satisfied little smile, proved irresistible. He'd kissed her, instinctively, passionately. She'd been warm and willing, as sensual as any fantasy should be, and exquisitely naked as well.

He'd come back to reality with startled blue eyes staring at him, questioning his intentions. Since he was wondering about that himself, he prudently escaped. Walking back with the towels, he thought the best plan would be to act as if nothing unusual had passed between them. Really, what was one kiss after all that frantic fucking on the floor? Nothing.

They dried off and dressed quickly. Ellie used the full-length mirror in the changing room as she ran her fingers through her hair, fluffing out the damp tendrils. He watched, wondering if he'd ever be able to look at that room and not remember her sitting naked above him, head thrown back and breasts arched toward him in the silver-gray shadows.

"Someone is sure to notice the wet hair," she said.

"They'll think we've been swimming."

"Good, because I don't think your mother would approve of what we've really been doing."

"Ellie, we're supposed to be engaged. They probably *expect* us to have sex."

"Maybe, but not on the floor of your mother's pool house. I get the impression she's the type who believes in a proper time and place for everything."

She was probably right about that. His mother ensured that everything in the Westfield house ran on an orderly schedule.

He folded the printouts from Banner's computer and stuffed them into his back pocket. Ellie noticed.

"What are we going to do about those?"

"*We* aren't going to do anything. *I'm* going to see what other dealings Westfield-Benton has with Michigan Janitorial Products. I'll call my friend in Colombia, too, and see if he knows any of the names on that other list, and if he thinks they might take money for sneaking drug shipments into our freight. *You* will wait for me to tell you what I find out, and you will not go off on some wild scheme on your own."

She narrowed her eyes at him. "I don't respond well to imperious commands."

He restrained the impulse to grab her by the shoulders and insist that she do as he told her. Taking a deep breath, he said, "Ellie, please. I'll go crazy with worry if I think you've aroused Banner's suspicions and put yourself in danger."

She looked at him for several seconds before she said simply, "Okay."

"Thank you." He refused to acknowledge the enormous relief he felt. "Now let's get back inside the house. I want to make sure Banner isn't throwing fits about someone using his computer again before I leave you."

They went back the way they'd come, walking boldly up to the patio and the library door as though returning from a stroll on the lawn. It was locked.

"Damn. What time is it?" He looked at his watch, the numbers glowing faintly yellow in the dark. "Just past eleven. The doors lock automatically at eleven. We'll have to use the front door and ring the bell. I have a key, but I don't have the alarm code. Apparently I'm not trusted after a certain hour."

"I know the code. We had to use it when we checked the system this morning."

He laughed. "Now, that's ironic. He gives the alarm code to the only person ever to break into the house without it."

They were walking back around the pool, cutting across the lawn toward the large fan of concrete beside the garage.

"How do you know I'm the only one? If they were successful, you'd never know how many others might have—"

She broke off abruptly as he pulled her into the shadow of a large fir tree. Fragrant branches brushed against them. Before she could protest, he put his finger to his lips and pointed at the front of the house.

The porch lights had flicked off just as the door opened, and for a moment two people were silhouetted in the light from the foyer. Before they stepped outside and closed the door behind them, he could easily recognize Ben Thatcher and his mother. Then they became two unrecognizable figures in the faint glow of the lights that lined the front walk.

"Why did they turn the lights off?" Ellie asked.

"I don't know." It was odd enough to make him

hesitate. "People turn lights on when they go outside at night. No one turns them off."

In the shadow of the tree, Ellie turned her face toward his. "We did."

He looked at her blankly for a moment, then realized what she was referring to. "Don't be ridiculous. I don't know what they're up to and I don't like the man, but trust me, Ben Thatcher has no designs on my mother."

"Are you sure?"

"Positive. The man never looks twice at a pretty woman. And believe me, I've seen a few look twice at him, and he ignores it. Get it? He doesn't like women."

"He's doing a good job of hiding it."

He turned back toward the porch, where the two figures had moved close together, as if they were embracing. He squinted and tried to see exactly what they were doing. His mother's blouse was white and had been easy to see, but Thatcher's bulk was shielding her from view. He frowned. "Maybe it's a good-night hug. They've known each other since I was in elementary school, and Mother probably needed reassurance about the fire. . . ."

His voice trailed off as his mother's arm came up around Thatcher's shoulder. He was right, it was a friendly hug. A hug that lasted a little longer than necessary, but still just a hug.

The two figures turned slightly and their pale faces caught the light. Except they were so close together, it looked more like one face. Jack felt Ellie's hand clutch his arm as they realized simultaneously that they were watching two people in an ardent kiss.

Jack swore under his breath, more from astonishment than anything else. His world had been gradually teetering farther out of balance each day, and this little scene shoved it right off its foundations. How had things become so confused? He'd gone away for two years and come back to find a daughter he'd never heard of, a brother turned murderer and drug smuggler, and his proper, reserved mother making out with the local cop. And, oh yeah, just to keep things complicated, the most uninhibited and temptingly sexy woman he'd ever known was masquerading as his fiancée while rattling his mind and overstimulating his hormones.

He turned to his sexy, fake fiancée, sighed heavily, and said, "Well, shit."

Chapter Nine

Ellie woke up with an itchy feeling of impatience, and the pouring rain only made it worse. She wanted to act on the information about Banner, but she'd promised Jack she wouldn't, and the curtain of rain outside only served to make her feel more confined. Now that she was close to proving Banner to be a sleazy, lying, worthless bastard, it was difficult to sit and wait while Jack did more research. It would be marginally better to shop and wait. Still, she felt the need to accomplish something.

She called Rocky.

A sleepy voice answered after five rings, and she heard a mumbled, "Hello?"

"It's Ellie." It was the first time she'd identified herself to anyone but Jack that way, and she felt liberated all over again. "Were you sleeping? It's nine o'clock."

"Ellie? What's wrong?" He still sounded fuzzy headed.

"Nothing. I have some business to conduct, and it's the beginning of business hours."

"I work nights."

"Not anymore. Welcome to the business world. Now, wake up so we can discuss Red Rose Security."

She heard grumbling and the squeaking of bed-springs. A minute later a voice sounding much more like that of the Rocky she knew said, "Okay, what's goin' on?"

"I want to get this business moving. Is there any reason we can't do Mrs. Hampshire's house tomorrow?"

He sounded more interested. "Make it Thursday and I'll be there."

"Good, I'll call her. I also have a design for our new business cards. It's simple but elegant, white with a black border and a half-opened rosebud in the lower corner. What do you think?"

"A rose?" She could hear the skepticism in his voice. "Sounds sort of sissy. I've gotta hand these things out with a straight face, remember."

"It's called Red Rose Security—what else would I use?"

He was silent for a few seconds. "Can't we at least make it long stemmed, with lots of thorns? Long, dangerous thorns, like barbed wire."

She pictured a long-stemmed rose lying across the bottom of the card. With medium-sized thorns. Not bad. "Okay, a dangerous rose. You've got it. I'll call you back about Thursday's job."

"Don't make it at nine o'clock, okay? We're busy professionals, Ellie. Pretend we can't get there until after lunch."

She laughed. "I'll try. Go back to bed."

"You know it." The phone clicked off.

Ten minutes later it rang again. She was in the

shower and heard it through the glass door, ringing inside the pocket of her bathrobe where it lay crumpled on the floor. She turned the shower off, found the phone, and pushed foamy hair away from her ear.

"Hello?"

"Good morning. How's your back?"

Jack's voice was so low and silky that hearing it was like being stroked by him. Already her body had a Pavlovian reaction to him, responding to his voice as if it were his touch. Unless that shiver up her back was simply from standing wet and naked on a tile floor. But that probably couldn't explain the tingling in her breasts and inner thighs.

"My back is fine, how's yours?"

"Dandy. Better than dandy. Am I interrupting anything?"

"My shower. What's up?"

After several seconds with no response, she said, "Jack?"

"Hmm? Sorry, you distracted me there. I wanted to let you know that I have to do something tonight, so I won't be able to see you after dinner. I want you to promise you'll be careful to stay out of Banner's way, in case he finds out we've been snooping around."

"Why would he find out?"

"Just be careful. I've had to ask questions this morning, and I'm not sure who I can trust. If he gets suspicious, I want you in a safe place. As long as my mother is home, the house should be safe."

"I've been here two days and so far he's stayed out of my way. I don't think I'm in any danger."

"Ellie, remember, you're the one who called him a murderer. Have you changed your mind?"

"No." He sounded more concerned for her welfare than he had last night. "Tell me what else makes you think I shouldn't trust Banner."

After several seconds of silence, she heard him release a loud breath, as if he'd reluctantly come to a decision. "I did some checking on that file he has on my accident. It took a while, but I found out who Tull is. He's Dr. Robert J. Tull, county coroner, and he filled out the cause-of-death papers on Benton after the accident. I can't think of any good reason why Banner would have anything to do with a cop, a lawyer, and a county coroner who are all tied to my accident. And all the reasons I *can* think of aren't good at all. I think Banner is as bad as you said, Ellie, and probably worse. Everything I find has me more worried. If he becomes the slightest bit suspicious of you, I want you out of there and back at my house, no matter how inappropriate my mother thinks it looks."

Except it wasn't his mother's opinion that mattered. If children's services found it inappropriate, he would surrender any chance of getting Libby. If he was risking that, he had her worried, too. "I want to know what the bad things are that you think might cause Banner to be involved with those three people."

"Later. We'll go over it and you can give me your opinion."

He wanted her opinion. She didn't think he was just saying it to brush her off, and the unexpected flattery caused a warm spot in her chest. She almost forgot about whatever it was he couldn't include her in this evening.

"Jack, what are you doing tonight?"

"I'll tell you about it later."

Now, that was a brush-off. His evasion decided it for her. "I want to go with you."

"No. It might be dangerous, and I don't want you involved. It's also slightly illegal."

"So you can take a risk but I can't?"

"I'm taking Rocky with me."

"Oh, good, you can both violate your parole. If it's in any way connected to Janet, you have to let me come along."

"You don't even know what I'm going to do."

"I'm going."

"We'll discuss it later."

He'd already made up his mind not to take her. She might as well let him think he was getting away with it. They could argue later. "Fine. When?"

"I'll come over for dinner. We can talk then; I have to call Rocky now."

She smiled to herself. "Tell him I said good morning."

Ellie flipped through the rack of clothes in her closet and frowned. A girls' day out, that's what they'd called it. A relaxed shopping day. As if Elizabeth Payton Westfield was ever relaxed, or had ever been one of the girls. She probably wore pearls in the shower.

Ellie selected a casual skirt and top, assuming she would still look dressed up next to Libby.

She was right. When they met in the hallway, loose jeans and a T-shirt hid the girl's slight curves in the unremarkable uniform of every teenager. Ellie impulsively pulled Libby into her room and began rummaging through her makeup bag. The girl's eyes widened at the sight of all the feminine accessories.

"When will you be thirteen, Libby?" she asked, trying to get a feel for what might be appropriate.

"October. Do you use all that stuff?"

"Not all at once." She smiled at Libby's undisguised interest. "Do you want to try some?"

"Do you have any eyeliner? My friend Tanya let me use her black eyeliner and mascara once. It looked really cool."

Ellie cringed inwardly. "I think that might be too dramatic for you today. Let's try some lip gloss and a little blush."

Libby wasn't excited about the muted colors but seemed pleased with the results. Inspired, Ellie pulled the dark mane of hair into a high, sassy ponytail with a sparkly red scrunchie, leaving bangs and wisps of hair around her face. Libby admired the results in the mirror.

"I look older, don't I?"

Brighter and fresher, Ellie thought, but knew what the correct answer was. "Absolutely. At least fourteen, I'd guess." She dearly wanted to change the faded T-shirt, but wasn't sure the suggestion would be welcome. She stood behind Libby at the mirror and gave her a critical look. "Let's see, what else could we do to perk up this look?"

Libby thought, too. "Mascara?"

"Hmm . . . No, I think a natural look is more stylish on you. Much more cool," she emphasized. "Maybe something to add color . . . ."

"Long earrings?"

Ellie pretended to seriously ponder the three studs Libby already wore in each ear. "No, I think we've got enough going on there."

They both studied the reflection again. "A different shirt?" Libby asked doubtfully.

"Yes! What a great idea! Or, if you're interested, I've got this red top that's too small for me. It'd look great on you, with your dark hair and that scrunchie."

The little cap-sleeved knit top that hugged Ellie indecently was looser on Libby and an improvement over the shapeless T-shirt. Better yet, Libby thought it aged her considerably.

"Wow, I look even older," she said, still young enough to think that was a good thing.

"You look a little bit older, and a whole lot classier," Ellie told her. "Let's get your grandmother's opinion."

Considering that Elizabeth could have raised hell about the makeup, her comment that they both looked "very nice" seemed surprisingly generous.

"Ellie let me borrow her top," Libby said, apparently proud to be sharing clothes with an older woman.

"Did she? It looks nice on you. I'm surprised it would fit Eleanor," she said, raising her eyebrows incredulously.

"It doesn't," Ellie said as she tried to decide if she'd been insulted. "You can keep it if you like it, Libby." She hoped Elizabeth didn't plan to spend the day taking not-so-subtle shots at the way she dressed.

They hit the boutiques in town first, exclusive stores where Ellie was afraid to touch the merchandise for fear of causing a snag or a stain that would force her to buy something. She tried to look indifferent as Elizabeth purchased a handbag or pair of shoes that would have left a permanent scar on her credit balance. The woman had impeccable taste and a fearless approach to spending.

She couldn't argue with an unexpected benefit of greed—Libby forgot her studied reserve and became a twelve-year-old girl on a shopping spree. At least Elizabeth enforced some restraint with Libby, making her justify the need for every purchase and rejecting some requests as frivolous. Happily, with tennis, golf, riding, theater, and school, Libby was able to justify a wide variety of clothing and accessories. Ellie helped carry the bags.

She was practicing restraint and doing well until a strapless black cocktail number whispered her name from the racks. Intending to merely dip her toe in the treacherous waters of temptation, she held it up before herself in the mirror. Elizabeth and Libby spotted her.

"Oh, try it on, Ellie!" Libby enthused.

"It'll look beautiful on you, dear. Model it for us."

Ellie bit her lip and hesitated, turning sideways to estimate how flat her stomach would look in the tapered cut.

"Please, Ellie, I want to see it on you. You'll look so hot!"

She'd heard that voice before. It was the little devil that sat on her shoulder and urged her into all the impulsive errors she'd ever made. The good angel who was supposed to kick him in the ass was evidently overcome by the beauty of the chic little dress, too, because she stayed dangerously silent.

Who was she to go against public opinion? She slipped into the dress and presented herself for inspection, turning in front of the mirror.

"It's very complimentary," Elizabeth judged.

"Oh my God, it's smokin' hot," Libby elaborated breathlessly. "You are *so* sexy in that dress."

Incredibly, it was true. The little dress flattered all the right curves and mysteriously eliminated her flaws. Even standing there in her bare feet and mussed hair, she could see the dress work its magic. She was sexy. She listened carefully, but the good angel was still speechless with wonder.

This was worth maxing out her card for. Assuring herself that one night in this dress would make up for a year of paying it off, she turned the little tag under her arm and read the price.

She blanched. Six hundred forty-nine dollars. Now she knew what had happened to her little angel: The devil had bound and gagged her. This was beyond temptation. This was impossible.

She gave them a sickly smile. "I can't."

"Why not? You gotta!" Libby pleaded.

Elizabeth understood her hesitation. "Yes, you can. Put it on Jack's card, Eleanor. That's why he gave it to you."

"Oh, no, I couldn't." There was that insidious devil's voice again. Elizabeth could not have purposely put her in this position, but Ellie knew she watched curiously to see how it would be handled. Maybe Elizabeth believed that it was truly all right for her to use Jack's credit card. Ellie knew differently. She might be willing to fool other people with her fiancée masquerade, but she couldn't fool herself. She would never be able to afford this dress.

She smiled brightly for Libby and Elizabeth. "Maybe when Red Rose Security is more established, this can be my reward. The dress can wait awhile." It would have to wait forever.

She dressed quickly, handing the piece of temptation to the salesclerk before she could change her mind.

Libby told her what a poor decision she'd made all through lunch.

The mall was a diversion for Libby, with an unexpected bonus. While Elizabeth purchased a silk scarf that cost what Ellie would have spent on an entire outfit, Libby wandered over to cosmetics and browsed with fascination through the displays. Since adolescents in blue jeans were not the typical customer at the Neiman Marcus cosmetics counter, a clerk hovered nearby, ready to sound the alarm and throw herself over the merchandise at the first indication of shoplifting.

Ellie exchanged looks with Elizabeth. Amazingly, they were in agreement on this one.

Another woman was heading intently for Libby when they approached the counter and she veered in midstride. "Mrs. Westfield! How nice to see you," she gushed, darting glances between Libby and her grandmother, trying to assess the situation before making a career-ending mistake.

"Good afternoon, Phyllis. My granddaughter is in need of some guidance in choosing the appropriate cosmetics for her age. Perhaps you could assist us?"

Voilà. Within seconds, Libby was seated before a mirror with two women hovering around her, explaining the basic principles of achieving a non-made-up look with makeup and applying cleanser to Libby's face in preparation for their anointments. Ellie watched with nearly as much amazement as Libby. All her cosmetic needs were met at the drugstore, with items a third the price of these. Libby had certainly been thrown into a world of privilege, but Ellie had to admit it wouldn't be too hard to get used to this life.

Libby walked away forty-five minutes later with two hundred dollars' worth of makeup and skin-care products, glowing like a beauty queen. It would have taken Ellie a year to spend that much on cosmetics. She felt torn between envy and the desire to run like hell back to Petoskey and the real world.

A question that had nagged at her from the beginning was becoming more significant every day. By helping Jack get custody of Libby, would she be doing the girl a favor, or would she be taking her from a pampered existence to life as the illegitimate daughter of an ex-con? Ellie knew she couldn't disrupt this fairy-tale-princess life unless Libby wanted it. Right now that didn't look likely.

She pondered the question as they sat sipping drinks at the food court. Elizabeth had gone off with a friend to debate the merits of a gown for some coming charity ball. While they waited for her to return, Libby took out her new compact and admired her reflection with wonder. Ellie made a stab at drawing out information while the girl was in a less guarded mood.

"How was your visit yesterday with your grandparents?"

Libby shrugged. "Okay, I guess."

Typically concise, she thought, and tried again. "Don't you miss them?"

"Not really." She tipped her head sideways, then down, looking at her faintly enhanced eyelashes from all angles. "I miss my aunt Jenny, though."

That was a name she hadn't heard before. "Did you see her often?"

"Sure, she lived with us. She was the one who took care of me when I was little. No one else really cared what I did. She was my mom's sister."

It was stated very matter-of-factly, and Ellie wasn't sure what to address first. "She *was* her sister?" she asked.

"My mom's dead."

This was news. "I thought no one knew where she was."

"That's just what my grandma told the child welfare people. My grandparents thought they might not give me back if they knew my mom was gone for good. She died of an overdose when I was little. Do you think my hair looks better behind my ear like this, or with some of it hanging in front?"

Ellie tried to keep the pieces of the story straight in her mind. "Behind your ear. So your grandparents wanted to give you up temporarily?" That didn't make sense.

"After Aunt Jenny got married and moved to Indiana, they said they couldn't handle me. But they would take me back if they could get money from my father's family. They knew he was rich."

Ellie was momentarily speechless. Had Libby's grandparents used her to get some sort of payoff? "Did they think the Westfields might pay them to keep you?"

"Uh-huh. 'Cause my mom told them when I was born that my dad wouldn't want me, and neither would his family, but they might pay us someday just so they wouldn't have to take me. That's why my mom named me after my grandmother Payton. She called it my insurance policy."

"Oh." She didn't know what else to say to such an amazing story. "So Libby is short for Elizabeth?"

"Elizabeth Michelle Payton, same as Grandmother. Except I'm glad they never called me Elizabeth, 'cause it sounds like an old lady's name." Libby pulled out her new pink-blush lipstick and carefully retouched the spot where her straw had rested.

Ellie watched, mesmerized by the simple action. She'd known Libby was a tough kid, but she'd thought it was because she'd been forced into a new situation. It seemed that she'd grown up with the knowledge that she was a piece of barter no one wanted, except, apparently, for her aunt Jenny. Thank God for Aunt Jenny.

"I'm glad you had your aunt. But what your mom said isn't entirely true. Your dad does want you, he just didn't know you existed."

Libby met her eyes over the mirror. "That's what he said."

Twelve was pretty young to be so cynical. "It's true, Libby," she said gently, wondering if she doubted everything she'd been told. "Is that why you're so hard on him?"

"My mom and dad are irresponsible people who don't deserve to have me. My aunt Jenny said so."

The kid was great at spitting back other people's analyses. Ellie hesitated to defend Jack's past, but someone should tell Libby she was being unfair. "Jack's a different person now."

"He went to jail for drunk driving," Libby observed.

"He doesn't drink anymore."

Libby didn't respond, closing her compact and taking a sip of her Coke. Ellie thought the conversation was over, when Libby said, "I guess when you marry him you'll be my stepmother."

Ellie started. "I guess so." This was definitely a subject to avoid. Fortunately, Libby's mental process had bypassed motherhood in favor of romance.

"Didn't you care that Jack had been in jail?"

This one was easy. "Yes. I thought it was awful. It wasn't exactly the kind of man I was looking for." She raised an eyebrow in a confidential, woman-to-woman manner and got a smile from Libby. "But I'm glad I gave him a chance, because he's a pretty great guy. He's responsible, and thoughtful, and you gotta admit, he's pretty handsome." She was selling Jack with such sincerity she was beginning to believe it herself. Maybe the sex had affected her judgment. Maybe she was running a fever.

She thought Libby's silence was due to a thoughtful reexamination of Jack's father potential, when she noticed the girl's eyes were riveted on a spot across the food court. Ellie followed her gaze to a group of boys buying nachos.

"Do you know those boys?"

"One of them." Her eyes shifted and became suddenly absorbed in the ice floating in her Coke. The group was coming their way.

Ellie watched them find a table, then saw one with overgrown blond hair and a silver stud through his eyebrow do a random scan of the room and stop at their table. He stared, then looked away. "I think he saw you. Five tables away to your right."

Libby slid a look in that direction, then went back to stirring ice cubes with her straw.

"What's his name?"

She barely caught the distracted reply. "Steven."

Ahh, Steven Beyer of the mysterious phone call. She tried to ignore the pierced eyebrow and shaggy hair. "He's cute."

Libby blushed as if the compliment had been aimed at her, then said, "I know."

The boy was darting glances their way. "I think he likes you."

She suddenly had Libby's attention. "How can you tell?"

"He keeps looking at you."

"But he saw me and didn't even wave."

Because you're with me, she thought. And he's with them. Maybe she should give Steven a chance and see if he was brave enough to take it.

"I have to use the ladies' room. Be right back." She left before Libby had a chance to answer.

She killed a few minutes combing her hair, then walked back, passing Steven, who appeared to be on his way to the restroom. She thought he'd totally blown his opportunity until she saw Libby's flushed and happy face.

"What happened?" she asked in a conspiratorial voice.

"He walked by and said, 'Hey.' "

From Libby's expression, it must have been the best "Hey" ever delivered by a male of the species. "Wow," Ellie said, hoping that covered the occasion. "What did you say?"

"I said, 'Hi.' "

Not the most pithy conversation, but obviously of great import to Steven and Libby.

"You were right, Ellie. I think he does like me."

It was said with such a serious look, all she could do was nod sagely in response. Too bad her relationships were never that simple.

Elizabeth returned a minute later and they continued shopping, no doubt leaving Libby's heartthrob wondering where she had gone.

Ellie had begun to think she'd actually get home without any damage to her credit card when they found the bra and panty sale at Victoria's Secret. The scantily clad mannequin torsos in the store reminded her that her underwear had also been on display lately. The ones Jack hadn't seen fell into the "stretched and frayed" category.

Buying three of each strained her card to its credit limit. Jack probably wouldn't mind if she put them on his card, but she couldn't do that. When she left she didn't intend to be indebted to him. Grateful, but not indebted.

Libby had so many bags that Ellie helped carry them into the house. If Elizabeth hadn't been trying to buy her granddaughter's affection, then she had a pretty strange view of casual shopping. Which, actually, might be the case, Ellie conceded. She'd probably never fully grasp the standard of living that Elizabeth took for granted.

It occurred to Ellie that Mrs. Hampshire's job on Thursday would net some actual income, probably enough to cover her underwear purchase. Happy to break even, she cut off the tags and laid them neatly in her drawer. Her hand hesitated on the knob as she took a second look at the disarray inside. Someone had gone through her underwear.

The notion that a maid might have an underwear fetish was creepy but harmless. She wondered if she should say something to Elizabeth, or maybe Mr. Peters. Ellie sorted through the pieces and was sure nothing was missing, which was no surprise, since no self-respecting pervert would want her worn panties and bras. If they had any fashion sense, they'd take some of the clothes Janet had given her.

Would she notice if they had? Methodically, she went through every drawer until she satisfied herself that nothing was missing. But she was fairly certain someone had gone through those drawers before her.

Ellie sat on the bed and went over the possibilities. Maids were in and out of the bedrooms each day, changing linens and towels, picking up and returning laundry, and cleaning. She couldn't narrow it down to one suspect. Maybe some maid was overly curious about the guest's lack of designer labels, and got a huge chuckle out of discovering the Wal-Mart brands. It was probably a harmless, one-time thing. After all, it was only clothes.

Her eyes narrowed thoughtfully as they moved from the briefcase on the writing desk, to the clothes closet, to the bathroom, where her vanity bag held all her personal items. She had to check.

Puzzlement changed to worry. Someone had gone through every item of clothing and toiletries she owned. She imagined a stranger fingering her pajamas, or her makeup, or even the box of condoms in her vanity bag. What a sicko.

She was still sitting on her bed thinking when Jack

knocked on her door, then walked in without waiting for a response. He closed the door behind him. God, he looked good. Instead of the expected business suit, he was wearing a tight-fitting long-sleeved black T-shirt and jeans, a dangerous look on a man with such a well-proportioned chest and slim hips.

"That was presumptuous. What if I were naked?" Why did she even say that word, *naked*? Things like that just popped into her head whenever she was with Jack lately.

"I should be so lucky. Mr. Peters was in the hallway, and I thought it would look odd if your fiancé had to stand there waiting to be admitted to your room."

She watched him closely. "Liar. No one was out there."

He grinned, looking especially rakish. The clothes made the difference, she thought. In a suit he was handsome, but in a T-shirt and jeans he was sexy. Also out of place—these clothes were appropriate for blending into the night, not for dining at the Westfield home.

"What's with the jeans?"

"I'm in a casual mood."

"No you're not. Those are your skulking clothes. What do you and Rocky have planned?"

"Skulking?" He seemed to enjoy the word. "That's more along your lines, isn't it? Sneaking through bushes, dashing across lawns, tripping over fences. I don't know how to skulk." He sat on the bed beside her. "Why are you sitting here, staring at the door? Waiting for me?"

She scowled at his face, which was no more than a foot from her own. "You can change the subject, but we'll get back to it." He gave her that impish smile again. He was in a good mood, and she was sorry to spoil it. "I was thinking. You can help."

"What are we thinking about?"

"We're trying to figure out why someone would go through all my drawers and personal belongings while I was out shopping today."

That got rid of the smile. "Are you sure?"

"Pretty sure. I'm sure that some things were moved that didn't have to be moved in order to dust or return laundry."

"Is anything missing?"

"I don't think so."

He wasn't reassured by that, so she knew he was thinking along the same lines she was. Either someone was especially nosy, or they were looking for something in particular.

"I don't like it," he said.

"Me either. It's creepy."

"Forget creepy, it's worrisome. I talked to a few people today about what other companies use Aims Air for shipping, and naturally I mentioned Michigan Janitorial Products along with several others. I hope it didn't raise suspicions."

"How does that make sense? You ask about MJP at work and someone searches my room?"

"I ask about the company that smuggles drugs, and someone decides to do more checking on my fiancée because they're suspicious about my sudden interest, and therefore they're suspicious about your coincidental appearance on the scene."

"You mean Banner. What would he suspect, that I'm an undercover DEA agent?" She laughed, but he didn't.

"It's not funny, Ellie."

Another knock on the door interrupted whatever admonishment he was about to deliver.

"See?" she told him. "This is how it's done." She raised her voice in demonstration. "Come in."

Libby opened the door and peeked in. "Ellie? I wanted to show you . . ." Her voice trailed off as she saw Jack sitting beside her. "Oh. Hi, Jack."

"Hey, that's your new outfit. Very cool," Ellie said appreciatively. "Come in and let us see it."

Libby walked in and stood awkwardly before them.

"What do you think?" Ellie asked Jack.

He hesitated. "What am I supposed to be looking at?"

"The whole thing—jeans, sweater, boots. New school clothes. You bought them."

"Oh, yeah? Well, they look good." He seemed just the tiniest bit uncomfortable. "That's the style now, that tight? Are you sure you're only twelve, Libby?"

Ellie and Libby exchanged smiles at his look of concern. He didn't even know he'd said the right thing. He'd simply reacted like a father to the developing figure apparent on his daughter, a father who used to be a twelve-year-old boy and knew how they thought. It was exactly what Libby wanted to hear. An older man thought she didn't look like a little girl anymore. Ellie wondered if he knew he'd just made significant progress toward acceptance.

"What else did I buy today?"

Libby seemed more eager to talk now. "I got another pair of jeans, two tops, tennis shoes, and Grandmother bought me a dress in case there's a dance or something. I bought a book bag, too. Ellie only bought underwear."

"Did she?"

"Yeah. We tried to talk her into getting a really hot dress, but she said it was too expensive."

"Really? Maybe I should have gone along. I'd like to see that. The dress, I mean."

She slid him a warning look. Libby was a little too smart for him to be playing word games in front of her, even with that innocent expression on his face.

Libby's thoughts had skipped on to something else, though. She was looking at Jack's jeans and T-shirt. "Are you wearing that to dinner?"

"Afraid so. I'm bending your grandmother's rules, aren't I?" He must have noticed Libby's hesitant look. "Want to bend the rules with me? It might make me look better if you wore your new jeans. I think she likes you better than me."

Libby smiled and nodded. "Okay." She started to leave, then stopped near the door. "Jack?"

"Yeah?"

"Did you, um, did you know my mother very well?"

Ellie was as startled as Jack. In the space of time it took for Jack to act as if the question weren't unexpected, she made the connection. They'd talked about Jack not knowing her mother had been pregnant. She could tell Libby doubted his story; the question must have been simmering in her mind all afternoon.

Jack cleared his throat. "I thought I knew her. Now I'm not so sure. We were only together for a couple months, and we were both pretty young and wild." He looked like he felt guilty about it now.

"If you'd known about me, would you have married her?"

She couldn't have kept him off-balance better if she'd tried. It was like a test, and the questions kept getting harder. Ellie watched him try to figure out how blunt his answer could be. She hoped he went with the cold, hard facts; Libby was old enough to hear it.

He did. "I doubt it. We weren't in love, Libby, and that's important. It's probably why she left without telling me about you. But if I'd known, I promise you I would have made sure I was part of your life."

He'd obviously said something unexpected. Libby straightened, blinked, and bit her lower lip. Cautiously, she said, "*She* left *you*?"

"Yeah. Just took off. Oh, I get it—you thought I left her. Well, I would have, so it's the same thing. She just beat me to it. We were both too young and irresponsible to have a child." He hesitated, then flatly stated his biggest fear. "If you hate me for that, I can't really blame you. I'd feel the same way."

Libby stood there, expressionless. She had new information to absorb, and it apparently took time to rearrange her opinions. Jack watched her, looking helpless, probably wondering if what he'd said would trigger a hatred worse than what she had already shown him. She finally mumbled, "I don't hate you."

Ellie was so proud she could have hugged her, and she knew Jack was exerting great control when he simply nodded.

Now that Libby didn't hate him, she seemed to want to find ways in which they were alike. With the mental agility Ellie had begun to expect from her,

Libby said, "Aunt Jenny told me I'm going to be taller than my mom, more like you."

Jack furrowed his brow, probably trying to remember how tall Libby's mother had been, and drawing a complete blank. He decided on the safe answer. "I think your aunt is right."

It gave her the courage to express a more daring thought. "Grandmother said I look like you."

"Really? Well, she never knew your mother, so she can't see that part in you."

"I guess I got my dark hair from you."

"Looks like it."

She chewed her lip thoughtfully and looked from Jack to Ellie. "So if you guys have kids, they wouldn't look like me, and they might have lighter hair, like Ellie's."

Ellie's mouth dropped open. She hadn't seen that one coming.

Beside her, Jack shifted uncomfortably. "Uh, we haven't really talked about having kids," he said.

Ellie shook her head, wondering if the girl was preparing for competition before she even got to know her father. "No, we haven't discussed it," she assured Libby.

"Well, you should," Libby said seriously. "Because, obviously, sometimes it happens."

Libby gave them a parental look, making sure the message sank in, before leaving. They both sat still, stunned. Ellie felt suddenly uncomfortable sitting so close to Jack, as though she might be inadvertently impregnated by being near such a potent masculine force.

Jack said something that sounded like, "Hmm."

"Uh," she began, and stopped. She knew what she wanted to ask him, but it felt awkward to say, "Exactly how did that pregnancy happen in the first place? Did a condom break or something?" Not very sensitive. She began gingerly, "Did you and Libby's mother, um . . ."

"She was on the Pill. That's what she said, anyway."

"Oh." She thought about it. "Maybe she missed one or two."

"I'd say that's likely."

It was mildly reassuring. She still wouldn't have been eager to pull back the covers and make love with Jack right now. Too much fertility in the room. Just the thought of pregnancy had her so skittish, she nearly jumped when he took her hand.

"Ellie, thank you. Libby's been more open with me this past week, and I know it's because of you."

She shrugged. "She just needed a friend."

"Yes, she did. Thanks for being one."

"I did it for her. I like her."

"So do I."

He smiled and looked so proud it made her smile, too. God, she was getting to be such a sucker for those smiles. "You're going to be a real soft touch as a dad, you know that?"

"Yes, and you know what's really weird? I don't care."

She enjoyed his silly grin for a while before saying, "Since you're in such a good mood, we're going to have that little discussion now about what you and Rocky are doing tonight. It has to do with that janitorial products company, doesn't it?"

"How'd you figure that out?"

"Well, it's pretty obvious. That's the information you've been trying to follow up on. You checked for evidence at your office, you made calls to Colombia, and the only other thing you can do is see what's being delivered to MJP. What's the plan, a break-in?"

He squinted one eye and seemed to be assessing her determination to stick her nose into his little midnight adventure. She gave him her best obstinate look. He wasn't going without her.

"A break-in would be illegal."

"Right, so you'd need Rocky, who could probably breach whatever security they have without getting caught."

"We're talking about drug dealers, Ellie. Very dangerous people."

"The whole damned operation is dangerous, Jack. That's why my best friend is dead, and that's why I came here. You're not leaving me home."

"I'm not letting you risk your life, either."

"I'm not giving you a choice. I can get into my own spiffy black outfit and follow you there."

"We can lose you. You don't know where it is."

"You think I don't know how to use phone books and maps?"

"Don't try it."

"Try to stop me."

They were in mid-glare when a rap on the door interrupted the standoff. Mr. Peters's muffled voice said, "Dinner is served, Miss Coggins."

"Thank you," she called out, and gave Jack one last firm scowl. "We're not done."

"That's what you think."

God, the man was as stubborn as she was.

They sat side by side and hardly spoke during dinner, each in a determined pique. Jack's and Libby's casual attire earned a long stare from Elizabeth but, remarkably, no comment. Ellie wondered if she had decided to encourage a closer relationship between her son and granddaughter. He had certainly drawn fewer disapproving remarks lately.

If Banner noticed the change in Jack's status, he gave no indication of going along with it. "A bit informal tonight," he said to Jack, ignoring Libby as he usually did.

"I'm in an informal mood."

"An offensive mood, I'd say." It drew no comment from Jack, nor reprimand from his mother, which seemed to irritate Banner. He turned his attention on Ellie. "Didn't you say you were from Petoskey?" he asked.

"Yes."

"My late wife spent many summers up there. Perhaps you knew her."

Ellie and Jack lowered their forks simultaneously and looked at Banner's politely blank expression. It was the first time Ellie had heard a reference to Janet since she'd intentionally mentioned his wife on the night of the party. Everyone seemed to avoid saying her name in the Westfield house. Hearing Banner mention her now was like a warning jolt. Even Elizabeth slid a questioning glance at Banner.

Ellie hoped she sounded nonchalant. "I have no idea. What was her name?"

"Janet Aims."

"Doesn't sound familiar."

"They belonged to the country club and kept their sailboat there all summer. It's called *Flight Path,* a very imposing craft. Perhaps you'd remember it."

He was watching her closely. His attention caused a sudden chill in her stomach, and beside her she heard Jack lay his fork down. This interest in her connection to Janet was too coincidental to be comfortable, coming just when Jack had begun asking questions about Banner's shipments on Aims Air Freight.

Ellie licked dry lips. "I'm afraid I don't know anything about sailing, so I never paid much attention to the boats. And we didn't belong to the country club." Did he already know that? Had he been doing some checking, too? The possibility was more than a little unnerving.

"Perhaps your parents would have known her."

He was ignoring his dinner now, waiting for her reply. Even Elizabeth seemed to find his questions curious. Oh God, he knows something, she thought. He's aware of the country club connection.

While she hesitated, Jack cut in. "How would they have met your wife if they didn't sail and didn't belong to the club? Not everyone has a life that revolves around leisure and luxury, Banner."

"I suppose my mother might have catered a party for them," Ellie offered helpfully. "She has a small catering business."

"Does she?"

Unexpectedly, Elizabeth came to her rescue. "I doubt their paths would have crossed, Banner. Eleanor would never have met Janet." It was slightly arrogant, and almost true. A friendship between the groundskeeper's daughter and the rich summer kid had been unlikely.

"I suppose you're right," Banner said. "Still, perhaps we could run through some names later, to see if we find a mutual acquaintance. It would be ironic if we did."

Elizabeth was openly irritated that he hadn't dropped the subject. Ellie was petrified.

"Sorry, she can't. We're going out tonight."

Ellie turned to look at Jack in surprise. He forked up some au gratin potatoes and looked his brother in the eye. "She'll be gone all evening. Maybe another time." Anyone but a simpleton would have taken that direct look to mean: *Don't ask again.*

Ellie stared at Jack, who spared her one stern look before forcefully stabbing more food and keeping his eyes on Banner while he chewed. She thoughtfully resumed eating.

Maybe Banner had been bluffing. Maybe he was suspicious but didn't have the facts and had hoped to scare her off. She didn't care. He'd said enough to worry his brother, and now Jack was taking her with him. Jack wouldn't let her stay home now even if she insisted.

She'd have to find some proper skulking clothes.

Chapter Ten

Jack had a horrible feeling he was going to regret taking Ellie along, but what choice did he have? He couldn't leave her with Banner, and she kept making it very plain that she wouldn't wait quietly at his house. Every time he thought he liked that spunky, independent streak in her, she reminded him how uncooperative she really was.

As soon as they reached his house, he sat her in front of the TV and turned it on.

"You'll just have to put your larcenous desires on hold for a few hours. It might even be a good idea if you examined this tendency you have to impulsively act on every wild idea that pops into your brain."

"You didn't say that when I impulsively dropped my clothes in the pool house."

She was probably trying to look innocent, but it was getting harder and harder to think of Ellie as innocent. Other people might buy it, but not him.

Jack gritted his teeth. "That wasn't impulsive, you planned it." And there was nothing innocent behind that smile, which was why his forehead was damp and his groin was aching pleasantly at the memory. He was never going to be able to control this woman if his body kept ignoring what his mind knew, that she was undisciplined and reckless, and quite possibly crazy. He should disregard every idea she had, just on principle. Instead, he got sucked in by that cute smile and wicked body, and ended up doing incredibly stupid stuff, like taking her along to break into what could, for all he knew, be the Midwest distribution center for the cocaine trade. Even now, with his rational self worried about her safety, his mindless libido was lusting after the hot little burglar sitting on his couch in tight black jeans and shirt.

The blond hair was pulled into a low ponytail, as if a plain hairstyle would make her less noticeable. "You'll have to cover your hair with a black knit cap."

She nodded seriously. She was so psyched for this escapade she'd probably smear a line of black paint under her eyes if he suggested it. His biggest challenge tonight was going to be keeping his mind on the job at the same time he was safeguarding Ellie and no doubt keeping an appreciative eye on her ass. She was going to be trouble.

"Wait here while I make some calls."

She didn't like it, but it was the only excuse he could think of to get away from her while he refocused on tonight's plan. They had at least four hours to kill and the bedroom was right down the hall. He didn't need that sort of distraction.

He phoned Rocky's pager and got a call back ten minutes later. His friend's voice was low and harsh.

"What?" Rocky asked curtly in response to Jack's hello.

"What's happening over there?"

"Nothing. The last employee left at seven and there are two security guards inside. Every hour on the hour one of them comes out and walks around the building, staying in contact with the other one by walkie-talkie."

"Are they armed?"

"Handguns."

"Shit."

"Did you figure out what we're looking for in there?" Rocky whispered. "I don't want to spend more time inside than we have to."

"Seeing that we're still a couple days from the next delivery, I'm hoping like hell there's no drugs there now. I don't want to mess with those people. The only evidence now should be the manifests in Shipping and Receiving. That'll be the office in back by the loading dock."

"Good, 'cause that loading dock is our best chance of getting inside. If we don't have to go creeping around the whole building, we'll get out of there faster. I want a nice, smooth operation."

Jack hesitated. "Uh, yeah, speaking of that, there's a bit of a complication."

"What?" Rocky snapped. The guy hated it when something messed up one of his plans, especially the ones like this that he had to throw together at the last minute.

"Ellie's with me."

"Shit! She can't come."

"I couldn't leave her home. I think Banner knows something, and I don't want to put her in danger."

"So you take her on a B and E? Good thinking. Leave her at your house."

"Can't. She figured out what we're doing, and she says she'll show up anyway. You know she will. I thought it would be better if we kept an eye on her than to have her barge into the middle of things."

"Damn. You know, Jack, when this is over, you and I are gonna have a little talk about women. You gotta learn how to control them, keep your business life separate from your sex life."

"Shut up, Rocky." It was their usual banter, but lately it wasn't funny. "You need me to bring anything?"

"Yeah, an umbrella and some insect repellent. I'm standing in the fuckin' drizzle and the goddamn mosquitoes are having a picnic."

Jack smiled. Rocky wasn't happy unless he could control every part of a job, including the weather. If he had resorted to griping about the rain, Jack knew that everything else must be satisfactory. "Thanks, buddy. I owe you for this one."

"I'll keep it in mind. Be ready for my call around midnight, okay?"

"Okay."

"That means have your dick in your pants and all your clothes back on."

"Hey, pal, shove it up your fuckin'—"

Rocky's low chuckle covered Jack's string of profanity before the phone went dead.

Jack slid the cell phone in his back pocket and returned to the living room, slouching in the easy chair. Ellie was stretched out on her side on the couch, head propped on one hand while she watched the TV, looking bored out of her mind.

"Rocky says he'll call about midnight," he told her.

Her face fell. "That long? What are we supposed to do until then?"

Jack studied the heavy-lidded eyes. Was that actually a hint of seduction he saw there? It had to be his sex-fogged imagination that had made her statement remind him of a flirtatious Southern belle.

"We can make ourselves comfortable and watch TV," he said. That sounded boring and safe.

"I suppose we can." She used her free hand to reach back and pull the elastic band from her hair while she watched the characters on the screen. She tossed the blond waves lightly.

"What are you doing?"

She lifted her eyebrows. "Making myself comfortable."

Definitely seductive. He watched her thoughtfully for another minute, while she pretended not to notice. They'd made love the night before and two days before that. With his sex life getting back up to speed, he shouldn't be feeling this uncontrolled rush of heat that pooled in his groin and strained against his jeans. It would apparently take more than two incredible, unforgettable episodes to get over two years of abstinence. Oh, hell.

Her eyes followed him as he got up, pulled the couch cushions from behind her, and lay down in their place, spooning against her back. His arm fell over her and his hand cupped her breast possessively. She hadn't moved.

"Isn't that a bit presumptuous?" she said.

"No, I believe I was invited."

Her throaty chuckle alone would have sealed her fate, but she helped by turning onto her back, her eyes laughing up at him. "You're a master of subtleties, huh?"

"There's nothing subtle about you, Ellie. You scream sex."

"My goodness," she said, feigning surprise. "You do read a lot into a conversation. Let's see if you catch this little nuance." Her hand dove into his pants.

His voice was low and gravelly when he choked out, "Find what you're looking for?"

"Yes." She smiled smugly, then unzipped his pants and proceeded to do things with her mouth that would have given even Scarlett O'Hara the vapors. By the time he was able to reciprocate, clothing was flung around the living room and their positions had changed from above to below several times, until finally Jack collapsed on top of her and they both lay naked, sweaty, and thoroughly sated.

He nuzzled his face into her out-flung hair, enjoying the clean fragrance. "Want me to get up?" he asked, too tired to move.

"No." She curled a leg around his and wrapped her arms over his back. "Stay here. It still feels good."

He snuffed a tired laugh into her hair, then raised up so he could see her face. "Ellie, I know it's none of my business, but has it possibly been as long for you as it has for me?"

"Why, do I seem desperate?" she asked self-consciously.

"No, you're wonderfully enthusiastic." He kissed her nose, then her mouth. "And I'm enjoying the hell out of it. But I can't believe it all has to do with my skill, although you can tell me it does if you want to," he added quickly.

She smiled mysteriously and he felt an intimate squeeze where they were still joined. "Maybe it does. Let's just say the last guy was merely competent. I wasn't sure what was missing until now. Does that satisfy your ego?"

"Every part of me is satisfied. Glad to be of help." It was a lie, because some part of his mind was distinctly uncomfortable with the idea of another man lying where he was now. "You deserve better."

"Better than what?"

"Than mere competence. Don't settle for him." He wasn't sure just whom she should settle for, but certainly not the man who couldn't make her look as contented as she did now. He didn't want to think about him. In fact, the whole subject made him damned uncomfortable.

He knew how to distract her. "Want some ice cream?"

Her eyes widened. "Sex *and* ice cream? You really are special."

He wished he were as easily distracted.

Ellie stood behind a Dumpster, rain dripping down her collar, rusty metal snagging her sleeve, and rank odors of oil and garbage making her nose itch. Something furry skittered past her feet and into the alley behind her.

She'd never been more pumped in her life.

The warmth of Jack's arm around her shoulders reminded her of other parts of him that had been warmly intimate with her just an hour before, a memory satisfying enough to make her body yearn for his all over again. It was amazingly different from the way she'd felt with Richard, the man who so concerned Jack. She'd been infatuated with Richard, but in bed he'd given new meaning to the term *anticlimactic*. Jack was just the opposite. She'd barely had time to become infatuated with him before he'd shown her what a true climax was, but she had to admit she was growing more fond of him with each repeated demonstration. Apparently love wasn't necessary for her to have unhinged, mind-blowing orgasms. It was an interesting new concept, and one she intended to explore further.

"Put these on," Rocky ordered in a low voice.

Ellie took the pair of latex gloves he handed her. His terse tone pulled her thoughts back to the drippy, dark alley behind the MJP building.

"We go in through the broken bathroom window," Rocky told them. "A workman's truck with a ladder sticking out the back had an unfortunate accident while backing up late this afternoon." She had a quick glimpse of white teeth. "By the way, Jack, you owe me a hundred fifty bucks for the window."

She heard Jack mutter a swear word.

"And let me remind both of you, I'm the boss here tonight. No arguments. You look at whatever files you need to, but only after I say you can, and when I say you're done, you're done. Got it?"

Ellie nodded seriously. He wasn't going to get any argument from her. The longer this took, the more cautious she became, and all the more eager to get it over with. But she'd learned enough recently to have questions. "How about alarms? Don't they have security?"

"Yes. But not on that window, as long as it's broken. Ready?"

Rocky had already turned away when she had another thought. "Wait. A place like this, with drug shipments coming in, would have more security than that. Are you sure there's nothing else?"

Rocky actually smiled. "Very good, grasshopper. They have two Rottweilers. They're napping peacefully."

"Hey!" She slapped him with one of the gloves, startling both men. "If you hurt those dogs, I swear I'll turn you in to the Humane Society."

"Relax, it's a simple tranquilizer. I'm an animal lover. Now, are we done with questions?"

She peered through the drizzle at the drab building, trying to imagine what sort of security someone would use to protect janitorial products. Or hundreds of thousands of dollars' worth of illegal drugs. "There should be guards."

"There are. If we hurry, we won't encounter them."

Jack stared at both of them. "My God, one day with you, and she's thinking like a burglar. What have I done?"

"She's thinking like a security expert. But, Ellie, time matters. You'll have to trust that I've covered everything."

It didn't take more than a second's thought. "I trust you." She pulled on her gloves. "Let's go."

Without further instructions, Rocky scrambled over the fence, covering the top rows of barbed wire with a jacket before helping her over. Jack followed.

They dashed across an unlit gravel parking lot, crouching before the boarded-up window while Rocky moved a crate into position beneath it. All three were inside the building less than a minute later.

Cat burglary lost the last of its glamour. They stood at the end of a row of urinals. From the smell, she judged that MJP was a little stingy with its own cleaning products. Rocky swung the plywood back into place, plunging the bathroom into total darkness.

"Now what?" Jack asked.

"Wait."

She heard a low rattle of static as Rocky listened to the walkie-talkie he had tuned to the same frequency as the guards'. He was deadly serious, a much different Rocky from the carefree young man who joked with her while explaining home security systems. She realized just how much nerve it must have taken for him to not only steal for a living, but to steal from other thieves. No wonder he'd gotten out of the business and was looking for a way to go straight. There was too much tension in this profession.

She reached for Jack's hand in the darkness and felt better when his latex-covered fingers clasped hers in a reassuring grip.

Rocky listened to a low conversation on the walkie-talkie, then said, "Follow me."

Once they stepped outside the men's room, they had the benefit of a faint gray light that filtered through the dirty windows from the security lights around the loading dock. To their dark-adapted eyes, it seemed brighter than it was, and they easily navigated the aisles of pallets and metal shelving in the storage area. Ellie didn't know what was stored here, but she smelled the fresh wood of the pallets and something soapy that reminded her of powdered laundry detergent. Her sneakers squeaked once on the concrete floor, and the sound echoed in the cavernous room.

Across the room, Rocky opened a frosted glass door but remained outside. "Penlights only," he said as he ushered them through, then closed the door behind them.

Ellie and Jack were alone in the MJP Shipping and Receiving offices.

The room seemed too light to Ellie's fearful senses. Yellow yard lights from the loading dock outside created an eerie tan atmosphere and cast brown shadows across desks and metal file cabinets. She looked around uncertainly.

"I'll start with the filing cabinets," Jack told her.

Large three-ring binders lined two desktops and looked packed with information. Knowing the clerks and secretaries usually kept track of operations, she decided to check the binders.

It took most of her time to find shipment distribution forms, which looked promising. In the middle of her search they stopped and crouched behind desks in the gloom while a security guard swept the room with his flashlight. It was cursory and ineffective, but her heart pounded the whole time.

When Rocky opened the door again, she had several binder pages folded and tucked into a back pocket and couldn't wait to get out of there.

Jack waited with her as Rocky checked the outer storeroom. She hardly noticed him until he reached out to tuck a stray strand of hair under her cap and give her a reassuring smile.

"Hey, how are you doing?" he whispered.

"I'm nervous as hell," she admitted.

"Yeah, you looked a lot tougher the night I met you. Maybe you're not cut out for a life of crime after all."

She knew he wanted to ease her tension, but all she could focus on was the next dash across the storeroom that would take them to the broken window and outside. That oppressive, muggy night air seemed wonderful to her right now.

Rocky motioned wordlessly for them to follow. Jack pushed her ahead, keeping her between the two men as they stepped back into the cavernous storeroom. They followed a route that kept them dodging between stacked pallets, weaving their way toward the hallway on the other side. Halfway across, their plan faltered. As they crouched in the shadow of pallets stacked at least fifteen feet high, a sudden scraping thud came from their right, as if something soft had fallen to the concrete floor on the far end of the room. All three froze.

Ellie and Jack looked nervously at Rocky. When no other sounds followed, he motioned for them to stay down, then disappeared into one of the narrow paths that wound between the shipping crates.

She strained to hear something, anything, but the silence pressed against her ears. To ease her cramped knees she stood, her back to the sturdy pallet of boxes behind her. Jack rose up beside her and kept a hand on her arm, as if she might dart out unexpectedly. She was more apt to jump into his arms in fear. For one long, breathless minute they waited for a clue but heard nothing. No more scuffling, no footsteps, and no sign of Rocky.

Ellie turned to Jack and whispered up toward his ear, "What will he do? He doesn't have a gun, does he?"

"No, no weapons," he said into her ear. "I imagine he'll have to search that whole end of the storeroom, so be patient. It was probably only a rat or a raccoon, dislodging something."

Right, it was probably a rat. She tried to convince her wildly beating heart of that while another minute passed with only the sound of their breathing, and her pulse pounding like a drum in her ears.

After three minutes, she began to fidget in the dark. Should they try to cross the last fifty feet to the hallway and the men's restroom, and wait for Rocky there? She didn't want to leave him, but she felt vulnerable in the center of this vast maze of crates. What if someone else was here and had caught Rocky, or worse? Maybe they should look for him. Or maybe someone was hunting them down, aisle by aisle. Her imagination was worse than the ominous silence.

Similar thoughts must have been going through Jack's head. He leaned close and whispered, "There's an open space up ahead. I'm going to see if I can see anything."

He stepped around her, and she grabbed his arm. "Not without me," she whispered fiercely.

He turned to object, took a close look at her determined face, and closed his mouth. She knew he didn't want to spend time arguing. "Stay behind me."

He didn't have to tell her. She kept a hand on his back as they crept across a narrow aisle, then moved between another row of pallets. The open space was before them. Jack stuck his head around the corner and stepped out.

"What do you see?" she asked nervously.

"Nothing."

He took a few more steps, walking in the direction Rocky had taken. Ellie followed, still clinging to his shirt. She didn't care how cowardly it looked; she *was* scared, and Jack's presence was reassuring. While he walked slowly forward, she looked behind them, peering suspiciously into the shadows, then beside them down the long, black paths between the stacked crates. The faint swish of denim as they walked was the only sound.

Jack stopped so abruptly she bumped into his back. He was staring straight ahead and she couldn't see what had startled him. She stepped out and his arm came up suddenly, pushing her back. But she had caught a glimpse of what had halted him, and she gasped, too. In that brief second, all that had registered of the person before them was the ski mask and the gun.

Jack's arm held her forcibly behind him, but she couldn't *not* look. Twenty feet ahead of them, a figure clothed in black had stepped out from between the pallets, arms forward and gun pointed directly at Jack's chest. Terror gripped Ellie and only one possibility hit her stunned brain: drug dealers. This storeroom housed illegal shipments once a month, and the gunman must be here for drugs. Except there were no drugs tonight, according to Rocky. Only Ellie, Jack, and Rocky were here. What had happened to Rocky?

The figure didn't speak but motioned with the gun for them to step further away from the crates, into the center of the open space. Jack took Ellie's hand, keeping her as close as possible as he stepped sideways. He moved slowly, eyes riveted on the masked figure while he tried to shelter Ellie with his body.

The figure moved an arm, and white light stabbed at their eyes. The thin flashlight beam hit Jack's face, then moved to Ellie's. She flinched, turning her face into Jack's shoulder, but the light lingered on her. After several seconds, it lowered and she was able to look toward the dark shape behind it. She held a hand up and squinted against the glare until the flashlight went out.

Darkness closed in again, then lightened as her eyes readjusted to the gloom. At first she thought her sight was still affected by afterimages from the flashlight. The gun was wavering. Ellie hugged Jack's side, mesmerized by the gun, which suddenly couldn't seem to decide on a target. After several nerve-racking seconds it lowered and an incredulous voice asked, "Nora?"

Ellie went cold. The gunman seemed to waver, and she blinked hard to bring him into focus. She knew that voice. Even as the figure in black raised a hand to the ski mask, she knew it wasn't possible but stared in disbelief as the mask was pulled off and brown shoulder-length hair was shaken out.

In a strangled voice, Ellie gasped, "Janet?"

Chapter Eleven

Ellie stood rooted to the concrete, breathing heavily and staring at the ghost before her. The image of Janet dropped the ski mask from trembling fingers and said, "Nora, what are you doing here?"

There was no question—she was real. Ellie didn't know how it was possible, but she didn't care. She choked, "Oh my God, Janet!" and threw herself at her best friend in a crushing embrace.

The gun clattered to the floor as Janet hugged her back, squeezing tightly and saying between tears, "I'm so sorry" and "I missed you so much!" Ellie could hardly make out the words between her own sobs and desperate inquiries of "What happened? What are you doing here?" and finally ended with "You're supposed to be dead!"

When she stepped back and wiped her tears, a hand fell on her shoulder. In a low voice Jack said, "Maybe you should save the joyous reunion for later. Rocky's still missing and we don't want to be discovered."

Janet blinked tears from her eyes and looked at

Jack. "Who are you?" she said, then noticed the gun he held. "Oh, my gun," she said, holding her hand out to take it.

"Oh, no you don't. You seem to have the same propensity for gunplay as your friend here. I think I'll just keep this."

Janet's brows drew together, more confused than anything. "Who are you? Who is this, Nora?"

"This is Jack Payton," Ellie told her, trying to readjust to her former name. Nora sounded odd after a week of being Ellie.

"Payton?" Janet repeated, recognition in her tone.

Jack smiled briefly. "Your brother-in-law. Glad to meet you."

Janet looked questioningly at Ellie, then back to Jack. "I don't understand."

"Me either," Jack assured her, then stiffened at a scraping sound coming toward them.

Ellie whirled, expecting guards with drawn guns, and was relieved to see Rocky. He shoved another man before him, a man who seemed to be having trouble walking, and not only because Rocky had a painful grip on the arm twisted behind the man's back. His head hung down as he stumbled along and his free hand rubbed it, as if he'd struck it and was trying to assess the damage.

"We've got problems," Rocky announced. "These idiots got the drop on the guards and tied them up. There'll be no way to disguise the fact that someone broke in here tonight. Goddamn amateurs," he added sourly.

"Did they set off an alarm?" Jack asked.

"No, by some miracle. We can get out of here, but

you better believe they'll wonder what these two were looking for, and they'll check everything."

"Shit," Jack said.

"Ow!" the injured man said as Rocky gave him a shove toward a stupefied Janet. He transferred his hand from his head to his arm, rubbing the elbow and glaring at Rocky.

Ellie saw his face for the first time. Her mouth dropped open. This was becoming more unbelievable by the second. "Richard?"

"Nora? My God, what are you doing here?"

Ellie stared at him, then at Janet. She shook her head slowly as if the fog might lift and things might become less surreal. "What. . . ?" She didn't even know what to ask.

"He came along to help me," Janet said. "I looked for you first, but you were gone, and no one knew where you were. Richard was concerned, naturally, and he said he'd help me."

The picture didn't seem any more clear. Help her do what? Steal drugs? Find Ellie? Before she could formulate another question, Jack interrupted her thoughts.

"Who the hell are you?" he asked Richard. "And how do you know Ellie?"

"Who's Ellie?" Richard asked.

"Me," Ellie said a little self-consciously. She was beginning to have too many names.

With that clarified, Richard turned an irritated face toward Jack. "Nora's my fiancée. Who the hell are you?"

"Who's Nora?" Rocky asked. The question was ignored as Ellie snapped a response to the other part of the statement.

"I am not your fiancée!"

"Well, almost," he corrected.

"Richard, you asked and I said no. That's not an engagement."

Jack's look of comprehension was not a pleasant one. "Is this Mr. Competent?" He looked Richard up and down critically. Considering the man's disheveled condition, he couldn't have made a favorable impression.

"Yes." Ellie was annoyed, but she wasn't sure if it was with Richard or Jack, who was looking as threatening as he had the first night she'd met him.

Jack's condescending smile was as good as his mother's. "Well, Richard, this is going to come as a shock to you, but Ellie is *my* fiancée." Before Ellie knew what he was doing, he lifted her left hand and dangled it before Richard, displaying the enormous Payton diamond that managed to gleam even in the dim storeroom. She snatched it away.

"Holy shit, Nora," Janet breathed.

"Why does he keep calling you Ellie?" Richard asked.

"Who the hell cares!" They all looked at Rocky. Janet and Richard cowered a bit at the volatile man who seemed to be in charge. Jack's lip curled with amusement. Rocky swiped an irritated hand through his mop of black hair. "Damn it, we're breaking a dozen laws just standing here. Can we have this conversation someplace else?"

Jack ordered Janet to follow his Jeep. Ellie desperately wanted to ride with Janet and find out just how her dead friend had come to be alive, but Janet was chauffeuring Richard, and Ellie definitely did not want to answer any questions from him just now. She tried to talk Rocky into taking Richard, who was too dizzy to drive himself, but Rocky firmly refused to have anything to do with the inept fool who had messed up his perfect plan. So Ellie sat in the Jeep, nervously turning every two minutes to watch the headlights that stuck close behind them.

"Relax, Ellie," Jack said. "You'll get your answers soon enough."

She slumped back in the seat in frustration. "Her parents buried her, Jack. The body was shipped to Petoskey, and they had a funeral, and they buried her." She amended that: "They buried *somebody*. God, who did they bury?"

He nodded. "The part that bothers me is not knowing where Banner fits into this. Does he know his wife's death was faked? Or was she supposed to be murdered, and no one told him it didn't work? I have questions, too."

"Whatever happened, Janet had nothing to do with deceiving her family and friends about her death," Ellie said firmly. "She wouldn't do that."

"Are you sure?"

She glared angrily. "Of course I'm sure! She's my best friend."

They rode in silence for several minutes while Ellie fumed over Jack daring to doubt her best friend's motives. He might not know Janet, but Ellie expected him to trust her judgment on that matter. Maybe that was the real problem—Jack didn't trust her. She shouldn't be surprised. No matter how good he could make her body feel, he was using her to win his daughter, just as she'd been using him for access to Banner. Their relationship was based on sex and blackmail, not trust. At least her relationship with Richard had been honest. Uninspiring, but honest.

Which reminded her of another irritating point. "You were trying to humiliate Richard with that engagement bit, weren't you? Why did you do that?"

"I'm not sure why I did it, but I know I enjoyed it." His lip curled with an evil little smile at the memory.

"You don't even know him."

Jack shrugged. "Some people are easy to dislike."

She opened her mouth to jump to Richard's defense, then came to her senses. She really didn't care to enumerate the good qualities of the guy she'd recently dumped. She settled for a disdainful sniff, then spent the rest of the drive with her eyes on the outside mirror, wondering about the chain of events that had ended with meeting her recently murdered best friend in the midst of a burglary.

Janet refused to sit down and talk until they had attended to Richard, who continued to finger the lump on his head and shoot suspicious looks at Rocky. She settled him on the couch and fussed over his wounded scalp while Ellie prepared a bag of crushed ice and tried to ignore the irony of her former boyfriend occupying the scene of her recent debauchery. Leaning against the kitchen doorjamb, Jack watched contemptuously as Ellie knelt and tenderly applied the ice. Rocky reluctantly helped by fetching the aspirin and glass of water Janet demanded. He handed them over while favoring Richard with a disgusted look.

Richard returned the loathing. "You hit me over the head, didn't you?"

"How do you know you didn't trip over your own feet and bash your head on a crate?"

Richard swallowed the aspirin and grimaced. "If I hadn't accidentally fallen over that empty pallet, you never would have known we were there."

"Yeah, then you could have accidentally shot us." With a contemptuous snarl, he left to stand by Jack.

Ellie placed Richard's hand on the ice pack, gave him an encouraging smile, and followed Rocky. In a voice low enough that Richard couldn't overhear, she said, "Why are you both so abusive? Neither of you know Richard. He's a good person. He's smart, and caring, and . . . and"—she searched for a noble word but could only come up with—"nice."

Rocky snorted, and Jack nodded agreeably. "And competent. Don't forget that."

She bit back a nasty retort and resigned herself to the fact that Jack would never like Richard.

Untroubled by further thoughts of the persecuted Richard, Jack turned to Rocky. "Are the cops going to be looking for us by morning?"

"I doubt it. The guards weren't tied that tightly and they'll probably get loose before then, but I don't think MJP will call the cops. We'll know more when we look at those papers you took, but if you're right about a drug shipment due to arrive Thursday, they can't afford to have the cops sniffing around in order to learn what a gang of burglars might have been after. They'll try to figure it out on their own. If we're lucky, they won't tell their buyer about it, 'cause he'd be bound to get all nervous and trigger-happy. You don't want to ever meet a trigger-happy drug dealer."

"So we're safe?"

"Maybe. The three of us weren't seen and we didn't leave a trail, but I don't know about Bonnie and Clyde here. They weren't exactly professional."

The two men gave Ellie's friends another baleful look.

That wasn't fair. "Of course they weren't professional," Ellie said. "You two are the ex-cons. They're just a couple of innocent victims who got dragged into this mess by Banner."

"Are you sure?" Rocky asked skeptically.

"Yes! Quit asking me that. You'll see when you hear their story."

"This should be good," Jack told Rocky.

"First," Rocky said, "could someone please tell me who they are? I got that the clumsy oaf is some ex-boyfriend of Ellie's, but why is he here, and who's the girl?"

"Good place to start." Jack walked to the back of the couch. "Rocky, this is Janet, my formerly dead sister-in-law." He smiled at Janet. "I'm sure you never heard of me, but I'm Banner's older half brother. I was in jail when you married Banner." He stuck out his hand.

Janet rose cautiously and reached over the couch to shake his hand. "Jail?" she asked weakly.

"Drunk driving and manslaughter. Rocky was my cellmate. Burglary. You're looking at an expert here."

She gave Rocky a half smile and looked uncertainly at Ellie. "You're engaged to this man?"

Under the ice pack, Richard's eyes sparked with interest and shifted expectantly to Ellie.

"Yes. Well, not really. Sort of." She looked at Jack helplessly, but he only smiled. The bastard was enjoying this. "Jack needs a wife in order to get custody of his daughter. I agreed to pose as his fiancée in order to get into the Westfield house and find out how Banner killed you so I could turn him in to the police."

Jack leaned toward Janet. "She's skipping the best part of the story—where we first met—but I'll fill you in later. Go on, sweetheart."

She'd kill him later. She didn't even want to think about dealing with Richard, who kept a calculating eye on Jack while he listened attentively to her story. "We learned that Banner was somehow involved with smuggling drugs, and we've been trying to prove it. That's why we were at MJP tonight."

Janet nodded slowly, and Ellie blew out a relieved breath. It was all so incredible, she hadn't been sure she could make it sound plausible.

Jack added helpfully, "Ellie has also started a business with Rocky."

Janet stared at him blankly. "Why do you keep calling her Ellie?"

"Because Eleanor sounds like a name for a sexually repressed old lady, and Ellie isn't—"

"Pay no attention to him, Janet. Besides, I'm getting used to the name. No one here calls me Nora." Janet nodded again but still looked suspicious. To keep her from asking the wrong questions, Ellie said, "So tell me what really happened to you and where you've been for the last two months."

"Wait, I want to hear this, too, but why don't we all get something to drink first," Jack said. "Can I get you a beer, Dick?"

Richard's eyes were cold as he growled, "Richard. No."

Rocky looked like he was beginning to enjoy the tension Jack kept stirring up. "I'll have one. Ladies?"

What the hell, Ellie thought wearily. It was bound to be a long story, and Jack didn't appear to be in any hurry. She sank into a chair and signaled Jack to bring one for her, too.

Janet shoved Richard's feet out of the way and curled up on the end of the couch. Ellie took a long, appreciative look at her friend. She seemed more healthy and vibrant than ever, the auburn hair a little longer than when Ellie had last seen it and the tan darker than she'd had after a summer on her parents' boat in Lake Michigan. No bullet holes or prison-pale skin. From her appearance, she might have spent two months on a Caribbean cruise instead of escaping death in Colombia. She had escaped a death plot, hadn't she?

"American beer!" Janet laughed, holding the Budweiser Rocky gave her as if it were the nectar of the gods. "You can't imagine how good this tastes after seven weeks of local brews and Coca-Cola. You can't get a decent beer in Guatemala."

"Guatemala?"

"That's where I was until six days ago. Gosh, I hardly know where to start, so much has happened."

"Start with Banner," Ellie said, desperate to gain evidence of something illegal. "In your last e-mail it sounded like you were worried about your marriage, or something you'd discovered."

"Both." Janet leaned back, still cradling the beer. "Okay, I'll try to summarize this, because it gets pretty complicated. It began with some papers Banner left lying around about the Aims accounts in Colombia." She looked at Jack and Rocky. "Aims is—"

"We know, the airline Westfield-Benton bought from your father."

"Yes. My dad used to take me on his South American trips, and since college I worked in Latin American Operations. Even though Banner wanted me to quit work when we got married, I knew all the customers. He had acquired a new one on this end, Michigan Janitorial Products." They nodded; obviously they all knew about that connection. "I was curious about what they shipped, but when I asked Banner about it he got angry, which I thought was odd, not to mention insulting. I knew as much about those accounts as he did, and I was his wife; it just didn't seem right. So naturally I tried to find out what he was hiding."

"Naturally," Jack agreed, amused.

"And I'm afraid I'm not a very good detective, because he caught me snooping, and that's when things started to get ugly. He yelled and ordered me to stay out of his business, trying to intimidate me into being a submissive, ornamental wife. That got me angry. That's not what I married him to be, and I don't respond well to bullying."

"Of course not. So you just got more determined to learn about MJP."

"Yes," she said, a bit surprised.

Jack waved a finger between Ellie and Janet. "You two think a lot alike."

Janet seemed to ponder that for several seconds, and Ellie knew what was really going through her mind. She was beginning to wonder just what sort of relationship they had. Since Ellie couldn't explain that one herself, she thought it best to stay away from the subject. Thankfully, Richard was beginning to nod off.

"How did you know they were bringing in drugs?" Ellie asked.

Janet turned back to her. "I didn't, not until I got to Colombia. Banner wanted me to go along, and he made a big deal over apologizing and promising to involve me more in the company business. He suggested I take on some of the work at Aims to show he wasn't hiding anything, then he said we could turn the trip into a second honeymoon. Oh, Nora, I was so gullible. Banner has this smooth way of making you think you're the most important thing in his life, but I know now it was all fake. He's really a lying, self-centered bastard. I mean a slimy, vicious, stinking piece of—" She stopped and glanced self-consciously at Jack, who was, after all, the half brother of the piece of shit.

Jack grinned. "Keep going. If you run out of adjectives, I've got a few choice ones myself."

"I think we're all in agreement on Banner, Janet." Actually, Ellie didn't understand how Janet had found the man attractive in the first place, but then she'd never been the target of Banner's questionable charm. Not that it would have worked. Cool perfection had never moved her. She liked a few nicks and flaws in the surface, something to add character. Someone more like . . . No! She squeezed her eyes shut and tried to erase the thought from her mind.

"Do you have a headache, Nora? I should let you get some sleep."

"No, I'm fine. Tell me what happened after you got to Colombia with the lying piece of shit."

"I was set up. Banner had to have planned it in advance. The first day there I went into the mountains to visit a medical clinic that Westfield-Benton was building for the local people. Banner arranged a guide to take me while he stayed behind."

Jack looked puzzled. "I never heard of that."

"I'm sure it doesn't exist. He just knew what to say to get me out there. So like the perfect victim, I let them lead me right into the trap. Saved them the trouble of kidnapping me. I can't believe how stupid I was. They took me to the home of the local mayor before visiting the clinic. That's who they said he was, but it was probably the drug lord who dealt with Banner. They were going to kill me."

"How did you know?"

"Pure, dumb luck—no one knew I spoke Spanish. Banner doesn't speak it, so they spoke English with him, and they just assumed they had to with me, too. Carlos, the guy he hired, spoke English well, and I never thought to switch to Spanish. Once he had me at the house, he began giving directions to other men in Spanish, and it became obvious they were only waiting for my host to tell them when to take me outside and shoot me."

"Oh, Janet!" Ellie felt the horror and shock that Janet had undoubtedly felt in the mountains of Colombia, even though she could recite it dispassionately now. Jack and Rocky had grim looks on their faces. She could tell Banner was going to pay for this. "What did you do?"

"I think some survival instinct must have taken over, because I didn't melt into a puddle of fear. I started looking for an opportunity to get away."

"Good for you," Rocky said, more interested now. "You used your one advantage."

"Exactly." Janet looked at Rocky gratefully, as if he was the only one who understood. "I just got very focused, you know? When there are no other options, it sort of quiets your mind."

Rocky nodded eagerly. "A moment of clarity. I know what you mean. How did you do it?"

"The so-called mayor finally showed up and told me that Carlos would take me to the clinic now. One man, walking me out toward the jungle. I knew what he would do."

She took a sip of beer while Ellie's stomach did flip-flops from the suspense. Rocky was smiling in anticipation. Richard snorted and mumbled something in his sleep.

"I started talking to Carlos, asking questions and not even waiting for answers, just chattering away like I had no idea what was going on. He tuned me out. When we were out of sight of the house, I pointed off to the side and said, 'Oh my God, what's that?' When he looked, I clasped my hands together and swung them at the back of his head like I was going for a home run."

Rocky loved it. "Excellent! The oldest trick in the book—'Look over there!'"

Janet grinned. "It would have worked better if I were six inches taller and sixty pounds heavier. I smashed my fingers on his skull and he staggered, but he didn't fall. So I kicked the back of his legs, then kept kicking when he was down. When he was unconscious, I found the gun in his pocket and fired it once so they'd think he'd killed me."

"Brilliant," Rocky said appreciatively.

"Holy Christ," Jack said.

"That's awful!" Ellie couldn't picture her cultured, sheltered friend kicking some guy silly, then searching his pockets and stealing his gun. "I would have been too scared to knock him out."

"He was going to kill me, Nora. You would have done the same thing. I always said you were a survivor, that you'd do whatever had to be done, and I guess I am, too."

She looked proud of herself, but Ellie was still feeling appalled at what Janet had had to do, and terrified all over again at how close her friend had come to dying. She caught Jack's eye and knew he understood.

Rocky apparently didn't. As Janet described her escape, he'd grown more animated, and he was looking at her now in open admiration as if they shared some professional rapport. "What did you do next?"

"I stayed in the trees and skirted the compound. They had their vehicles in front and I found a truck with keys in it. I drove out quietly, then took off like the Colombian version of the Indy 500. The roads are horrible out there, and I hit the ruts so hard, I kept bumping my head on the roof and scraping trees, but I got away. I don't even know if they chased me. When I got into Bogotá I ditched the truck. I was afraid to go back to the hotel, so I looked up a pilot who worked for Aims. He was the only one I knew I could trust. That's about it." She shrugged, as if the rest of the story were too simple to bother telling. "He took me on his regular run to Guatemala and left me with some friends until they could get a fake passport. That's what took most of the time. Once I had the passport, I took a commercial flight home."

Ellie and Jack were still staring in amazement, and

Rocky was grinning from ear to ear. From the couch, Richard snored softly.

"I hope you don't mind that I got Richard involved, Nora, but I needed help. I suppose I could walk back into the Westfield house and say, 'Surprise, honey, I'm home,' but I don't want to simply divorce Banner and walk away. He tried to have me killed, and he probably thinks I really am dead. That's the advantage I have to use, but I don't know how yet."

Ellie nodded and pulled the folded papers from her pocket. She'd nearly forgotten about them. "This might help," she said. "Did you get anything, Jack?"

"Maybe. We'll go over it tomorrow. Right now I'd like to get some sleep. Come on, I'll take you home, Ellie."

"Home?" Janet stood as they got up.

"I've been staying at the Westfield house." At Janet's look of fear, Ellie added, "Don't worry, Banner won't touch me with Elizabeth there."

"I hope you're right, Nora, but don't underestimate him. He only cares about himself. He's dangerous."

"I'll be careful." The thought of what Banner was capable of and what Janet had gone through terrified her all over again. "Oh, Janet, I'm so glad you're not dead!" she blurted, and clung to her friend for several seconds, reluctant to let go.

Janet finally laughed and pulled away. "I don't know why I didn't think to look for you here. I should have known you'd come after Banner if you thought I was dead."

"That would have been *my* first guess," Jack said dryly. Ellie made a face, which amused him and had Janet watching with interest.

When Jack reached for Ellie's hand, she took it without thinking. Janet's eyebrows went up.

Jack turned toward Rocky. "We have to keep Janet out of sight. Give her the guest room. Prince Charming can stay right where he is."

"No problem," Rocky agreed, suddenly a full member of the let's-get-Banner team. "You see that Ellie's safe, and I'll take care of Janet."

Apparently, Richard was on his own.

Ellie's gaze fell on Richard and she shook her head, smiling fondly. He'd made a pathetic burglar, even if his intentions had been admirable. She hadn't even thanked him for worrying about her safety and for unhesitatingly coming to Janet's aid.

"Shouldn't we wake him up?" she asked. "I think you're supposed to avoid sleep after a head injury."

"Nah, I didn't hit him that hard. He's fine."

Ellie bit her cheek but decided to trust Rocky. "Tell Richard I'll come by tomorrow," she told Janet softly.

Jack tugged sharply on her hand, urging her to leave, then glanced back at Richard with such disgust, she was glad to separate them for a while.

The rain clouds had cleared and Ellie rolled the window down, letting the light breeze fan her hair while she stared vacantly at the dark streets. She could use about an hour of this, going completely blank while the night air cleansed all the conflicting emotions from her mind. No talking, just fresh night breezes and glittering starlight.

"Why do you need to see Richard tomorrow?"

She looked at Jack, but he didn't meet her eyes. "I

don't *need* to, I *want* to. I think he at least deserves a thank you."

"For what?"

"For caring enough to help! Caring about someone besides yourself is admirable."

That earned her a look, but no comment. Fine, she didn't want to talk to Jack about Richard, anyway.

It was nearly four A.M. when they pulled into the Westfield driveway. "I'll walk you in."

Some contrary instinct roused itself. She couldn't seem to stop drawing boundary lines through their relationship. "It's not a date, Jack. I can see myself in."

"I'm not walking you to the door so I can kiss you good night," he snapped. "I'm walking you to your room because you live with a murderer."

As they opened their doors and stepped out, a man crossed behind the Jeep, eliciting a frightened gasp from Ellie. He looked startled, then nodded stiffly to Jack and walked to a black car nearly hidden in the dark shadows.

Jack didn't move while Ben Thatcher started his car and drove off. Ellie could only see his back, but it was rigid with tension. "Guess we're not the only ones out late," she said.

She could practically hear his teeth grinding. "There's only one reason he'd be sneaking out of here at four A.M."

"He wasn't sneaking."

He turned and growled, "He wasn't selling tickets to the policemen's ball, either."

Chapter Twelve

"Grow up, Jack. Your mother has a right to her own life. Besides, he seems like a nice man."

He turned, his eyes gleaming darkly. "A nice man," he said, curling his lip as if the words left a bitter aftertaste. "I've had it up to here with nice men."

If he was going to be unreasonably cranky, she didn't have to talk to him. Wordlessly they walked to the front door, unlocked it, and canceled the alarm. When she started up the wide sweep of stairs, he was right behind her, and when she reached the bedroom, he walked past her and looked in every corner of the bathroom and walk-in closet while she waited impatiently at the door. It seemed unnecessary, an exaggerated spy game, but she let him do it.

Having satisfied himself that Banner was not lurking in the towel heater or behind the rotating shoe rack, he returned to her. She stood with the open door at her back, and he stopped so close to her they nearly touched. His body heat electrified the hairs on her arms, and she had to tilt her head to meet his eyes.

That was a mistake. His gaze was intense, with an almost magnetic pull. She knew he was going to kiss her, and when he did it would be hard and possessive, claiming her whole body, not merely her lips. She didn't want to kiss him, didn't want to be part of his primitive territory-marking, but her neurons must have shorted out because the message was not getting through to her body. Her heart pounded and her skin shivered as she readied herself for a full-body experience.

She waited for it to happen. His face was so close her head bumped the door behind her, and energy seemed to radiate from him with each visible rise and fall of his chest. His gaze fell to her lips, then back to her eyes.

"Good night, Ellie." His voice was low and rumbly.

She watched him walk away, every expectant nerve fiber left unfulfilled. Damn, she'd wanted that kiss after all.

Sleeping late in a luxuriously decadent bedroom suite made her feel like one of the idle rich. Idle was too much like useless. Ellie hurried through lunch and drove her Toyota to Jack's house.

He was gone. Janet, Richard, and Rocky sat around the kitchen table ingesting caffeine and waiting for it to take effect. Rocky looked more alert than the others, probably due to his shirt—pink this time, with lime-green vines crawling around it. The California surfer was back.

Richard perked up when Ellie took a chair next to him. He wore last night's rumpled clothes, but was washed and shaved, and seemed to have gotten over his failure as a burglar.

"How's your head?" she asked him. "Does it hurt?"

"It has a lump. I'll feel better when you explain to me why you left Petoskey without telling anyone, and why you're pretending to be engaged to someone you don't even know."

"I do know Jack," she defended herself. Intimately. In fact, she knew his naked body better than she knew Richard's. Which she was not going to think about.

"It's not a big deal, Richard. We met, we figured out we both hated Banner, and we could both benefit from pretending to be engaged," she said, neatly summing up her criminal activity and Jack's blackmail. "It got me into the Westfield house, and that's how we found out about Michigan Janitorial Products. And I didn't tell anyone why I left home because you'd all try to stop me, or come after me."

"Damn right. That impulsiveness has always gotten you into trouble, Nora. You know you need to consult someone more level-headed and objective before jumping into these things. It's dangerous."

"We're supposed to call her Ellie now," Janet said.

"Do you always try to tell Ellie what to do?" Rocky asked him, as though wondering just how crazy her friend was.

Richard scowled at both of them, less perky now. "*Nora*," he emphasized, "knows she makes hasty decisions, and she has always appreciated a more prudent analysis of the situation. I think she could have benefited from some judicious advice before taking off after a possible killer."

"Prudent analysis?" Rocky seemed to enjoy the words.

"Banner isn't a possible killer, he *is* a killer," Ellie insisted. "Attempted murder is as good as the real thing. And sometimes I get tired of doing the prudent thing, Richard." She said it kindly so she wouldn't offend him, but it felt good to say. Liberating, like her new name. Nora had tried to be a prudent person; Ellie didn't. She liked Ellie better than Nora.

"Please call me Ellie, Richard. I like it better."

He frowned. "You never did before."

"People change."

"They don't have to." He gave her a long, hard look.

Whoa. This was a deeper issue than she cared to get into right now. Janet and Rocky were riveted by the real-live soap opera unfolding in front of them.

To change the subject, she asked, "Does anyone know what was in the papers we stole last night? Were they helpful?"

Rocky nodded. "You did good, kid. Lots of bills of lading that look completely innocent, but one of them gave us a good lead. One of their sources of cleaning compounds comes in by air freight from Colombian Chemicals. Jack and I went over the papers this morning, and we both think those shipments are the likely source of the smuggled drugs."

Now that he mentioned it . . . "Where is Jack?"

"He said he wanted to put in an appearance at work," Rocky told her. "He'll be back any time now."

"Right now," Jack's voice announced. He'd used the garage door and she hadn't heard him come in. "Was someone asking about me?"

"Ellie was," Janet offered brightly.

Ellie peered at her friend closely. What the hell?

Jack smiled. "Miss me, sweetie?"

She refused to answer. He might not mind an audience, but she wasn't about to become part of the morning's entertainment.

Jack dragged an extra chair to the table, threw his suit coat over the back, and sat next to Ellie. She deliberately turned and smiled at Richard, who was developing furrows in his forehead as he tried to prudently analyze the situation.

Jack pulled the tab off a Diet Pepsi, joining the caffeine party. "Did you guys come up with anything?"

Janet leaned across the table toward Ellie. "Jack wanted us to think about how we could use the fact that Banner doesn't know I'm alive. We'd like to get him upset, make him do something that would give himself away."

"I think we can do better than that," Rocky told Jack. "I think we can get him in trouble with his drug dealer friends. Make them very unhappy. The only problem is it exposes Janet, and she'd be in danger."

"Can we protect her?"

Rocky nodded firmly. "I'll take care of it."

Ellie didn't find his lack of detail very reassuring, but Janet seemed satisfied. Of course, Janet probably felt like Superwoman after kick-boxing her way out of Colombia, so she might not be thinking clearly.

"Are you sure, Rocky? Banner knows you're connected to Jack and to me, so she might not be safe with you, either."

"I have connections and friends if I need them."

Janet said, "Don't worry about me, Ellie. I trust Rocky."

"Really." Talk about impulsive decisions; she hardly knew the guy.

Rocky was unfazed by Ellie's doubts, ignoring her to get back to the issue of exposing Banner. "Janet knows how Aims's Latin American division works. I'm sure there are some employees who would be thrilled to find out she's not dead and would gladly help her out." He raised his eyebrows at Janet, who nodded her agreement. "We can use those contacts to make changes in the drug shipments."

He had Jack's attention. "How?"

"We're assuming it's a tight operation. The drugs arrive already packed for shipment along with other supplies. No one has to be bribed to look the other way, it just gets loaded onto a plane. So the only way to stop it is an all-out search of the cargo by police with drug dogs."

"And I can arrange that," Janet said. "The Colombian police won't barge into our hangar and do a random check, but if I *request* a drug search by the police, especially if I can pinpoint a particular shipment, they'll do it."

"We just need to be sure about which company the drug suppliers used as a cover for shipping," Rocky added. "I doubt the boxes are labeled 'Illegal Drugs, Do Not Open.'"

"I can help you there," Jack said. "That's one of the things I checked out at the office this morning. The Aims relationship with Colombian Chemicals started shortly after my accident, when I was dismissed from the company. That coincides with the unusual profits Banner started raking in. It's exactly what I expected to find—as soon as he was in charge, the corruption started. I'm sure they're using Colombian Chemicals. They ship every other Thursday, and tomorrow's package would be the one with the big prize."

Something in Jack's report nagged at Ellie's mind, but Rocky and Janet interrupted her thoughts.

"Got 'em!" Rocky exclaimed as he and Janet grinned at each other. Ellie smiled at how much her friend's spirit of adventure meshed with Rocky's. She couldn't help wondering if she'd rebound from a crisis as well as Janet had. Well, she'd find out soon enough. Leaving Jack was going to precipitate the biggest emotional crisis of her life.

"No." Richard's flat statement brought her attention back. "It can't be that easy," he objected.

"Yes, it can. The best plans are simple," Rocky told him. "If the drug shipment is confiscated, the bad guys get mad at Banner and Banner backtracks and finds out who ordered the search. Once he's convinced it really was Janet, he'll go after the Colombian guys who were supposed to have killed her but neglected to mention that she wasn't dead. What could be better than turning them against each other?"

Ellie had no desire to put her friend in jeopardy again. "I don't like Banner knowing Janet is alive. What if he tries to have her killed again?"

"He won't know where to find her. For all he knows, she could be in Colombia."

"I don't care what Banner knows. I'm doing it anyway," Janet said. "Nothing else will expose him as a murderer. I don't care if he's connected to drug runners. I hope he does try to kill me. Because you can protect me, and then I can see him go to jail for the rest of his life."

Ellie assumed by "you can protect me" she meant the plural form, all of them, although Janet was looking at Rocky, waiting for a response. It hadn't taken Janet long to figure out who the daredevil action hero was in their little group.

He finally nodded once. "Okay."

"This is stupid," Richard said. "You have to give it more thought before you take such a big chance."

Rocky stood up. "You analyze it, Professor. Janet has some long-distance calls to make." Before he followed her to the living room, he smiled at Jack. "You don't mind a few prime-time calls to Colombia, do you? What's another couple hundred dollars?"

"Sure, go ahead." Jack waved him off. "My daughter doesn't have to go to college."

"You're all crazy," Richard grumbled. "And too goddamned impulsive."

"Rocky doesn't act on impulse, Richie. It's called being decisive."

Richard glared at Jack's flat stare. To Ellie, caught between them, they looked like every nature special she'd ever seen where two males faced off for territory and dominance. She didn't care for her position in the middle.

She left the wildlife to work out their aggressions and followed the others to the living room. Janet was on the phone, already explaining her resurrection to someone in Bogotá.

"I know, I wish I could have told you, but we had to let certain people think I was dead. It's a long story, and I'll come down and give you all the details as soon as I can. Right now I need you to do something for me. There's a shipment going out on flight twenty-nine tomorrow, and I need you to call for a full-scale drug search of the cargo." She listened, smiled at Rocky, and nodded. "That's a very interesting guess, Enrique, but you realize I can't give you any information yet. Can you just trust me and make the arrangements? No, don't tell *anyone* else. You'll be the only one who knows it's going down until it happens. After that, tell anyone who asks that I ordered it." She lifted her eyebrows at Ellie and Rocky and beamed. "No, I'll call you. And remember, if you pick up any flak, just blame it on me. Bye."

As soon as the phone hit the cradle, Janet and Rocky were laughing and high-fiving. "He thinks the rumor of my death was all part of an elaborate sting to catch drug runners."

"As it turns out, it was," Rocky told her. "When will it happen?"

"Probably tomorrow morning before nine o'clock."

Being around Richard again must be rubbing off on her, Ellie thought. No one seemed to be concerned enough for Janet's safety. "We have to be ready for repercussions," Ellie said. "How will we know what's happening?"

Rocky had obviously thought it through farther than she had. "Once the shit hits the fan in Colombia tomorrow morning, the bad guys will be trying to avoid the authorities there. Meanwhile, the drugs don't arrive on the Thursday flight. If the Colombian boys don't bother to tell Banner the shipment was confiscated, then for sure MJP will be calling him when it doesn't arrive. Either way, Banner will follow up, but he'll care more about the screwup with Janet than he will about one shipment of drugs not getting through.

I'd expect him to hop the next flight to Bogotá and confront the men he paid to dispose of his wife. He'll try to figure out where she is, but he'll be looking in Colombia, not here. Or if he doesn't go, at least he'll be making frantic calls and screaming enough for Jack and half of the W-B Administration wing to know about it. That could be as late as tomorrow evening, so you might want to stay out of his way, Ellie. He'll be pissed and out for blood."

Janet looked worried for the first time. "I don't want anyone else to be in danger. I married the bastard—this is my problem."

"Yeah, but you can't get out of this one by yourself. Ellie knows how to handle herself around Banner, and Jack will be there with her."

Janet studied Rocky, then surprised Ellie by nodding. "Okay. Thanks for your help."

"Hey, you're my boss's friend and my friend's sister-in-law. How could I refuse?"

The connection confused her. "I'm your boss's friend?"

"Sure. Ellie's my new boss. I'm working for her security company."

"I'm not your boss," Ellie began, but Janet spoke right over her.

"Oh! That's what Jack referred to last night. Tell me about this company. I think I missed a lot while I was dead."

"Don't you hate when that happens?" Rocky said. "You fill her in, Ellie. I'll go see if Jack has killed your ex-boyfriend yet."

While she tried to decide if that was a possibility, Janet tugged on her arm, landing them side by side on the couch. "I think you've got a story of your own, Nora. I mean Ellie." She smiled dangerously. "There's more to that name change than you're telling, too."

Ellie wriggled uncomfortably. That name change connected her to two men in the next room in an embarrassing way. Steady, stable ex-boyfriend Richard, the caring, competent lover, and her impulsive, once-in-a-lifetime fling, Jack, whose breathtaking sexual skill left mere competence in the dust. "It's nothing, really," she protested.

"I'll ask Jack. He seems willing to talk about you."

Ellie groaned. "Okay, but you can't tell Richard anything. I met Jack when I was breaking into his mother's house, so he kind of blackmailed me into posing as his fiancée."

"My God, what were you thinking? Is he forcing you to be part of this mess with Banner?"

"No, no. No one's forcing anyone. I thought I could get some incriminating information from Banner's files. Stupid, I know. I'm exactly as impulsive and reckless as Richard said. But then Jack became a way for me to be in that house and really search, and he knew Banner was into something illegal, too, so he wanted to help me. And . . ." She faltered at the next part. "He's pretty handsome, and he has this way of looking at me like I'm a piece of chocolate cream pie and he hasn't eaten in a week, and . . . I slept with him," she finished helplessly.

"Ahh."

"Three times."

"Ahh!" Janet grinned. "That good, eh?"

Ellie took a deep breath and sighed, "Oh my God, Janet."

Janet was laughing now. "Really? Good for you! I

obviously met the wrong brother." She looked at Ellie shrewdly. "And he's the one who calls you Ellie, and when he says it, it sounds pretty good, right?"

"It's more than the name. It's the way I act and the way I feel when I'm with Jack, compared to how I felt with Richard. I don't want to go back to being boring old Nora, the kind of girl who would marry Richard and live comfortably ever after. I want to be exciting and reckless sometimes, and feel as alive as I do when I'm Ellie."

"And marry Jack?"

She flushed. "No! I'm not in love with Jack, and he's not in love with me. We're just a good, temporary fit. Emphasis on *temporary.*"

"So where does the part about being Rocky's boss come in?"

"Oh. Jack invented this career for me as the owner of a security company, and Banner either knew it was a bluff or thought he'd make me look bad, so he asked me to review the Westfield security system. Jack got Rocky to help because he's the only one who knows what he's doing. So I gave the company a name and we did the job, but now this Mrs. Hampshire, a friend of Elizabeth's, wants us to do her house tomorrow, so we have to carry on the illusion of having a business. See?" She pulled a small white rectangle from her pocket. "Jack's daughter made up this card for us. I meant to show it to Rocky."

Janet examined the card and raised her eyebrows. "Nice. So why don't you want to keep going with this company?"

"Obviously, because I have to go back to Petoskey as soon as we catch Banner."

"Why?"

Ellie stopped with her mouth open. Why *did* she have to go back? She didn't have a job to return to, and she certainly didn't want to go back to Richard. She could stay here and maybe for once in her life have a job that she didn't suck at.

And Jack was here.

"I have to go," she repeated firmly. Jack would be raising Libby and dating Christina or some other properly connected bedwarmer, and she didn't want to be around for that. When it's over, it's over, and the mature woman knows how to leave without regret and get on with her life.

"Rocky can have the business. He's the one with the expertise, anyway. He doesn't need me." She didn't want to talk about it anymore. "What will you do?"

Janet shrugged. "I'll probably have to get myself bureaucratically un-dead, which could take a while. I suppose I could keep my position at Aims, but I'm not sure I'll want to stay there, either. It wasn't a good time."

They were pondering their unknown futures when Richard asked to borrow Ellie's Toyota. "All our stuff is at a motel," he grumbled. "If we're going to stay here, I'll have to go get it, and your friends think we have to keep Janet's car hidden in the garage."

She nearly asked why he wanted to stay at Jack's when he could go back to Petoskey, then decided she didn't want to deal with the answer. He was staying because of her. He hoped her leaving had been another of her impetuous reactions in response to the shock of Janet's death.

He didn't get it. She should tell him it was over, that he didn't stand a chance in hell of getting her back.

She'd never been in love with him, and if she'd known that really good sex was supposed to fuse her brain cells and melt her body to blissful mush, she would have been gone even sooner. Telling him would be harsh, but mercifully quick. Only a coward would let him hang around until he figured it out for himself.

She opted for cowardly and handed over the keys. "Be careful, the brakes are touchy."

"I remember. Did you think I'd forget the time at the beach when you nearly put me through the windshield?"

She couldn't help laughing at the memory, and naturally Jack had to walk in at that moment, while her hand holding the keys reached up to meet Richard's and her face tilted happily up at his. From Jack's expression, Richard should have combusted and burned to a lump of charcoal on the spot.

Damn. Not that she cared if Jack was irritated with her, since that happened on a daily basis. But they didn't need any more tension crackling between those two men.

She deliberately turned away from them and in her best perky-blond voice said, "Go on, Janet. You were telling me about that dress you wore. Did the embroidery cover the whole bodice, or just the neckline? I think those little beaded flowers are so precious."

Playing with Colombian criminals hadn't dulled Janet's feminine sensibilities. She smiled brightly. "Oh, you'd absolutely love it! It has a very daring décolletage, and the embroidery follows the neckline. This woman does the most exquisite work with tiny pearls and silk embroidery, and she tailors the bustline to fit each individual customer, so the effect . . ."

Two doors closed at once as Richard left through the front and Jack and Rocky escaped out the sliding patio door to the backyard.

Ellie grinned. "Nice working with you again, Jan. I think you really got them with the way you rolled your eyes when you said *exquisite.*"

"Nope, Jack was already on his way out when you said *precious* and did that breathless little sigh."

They giggled and hugged, and for the first time Ellie felt she had her old friend back instead of some undercover Colombian narcotics operative. They spent an hour talking about every irrelevant, silly thing they hadn't had a chance to say for the past two months, and Janet looked as relaxed and happy as she had before Banner screwed up her life.

When Jack and Rocky finally returned, Janet grew thoughtful. "How has Elizabeth handled all this?" she asked, looking from Ellie to Jack.

Jack shrugged. "I wasn't around when you supposedly died. Your picture is still on the dresser in her bedroom. I saw it, but I didn't know who it was until last night when I saw you."

"Is it?" Janet asked wistfully. "I wish I could tell her I'm all right, but she may not be glad to see me when I have to implicate her son in murder and drug dealing. This is going to be so hard for her."

Ellie was surprised at the depth of feeling she sensed for the woman who had given Ellie such a chilly reception. Jack didn't seem concerned.

"She'll handle it," he told her. "She accepted my guilt easily enough when I was convicted of vehicular manslaughter. She's tough as nails."

"Not as tough as she wants you to think," Janet

said. "She sets a difficult standard for everyone, including herself, and sometimes it hurts her to live up to it. I always thought she seemed sad about something she wouldn't mention. It must have been you."

Jack made a noncommittal sound and shifted uncomfortably. He'd been at odds with his mother for so long, he probably never thought of her as sensitive.

Ellie's mind wandered to a more immediate problem. Richard would return soon, and she'd like to avoid another glaring confrontation.

"I probably should get back soon," she told Jack, who was going to have to drive her since Richard had her car.

He nodded, then turned to Rocky. "You don't have to stay. Nothing will happen before tomorrow, and Richard will be here with Janet."

Rocky waved them off. "No problem. I keep a change of clothes in my car in case of, uh, emergencies." Ellie took that to mean in case of overnight opportunities with a girlfriend, and from Janet's smirk, so did she. "Hey, if I run out of clothes, I'll borrow some of yours. I'll just call my sister and ask her to feed my cat."

"You have a cat?" Janet looked as interested as if he'd pulled a kitten out of his pocket.

Great, they could talk about cats and swap harrowing escape stories. Ellie reminded Rocky of their appointment tomorrow with Mrs. Hampshire, then practically pulled Jack out to the Jeep, in a hurry to leave before Richard got back.

There was no pressing reason to return to the Westfield mansion, but she needed to get Jack alone. His research on Colombian Chemicals had nudged her memory, and that piece of the puzzle was starting to fit with some other pieces. Since finding Janet, they had been distracted from the information they'd found in Banner's files. Ellie had a feeling that they were both parts of the same puzzle, and what they were ignoring about Banner was just as important as what they were pursuing.

She waited only until Jack backed out of the driveway.

"We need to talk about the information in the 'Bad' file."

He frowned. "The accident? Why? It can't be as important as drug dealing, no matter who Banner paid to do what."

"I think it is. It might even be more important. It's just a hunch, but with Banner behind it, I think my suspicions are justified."

He drove without looking at her and without a change in his implacable expression. "No. I don't want to discuss it, Ellie. I'm going to spend the rest of my life trying to forget it, and I don't need to rehash the details one more time. It won't change the outcome."

"Maybe it can."

He scowled. "Joe Benton is dead. Nothing can change that."

"I know we can't change the fact that a man is dead. But I don't believe you killed him."

"Don't be ridiculous. I hit him, there's no question about it. Just drop it."

She shook her head. Her voice echoed the urgency she felt to make him understand. "Don't you get it? This all hinges on your accident. You told me yourself that Banner got the South American division because you went to jail. If you hadn't, he couldn't have arranged the drug smuggling and his big bonuses. He needed you out of the way and, wow, what a coincidence, you accidentally killed someone and got sent to jail. You don't find anything suspicious there?"

Jack ground his jaws together, as if fiercely resisting his thoughts. She knew the idea that his half brother could be responsible for his two years in jail was difficult to believe. "How?" he finally asked, anger in his voice. "I hit Joe Benton with the car. I didn't imagine it, and Banner couldn't have made me do it."

"You remember it clearly?"

"Yes, damn it, too clearly. I can replay it in my head in slow motion. I wish I couldn't."

"That's pretty good for someone who was too drunk to drive."

He gave her a hard look. "It doesn't take much to impair your reactions."

She recalled her conversation with Pam, the bartender at the club, who'd known the truth all along, even if her reasoning was wrong. "And you'd had that much?"

He hesitated. "That's what the police report said."

"The report written up by the cop named Messner, who was possibly paid ten thousand dollars by Banner, if we believe the file?"

He took a long look at her this time, and she was thankful they were on a quiet side street where there was no traffic and no parked cars to hit, because he was no longer paying attention to his driving. The Jeep slowed to a crawl as he studied her face. "You think those amounts are money Banner paid to bribe public officials to convict an innocent man? Assuming there's some incredible way I could be innocent, do you know what a serious crime you're talking about?"

"Gee, you don't think he's capable of it? A guy who launders drug money, takes payoffs, and arranged to have his wife murdered? Maybe I'm way off base here, but I'd say serious crimes are Banner's specialty."

They had rolled to a stop in the middle of the street.

"You want me to believe I spent two years in jail for nothing?" He shook his head. "No, it's not possible."

She hit her palm against the dashboard in irritation. "Damn it, Jack, quit being so stubborn and just trust me for once, would you?"

"Ah, there's that word again, *trust.*" The strain left his face and was replaced with a tiny lift at the corner of his mouth. "That seems to be our cornerstone. Trust you to prove my innocence and save my reputation?"

"Why not?"

She waited for him to say, *Because I've only known you a week and you couldn't possibly understand everything that happened two years ago.* He didn't. He studied her for several seconds and seemed oblivious to the silver BMW convertible that shot around them with a squeal of tires and a raised finger. He finally mumbled, "What the hell," to himself, then said aloud, "Okay, Ellie, my future with Libby is in your hands, so you might as well have my past, too." He downshifted and started forward again. "But you're going to wait until we get to my mother's so I don't cause another accident."

When they pulled onto the wide curve of the driveway, Jack cast a suspicious look at the house. "Let's stay out here," he said. "I never feel comfortable in that place."

She unfastened her seat belt and turned to face him. "Fine. Tell me about the accident, in detail this time."

He took a deep breath and ran both hands through his hair, then dropped them to his thighs, where he rubbed them slowly toward his knees. He looked like a diver about to plunge off a high cliff, nervously readying himself for the fall, and she felt a pang of guilt for making him relive the scene.

He drew a deep breath and stepped over the edge.

"I was at the club, and my stepfather, Leonard, asked me to run home and pick up my mother. He'd been drinking steadily and said he shouldn't drive. He was probably right. I'd only had two drinks, and the last one was a half hour before. I couldn't feel any effect from it."

"Did he know you'd had a couple drinks?"

"Yeah. He probably figured I was sober enough. Anyway, I left him at the bar. I may have been a bit distracted when I started out, because I was thinking that my mother was going to hate riding in the Maserati."

"Why didn't you ask to take Leonard's car?"

"I did, actually, but he didn't want me to drive it. Are you going to keep interrupting me?"

"Maybe." She leaned closer, holding his attention. "You didn't mention Leonard's car. Don't leave these details out. Why didn't he want you to take it?"

Jack rubbed his forehead and frowned in irritation. "I don't remember. It was new, and I think he said something about not wanting me speeding in it. He said Mother was always complaining about something, and she could ride in the Maserati for the ten fucking minutes it would take to get to the club. His words. He was in that half-drunk state where the slightest thing sets off an argument, and it wasn't worth it. I took my car."

She nodded for him to go on.

"About a half mile from the club there's a tight curve, and just around the bend I recognized Joe Benton's Mercedes. I came on it so quickly I didn't have time for a long look, but I saw that the trunk was open and the rear driver's side was jacked up, so obviously he was changing a flat."

"Did you see Joe?"

"Not right away. I was concentrating on not hitting the car because it wasn't all the way off the road. Then just as I was going past, the driver's door opened and Joe leaned out." Jack squeezed his eyes shut briefly and recited in a dull voice what he was seeing in his mind. "I tried to swerve, but I caught the open door. There was a loud crash as it ripped off and slammed against the front of the car. I pulled over and ran back to Joe. He was lying on the cement just outside the car." Jack's hands gripped the steering wheel in front of him and she saw his knuckles turn white. "One foot was still inside the car. I remember that clearly because it looked so ridiculous. His eyes were closed and when I put my hand under his head it was sticky with blood. He wasn't breathing, and I panicked. I started mouth-to-mouth, then I heard another car come up, and Banner and his father ran toward me."

"His father? Your stepfather, Leonard, the one who told you to get your mother? How did he get there?"

"I didn't know at first. Later Banner told me he'd decided to take his dad home because he'd had too much to drink. I hadn't even known Banner was at the club. He called nine-one-one, and Leonard pushed me aside and checked Joe's breathing, then started slapping his face. I think he was more panicked than I was. He was yelling Joe's name, and I was trying to get him to stop slapping him in case there were neck injuries." He grimaced. "It didn't matter. Joe was probably already dead."

"When did the police get there?"

"Soon, before the ambulance. It was that cop, Messner. He'd actually been at the club on another call, so he was nearby. Then the ambulance came, and then Messner was asking me to take a sobriety test, which I did, because I was sure I'd pass. I didn't." He looked at her, his jaw set grimly. "Do you want the details of the booking, too?"

"No." What she wanted was to take the look of pain off his face.

"So what is it about the accident that makes me innocent? Because I still don't see it."

She shook her head in frustration. "I'm not sure. You have to help me figure it out."

"Look, your faith in me is very touching, but coincidences happen. Just because Banner took advantage of the situation doesn't mean he caused it."

"No, no, no. Banner appears all over this story, and that's too much of a coincidence. He just happens to be at the club, happens to decide to drive his father home, happens to come along right after you hit Joe Benton, and later he happens to get promoted into your former position in the company. It's just like when Janet supposedly died—he was with her when she was kidnapped, he got her life insurance money and her father's airline, but he's not responsible. Bullshit. We know he arranged to have Janet killed, and I know he somehow arranged to have you sent to jail."

That shut him up, and he thought it over. "Okay, let's look at it another way. If he paid those people bribes, what was Messner paid to do?" Before she could respond, he answered it himself. "To fake my Breathalyzer results. That's his only function in this scenario. Let's assume he did that, and I wasn't driving drunk. What difference does it make if I was drunk or sober? Joe is dead either way."

She chewed her lip and thought about it. Drunk or sober, the whole idea of a setup only worked if Banner could ensure that Jack killed Joe. How did you arrange for someone to die in an auto accident? You couldn't. Even if they could be sure Jack would hit him, they couldn't be sure he'd die. The only way to ensure Jack could get blamed for his death was—

"Joe was already dead."

She said it tentatively, then looked at him and repeated it. "He had to already be dead. That's the only way to ensure you'd be blamed for his death."

"That's crazy. I saw him open the door and get out—"

She held her hand up in front of him. "No, wait, that's not what you said. You said the door opened and he leaned out. Think about it. He didn't step out, he leaned. Why? And what was he doing inside the car if he was changing a flat?"

Jack frowned. "There's any number of reasons he'd be in the car. Maybe he wanted a rag to wipe his hands. Maybe he gave up and decided to call the auto club."

"Well, what about the way he leaned out?"

He thought. "I don't know. It *was* odd, now that you mention it. It was more like he was looking for something that fell on the ground than intending to stand up."

Ellie pictured it and grew more excited. "What if someone were inside the car and pushed him out? If he was already dead, he'd slump over just like you described, right?"

"Right," he agreed cautiously. "It would have to be timed perfectly, but it could work. What about the person in the car with him? No one else was there."

"Forget that for now." She waved her hand dismissively. "Let's be brutally honest here. What would happen if Joe were alive and starting to get out of the car? I mean physically, what would the injuries be?"

Jack grimaced distastefully but told her, "It wouldn't be pretty. The back of his head would be smashed by my car. I told you there was blood under his head."

"What else? Come on, think. Does he just get conked on the back of the head?"

"No," he replied, angry at having to describe it. "His face would be driven against the door and smashed into it. His nose . . ." He paused, then continued more slowly. "His nose would be broken, facial bones would be crushed . . . Joe's face wasn't injured. I did mouth-to-mouth on him, and there wasn't a drop of blood on his face." He looked at her intently as he thought it through. "He never got pushed into the door. He had to have slumped over so abruptly that the car missed him and just took the door off. Not like he was getting out of the car, more like falling out."

"Like a dead body falling out," she said, meeting

his eyes just as intently. "It wasn't timed that well after all. The body fell over in time for you to see it, but it couldn't hold itself steady like a living person, it just kept falling, and then your car clipped the door and took it off, missing the body."

He stared at her for several seconds. "You're right. The body would have been battered if I'd hit him with the car. Why didn't I think of that before?"

"Because Banner and his father were there immediately, panicking and yelling that you just killed a man."

He nodded slowly. "That means someone had to push him out of the car. I didn't see anyone else there."

"Yes, you did." Pieces were falling into place now. "You said a car pulled up while you were bent over Joe. You didn't look up because you were giving him mouth-to-mouth. When you did look, you saw two people, Banner and Leonard Westfield. Only one of them had to have driven the car."

"Jesus. I assumed they came together." He was breathing faster as the plot became clear. "Only one of them drove up in the car. It was my stepfather's car, and he's the one who was at the club, so it had to be him. That means Banner . . ."

He looked past her to the house where Banner lived with their mother and swore again. "Christ, he pushed Joe out of the car. He pushed a dead body out of the car." His eyes went back to hers, and his voice dropped. "They must have killed him. That's how he got the wound on the back of his head. Leonard and Banner killed the president of Westfield-Benton, then set me up to take the fall for it."

She sat motionless in the Jeep, frozen in shock. Even though she'd expected to find Banner's machinations behind Jack's accident, this had an even stronger scent of evil. She knew what he must be feeling. His own family had plotted an overthrow within the company, murdered a man, and framed him for it, getting them both out of the way. Two birds with one stone. Two vacancies in the company's management, and no one to stop them from further predations. Unless Joe's son Allen could be a threat to them.

"What about Allen Benton? Didn't you say he moved into his father's position as president? Is he involved, too?"

Jack shook his head. "Allen is a figurehead. A nice guy, but not the businessman his father was. Leonard controlled him as CEO, and I'm sure Banner does as well. He's an asset because everyone likes him, and they know Banner is a son of a bitch. They'd much rather deal with Allen. I'm sure they wanted him right where he is. But Joe had to go. Joe never would have supported the purchase of Aims, and he would have been suspicious of the excessive profits, just as I was." Jack sat back and leaned his head against the back of the seat. "My God, Ellie, you were right." He looked back at the house. "And I have a daughter living there with that goddamned son of a bitch. Christ, and I've been letting you stay there, too. I have to get both of you out."

"No, wait." She put a hand on his forearm. "That would look suspicious. If Banner doesn't think we're a threat, he won't bother us. And as you keep saying, your mother is there. I can't believe she knows anything about this."

He thought, then grudgingly said, "No, neither can I."

He didn't look relieved. His hands clenched, stretched, then clenched again, as if he were looking for something to grip. Banner's neck, probably. He finally threw his door open as if it were an escape hatch.

"Come on, let's walk around. I need to move."

She followed him across freshly cut grass, the green clippings clinging to her sandals. They wandered through the large plantings and trees of the east lawn, then walked the mulched path around the koi pond and waterfall. If anyone saw them, it would look like a companionable stroll, but Ellie could see the drawn brows and stress lines around his eyes as Jack brooded, probably planning different ways of getting her and Libby out of the house.

Ellie was thinking, too, going over the details of Jack's story again. Everything made sense now. When Jack stopped by the little tumble of water that fed the pond, she spoke aloud and pulled him out of his reverie.

"You said the blood was sticky on the back of his head. Fresh blood isn't sticky."

He looked at her blankly, then nodded as he understood. Joe had been dead long enough for blood to begin to congeal.

"And I don't believe Messner just happened to be open to bribery," she continued. "I think they found a cop who'd take a bribe, then arranged for him to be there. Whatever brought him out there was just a ruse to have him in the area." She kicked a tiny wood chip into the water and watched the fish swarm around it.

"And Joe's flat tire—I'll bet that was arranged, too. In fact, I'll bet Banner was in the car and killed Joe just before setting up the scene for your appearance."

"Shit." He looked at her. "I sure could have used you two years ago when I was convicted and sent to jail. My lawyer didn't figure out any of this. But we know why, don't we?" he said wryly. "He was on Banner's list, too. He probably wouldn't have agreed to cover up evidence, so my guess is they paid him to close the case quickly without asking questions. Make it easier on poor Jack."

"Lundberg," she said, recalling the lawyer's name. "And what about Tull, the coroner?"

"He was bribed to fudge the cause of death. I imagine any competent coroner would know the injuries didn't match with the police report. Hell, you figured that out."

He turned away, skirting the mounded rocks of the waterfall while theorizing about Tull's part in the conspiracy, and Ellie followed. He was on a roll, absorbed in his line of detection.

"He must have wondered why they didn't want him to look too closely at the cause of death. I wonder if Banner and Leonard made up some lie about me being the one who murdered Joe, then tried to make it look like an accident. Doesn't matter. He took a bribe, and so did Messner. And I'm the one who paid for it. I swear I'll find some way to expose what they did, even if I have to personally beat it out of him." Jack stopped and took an abrupt step back into the foliage. "Shit. What the hell is he doing here?"

Ellie bumped into his back, then stepped around him to look through the thin screen of lilac leaves.

The fence of hedges, brick walls, and wrought iron that surrounded the pool lay ahead of them. Through the wrought-iron section in front of them, she saw Elizabeth and Ben Thatcher at a poolside table, sipping drinks and talking quietly. As they watched, Ben briefly covered Elizabeth's hand with his own, and Elizabeth smiled at whatever he said. Beside her, Ellie saw Jack stiffen like a guard dog spotting an intruder.

Ellie smiled. "I think it's obvious what he's doing here, and quit being such an old fuddy-duddy."

"Shouldn't he be at work? He's a public servant, wasting the taxpayers' money while he's sniffing around after vulnerable, rich widows."

"Wow, and I thought your mother was cynical about me."

He gave her a critical glance, then narrowed his eyes at the couple by the pool. "I take it you don't think there's any reason for concern."

"No, I don't. Your mother is not vulnerable, she's sharp, and savvy, and entitled to a sex life." She saw his jaw clench when she said *sex*, and wished she'd left that word out. She tried to soften it a bit. "Don't you think she misses the romance now that your stepfather is gone?"

Jack gave her a pitying look. "Obviously you have no grasp of the Westfield marriage. Picture Banner older, smarter, and more coldly calculating, and you've got Leonard. If their marriage was ever romantic, it ended before my memory of it. It was a business partnership, with Leonard providing the money and prestige and my mother providing more of the same, plus the heir."

Ellie looked at the two relaxed people by the pool,

comfortable in each other's company. "How sad for her."

"Don't be naive. She must have wanted it that way."

"Of course she didn't want it that way." God, this family could be dense about relationships. "Yes, she sacrificed her happiness for her children's social fortunes, but I'm sure she would have preferred a loving husband and a normal, happy family. Who wouldn't?"

"I don't expect you to understand, coming from your perfect little family, with your perfectly normal, law-abiding boyfriend, but in my experience families are destructive, and love is a front for personal ambition."

It was a purely Westfield sentiment. It was also the basic dichotomy of Jack Payton. She didn't understand how a man could make love so passionately yet understand nothing about being in love.

He glanced briefly at Ben Thatcher and his mother, then looked away. "I have more important concerns right now than who my mother is sleeping with."

At least he recognized that. "Yes, you want to beat the crap out of Dr. Tull and Officer Messner."

"Damn right I do," he said with renewed anger. "You think yanking me out of my life and putting me in jail for two years, not to mention making me think I was responsible for killing a man, isn't enough to justify breaking a few bones and pounding their faces to a pulp?"

"Go ahead, they deserve it. But what do you get out of it?"

"I get to feel a whole lot better about being set up."

"And then you get to go back to jail for violating parole and committing assault." She met his glare stubbornly with one of her own. "Use your head, Jack. You have to go after them with facts, or at least with a convincing bluff, and get them to confess their involvement in the plot. That's the only way to make them pay."

He looked angry. "And how do I do that? All we have are theories based on a stolen computer file. No one would believe me. I'd rather beat them senseless and damn the consequences."

She was about to argue that their theories weren't exactly groundless when Elizabeth's voice called out, "Jack? Eleanor?"

Through the screening leaves, Ellie could see her standing beside the pool, shading her eyes and peering at the lilac bushes.

"Damn it," Jack muttered beside her as they stepped out. "I don't feel like being sociable to that man right now." His arm went around her waist, holding her close, as he waved back.

Apparently now that someone was watching, they were going to play lovey-dovey again. Ever since Richard had shown up, Jack had been grumpy and distant with her. She sighed wearily, snuggled close to play her part, and smiled at Ben and Elizabeth.

They began strolling slowly toward the pool. "Let's make this quick," Jack said, his voice low. "I need to take some time to find the best way to confront Tull and Messner without getting caught."

"Uh-huh," she responded absently. It had suddenly occurred to her that Jack didn't have to risk his freedom to get back at the men who'd helped conspire against him. "Too bad you don't have some authority to use against them. You know, something more worrisome than being confronted by a Westfield-Benton accountant."

Jack growled, "A pretty goddamned mad accountant, with a huge grudge to settle."

"Still, it would be nice to leave them with more than a broken nose. Perhaps if you could make them worry about the legal consequences of what they did . . ."

"Ellie, I'm not putting them under citizen's arrest, I'm beating the shit out of them."

"Don't you think you could accomplish more if you had a little help?"

He gave her a warning look. "You're not coming along!"

"Not me, silly."

"If you expect me to include that whiny, incompetent boyfriend of yours, you can—"

"He's not my boyfriend, damn it! And I'm not talking about Richard. I meant someone with enough influence to be threatening. Like a cop," she added, giving him a heavy-handed clue.

"Who . . . ?" He broke off and looked at her suspiciously.

Attaboy, she thought as his brows drew together.

"Hold on. Thatcher? Hell no, no way." She was unmoved, and it seemed to bug him. "Why in the hell would I want to involve the police chief in assault and battery, especially when he's never been friendly to me before?"

"You don't have to commit assault. Or you could pulverize them later if you still need a little primitive gratification."

He spoke between gritted teeth, purposely turning away from the pool, where Ben and Elizabeth were watching their stalled progress curiously. "Ellie, Ben Thatcher has been a pain in my neck ever since I can remember. I couldn't jaywalk in this town without it getting back to my mother, and the few times he didn't tell her what I'd done, he took it upon himself to throw me up against a wall and threaten a little police brutality."

"See? He'd be perfect for the job."

"No, he wouldn't. I'm not making this clear—he hates me. He always has, and I can't say I've given him any reason not to. We aren't exactly friends, and he wouldn't help me threaten a cop and a county coroner, even if he were. He believes I was guilty."

His resistance was starting to irritate her. "Of course he does, you idiot—even you did. You have to tell him what we figured out, how you were set up."

"Oh yeah, he'll believe that."

"Yes, if he's as smart as he seems, he will. I think he is."

Jack gave her an exasperated look. "What in the hell makes women like that man? You hardly know him, and you assume he'll go against years of history and take my side."

"Your mother trusts him, and she knows him better than anyone."

He clenched his jaw and made sure his back was to the couple across the pool. "It seems she's not exactly impartial," he said, spitting out each word with distaste.

She got close to his face and hoped it looked like an intimate moment from a distance. "Damn it, Jack, you have a close connection to the best person to help you put pressure on Tull and Messner. Use it. Just tell him what we know and see what he says. What have you got to lose?"

"Everything, when I lay out my motive ahead of time and he gets to arrest me for assault."

She peeked around his bulk and smiled cheerfully at the puzzled expressions from Ben and Elizabeth. "Do it," she growled at him, still smiling. "Take a chance on someone else for once."

He shook his head. "You're really big on this issue of trusting other people, aren't you?"

"It works for me."

"It hasn't worked well for me."

"Really? You trusted me. How's that working for you?"

They both knew the answer. No matter how big a pain she'd been, trusting her had worked. He'd found the illegal source of Banner's excess money, and he'd made huge progress in his relationship with Libby.

He shook his head. "Why do I have the feeling I'm going to regret this?" he muttered.

Chapter Thirteen

It wasn't until they were inside the fence that Jack saw Libby lying on a chaise lounge, flipping through a magazine. Her dark hair was still damp from swimming, which explained why Thatcher and his mother were sitting by the pool. They'd been watching her. He felt the usual mix of jealousy and irritation that everyone else seemed to play a larger part in his daughter's life than he did.

When her eyes met his, Jack smiled. "Hey, Libby."

She smiled back briefly, said, "Hey, Jack," and returned to skimming her magazine. No hostility, no exaggerated indifference. He considered it a small victory.

"You're home early, Jack," Elizabeth said as they joined her, and he remembered he was supposed to be at work.

"I had some personal business to take care of."

Thatcher stood to greet Ellie and turned a polite smile on Jack. "It's nice to see you two. Please join us."

Jack felt a familiar, prickly irritation that Ben Thatcher could invite him to sit with his own mother, a reminder that Thatcher was more welcome at this house than he was. He repressed the feeling, telling himself that it wasn't Thatcher's fault he had ended up in jail.

It wasn't his own fault, either. He took a deep breath and tried Ellie's approach.

"Actually, I need to speak with you about something," he told the police chief. Noting his mother's curious look, he added, "In private."

Thatcher's expression changed immediately, a cool hostility covering the former pleasantness. Jack saw his mistake. Thatcher expected a confrontation about his early-morning departure from the house. An accusation wouldn't even be necessary. The cold eyes already said, *Yes, I'm sleeping with your mother, and it's none of your business.*

Jack shook his head slightly and watched Thatcher's expression cautiously relax. "It's about a police matter," he said. He didn't want the man siding against him before he even broached the idea of a conspiracy and a setup.

Jack led the way outside the gate where they could be seen but not overheard.

Ben waited silently while Jack searched for a way to begin. Ellie had made it sound so easy: Tell Thatcher he'd been framed and get him to help convince Tull and Messner to talk. He'd forgotten it had been a simple matter for the two of them to accept Banner's guilt as a murderer when they already knew he was an accomplice in Janet's attempted murder. But no one besides Ellie had even suspected Banner of conspiracy in Janet's supposed death. Thatcher probably saw Banner as Elizabeth's good son, the one who did everything right and never embarrassed his family with a wild lifestyle and a jail sentence.

Jack ran a hand through his hair, unsure how to make his story believable. Ben watched patiently, waiting for him to say something.

"Look, I know we aren't friends and you never liked me much," he began.

"I'm sorry you feel that way."

He paused in mid-thought. "What?"

Ben gave him a hard look. "I like you, Jack, I just never cared for some of your stupid pranks. Your sorry-ass excuse of a stepfather didn't provide much guidance when you were growing up, so I came down pretty hard on you to make up for it. I guess I can see how you'd misinterpret that. It wasn't personal."

Jack studied Thatcher's bland expression and recalled all the lectures on speeding, teenage parties, and irresponsible sex, and thought they seemed pretty personal. Not that he didn't deserve them. It was true that Leonard Westfield hadn't helped, buying him a new Corvette for his sixteenth birthday and, when his mother wasn't looking, handing him a box of condoms. Definitely not responsible parenting, although at the time Jack had thought it eminently progressive.

He wasn't buying the impersonal part. "It seemed personal when you slammed me up against the wall at the police station after I'd been arrested for drunk driving and manslaughter, and called me every name in the book."

Ben's lips pressed together sternly at the memory. "Yeah, I guess that time it was. I never thought you'd go that far, and I knew what it was going to do to your mother."

If Thatcher had expected Jack's mother to be heart-broken, then the police chief knew a different Elizabeth Payton Westfield than he did. He was beginning to think that was entirely possible.

Jack grabbed at the positive part of Ben's comment. "I'm glad you find drunk driving and manslaughter out of character for me, because it might help you believe what I have to say. Ellie and I have been doing some digging, and we think it's possible that I was framed for Joe's death. That he was murdered, and I was set up to take the fall."

That got his attention. Ben went instantly into cop mode. "What sort of digging did you do, and how could you have been framed?"

"Do you know the cop named Messner who arrested me at the scene?"

Ben nodded. "I remember him. I spoke to him afterward, questioned him at length about who saw you leave the club, what condition you were in, and how fast you were going. I even measured the skid marks on the pavement myself to check his notes. He was a young kid, kind of nervous, but his facts checked out."

Jack was impressed—he hadn't known Thatcher had looked into the investigation at all. But he wouldn't have been able to double-check the fact that mattered. "We think he was bribed to alter the Breathalyzer results, because I wasn't drunk."

"Bribed?" Ben's eyes narrowed to mean slits. "You have proof of that?"

That was the weak part of their theory. "Not

exactly. But you could check it out. He would have made a large bank deposit shortly afterward for ten thousand two hundred and thirty dollars. I'm not sure why it's such an odd amount."

"I am. If it's true, the amount makes it easier to explain. He'd say he sold a car, a boat, a coin collection—something like that. Bribery's a serious charge, Jack, and you better be sure before you go throwing accusations around. Who would bribe him?"

"Um, let's get back to that later." Ben frowned, but Jack rushed on. "There's also the probability that the coroner, a Dr. Tull, was bribed. He could explain the skull fracture as the cause of death, but he'd have to ignore the fact that there were no other injuries consistent with that type of accident. No broken bones, no internal bleeding, no facial lacerations."

"Is that true?"

"I don't remember any lacerations, and I saw his face. You'd have to check with the funeral home about the rest. Maybe they keep records on that sort of stuff."

"I know Tull. Arrogant bastard, but smart. You claim he was bribed, too?"

Jack nodded. "Twenty-seven thousand-something."

Ben looked dangerously angry. "Who bribed them?"

Jack hesitated for a few seconds, trying to get past his amazement that Thatcher was accepting his innocence so quickly. "The person who really killed Joe Benton and had a good motive to want him dead."

"Goddamn it, Jack, who?"

"Banner, with help from his father."

Jack watched him absorb the information, trying

to gauge his reaction. Ben didn't so much as lift an eyebrow in surprise, just stared back at Jack while he let the idea settle in. Maybe cops got used to hearing about incredible crimes committed by people they knew. Or maybe he had no more love for Banner and Leonard Westfield than Jack did.

"What's your proof?" he finally asked.

"It's circumstantial," he admitted. "We pulled the names and numbers off a file in Banner's computer."

"Names and numbers, that's it?"

"The file is called 'Bad.' That was—"

"I know, it was the vanity plate on that fuckin' insane Maserati of yours. That's not proof. That's not even circumstantial evidence. That's conjecture. What do you expect me to do?"

"You could put a little official pressure on Messner and Tull. That might scare them more than me beating the crap out of them. Either way, I want them to talk, and I want Banner to pay for this."

Ben crossed his arms and leaned a shoulder against the iron gate. He was quiet for several seconds while he digested the information. "That's a pretty good story, Jack. You're telling me four people covered up a murder and conspired against you, but you have no real evidence of it."

"Five, actually. My lawyer was paid off, too, but he probably didn't know it involved murder."

He raised an eyebrow. "That's a big conspiracy."

He didn't care for the implication. "I'm not just trying to shift the blame for Joe's death."

"That's how it sounds."

Jack's brows pulled together and he stepped closer aggressively. "You know damn well I was willing to accept the blame and take the punishment for that accident. I never denied it and I didn't fight it in court."

"True."

"It never occurred to me it could have happened any other way. But now I know why they sent me to jail. And I know why they wanted Joe dead."

"Why?"

Jack laughed once, cynically. "You wouldn't believe it. It sounds even more preposterous than the accident theory. It involves money laundering, drug running, attempted murder, and janitorial products that come packaged with cocaine. Pretty outrageous, except in a couple days things may shake loose and all the rats will come out of hiding. I think I'll save the details until then, when you're more likely to believe me."

Midway through his answer Ben's skeptical look had hardened to one of sharp concentration. His arms dropped now, and his shoulder came off the fence. "Did you say janitorial products and cocaine?"

"I know, it sounds far-fetched. Forget it."

Jack began to turn away, but Ben clutched his upper arm in a firm grip. "Would that be Michigan Janitorial Products?" he asked harshly.

Annoyed, Jack nearly knocked the hand off when the question registered and he gave Ben a hard look. "Yeah. How did you know?"

"I think you'd better tell me how *you* know first."

He looked pointedly at Ben's hand. When it dropped, he said, "I know because it involves Banner and Westfield-Benton. It seems my brother has acquired a large, illegal income. The company's fortunes also affect my mother, if that makes any difference to you."

Ben looked him directly in the eye. "Yes, it does, and we can discuss that later if you want to. Right now I want you to tell me how you know about a joint operation investigating drug trafficking in southeast Michigan, and exactly how it ties in to Westfield-Benton."

A drug-trafficking investigation? If the police were investigating MJP, he and Rocky had to be the luckiest burglars in the world for not getting caught breaking into the main office. Also the stupidest. Briefly, he told Ben about the Aims connection and the alternate-Thursday deliveries, while the police chief listened with increasing concern. At the end, Ben shook his head.

"You and Ellie have no business being mixed up in this."

"Couldn't help it. I have an interest in the company, and Banner's wife is Ellie's best friend."

Ben winced with regret. "I knew Janet. Nice girl."

"Yeah. By the way, she's not dead."

"What?"

"Banner tried to have her killed, and now she's out for revenge. We have her stashed at my house."

Ben stared, then shook his head. "If she's fingering Banner for murder, I want to talk to her."

So they both wanted something. "You plan to help me with Messner and Tull?"

They took each other's measure. They hadn't always seen eye to eye, but Jack had never doubted the other man's integrity. If Ben said he'd help now, he'd keep his word.

Ben finally nodded and held up a warning hand. "I get to talk to Janet first. If I believe her, and I don't know why in the hell I wouldn't after Banner identified her dead body, then I'll help you lean on Messner and Tull."

"I'll take you there now." Now that he had a plan, he didn't want to wait.

"I want to check with some people first. I'll meet you there at five." Ben reached for the latch on the gate, then cocked his head at Jack. "Drugs, money laundering, and murder—you lead an interesting life, boy."

Jack smiled wryly. "No shit."

Ellie sat across the table from Elizabeth and tried to relax. The morning had been more stressful than she realized. Every time Jack brought up Richard, anger crackled between them like static electricity. He was completely unreasonable on the subject, and it gave her a headache. When Mr. Peters brought her an iced tea, she smiled gratefully and held the cold glass against her forehead.

While the men were gone, Libby had decided to join the women on the pretext of getting out of the sun. With the generous slathering of lotion on Libby's body, Ellie doubted she was in danger of burning. Either the girl was desperate for friends or she genuinely liked their company. She chatted happily about the articles in her teen magazine and asked Ellie's opinion on the makeup section.

Ellie was flattered. She was also surprised at how easily she was drawn into Libby's teenage concerns about makeup and boys, clothes and boys, hair and, especially, boys. But if maturity had eluded her, she wasn't alone. When Ben returned, announced he had to leave, and dropped a brief kiss on Elizabeth's cheek,

Ellie was surprised to see a blush creep over the older woman's face. Elizabeth said a flustered good-bye, then glanced hastily around the table as if they might all be staring at the overt display of affection.

If Jack had seen, he ignored it. Libby watched thoughtfully, chin propped on her hand, and smiled broadly at Ben as he walked past and ruffled her hair. That did elicit a cynical look from Jack and a muttered, "Are there any females on the planet who don't respond to that man?"

"None in their right minds," Ellie assured him, and Elizabeth flashed her a surprised smile.

"This is perfect," Libby announced, her mind already on another subject. "I need a guy's opinion for this survey on relationships. You can be the guy, Jack."

He rolled his eyes at Ellie, and she said, "Think you can play the part?"

He told Libby, "Bring it on."

She was paging through the magazine, looking for the article in question. "Don't worry, it's just a few questions. Grandmother answered the girl part for me. Okay, first question: Can a girl ever ask a boy on a date?"

Libby picked up a pencil and looked at Jack expectantly.

He glanced at Ellie and Elizabeth for clues. Elizabeth took a sip of iced tea. Ellie raised an eyebrow and waited for his answer.

Jack shrugged. "Sure, why not?"

Libby filled in a circle. "Do you currently have a girlfriend?"

He appeared to relax, as if reassured by the easy

question. Avoiding the eyes of the girlfriend in question, he said, "Yes."

"If so, how long did you know her before your first kiss?"

Jack paused and shifted in his chair. Ellie knew what he was thinking—he had pulled her into a passionate kiss less than five minutes after finding her in the library, when he hadn't even known her name. He couldn't say that to Libby.

Elizabeth stopped stirring her drink and looked at him with mild interest. "Well, Jack?"

"Um . . ." He looked at Ellie helplessly. "I don't remember."

"Gee, thanks." What a coward. She answered smoothly, "I think it was two days after we met, on our first date."

Libby made another mark on the page while Ellie gave Jack a disapproving look. Across the table, Elizabeth watched them with interest.

"One more question," Libby said. "Is it ever okay to have sex with your boyfriend-slash-girlfriend?"

Ellie darted a surprised look at Libby, whose innocent expression obviously hid a sneaky intelligence.

Jack snapped, "That's not on the survey."

"Yes it is. See?" Libby handed him the magazine, pencil pointing to the page. "Right here, question twenty-five."

Jack read the indicated line and frowned.

Ellie didn't believe for a second that Libby hadn't been hoping for an opportunity to put him on the spot with that one. She couldn't blame Libby for wanting to feel out what sort of man her father was. And a father had to take the difficult questions as well as the easy ones. Ellie nudged his shoulder. "Answer the question, Jack."

He passed the magazine back to his daughter. "The answer is, none of your business, kid."

Elizabeth smiled and looked away.

Libby said, "That answer isn't on the survey."

"Too bad."

"This survey is designed to give me input on the topics most often neglected by parents of teenage girls. I'm almost thirteen, so I'm supposed to know how you feel about premarital sex in order to help me form my own opinions. It's imperative that I have confidence and a positive self-image, you know."

It was a pretty impressive mouthful of psychology to recite without consulting the magazine. Ellie recalled the "average" school grades Libby had received and wondered why she'd been hiding her abilities. Despite her benign expression, the girl was far beyond average.

Jack peered at his daughter, squinting against the sun, then looked at his mother. "I think you can stop sending her to therapy. The kid's mastered the subject."

Libby grinned, apparently content that Jack had not taken the bait. Even more surprising, Elizabeth nodded seriously and said, "You may be right. I'll speak to the social worker about it."

Ellie watched as Jack slowly realized his status had risen. Both his mother and his daughter valued his opinion. He sat back, absorbing this new development, while Ellie tried to hide her smile. She'd promised to look out for Libby's welfare, but the girl was obviously comfortable with Jack and more than capable of looking out for herself. Libby seemed to take the same suspicious approach to families and relationships as her father, but they were definitely forming a bond. Ellie hadn't done much to facilitate it, either. Soon they'd be comfortable enough together that they wouldn't need her around, pretending to be part of the family unit.

She tried to be happy about that, too.

Libby closed her magazine and rose. "I have to call my friend Deanna. She wants to know if I'm going to meet them at the Junkyard Dogs concert. So can I go?"

She was speaking to Jack, not her grandmother.

He looked surprised. "You're okay with me going along?"

Libby shrugged and tried to look unconcerned. "Deanna and Tanya said they want to see what my father is like. So I guess it's okay if you go."

Jack nodded solemnly at being displayed for the approval of twelve-year-old girls. "When is it?"

"A week from Saturday." She licked her lips, then added, "Could we take one of my friends with us?"

"Sure. I didn't know you'd made any friends here. Who is it?"

She averted her eyes and said evasively, "Just some guy I take golf lessons with."

Steven Beyer. Ellie bit her lip to hide her amusement as Jack's eyes narrowed at the same thought.

"Yes, I'd like to meet your friend," he said seriously, and Ellie felt sorry for poor Steven. Jack would probably introduce himself as Libby's convicted-killer father and have the boy so nervous he'd never so much as look at Libby again. She'd have to have a stern talk with Jack before next Saturday.

"If you have your credit card, we can order the tickets online right now," Libby said eagerly.

Jack gave Ellie a helpless smile and stood, saying, "I'll be right back."

Elizabeth and Ellie watched until the two were out of sight. Elizabeth's iced tea glass clinked against the glass tabletop as she set it down and turned toward Ellie. Sharp blue eyes scrutinized her, and Ellie shifted uncomfortably.

"I may have misjudged you, Eleanor."

Ellie looked at the other woman, surprised.

"When I first met you I thought your motives were entirely selfish, but I believe you truly care about my son and my granddaughter."

"Of course I do," she said.

Which didn't eliminate the guilt. She did care about Jack and Libby, but Elizabeth's first impression hadn't been that far off. Ellie's motives *had* been selfish, using Jack to get into the Westfield home to accomplish her own goal. She hadn't cared a thing about Jack or his daughter. Except now that her goal of discovering Banner's secret and avenging Janet was almost complete, she should be ready to get the hell out of their screwed-up family. When had she become so emotionally entangled in their lives?

That answer was obvious—when she slept with Jack. She *knew* she should have kept the relationship professional, *knew* she couldn't play the modern sophisticate, indulging in a wild affair, then breezing out of town with her sexy new underwear and man-killer attitude. Oh no, she had to follow her horny little instincts right into the very emotional quagmire she'd wanted to avoid.

"Your presence has made an enormous difference to Libby."

"I'm glad." She forced a smile. Oh good, more guilt. One more abandonment issue for Libby, coming right up. Better not dismiss that therapist yet. She wished Elizabeth would shut up and stop looking at her so closely. Ellie closed her eyes and pretended to serenely soak up the sun until Jack returned.

She barely listened while Jack and his mother discussed private schools for Libby and who should be invited to some boring upcoming dinner party. She simply watched him. The sensuous curve of his upper lip, the firm chest evident under his shirt, the way he would arch an eyebrow and smile at a comment—all the things she'd noted under other, more intimate circumstances. It might be a long time before she found another man who stirred her sexually the way Jack did, and she was determined to appreciate every inch of him while she could. She stretched her leg so it touched his under the table, and he dropped a hand briefly on her thigh as he talked, sending shivers of awareness all the way up. From the quick twitch in his lip she knew he was conscious of her reaction and knew she had planted a similar thought in his mind. They never had any trouble communicating on a sexual level.

They barely spoke when they left Elizabeth, or during the drive to Jack's house. Their communication was more basic, through looks and unnecessary touches. It would be several hours yet before they had an opportunity to be alone, and Ellie planned to spend the entire time gearing her body language to one simple thought—sex. It would be wonderfully torturous. By the time they got together, desire would be sparking between them and the resulting sexual explosion should be incredibly satisfying. It might actually be memorable enough to last for the years it would probably take to equal the experience with someone else.

Ben Thatcher pulled into Jack's driveway ten minutes behind them. Ellie allowed herself the momentary distraction of enjoying Janet's reunion with Ben, the first person from her former Westfield circle of friends to learn of her erroneous demise.

Ben spent the next hour listening with absorption while Janet recounted her discovery of Banner's activities.

Ellie spent it in heated flirtation, sitting on the arm of a chair next to Jack. The hand she draped behind his shoulders rubbed a slow, light massage along his upper back and played absently with the hair above his collar. When he turned toward Ben, she traced her finger around his ear and saw a muscle shiver beneath the skin.

His eyes remained on Janet, but she had his undivided attention. If he'd moved away the slightest bit, she would have stopped. Instead, he angled closer until his upper arm touched the side of her breast. She made sure to shift position a couple times and let him feel the contour of her breast slide over his arm. Not very subtle, but nicely effective. When she draped her arm across his shoulder, he reached up to idly stroke her hand and fingers. Heat flared low inside her at every touch. He'd definitely received the message. This was going to be good.

By the time Janet finished, Ellie could tell Ben had been thoroughly convinced of Banner's guilt in every area—Janet's attempted murder, Joe Benton's death, and Jack's rigged accident. Grim-faced, he motioned for Jack to follow him to the kitchen.

Ellie watched their discussion, punctuated by nods from Jack and one long gaze in her direction. Finally, Jack motioned for her to join them.

"Ben says Messner is on duty now," he told her, drawing her close. "We're going to go have a little talk with him."

She nodded.

"I'll be back as soon as possible," he said with another long, significant look at her.

"Okay." She met his gaze directly, letting him know through every tingling cell in her body that she wouldn't have cooled off one degree by the time he got back.

He got the message. His eyes flashed darkly and he pulled her into a hard kiss good-bye, which Ben might have interpreted as romantic, but Ellie knew was a promise of pure lust. She smiled wickedly and whispered, "Hurry back."

She almost felt sorry for Officer Messner. That was one lathered-up and impatient accountant he was about to deal with.

Rocky, Janet, and Richard repeatedly invited her to share the pizza they ordered, but it didn't satisfy the sort of appetite she'd worked up, so she nibbled at a bread stick while she waited for Jack to return. Richard gave her a few tight, disapproving looks, as if he knew her plans for the evening.

When she'd been with Jack she'd been taut with anticipation. With him gone, she was restless and distracted. *Antsy*, Janet called her, watching her friend with amusement. It was their private euphemism for *horny*. Ellie gave her a sidelong glance without comment, and Janet laughed, knowing she'd guessed correctly.

Jack returned two hours later, quickly assessed the level of privacy in his own house, and announced, "I have to take Ellie home." They were out the door within a minute, ignoring Richard's glare, Janet's smirk, and Rocky's indifferent wave.

She asked about his talk with Messner, but Jack dismissed her question with an intense look and a brief, "It went fine. I don't want to to talk about it now." Obviously, he had other things on his mind. More important things. As they sped wordlessly to the Westfield house, Ellie's level of anticipation rose with each tense minute that passed. By the time they arrived, she could practically hear the air crackling between them. His hand on her back as he guided her up the front steps seemed to burn a hole right through her shirt. She ached to turn and press other parts of her body against it, parts that were already burning for his touch. Her morals seemed to have taken an alarming shift toward the licentious, and she couldn't have been happier about it.

By unspoken agreement, they headed for her bedroom. They had crossed the gleaming marble entry and started up the long sweep of stairs when the butler stepped silently from the dining room and spotted them.

"Excuse me, Mr. Payton."

One step below her, Jack stopped. "Yes, Mr. Peters?"

"Miss Payton asked to see you if you came to visit. She said it was very important."

Cold water splashed onto Ellie's flames and cooled them to sizzling embers.

Jack asked, "Do you know what it was about?"

"I'm sorry, sir, she didn't say." Seeing Jack's hesitation, he added, "In my experience, most things fall into the urgent category for twelve-year-old girls."

"Yes, they seem to," Jack said. "Thank you, Mr. Peters."

As the butler disappeared around the corner, Ellie felt the heat slowly dissipating from her body.

Jack looked at her. "It's probably not important."

She shook her head. There was no way she would come between Libby and Jack. "If your daughter wants to see you, that's important." She smiled regretfully. "Go on. You know where to find me."

He took one step up, caught her hand, and squeezed. "I'll hurry." His intense gaze held hers long enough to make sure she knew he was fully aware of what she wanted, and that he was more than prepared to oblige her. Then, for emphasis, he slipped his arm around her and kissed her long and hard enough to satisfy any doubts that his thoughts were as lustful and risqué as hers. Stepping back abruptly, he ran up the rest of the stairs toward Libby's room, leaving Ellie to look around self-consciously before readjusting her shirt and walking calmly to her bedroom.

All that flirting for nothing—there was no way he could maintain his fevered, sexual thoughts while he was with Libby. She was going to have to get him worked up all over again. She wandered the room restlessly, then sat at one of the window seats, swinging her foot nervously and biting a fingernail.

She didn't know he was there until she heard the

door close and the lock click. He didn't seem in the mood for pretenses. He strode across the room, pulled her to her feet, and growled softly, "Remind me why we're here." Without waiting for a response, he placed a hand on each side of her face and kissed her with a studied slowness, before pulling her into a tighter, steamier embrace that immediately reminded her entire body why they were there.

Her heart soared—she knew he'd gotten the right message. She had not been looking for tender love-making. This would be raw sex, powerful enough to flutter her insides at the mere memory long after she'd left Bloomfield Hills and Jack Payton behind her.

He still wore the suit pants and white shirt he'd worn to the office that morning. She kept her lips firmly against his as she pulled away, undid his belt, then reached inside the loosened pants to cup his butt and pull him into her, grinding herself against the hard line of his erection.

He groaned his satisfaction. "I think I've got the idea, sweetheart."

"Good," she told him, unbuttoning his shirt. "But if you need a little more inspiration," she said as she ran her tongue slowly over the hard nub of his nipple, lick-ing and nipping, "I'll be glad to provide some." She bent her knees, taking his pants down with her and adding a few more flicks of her tongue on the way.

He swore, helped by kicking free of the pants, then hauled her up roughly by her arms. His face was two inches from her own. "Ellie, if you think you have to do anything special to get me aroused, you're mis-taken. One look from you is all it takes to get me hard. Don't get me wrong," he said, leering, as he pulled off her shirt and reached for her breast without bothering to unfasten the bra. "You can be as uninhibited as you want. Just don't think I need that to get out-of-my-mind crazy over making love with you."

Her bra strap hung off her shoulder and her breast was out of the cup and in his warm hand. He lowered his mouth, sucking and licking, and her knees turned to jelly. Lines of fire streaked down her body, settling into a heated, swollen flush below. As if he were following the trail, his hand stroked her sensitive folds through her shorts, further inflaming her tingling flesh. She moaned and pushed toward him, shamelessly eager. At the same time she reached into his Jockeys, trying unsuccessfully to free his erection and excited by the heavy fullness of him.

He did it for her, stripping off the Jockeys and moving her toward the bed. She dropped her sandals, shorts, and underwear along the way, falling naked onto clean white sheets. Jack was above her, supporting himself with one arm while his free hand roamed from her hair to her breast, then slipped between her legs as his fingers slid in and out, teasing and exploring while his mouth covered her gasps.

Her body responded enthusiastically. He was driving her there too quickly, and she wanted to hold back, make it last, but her body was not in favor of anything that would make him stop the incredible things he was doing. She arched instinctively into his palm at the same time she twisted her face away from his and cried, "No, no, don't! I want you in me. Now, Jack, please, now!" Her plea died on a whimper.

Some detached part of her was appalled—she was actually begging for sex. Not cool at all. But her heart was pounding and her body was burning, and at the moment she didn't care how needy she sounded, she just wanted to feel him moving inside her. Her desperation probably didn't matter because she saw the same fire burning in his eyes and the same irresistible desire moving him to place his legs between hers. She waited, panting, to feel him fill that wonderfully aching space.

He didn't. His face hovered above hers and his body moved sensuously up and down, but he was not inside her. She felt his erection slide over her, down, then up, teasing the sensitive folds that were pulsing with hunger for him.

"Oh God," she groaned, closing her eyes. It was like an itch she couldn't scratch, and he was making it worse with every delicate, wet pass across her. She lifted her hips to find the right angle to draw him in, but when she opened her eyes and tried to reach between them, he smiled wickedly and inched away.

"Uh-uh, not yet," he whispered, pinning her with his weight while he continued his slow movements.

She released a shuddering breath. It was exquisite torture, and he wouldn't stop. She wanted to laugh and cry at the same time, but all she could do was dig her nails into his back, whimper softly, and hold on. She wouldn't have thought she could balance on the edge of ecstasy for so long, but Jack seemed to know her limits better than she did herself.

He didn't make her wait long. She realized it had been a sweet torture for him as well, because his eyes were glazed with desire when he finally raised up and used his hands to deliberately bend her knees and spread her legs apart. She saw him kneeling, erect and ready.

She threw her head back and closed her eyes, eager to receive the thrust she'd been waiting for.

That was when he changed the rules.

"No, look at me," he whispered. "I want you to look at me."

She opened her eyes to his intense gaze. He still didn't deliver the hard coupling she'd expected. His hands moved slowly up her inner thighs, moved to cover her breasts, then higher still to join with hers. He lowered himself easily, holding her mesmerized eyes with his own while he fit over and into every part of her.

Oh no, she thought at the last desperate moment. She should have closed her eyes, should have looked away. Those steady brown eyes had undone her, took the feelings that she'd kept safely apart and opened them in a rush as he joined their bodies. She cried out and came as soon as he filled her, and continued to spasm as he stroked to his own release. And by the time he collapsed onto her, melding their sweaty bodies in an exhausted union, it was too late. He'd ripped away the veil of lust and exposed the emotion underneath, ruining her perfectly good illusion.

She knew he'd been claiming her, marking his territory in a primitive, male way, without realizing how unnecessary that was. She could no longer pretend they were just friends, having incredibly good sex. She loved him, and the big jerk had to make her see it with that final, impassioned "Look at me" move. She turned her head and felt a tear trickle into her tangled hair.

She hated him for stripping away her denial.

For everything else, she loved him, and knew she always would. Damn it!

Jack lifted his head and framed her cheeks with his hands, forcing her to meet those gorgeous chocolate-colored eyes again.

He kissed her and murmured, "My God, Ellie, you make me do things I've never done before. Have I told you you're a fantastic lover? You make me crazy." He smiled happily.

Good for him. Crazy was better than in love. You could walk away from crazy without regrets.

He rolled off her and disposed of the condom, then lay back down, his bare body tucked against hers. Oh swell, the perfect man who wanted to cuddle after sex. Just when she needed to establish some distance between them.

She propped herself on one elbow and tried to look as uninterested in bodily contact as she could while naked and glowing from recent sex. "What did Libby want?" she asked. There, thoughts of his daughter ought to take his mind off any further intimacy with her.

Jack snorted. "She wanted to know if we could drive my mother's Jag to the concert next weekend. I think she wants to impress the lecherous little Don Juan she invited along."

Ellie smiled. "He's probably a very nice boy. And don't you dare embarrass Libby by being the slightest bit threatening." Maybe she should leave instructions on parenting teenage girls before she left him. "What did you tell her?"

"No, of course. I explained that her grandmother's the one with the gobs of money, not me, so she has to settle for the Jeep." He added reluctantly, "I also explained that it's more cool to be unpretentious, and the twerp is probably jaded enough that Jags don't impress him, anyway."

He was going to do fine. It would have been fun watching him struggle with female adolescence, she thought wistfully, twirling a few of his chest hairs. He and Libby would no doubt clash a few times, especially over dating and curfews, but his instincts were good and—

He flipped her onto her back and rolled on top of her. "I don't want to talk about Libby," he said, easily overcoming her distracting maneuver. "Not when I've got you alone and naked." He nuzzled her neck, sending shivers both up and down. "Tell me what you like, Ellie. Tell me what I haven't done yet that you want me to do."

She laughed hoarsely. "You've already done more than I ever thought of, you moron." She tried to make light of the breathless heights he'd taken her to. "I was an innocent, a babe in the woods, before I met you."

"Were not."

"Was too."

"You mean no one's ever done this to you before?" He slid lower, shaped her breast with his hand, and put his warm mouth over the nipple.

She went all squishy inside. "Not exactly," she said weakly. It had certainly never felt like that. She looked down at the tousled brown hair and gently laced her fingers through it.

He raised his head and his face grew serious. She wondered if she'd voiced her thoughts aloud when he said, "You're right, this is different. Better." He kissed her mouth. "Sexier." Kissed her again. "More fun." He licked her earlobe. "More stimulating," he added innocently, and shifted slightly so she felt the evidence against her thigh.

His kisses were infinitely tender, and for a fleeting moment she wondered if he felt the same sharp tug on his heart, the same giddy warmth that had startled her. But as his touches became more erotic, she realized that the tenderness wasn't love, it was just his way of driving her mad with desire, gently stoking the fire until it consumed her with lust. It was maddeningly effective, and she gave herself up to it, wrapping her legs around him and caressing every part of him she could reach while he made slow, breathtaking love to her again.

She didn't pull away from him this time. They drew up the comforter and, wonderfully exhausted, Ellie snuggled against his side. If she couldn't have his love, she'd settle for driving him crazy, and for being all those things he'd said: different, sexier, more fun. For a man who'd shut himself off emotionally from everyone else, including his own family, it was a big commitment.

It just wasn't the one she needed.

Jack woke to darkness and a painful warmth in his shoulder. He couldn't feel his arm. Confused, he turned his head to see why and found his face covered in silky, fragrant strands of hair. He drew back and blinked. Faint moonlight illuminated the pale gold hair that tickled his face and chest, and pinned his arm to the bed.

Ellie.

He remembered the sated and utterly contented feeling of falling asleep with her warm, naked body tucked against his. Sometime during the night they had changed positions, and now he lay looking at the shadowed ceiling with her tousled blond head over his outstretched arm and her soft, bare bottom pressed against his thigh. He moved his leg and felt the smooth skin of her lower leg rub against his hairy one. She sighed in her sleep and flexed her leg, slipping her foot around his. He didn't want to move, ever.

Unfortunately, his shoulder ached and his stomach was making angry, growling noises. Raising his head, he looked at the illuminated clock over Ellie's shoulder—ten after two. No wonder he was hungry. He'd missed dinner in favor of some mighty invigorating exercise with Ellie. Just the thought of it, along with the silky brush of her hair and satiny-smooth touch of her bare skin, had him rising hopefully beneath the covers.

No, don't think about it. As nice as it would be to bury himself in that luscious, willing body again, he'd end up falling back to sleep afterward and he needed to leave before the household began stirring. Some vague parental instinct told him he shouldn't be in Ellie's room when his daughter woke up, or even in the house in the same clothes he'd worn last night. After Libby's poolside inquisition, he didn't need to provide such an obvious sexual clue for her devious and impressionable twelve-year-old mind.

He had to slide his whole body sideways to remove his nerve-deadened arm from beneath Ellie. She made a few sleepy, kittenish sounds, burrowed her head into the pillow, and smiled in her sleep. If she'd so much as opened her eyes, he knew he would have climbed right back under the covers, wrapped his body around hers, and made love to her again. He grimaced with pain, both from having to leave and from the sharp pinpricks shooting down his arm. He got up and, after dressing quickly, bent close to her face and whispered in her ear.

"Ellie, sweetheart, I'll call you later."

"Hmm?" she murmured, still mostly asleep.

"I have to go now."

"Go?" Faint lines crossed her forehead as she struggled to concentrate on the words.

"I have to go, honey, but you can get more sleep." He kissed her cheek lightly.

"'Kay. Love ya," she mumbled, and was sound asleep two seconds later.

For a few stunned seconds Jack paused, then smiled tentatively. It was meaningless. She'd barely been awake, hadn't known what she was saying. So that otherwise weighty word, one he'd habitually fled from over the years, was nothing more than an automatic response, a friendly good-bye. He shouldn't give it another thought.

He crept silently down the stairs, remembering to switch off the security system before closing the front door gently behind him. The Jeep was covered in dew, and he let the wipers clean it off while he glanced back at the dark house.

Weird. He'd never felt reluctant about leaving this place before. With Ellie and Libby in there, it didn't feel like he was going home. It felt more like leaving home. Very weird.

Bloomfield Hills was dead, the streets empty and lights flashing yellow. His heavily treed street absorbed the sound of his engine without disturbing the chorus of frogs and crickets that pulsed all around him. After parking in front of the darkened house, he quietly let himself in.

He didn't bother with lights, feeling his way by memory and moonlight past the softly snoring form on the living room sofa and down the hall. His bedroom door stood open, the bed empty. Odd. He'd expected Rocky to be there. The Lexus was out front, so his friend was somewhere around, probably prowling the grounds or lurking in bushes, diligently ensuring Janet's safety. Rocky had jumped into the role of protector and took the job so seriously that Jack didn't worry about leaving Janet at the house. Thank God for Rocky.

Grateful that he could claim his own bed instead of the floor in the empty third bedroom, he shed his clothes and crawled under the covers. The scent of Ellie lingered on his skin, a light, fragrant mix of cologne and shampoo. He breathed it in deeply and fell asleep with "Love ya" whispering in his mind.

Chapter Fourteen

Janet and Rocky stopped talking when they heard the car engine out front, listened as the front door opened and footsteps crossed the floor. When the bedroom door shut at the far end of the house, they relaxed. It was only Jack, not some vengeful drug lord or a hired goon sent by Banner. She smiled at Rocky with nervous relief, and he shook his head seriously.

"It's too soon," he said, keeping his voice low so it wouldn't carry beyond Janet's bedroom. "If they come here at all, it won't be until tomorrow evening, soonest. Banner won't know it was you who gave the orders for the search and seizure until the drugs don't show up at MJP and the bad guys start asking why."

She bit her lip and nodded.

"Hey, are you gonna be okay with this?" he asked, watching her closely.

"Yes, honest, I will. I am. It's just that the waiting gets to me."

Rocky smiled. "I know. Action is easier because it lets you take control."

"Yes!" She smiled back, surprised again by the feeling that he was the only one who understood. Even Nora—*Ellie,* Janet corrected herself—hadn't been able to understand the thrill of taking a risk, though her friend had been supportive of whatever Janet wanted to do about Banner. They'd all been supportive.

Especially Rocky. It was hard to believe she'd met him only . . . what? Barely more than a day ago? They'd talked constantly, about everything, and he even made her laugh about her catastrophic marriage to Banner. Everyone else gasped in shocked sympathy over Banner's deceptions and manipulations, depressing her even more than she already was over her incredibly stupid mistake of a marriage. Everyone but Rocky. He took such a healthy approach to shrugging off the bad parts of life and getting on with the good that she felt wonderfully relieved of guilt over her failed marriage and free to fix her mistake and move on. He was like a huge dose of therapy, only more fun.

Cute, too.

Whoa. Don't even think it, she warned herself. She might have been emotionally separated from Banner for quite a while, but the legal connection was still there. And the little matter of him trying to kill her. The last thing she needed right now was a new relationship.

He was tempting, though. Which had to mean her libido had survived intact. Good to know.

Elizabeth was getting suspicious.

Ben Thatcher's arrival during the middle of breakfast was unexpected enough to cause her to drop her croissant and rise from her chair in concern.

"What's wrong?" she asked, as if his appearance at her house in the morning could only mean something bad.

"Nothing. Where's Jack?"

"Jack?" Elizabeth looked at Ellie, who shook her head, then back at Ben. "He's not here. Why?"

"He said he'd meet me here."

"He did? Why? Is something wrong?"

Ben smiled reassuringly. "Nothing's wrong, Liz. Relax. I'm just helping him with something and he said he'd meet me here."

"May I ask what you're helping him with?"

"No." Ben smiled at her.

Elizabeth frowned and settled slowly into her seat, obviously unhappy with his answer. Libby watched with open curiosity.

Ellie kept her mouth full and her expression blank, hoping she looked clueless. This had to be about the coroner.

Yesterday's lengthy seduction of Jack had prevented her from asking him about their talk with Officer Messner, but she knew Tull was next on their list. She couldn't blame Ben for not wanting to tell Elizabeth that he was looking into the possibility that her younger son had paid bribes to implicate her older son in a man's death. Not until he had proof. But his flat "No" had not exactly diverted Elizabeth's suspicion that he was up to something.

Before Elizabeth could formulate a new question, Jack strode into the breakfast room looking well rested and incredibly cheerful. Ellie was immediately smacked with mental images of him in her bed last night, his face hovering over hers, eyes smoldering, while he slowly entered her body. Heat rose to her face and she reached for the chilled glass of orange juice, hoping it was sufficient to bring down her soaring temperature.

"Hey, Libby," he said, grinning at the immediate, "Hey, Jack," he got in response.

"Mother." He favored Ellie with a large smile as he stopped behind her chair, placed a hand on her shoulder, and kissed the top of her head. "Morning, El," he said in a much softer, intimate voice.

Pleasant chills ran from the spot he'd kissed down her arms. Could anyone, even Libby, possibly not know how they'd spent the previous night after that greeting? She glanced sideways at Libby. Jack's daughter was munching a mouthful of cereal while keeping bright, animated eyes on Ellie and her father.

Oh, God, she knew. Ellie blushed again, lowered her gaze, and concentrated on rearranging the slices of fruit on her plate.

"Ready?" Jack asked Ben.

Before Ben could answer, Elizabeth said, "Ready for what?" Looking pointedly at Jack's casual outfit of khakis and knit shirt, she asked, "Aren't you both supposed to be at work?"

"I am at work," Ben told her with another smile, which earned him a tight, suspicious stare. "Police business, I can't talk about it."

"Police business that involves Jack?" She was on her feet again.

Her voice held enough worry that even Jack couldn't mistake her concern. "I came across some information that I felt Ben should know about," he told her. "That's all. I'm not in any trouble."

"Liz, we'll talk about it later," Ben said in a more reassuring voice. "Okay?"

She hesitated, then sighed and sat down.

Ellie touched the hand that still lay on her shoulder and looked up. "Let me know, too, Jack."

"Me too," Libby added, aware that something important was going on and determined not to be left out.

Jack smiled. "I'll let both of you know." His hand trailed a slow caress along her neck as he left.

She turned to watch the two men leave, glad to see that Jack had let go of the usual hostility he displayed toward Ben. It was ridiculous, really, that he should resent the man for trying to make up for the parenting Leonard Westfield didn't provide. Maybe stepping into that role for Libby made him see how important a father figure could be. And after all, they were almost enough alike to be father and son. The same height, the same build, the same killer smile that could devastate any woman . . .

Ellie narrowed her eyes at the two men disappearing around the corner, then looked back at Elizabeth, who met her eyes with her usual cool demeanor. Was it possible?

She picked up her knife and casually began spreading butter on a cold piece of toast. "Jack said you've known Ben most of his life. Is he from around here?"

The sharp blue eyes watched her steadily. "Ben is from Massachusetts, originally. He moved here when Jack was three years old and Banner was just a baby. We met when we worked together on a committee to form a women's shelter."

Very concise, almost rehearsed, Ellie thought. She

tried to look interested in the pitifully dry toast as she asked, "He'd never been here before?"

"No." Elizabeth sat back and sipped her coffee.

"Hmm." Ellie studied the toast and its coating of unmelted butter with distaste. "I wonder why he chose Bloomfield Hills."

"I couldn't say. I know he'd just returned from a four-year hitch in the navy and was looking for a job in law enforcement. I suppose he heard about openings here."

"Oh." That sounded reasonable. It also sounded as if Ben and Elizabeth could not possibly have met before Jack was three years old if Elizabeth was in Bloomfield Hills and Ben was in Massachusetts or somewhere at sea.

It had been a long shot, anyway. Maybe Jack was right and his father was someone too embarrassing for his mother to name. She bit into the toast, which tasted like buttered cardboard, and slid a surreptitious glance toward Elizabeth, trying to imagine the proper, formal woman falling into a heated affair with some low-bred jerk (never!) or a rich, well-bred man who turned out to be a jerk (possible). A married man? Now, that was entirely possible.

While the Payton-Westfield soap opera had distracted Ellie, Libby had, as usual, forged ahead with her own agenda. Ellie toyed with the sad piece of toast and half listened as Libby wheedled her grandmother into excusing her from her morning lessons in order to spend more time with her future stepmother. It took several seconds for Ellie to realize that the word *stepmother* referred to her.

She looked up at Libby's pleased expression as a ton of guilt smashed down on her.

Libby liked her. Worse, Libby trusted her. The one person she had sworn to protect from emotional harm in this charade was the one who would be hurt the most when she left. She couldn't let that happen. No matter how much it would hurt to see Jack once their fake engagement was over, she could not sever her ties with Libby. It was not just a feeling of responsibility; she realized she truly cared for the girl.

Ellie smiled warmly at her. "Sounds great. What would you like to do?"

She should have guessed that anything Libby did would involve a computer. They started out playing an interactive game that had Ellie baffled with its complexity, until they were interrupted by an instant message to Dragonfly from someone named Hotchic.

Ellie turned a questioning look at Libby. "Hotchic?"

"That's Tanya. She thinks she's hot." Libby's wrinkled nose said she disagreed.

They responded and soon picked up another IM from Sexilicious.

"Deanna," Libby said.

"These are your friends?" Ellie heard echoes of her mother and felt ancient. She kept her face straight and her opinions to herself during the following discussion of hot movie stars, hot rock stars, and hot boys at school. By the time Jack called, she was tired of boys and sex.

Ellie flipped open the cell phone and asked eagerly, "What happened?" while Libby continued her online conversation.

"Exactly what we hoped," Jack said with satisfaction. "You are not only sexy, Ellie Coggins, you are brilliant as well."

She laughed, thinking she wasn't *completely* tired of boys and sex. "Thank you. Now, start at the beginning. You never told me about Officer Messner last night."

"I noticed that. You seemed to be preoccupied with other areas of interest. . . ."

She cleared her throat.

"Not alone?"

"I'm with Libby. Get on with the story."

"Tell her hi."

She relayed hellos between them, smiling at how wonderfully normal their relationship was becoming. "Now, tell me before I explode. What happened?"

"Messner denied everything. He looked scared shitless, though, so Ben figured we were right. *You* were right. He came down hard on Tull this morning, and the good doctor got so scared of losing his medical license, he was only too happy to implicate Banner. He claimed Banner convinced him that if he reported that Joe Benton had died from something other than the accident, they'd never be able to convict me, even though I was obviously the one who had murdered him. But they could get me on manslaughter if he said Benton died in the accident. So he did."

"I can't believe he just accepted that you would murder someone."

"Banner gave him some story about me embezzling funds from Westfield-Benton, and he bought it. He didn't know me, didn't care, and Banner was offering big money."

"Will he lose his license?"

"I don't know. We left him with his attorney. Ben says they may have to cut a deal to give him a reprimand and a fine if he'll testify against Banner. I'd rather get Banner, so that's okay with me."

Ellie released her breath and leaned back in her chair. "I'm glad, Jack. I can't tell you how happy I am for you."

"Really? Well, you can show me, sweetheart. But I really think I'm the one who owes you something. How about if we start with a nice dinner at a terribly expensive and snooty restaurant?"

Ellie smiled. "Okay." She caught Libby's bemused expression as the girl tried to puzzle out what had happened. "Can Libby come, too?"

Jack's voice sounded surprised. "Sure."

"Good. I'll let you explain why we're celebrating when you see her." She paused, realizing that for Elizabeth this was both good news and bad. "How are you going to explain this to your mother?"

"That's the hard part. Ben said he wanted to be there, and I guess that's a good idea." There was a long moment of uncomfortable silence from Jack. "He's a pretty good guy."

"I think so, too."

"You think he's handsome."

She laughed. "Devastatingly handsome. Jealous?"

"Hell, yes."

She waited, but he didn't add anything more. Something like, *Hell, yes, I'm jealous, I'm in love with you.* Nothing.

It was disappointing but not surprising. She imagined that when two thirds of your family hated you and had you unjustly sent to jail, you might become a bit disillusioned by love. And his mother, the only emotional support he had, believed the lies and turned

away from him. It was probably amazing that he
would even risk loving his daughter. And it *was* a
risk—she'd seen the pain he felt when Libby had been
indifferent toward him. She couldn't expect him to
take another chance by loving her, too.

Ellie forced herself to smile for Libby's observant
eyes and said into the phone, "I have to get ready to
meet Rocky at the Hampshire house." She hoped he
made the connection that Janet would be left with only
Richard to guard her. She wouldn't need to explain
how ineffective Richard would be as a bodyguard.

"Gotcha. I'm going to hang out at the office for a
while and see what the mood is in Administration, just
to make sure Banner hasn't heard about this morning's
drug bust at Aims. I'll get back home after that."

"Thanks."

"Be careful, Ellie. I know you'll be with Rocky,
but these drug pushers are serious about their business. And Banner's no amateur at intimidation, either.
Maybe you should take Janet with you."

"Okay. But I thought nothing would happen before
late afternoon when they realize the shipment didn't
get through."

"Yeah, but still . . . Just be careful."

She didn't know what being careful constituted but
liked the sentiment. "Okay."

Ellie had hoped for a fast, easy security assessment at
the Hampshire house. She should have known there'd
be complications; nothing in her life was easy anymore.

The complication was Mrs. Hampshire's son. Mr.
Hampshire might be gone, but his son had assumed

the job of taking care of his mother and resented any implication that his efforts might be less than perfect. *Nothing* in the Hampshire house was less than perfect. Except, temporarily, Ellie, Rocky, and Janet. They were obviously not up to Hampshire standards, at least not in the opinion of Dr. Edward J. Hampshire, Jr.

"Please don't touch the artwork," he said, placing himself between Rocky and the picture frame he'd been discreetly peering behind. "Even the frames are valuable, and the human hand carries oils."

Rocky gave him an even look. "I need to check the wiring on the sensors."

"We have to let them do their job, Eddie," Mrs. Hampshire reminded her son. "I'm sure the frame will be fine."

"You can't be too careful, Mother. I'll do it."

Ellie wasn't sure if he was being cautious about people handling his family's priceless art, or just Hispanics and women. She suspected the latter.

If Rocky resented the attitude, he didn't show it. He examined the back of the picture without comment while Edward used two immaculately scrubbed fingers to hold the bottom away from the wall. "It's good," he told Ellie.

She noted it on the legal pad she carried. Not that she wouldn't have remembered. Every minute detail of the Hampshire security system had passed with flying colors. The house was a fortress.

"Eddie is very particular about cleanliness." Mrs. Hampshire gave her son a benign smile. "That's one of the things that makes him such a good surgeon. Just like his father was."

"Hmm." Ellie had resorted to making agreeable

sounds when she could no longer find agreeable words. Rocky had become silent. She found that more ominous than if he'd put the stuffy doctor in his place. Janet looked like she wanted to kick the good doctor, but a stern glance from Rocky kept her on simmer.

"You said you keep your guns in this room, Dr. Hampshire," Rocky said, his gaze scanning the den. "Where are they?"

The doctor hesitated, and Ellie wondered if he was having second thoughts about showing them his precious guns.

Rocky waited him out.

"Over here," Dr. Hampshire said finally, and led the way across the room.

Janet hung back, pulling on Ellie's arm. "The man's a jerk-off. Why don't you guys just tell him to stuff it and leave?"

"Shh." Ellie brushed off Janet's hand. "Because it's a job, and we're building a reputation. Try to act like an apprentice."

"This man is not going to help your reputation," Janet muttered, following Ellie.

She joined the others at a tall armoire. Dr. Hampshire used a key to unlock the double doors, swinging them wide open. Inside, three rifles and two handguns hung on mountings.

"Please don't touch them," he said.

Rocky gave him a long look. "I know." He held up his hand as if something might be evident on his clean palm. "Oil."

The man's eyes narrowed as he watched Rocky examine the lock on the cabinet and rattle the handle on the drawer beneath the guns.

"Bullets in here?" Rocky asked.

"Yes. It seems logical to keep them in a handy place." Dr. Hampshire's voice was stiff and defensive.

"Handy for thieves, too."

Hampshire took offense, just as Ellie knew he would. "I doubt a thief would have the opportunity to look for bullets. In fact, I doubt a thief could ever get into this house. If you think one could after what you've seen, then you don't know what you're talking about and have no business pretending you do."

Oh, shit. Ellie knew the irony would be too much for Rocky to pass up. She could already see a serene smile twitching at the corner of his mouth as he antici- pated telling the good doctor that a thief was currently standing in his house, eyeing his concealed weapons. She couldn't let him do it. A moment's satisfaction would ruin any chance he had of making their business work.

"You're right, Dr. Hampshire," Rocky said. "You have an excellent security system. There's nothing wrong with the electronics. It always comes down to the people, doesn't it?"

"What do you mean?"

"He means there's no one clever enough to get by your system," Ellie said.

Rocky ignored her. "I mean you never can tell who you're inviting into your house."

"I assure you, my friends are more than trustwor- thy," Dr. Hampshire said with a snootiness even Eliza- beth Westfield couldn't have achieved.

"I'm sure they are. I'm not talking about your friends."

"You know, a friend of a friend," Ellie interjected.

The doctor spared a glance at her, and she tried again. "A friend's date, something like that, right, Rocky?"

"Not exactly."

He wasn't going to be deterred from shocking the stuffy Hampshires with the truth of his background. Ellie closed her eyes and said, "Don't."

That earned her another glance from the doctor, more suspicious this time, but Rocky wasn't listening to her. "You might have a thief standing right in front of you and not know it."

Even Mrs. Hampshire looked concerned now. Ellie stepped closer and jabbed her pen in Rocky's side, but he didn't flinch.

"In fact—" Rocky began, a satisfied smile already on his face.

"In fact," Ellie said, louder and more forcefully than Rocky, "maybe you do." She saw Rocky's eyebrows go up as she apparently stole his line. At the same time, she reached into her purse and closed her fingers around the largest object she could find. Pulling it out in one quick move, she pointed her sunglasses at Dr. Edward J. Hampshire, Jr.

"This is a gun," she said. The Hampshires blinked at the sunglasses in her hand. She aimed them at the doctor's chest. "Bang. You're dead, Edward."

Mrs. Hampshire's mouth dropped open. Her son's pulled into a stern line. "I beg your pardon?"

"You just fell for the perfect setup, Doctor." She spoke rapidly, trying not to sound as jittery as she felt. "You invited us into your home, not knowing anything about us, and showed us every security device and every valuable item it protects. We're taking them all. And you've seen our faces and know our names, so we have to kill you." She pointed the sunglasses at Mrs. Hampshire. "Bang."

No one said anything, but Ellie thought she heard a snicker from Janet behind her. She took a deep breath to calm the hammering beat in her chest. "Forgive me for being crude. I—" She motioned to Rocky. "We were simply making a point. Even with the best security system—and you have the best, Dr. Hampshire—there are ways around it. This is the only vulnerability we can find. You just need to be aware that you do sometimes invite people into your home without knowing much about them." She stuck the sunglasses back in her purse. "Sorry, I hope I didn't scare you." She looked at Mrs. Hampshire as she said it, concerned for the old lady's health. Maybe she should have been more subtle. At least they had a doctor close by.

Mrs. Hampshire's stunned expression gradually changed into one of awe. "Brilliant!" she exclaimed. "I never would have thought of that. Aren't they clever, Eddie? And thorough. I told you they were good."

Eddie didn't look quite as pleased as his mother, who clapped her hands joyfully.

Rocky accepted a pat on his cheek as Mrs. Hampshire marched off to write them a check. They followed her as her son stayed to lock up his guns and wipe imaginary oil off the armoire.

Sliding a look at Ellie, Rocky allowed a tiny smile and a disbelieving shake of his head. She grinned back. "Idiot," she whispered, so Mrs. Hampshire wouldn't hear.

"It would have been worth it."

"No it wouldn't."

His grin broadened as he winked. "Whatever you say, boss."

"Partner."

He surprised her by pulling her against him in a quick hug as they walked. "The best one I could have."

Ellie knew he hadn't intended to put a damper on her mood, but she couldn't help thinking that their new partnership wasn't going to last long. At least Rocky would get something good out of her time here.

Outside, Mrs. Hampshire preened as Rocky praised her security system, fluttering her false lashes in a manner that looked remarkably like flirting. Ellie hid her smile behind her clipboard and turned toward Janet.

"If all the women react to Rocky like that, he won't even need me as a business partner. She's barely looked at me since I said hello."

"He's a natural charmer. He's going to be a great business partner, Ellie."

"Hmm."

"This thing has potential," Rocky said as he joined them. "Mrs. Hampshire wants us to set up the security system at her daughter's new house, and she said she knew a couple other people who might be interested in our service."

"It's you she's interested in," Ellie teased.

"The woman knows quality. I think I could have gotten a date." He wiggled his eyebrows suggestively.

As they laughed, Rocky's gaze went past them to the street beyond. A thoughtful look replaced his smile.

"You ladies wait right here," he said. "I want to check on something."

Ellie looked at Janet, who shrugged, and watched Rocky stroll across the lawn parallel to the street, then cut through the bushes to come out behind a parked car. He had a brief conversation with the driver, then walked back up the driveway while the car drove off.

Ellie saw his look of concern. "What's wrong?"

"I know that guy. He's a small-time burglar."

She doubted this neighborhood qualified as small-time. "What did he want?"

"He says he was hired to hit this place, so he was casing it. He figured I was doing the same thing."

Ellie frowned. "Why would someone hire him to burglarize Mrs. Hampshire?"

"To make us look bad would be my guess." He turned to Janet. "The guy who hired him works for Westfield-Benton security."

Janet's expression became stony. "Banner wants you to look bad."

Rocky nodded, but Ellie didn't get it. "Why would he care about Red Rose Security?"

"I'm not sure. Maybe Jack and Ben Thatcher have him worried about all the questions they've been asking."

She shook her head. "I don't think Tull or Messner would tell Banner that they were about to spill their guts about taking a bribe. That wouldn't—"

A ring from her cell phone interrupted her, and she answered it.

Jack's voice was curt. "Where are you?"

"Just ready to leave the Hampshire house. Why?"

"Is Rocky with you?"

"Yes."

"Good." He hesitated. "How about Janet?"

"She's here, too. What's going on, Jack?"

"Get everyone to my house right away. I'll explain when I see you." Another brief pause. "You'd better put Rocky on."

She handed the phone to Rocky and watched his expression grow stern and cold. When he flipped the phone shut and handed it back, she demanded, "What'd he say?"

"They know."

"Who knows? What do they know?"

"Banner. The Colombian connection. MJP. Everyone. They know Janet's here."

He had a hand on Janet's arm, attempting to guide her toward the Lexus, but she resisted. Planting her feet firmly, Janet said, "It's not possible. Even if they found out the shipment was confiscated, they should assume I was in Colombia. How could they possibly know I'm in Bloomfield Hills?"

"I don't know, but it would be a lot easier to protect you if you weren't standing in the middle of a driveway. Please get in the car."

Responding to the urgency in his voice, Janet got in the Lexus. Rocky turned to Ellie.

"Do you know how to get to Jack's from here?"

She nodded.

"Then drive the Toyota. I'll be right behind you."

Adrenaline surging, Ellie dashed to her car. Events were just beginning to unfold, and already they were out of control. Anxiety increased her speed through the winding streets, and one thought took over her mind: If they hadn't anticipated how quickly Janet would be found, what else had they overlooked?

They found Jack standing in the living room, arms folded, watching dispassionately as Richard held an ice pack to his head. Since Jack looked fine, Ellie rushed to the moaning Richard and knelt in front of him, easing the ice pack aside to look beneath. A large swelling reddened the scalp under the fair hair.

"Are you okay?" she asked, fingering the bump.

"Ow! Don't do that." He replaced the ice pack with a wounded look.

"He's fine," Jack answered for him.

Richard's expression turned angry. "I am not. I'm in pain and probably have a concussion. And I'm getting sick and tired of what appears to be the traditional Bloomfield Hills greeting."

Ellie turned a horrified glance toward Jack. "You didn't . . ."

"Of course I didn't." She believed him, even though his look said he wouldn't mind whacking Richard. "I found him tied up and unconscious in the kitchen."

"Shit," Rocky growled, then elaborated with a string of profanities in Spanish.

"Exactly," Jack said.

Janet laid a hand on Richard's shoulder. "I'm so sorry," she told him. "I shouldn't have put you in the middle of this."

He gave her a weak smile. "It's okay, Janet. It's not your fault." His eyes flicked past her to Jack with a look of disdain, as if somehow he were the one to blame.

Ellie stood and faced Jack. "Do you think whoever did this was looking for Janet?"

"I'm afraid so."

Rocky didn't spare any sympathy for Richard. "Did you tell them anything?" he demanded.

"I didn't get a chance. One second I was sitting there reading the *Free Press,* and the next thing I knew, Payton was slapping me while elephants tromped inside my head."

Jack's lip twitched. "I had to make sure you weren't comatose."

Jack might be amused, but Ellie felt sorry for Richard. "Why did they have to hurt him? They didn't even ask him where Janet was."

Jack shrugged. "I'm sure whoever Banner sent didn't expect Richard to give her up, they just wanted him out of the way. They wouldn't even know who he was. I'd say it was a search-and-destroy mission with one goal, and it's a good thing Janet wasn't here."

Ellie blanched. Just when she thought Janet had survived the worst Banner could do, she was right back in his sights.

Janet turned to Rocky, her partner in planning the drug sting. "I don't get it. How did they already figure out that I'm alive and in Michigan?"

Rocky shook his head and frowned, as puzzled as she was. "I don't know."

"I do." Jack nodded his head toward Richard. "As soon as I untied your friend here, I made a call to the Aims office in Colombia. I thought the drug bust must have caused the Bogotá supplier to panic and tell his distributor at MJP not to expect the shipment, or even to lay low for a while. It didn't. In fact, there was no drug bust."

Janet's mouth opened in surprise. "Enrique promised

he'd arrange the bust. He would have told me if he couldn't."

"Oh, the police showed up, all right, but they didn't find any drugs. No cocaine, no heroin, no marijuana, nothing. The shipment was clean. Just five crates of the usual chemical compounds for MJP."

"They were tipped off?"

"Probably. It wouldn't be that unusual for a cop to take money in exchange for information. The question is, why did someone come looking for you on this end as soon as the drug bust was arranged in Colombia? And I can only come up with one answer. He knew you weren't dead, Janet."

"Of course he did. I escaped from one of his murdering thugs—"

"Not the Colombian drug lord. Banner. Banner knew you were alive. No one in Colombia cares whether you know about drug running down there. Hell, everyone knows who controls the drugs in that country. But you were a big problem on this end, knowing about the drugs coming in and the payoffs to Banner. They must have told him you escaped, and all he could do was wait for you to make your move. Unfortunately, Ellie and I seem to have aroused his suspicions by snooping around, because he knew right where to look—my house." He looked past her to Rocky. "It's a good thing she wasn't here," he added softly. "She might really be dead by now."

Janet shivered, and Rocky stepped up behind her, rubbing her shoulders. Ellie suspected it could have a little to do with the affection he seemed to feel for Janet. But she was grateful for the gesture, because it also reminded Janet that she wasn't alone, that they would all help her fight whatever Banner had in mind for her next. Janet sighed and looked a little less tense.

Ellie looked away, suddenly uncomfortable with how natural their simple touching seemed. If Jack cuddled her like that, it would be related to sex or because his mother was watching and he was playing a role. In front of their friends where they didn't have to pretend, he never touched her with affection. That hurt more than she wanted to think about.

Jack didn't seem to be bothered by such thoughts. "We need to get you out of here, Janet, as soon as possible."

"But I want—"

"I'll take her." Rocky spoke to Jack, ignoring Janet's protest.

Janet's gaze moved toward Ellie in appeal, but she shook her head. "I thought I lost you once," Ellie said. "It was too horrible to risk again. Please go, Janet."

Janet sighed with resignation. At the same moment, the phone on the end table rang and Jack crossed the room in four quick strides. He glanced at the caller ID, grimaced, and picked up the receiver.

"What," he said, his voice flat.

As he listened, Ellie saw his jaw clench and his posture stiffen. His eyes met hers, then went past her to Rocky and Janet. While they watched, puzzled, he punched the speaker button, put the receiver down, and said curtly, "Go ahead."

"Thank you," a smooth male voice said from the speaker, and Ellie went cold. She whipped her head around to see Janet's frightened eyes widen as Banner's voice said, "I trust you are there, too, Janet darling. How remarkable to speak to you again."

Chapter Fifteen

Janet's face turned red and she started toward the phone, but Rocky grabbed her arm and motioned for her to stay quiet. Ellie heard him whisper harshly, "He wants to get you upset. Don't let him."

Janet seethed but remained silent.

"What do you want?" Jack demanded.

"My wife, of course." The disembodied voice was a creepy presence in the room, sending shivers up Ellie's spine.

"You're done using Janet, Banner."

"Now, Jack, don't be judgmental. I haven't questioned your timely engagement, have I? We both know your reasons for acquiring a pretty little fiancée are more than they seem. A more cynical person might say you were using Ellie."

Jack's eyes met hers, but she couldn't read his hard expression. "You don't know what you're talking about."

"Perhaps not," the silky voice continued, unperturbed. "By the way, have I mentioned that I'm here with your charming daughter? Say hello to your father, Libby."

Ellie sucked in a shaky breath and Jack's face paled. A cautious voice in the background responded, "Hi, Jack."

Rising panic clutched Ellie's throat as Banner's intention became obvious and chilling. He wanted to trade Libby for Janet. She finally had the answer to the persistent fear that they had overlooked something in their scheme to get Banner. Libby was in his house, vulnerable, and was the best leverage against Jack that Banner could have. They had overlooked Libby.

Janet pulled away from Rocky and whispered fiercely to Jack, "You have to let me go to him."

"No," three voices responded immediately, and she fumed.

"I beg your pardon?" Banner said.

Jack ignored him and closed his eyes in concentration. Ellie knew he was wondering if the threat to Libby might be a bluff. Elizabeth rarely left her alone in the house with Banner, assuming he had better things to do than babysit a surly pre-teen. Jack began, "Mother—"

"Is unfortunately not here. Some business about an impostor in our house—I believe her name is Nora. There's a nasty rumor that she attempted to make off with a valuable family keepsake."

Oh, God. He not only knew who she was, he had used it to turn Elizabeth against her. The way Jack's mother kept watch over the family inheritance, the idea that Ellie might steal that blasted ring would inflame her like nothing else.

Banner had paused just long enough for his words

to have the calculated impact before continuing his narration. "Naturally, Mother was terribly annoyed. She hurried off to see her policeman friend. Don't worry, I'm sure it will be resolved soon. Isn't it lucky that your fiancée has made us so conscious of home security? Background checks on everyone with access to the house turned out to be a valuable suggestion."

While Banner savored the irony of outing Ellie through her own advice, she struggled to ignore the sick feeling in her stomach and concentrate on helping Libby. If they could get her away from Banner, he would lose his only leverage over Jack. She had no doubt that the girl was resourceful enough to hide from her uncle if she knew the danger she was in. She already sounded suspicious about Banner's presence in her room. She had probably been chatting with her friends as usual on the computer, unaware of— Ellie's mind slammed to a halt. If Libby was on her computer, they could talk to her. Libby was *always* on her computer. They could warn her about Banner and at least make her wary, maybe even give her half a chance to escape.

Ellie whispered to Jack, "Keep him talking," then, ignoring his confused look, bolted for the bedroom, pulling Janet with her.

Janet stumbled down the hall, unwilling to leave while Jack and Rocky tried to negotiate her fate with Banner. "Ellie, what's going on? If you think you can keep me away from Banner by locking me in the bedroom, I can assure you it's not going to be that—"

Ellie cut her off. "If this works, I need you to let Jack know what I'm doing." She turned on the computer and watched impatiently while the monitor flashed through incomprehensible names and codes. "Do you think this thing is connected to the Internet?"

"Are you kidding? This family doesn't know how to do anything without all the bells and whistles. This computer can probably hack into Westfield-Benton and launch the space shuttle at the same time."

"Just help me find the program that gets me onto the Internet."

A minute later she opened the IM program, filled in the user name Dragonfly, then hesitated at the message box. If Libby was using her computer, Banner might very well be looking over her shoulder. Trying to sound like one of Libby's twelve-year-old friends, she typed, "Top Secret message about a BOY. Respond!" If Libby recognized the user name, she'd understand that BOY referred to Banner. She pressed *Send*, watched the message disappear, and held her breath.

Half a minute passed before the box popped up again with a message: "Hi, Special-One. What's going on???"

Ellie and Janet let out a small cheer before Janet rushed off to tell Jack what they were doing. All he had to do was keep Banner distracted and on the line long enough for her to warn Libby. Then it would be up to luck and Libby's inventiveness to escape Banner.

Ellie smiled at the user name, Special-One. Jack had to have programmed that into this computer for Libby. When it came to his daughter, the man was pure mush.

From Dragonfly's response, Libby obviously knew something wasn't right but hadn't said anything specific. Good girl, Ellie thought. She typed, "My b/f told me that other BOY we both know is bad news. Stay away." Referring to Jack as her "boyfriend" would at least let Libby know the information came from Jack. She pressed *Send*.

Seconds later, the IM came back, "How?"

Good question. If Ellie could give her a hint about how to get away for a few seconds, Libby was smart enough to find a place to hide. But she couldn't spell it out for her. If Banner looked over Libby's shoulder and saw Ellie's instructions on how to escape him, the whole plan would be useless.

She thought about what options were open to Libby. Banner might not have threatened her, preferring a calm, willing hostage, but neither would he let her out of his sight. All the hiding places in the world wouldn't help if Banner didn't let her do more than sit at her computer or go to the bathroom.

Ellie brightened, recalling Libby's attached bathroom, which continued through to Elizabeth's room. Libby had a way out. And Ellie even had a way to tell her to use it, if Libby was bright enough, and devious enough, to catch on. She was willing to bet all her money that Libby was.

She typed in the message box, trying to sound like a girl on the verge of an obsession with boys. "Hey, I saw that cute boy you like in the food court at the mall. He came over to our table, but I didn't get to talk to him." It was a deliberately incomplete thought and she counted on Libby's memory to supply the rest: *because I went to the restroom.* She pressed *Send* and waited.

And waited.

Ellie chewed a fingernail and tapped her foot nervously against the floor.

Janet came up behind her, looking as concerned as Ellie felt. "How's it going?"

"I don't know. I think she knows she should try to get away, and I hinted that she should make an excuse to go to the bathroom because it connects to another room, but she hasn't answered. Is Banner still on the phone?"

Janet nodded. "He's still using that cool-as-ice voice, but he sounds a little edgy, different than I remember. Like something has snapped." She hesitated, then added, "He has a gun, Ellie."

"Oh, God." Libby had to get out of there, fast. She looked at the monitor, wishing she could reach through and yank Libby out of Banner's grasp. The fantasy shattered when the IM box reappeared with a brief message.

" 'POS,' " Janet read aloud. "What's that mean?"

"Kid terminology Libby and her friends use for 'Parent Over Shoulder.' It must mean Banner is standing right beside her and she can't answer." It also meant Ellie couldn't tell her to run away without Banner reading it. But he probably didn't know the Internet slang Libby used. Searching her memory for acronyms she'd seen Libby use, she typed, "UGTR."

"What's that?" Janet asked.

" 'You,' and the abbreviation for 'gotta run.' I don't know how else to say it, but I think she'll get it."

She hoped she would. They waited again, Ellie's heart filling with dread for every minute that passed with no further response from Libby.

Libby snuck a look at her uncle, then fastened her eyes back on the computer screen. He was still standing by her dresser, speaking to Jack in that friendly voice that made her think of the satin sheets they'd given her, all slippery and cold. He gave her the creeps.

She'd nearly freaked when he'd come in her room without even knocking, then ignored her while he phoned Jack. Their conversation didn't make sense and she decided to ignore him in return, but then she'd received that weird IM from Ellie, who was using Jack's computer.

She understood immediately. Ellie was with Jack, Jack was talking to Banner, so the "boy" Ellie wanted her to stay away from was the man in her bedroom. That meant Banner's creepiness wasn't just her imagination. Not good news.

Libby's finger tapped nervously on the mouse pad as she tried to figure out why Ellie was talking about seeing Steven Beyer at the mall. It had to mean something, but she didn't want to stay and figure it out, she just wanted to get away from Banner. His voice was developing a sharp edge, and his hand played with something large in the pocket of his suit coat, and she didn't think what he was saying to Jack was nearly as nice as he wanted it to sound. If she could just think of an excuse to leave . . .

Duh, what an idiot she was. That was the hint Ellie had been trying to give her. All she had to do was go to the bathroom, then escape to the adjoining room.

Her hand poised over the keyboard to let Ellie know she understood, when a voice spoke right above her head.

"Who are you talking to?"

She didn't jump, but the back of her neck got all prickly and cold. "My friend Deanna."

Banner's head lowered near hers as he peered at the screen. Quickly she typed, "POS," pressed *Send,* then leaned closer to the monitor to block his view. "It's a private conversation. Do you mind?"

She risked a look at his face and saw his upper lip curl with amusement. He thought they were discussing boys. Libby took a deep breath and pushed her luck further. Even though it caused her to nearly brush against him, she pushed the chair back and stood. "I have to go to the bathroom."

She expected resistance, or at least suspicion, but he stepped aside and said, "Go ahead."

Perfect! Maybe he didn't remember about how the bedrooms connected. She crossed her room as calmly as she could while the creep watched her, then locked the bathroom door behind her. Hurrying past the sinks and shower, she ran into the small, feminine sitting room on the other side and pulled on the door that connected to her grandmother's bedroom.

It was locked.

Libby stifled a cry of despair and twisted the knob harder, but it wouldn't budge. No wonder her scary uncle hadn't been concerned about her escaping. He'd already anticipated it and made sure she had no way out.

Libby's heart pounded in her chest as her eyes raked the room, searching for other possibilities. She'd stay locked in here if she had to. No way was she going back into her bedroom with Banner. The guy was probably some kind of pervert, and Ellie must know something bad about him, because she wanted Libby to get out.

She trusted Ellie. She trusted Jack, too. After all,

he was her father, and parents were supposed to care about their kids. Okay, maybe her mother hadn't cared too much, but like Deanna said, that didn't mean Jack was a loser parent. She wasn't even so sure he was a loser as a person. He didn't seem like the type of guy who'd been in jail. And he acted like he cared for her, even when she was rude to him. He certainly didn't care for Banner, and right now that was the most important point in his favor. Jack and Ellie wanted her to get away from Banner, and she agreed with that plan. But how?

The bathroom and lounge held only one possibility—a window that overlooked the backyard. Unlike the windows in her grandparents' home, the ones in this house all slid open easily and noiselessly, and screens would pop out with a good kick. The problem was what was on the other side of the window—nothing. Her grandmother's private balcony ended at least eight feet to the left, too far to reach. Hers was even farther away to the right. The only thing nearby was one of the upper branches of the huge oak tree that grew outside the breakfast room. She'd never be able to climb down the tree and run for help; the branches were too high up and the trunk too thick to shinny down. But she could climb from one of the sturdy branches to another and drop onto the edge of her grandmother's balcony. From there, she could escape into another part of the house. Or out the front door if Banner wasn't close behind her. She'd worry about that later. First, she had to get out of the bathroom.

The branch was near enough to touch, but a good three feet above the level of the window. If she stood on the window ledge and grabbed a handful of leaves and stems, it might be like mounting Tango at her riding lessons. Except if she slipped, the ground was a lot farther down than a fall from Tango's back.

Across the length of marble and plush carpet, a knock sounded on the door to her room. "Come on out, Libby. No more games." Banner's voice was tense and impatient.

Standing on the brocade love seat, Libby kicked out the screen, watching it sail outward before it clattered to the terrace below. She stepped onto the sill. The tree branch was at eye level an arm's length in front of her, leaves hanging limp in the still, midday heat. Two stories below her, a freshly washed stone terrace gleamed in the sunlight.

As she hesitated, one hand gripping the upper edge of the open window, a loud explosion sent wood chips hurtling all the way across her bathroom and onto the soft white carpet of the lounge.

Terror overrode caution. Clutching a handful of leaves and twigs, Libby rocked back once to get the feel of it, then let go of the window frame and vaulted into open air.

Jack rushed into the bedroom, Rocky right behind him.

"Did she get out?"

"I don't know." Ellie knew her voice trembled, but she couldn't help it. As much as she wanted to reassure Jack, she had no idea if Libby'd had time to act on her message. She stood, abandoning the computer. "Did he hang up? Did he say anything about her?"

"He started swearing, then we heard a gunshot. He told us we had fifteen minutes to get over there with

Janet before he . . ." Jack's voice faltered, then continued, "Before he started doing things to Libby."

Ellie's hand flew to her mouth while the other reached for Janet's hand beside her. "What will we do?"

"We'll drive over there, of course, right now." Janet looked firmly at each of them. "I won't let you put an innocent little girl in jeopardy in place of me. You either take me there now," she said to Rocky, "or I'll go by myself."

"I'll take you," Jack said.

"You will not!" Ellie turned on him in outrage. "Call the police, call the SWAT team, do anything but give Janet back to that monster. He's insane!"

"Maybe. That's why we have to get Libby away from him. Richard's already calling the police, but by the time they get a team in position, Banner will have done something to Libby. He'll do it, you know he will. The only way he'll release her is in exchange for Janet. I have to save her."

"But not that way!" Ellie turned to Rocky, furious that he had suddenly abandoned his role of bodyguard. "Don't tell me you're willing to let Janet walk back into Banner's clutches like a good little victim."

Rocky's mouth hardened. "I don't like it. But we don't have a choice."

Before she could explode, Jack gripped both her arms and looked her in the face. "Calm down, Ellie. It's not what you think. We're not going to simply hand her over and walk away with Libby. But it has to look like that."

Janet asked, "Then what *are* you going to do?"

"Banner doesn't know I'm here," Rocky told her.

"And he has no reason to think I'd give a damn about keeping you away from him. Jack can go in with you, do the trade, then I'll be waiting when he walks out with you."

"No police?" Ellie asked. Jack and Rocky were capable, but their plan seemed to rely too much on the macho approach.

Jack shook his head. "There's no time and no way to hide them. If we had half an hour to get a team into place, yeah, I'd wait for them. But we don't have time. Libby is in danger now. If we're lucky, we can stall Banner long enough for the police to get there. But we go in, whether they arrive on time or not." He looked from Ellie to Janet. "Are you both okay with that?"

"Yes," Janet replied.

Ellie glanced at her friend, then back at Jack. "I'm okay with it if she is."

"Good." He smiled at her, for the first time showing a small release of tension. "I'll take my phone, and I'll call you as soon as it's over."

"Excuse me?"

"Stay here with Richard, where I know you'll be safe. I'll call you as soon as we have Janet and Libby back."

She shoved her face up close to his. "I go with Janet."

While Jack's smile dissolved and Rocky rolled his eyes, Janet protested, "No, Ellie, it's not necessary for you to risk your safety—"

"Forget it. I'm not risking any more than anyone else, and I'm not getting left behind like some inept little girl while my friends do all the dirty work."

"I can't take you, Ellie," Jack said through gritted

teeth. "And I don't have time to argue about it. Banner specifically asked that you be there, and that can't mean anything good."

"He probably wants all his enemies where he can see them."

"Or where he can shoot them."

Ellie pressed her lips together. "You just said you have to give Banner what he wants. He wants Janet and me. Take me, or I go on my own. What's it going to be?"

From the doorway, Richard said, "I'll take you, if that's what you want."

She allowed a mean smile while Jack fumed, probably despising her but powerless to stop her, just like when he had first included her in his engagement farce.

She figured their relationship had come full circle.

They reached the Westfield mansion a minute past the deadline. Instead of stopping on the front drive, Jack parked by the garage, allowing Rocky and Richard to sneak out of the car undetected. As Jack, Ellie, and Janet walked to the front door, the two men crept past bushes to the large clump of greenery at the base of the front steps. Ellie looked back before they walked through the large double door. They had vanished into the dense growth beside the steps.

Rocky had been right about removing the excess shrubbery that offered concealment. Too bad Banner hadn't taken his advice.

Ellie fought to calm her trembling as they walked up the steps. "When will the police get here?" she whispered to Jack.

"I don't know. Ben said he was on his way, so it shouldn't be more than five minutes."

"We can't wait, we're already late," Janet said, motioning impatiently at Jack. "Open the door."

He stood with his hand on the brass door handle. "I can't let you be part of this, Ellie. Stay here. I'll stall him somehow."

"Or he'll be so mad he'll shoot you. No, Jack."

He didn't budge. She thought he was about to say something else, when Janet pushed past him and opened the door.

"I'm here, Banner!" she called out as she strode inside.

They had no choice but to follow her.

They walked through a silent house, footsteps echoing across the marble foyer, then absorbed soundlessly into thick carpets. Ellie saw no sign of Mr. Peters, the kitchen staff, or the downstairs maid and knew they had been dismissed for the day.

At the library, their designated meeting spot, both carved wooden doors hung open. Banner stood in front of his desk, leaning casually against the very spot where Jack had first assaulted Ellie, then backed her into the most staggering kiss of her life. It wasn't exactly like desecrating an altar, but she resented his butt being where hers had happily rested.

Jack's eyes swept the room. "Where's Libby?"

"Nearby." He motioned with the gun. "Come all the way in, Jack. You too, Ellie." His eyes went beyond them and his teeth showed in a feral smile.

"Hello, Janet, how good to see you. You're looking well."

"For a dead woman?" she asked, brushing past

Ellie. Jack made a grab at her arm, but she eluded him, walking right up to Banner. "Sorry I missed the funeral. I hope it was lavish."

"Naturally, my dear, you're a Westfield."

"Not for long. What's the plan, leave the country?"

"Of course."

"I didn't bring my passport."

Jack interrupted, "And Banner didn't bring Libby, so no one's going anywhere. Where is she, Banner? I have to know she's okay before you can take Janet."

"Really?" Banner raised the gun he'd been holding casually and pointed the long steel barrel at Jack. "I don't think I have to do *anything* you say, Jack. Maybe I won't tell you where she is, just so you'll have something constructive to do while I make my escape."

"Maybe you don't have her."

Banner's face became stormy with sudden loathing for Jack. "And maybe I shot her! Did you think of that?" he yelled, relishing the flush of anger Jack fought to control. Ignoring Janet, he walked toward Jack as he spoke, the gun pointing steadily ahead. "I can see you're worried about that. Well, let me give you something else to worry about."

In a rapid move, his arm shot out and he pulled Ellie to his side, the gun never wavering from Jack's chest. Ellie gasped, and Jack reached toward her.

"Uh, uh, uh," Banner warned. "Back off, brother." The gun swung toward Ellie's chest, digging painfully into her ribs below her right breast. She tried to move away but he held her fast.

Ellie's senses narrowed. She saw the blue steel burrowing into her, felt the hard grip of Banner's arm around her, and smelled the light spice of an exotic aftershave on the cheek that brushed her hair. Raising her eyes, she met Jack's alarmed look.

His chest rose and fell visibly as he shifted his eyes from hers to the gun to Banner. They hadn't anticipated this. "Let her go," he said, his voice a low growl.

"What are you doing?" Janet cried, rushing around from behind them. "I'm the one you want. Let her go!"

Janet grabbed for the arm that encircled Ellie, but Jack yanked her back against him. She struggled and flailed, but he held her tightly.

"Don't touch him, Janet," he ordered. "The safety might be off, and that gun has a hair trigger."

"Very wise," Banner said, taking a precautionary step backward.

Janet quieted instantly, staring at the gun in horror, and Jack released her. Ellie had no idea what a safety looked like, never mind how to tell if it was on or off, but she believed Jack and canceled her plan to kick, claw, and bite her way free. She would have to trust him to come up with an idea to get her away from Banner.

"I'm the one you want," Janet croaked at Banner through a fear-tightened throat.

"No, my sweet, I'm afraid not. Ellie is the one I want. You see, my big brother here is the one who wants to stop me. He never knew his dear departed sister-in-law, and he's never been one to waste sentiment on family members, have you, Jack?"

"I wonder why," Jack muttered.

"I found that rather sensible. But then his little bastard showed up and found his weakness, which I am only too happy to exploit. He might allow you to get killed, Janet, but not his precious Libby. And I believe your friend Ellie here—or is it Nora?—has managed to wiggle her way into his new soft spot, so she makes a far better hostage than you, my dear. When I'm safely away, maybe I'll release Ellie. And when I'm out of the country, I'll tell you where to find Libby."

He turned slightly to face Jack, who had taken a couple steps to the side. The gun barrel slipped lower and now dug into Ellie's liver, not an improvement. "Do we have an understanding?"

"Not really." Jack no longer looked disturbed, which Ellie found annoying, since she was becoming more protective of her liver by the second. "You're assuming that threatening Ellie will keep me away from you, when you know she's not who I said she was. She did me the favor of posing as my fiancée so I could get Libby. She's a ringer, Banner. An impostor." He smiled smugly, and Ellie's faith wavered.

Banner shoved the gun harder against her side and it burrowed deeper, which Ellie would not have thought possible. She gave a small cry of pain, but Janet was the only one who showed concern. Banner's attention was on Jack.

"I'm walking out of here, and if anyone tries to stop me, Ellie dies."

"Okay."

"Stand aside."

"No. Go ahead and shoot her."

Ellie nearly forgot about the gun impaling her liver. *This* was his plan?

While Banner narrowed his eyes at Jack, trying to judge his seriousness, and Jack stared back, Ellie sucked her stomach flat and tried to execute a belly-dance ripple that would shift the pressure to some other internal organ. A couple inches lower and a gunshot would merely perform an appendectomy and take out a kidney. She could spare a kidney.

The staring contest had her so tense, Ellie thought the rhythmic tapping she heard was her heart knocking against her bruised ribs. When the tapping faded to soft pads and heads turned toward the doorway, she knew it was footsteps in the hallway and not her heart. Elizabeth Westfield breezed through the doorway as if whatever was transpiring could not be worthy of her notice. She walked past Jack and Janet without acknowledgment, and trickier yet, stared right through Ellie with her upper-class gaze that granted visibility to only a select few. Her eyes fastened on Banner.

"What is going on here?" she demanded.

Ellie relaxed with relief, or at least as much relaxation as the intruding muzzle would allow. Whatever happened, Banner wouldn't shoot anyone in front of his mother.

"Hello, Mother. Sorry for the disturbance. I'm just taking care of an embarrassing family problem without creating a police scene."

Elizabeth's cold gaze took in Ellie and Janet for the first time, then went back to Banner. "I appreciate your discretion."

Ellie groaned and closed her eyes. She was toast.

Jack wasn't taking it well. "Discretion! He's threatening to kill Ellie, and he may already have harmed Libby. There's no way the police won't know about this."

"Is this true, Banner?" Elizabeth's eyebrow raised in a tiny show of concern.

"I'll be gone before they know anything happened. And Libby and Jack will be just fine if they do what they're told."

Ellie and Janet were conspicuously missing from the list of survivors, but if Elizabeth noticed, she wasn't bothered. She simply nodded once, no doubt agreeing that if Jack obeyed the rules more often, they'd all be better off.

"You aren't going anywhere until I have my daughter," Jack said, fury tightening his jaw and shadowing the dark brown eyes.

Don't forget about me, Ellie wanted to yell, then decided it might be better if everyone *did* forget about her. She kept silent and listened to Jack turn his outrage on his mother.

"I can't believe you're letting him do this! He tried to kill Janet, he may have killed Libby, and he's threatening Ellie. Are you blind?"

Jack didn't wither and die at his mother's look, but a lesser man might have. "You heard your brother say that Libby will be fine. As for the others, they are not family."

"Family! Is that all that's important to you? Then you may be interested to know that Banner is using the family business to launder drug money and take a nice cut for himself on the side. How do you think that makes your precious family look?"

"Westfield-Benton has prospered under Banner. I believe that reflects well on our family."

"It won't prosper when the shareholders learn that Banner bribed public officials and arranged Joe Benton's death."

Ellie felt Banner's grip tighten as Elizabeth turned her frigid gaze on Jack. Standing even more ramrod straight than before, she lectured him in a voice as hard as steel.

"Enough! Jack Payton, I will not allow you to spread vicious rumors about your brother. Banner has led an upstanding life while you have embarrassed this family at every turn with your excessive lifestyle and public flaunting of rules. You have proven that you have no respect for decent society, and I refuse to listen to more of your lies. Furthermore, if you hope to have continued contact with your daughter, I expect you to drop these slanderous accusations immediately."

Ellie groaned. Just when Elizabeth had begun to seem human.

Ellie heard a chuckle in her ear as Jack turned red with rage. "Breeding shows, big brother. You never had enough class to run Westfield-Benton. Too bad—we all hoped the Payton genes would dominate. It might have justified Mother's early departure from Wellesley just because of you."

Wellesley?

As Jack unleashed a string of profanities, Ellie looked at Elizabeth with dawning insight. Elizabeth had been away at college when she became pregnant with Jack, not here in Bloomfield Hills. Wellesley was in Massachusetts.

Elizabeth's eyes met Ellie's, then flicked back to Banner. It was enough.

Elizabeth saw it. Jack hadn't made the connection, but Ellie had.

Elizabeth spoke sharply to Banner. "Leave now. We can take care of the details later."

Ellie assumed she and Janet were the details. Banner nodded, moved the gun out of her side, and shoved her toward the door.

"Wait."

Banner turned at his mother's order.

"Leave her here and give me the gun. You'll travel faster without her."

A frown creased his forehead. "She's my insurance."

"You don't need any as long as they don't talk to anyone. I'll see that they don't."

"What will you do about—"

"Your father knew people. Our hands will be clean."

The handsome face became thoughtful, then nodded. The hand that gripped Ellie's arm spun her toward Jack.

"Here, brother. You can have her back."

Jack tensed and looked ready to leap at Banner. Ellie expected another shove, but was stunned by a sudden blow to the back of her head. She staggered forward and sprawled on the floor at Jack's feet.

Her brain registered Janet's scream, but her eyes were having trouble focusing, watching Jack's two feet become four, then two, then four again. He knelt and pulled her to a sitting position, holding her spinning head in his hands. Steadying her wobbly head seemed to help her eyes, which stopped splitting Jack into two people, and allowed her brain to register the sharp pain at the back of her head.

Jack held her shoulders and forced her to focus on his face. "Ellie, look at me. Are you okay?"

"Ow," she replied, raising a hand to her throbbing head.

That was apparently good enough for Jack. He stood and took two long strides toward the door.

"Stop!"

Ellie turned and blinked up at Elizabeth. Banner's gun was now in her hand, and it pointed at Jack. In a steady voice she told him, "You will wait here."

"You're crazy. If you won't stop Banner, I will. Or you can shoot me. Would you go that far, Mother?"

The gun swung toward Ellie where she sat on the floor. "Of course not. I'd shoot her."

For a fleeting moment Ellie had hoped that all of Elizabeth's arrogant talk had been a ruse to get Banner to give up the gun. If it had, it didn't do her any good. The hand that pointed the gun at her now was as unwavering as Banner's had been, and the face as determined. It was an unlikely change from the pleasant woman who'd sat with Ellie beside the pool yesterday, but she wasn't about to argue with a gun.

Jack was having a harder time accepting it. More stunned than anything else, he shook his head as he looked at his mother. "I don't believe this. This isn't you."

"Don't test me, Jack." Both hands went around the butt of the gun in what appeared to be an experienced brace.

Jack helped Ellie to her feet without taking his eyes off his mother. From the look on his face, he still doubted his mother's threat, but he was careful to stand between her and Ellie.

"What happens now?" he asked.

Elizabeth didn't answer. For several seconds more she held the gun on them while Ellie listened to her own hammering heart and nervous breaths. What was she waiting for?

Sudden yelling erupted outside, and all four whipped their gazes toward the library door. Ellie remembered Rocky and Richard, and pictured them tackling Banner as he left. The police had probably arrived by now, too. That had to be the cause of the shouting. Elation lasted two seconds before Ellie remembered that Elizabeth still had a gun pointed at them. At her. She turned wary eyes back to Elizabeth, braced for an angry reaction.

It didn't happen.

As if the commotion had been a signal, Elizabeth's hand wavered, fell, then dropped the gun. Her three hostages stared as the controlled expression sagged and one tear rolled down a cheek. Dazed, her eyes found Jack's.

"Mother?"

"I'm so sorry," she whispered.

He stepped forward. Elizabeth pressed her eyes closed and leaned into her son as he gathered her in his arms. She didn't cling or sob hysterically, but her quiet despair was more painful to watch than hysterics. A soft tremor shook her body, and Jack raised his eyes to Ellie in a helpless glance.

She shook her head, as confused as he was about what had just happened.

He pointed at the gun. Ellie handed it to him gingerly and watched as, with one deft movement, he released the bullet clip. It hit the Oriental rug with a dull thud, followed by a sharper thump as Jack tossed the gun in the other direction. It landed near the door, beside someone's feet.

"Jesus!"

Richard jumped aside and looked at the gun as if it were a poisonous snake.

"Richard!" Ellie cried. "What happened?"

"Where's Rocky?" Jack demanded.

With a cautious look, Richard sidestepped the gun. "He's helping Ben take Banner to the police station. They sent me to find you guys."

"Ben?" Jack looked at his mother, who had taken a step back and was doing her best to look composed in front of the stranger in her house.

She nodded, her eyes on Jack. "When Banner implied that Eleanor was trying to steal from us, I knew something was wrong. With Banner," she added, glancing at Ellie to make sure she hadn't been misunderstood. "I went to Ben, and he told me about your accident, Jack, and everything you suspected Banner of doing." The look she gave Janet was raw with pain, and Ellie remembered that Elizabeth was seeing her daughter-in-law for the first time since Janet's supposed death. "I'm so sorry," she said to her daughter-in-law, her voice whispery with grief. "I don't know what else to say."

While Janet nodded, Elizabeth turned to her son. "I'm sorry I said those things about you, Jack. I had to let Banner think I was on his side. He's . . . I think he's crazy."

He put a hand on her shoulder. "It's all right, Mother, I understand. In fact, you probably saved Ellie's life."

He actually looked grateful. He'd better. After daring Banner to go ahead and shoot her, a little reassurance that he cared wouldn't hurt.

"We can talk about it later," he told Elizabeth. "Right now I have to get Banner to tell us what he did with Libby, and I hope I have to break some bones to do it."

Elizabeth shook her head. "Ben will have taken him away by now. He said he'd make sure the arrest was quick and quiet."

Ellie rolled her eyes. Heaven forbid that the neighbors learn a Westfield had been arrested.

Jack turned anxious eyes to Richard. "Did he say anything about my daughter? Did anyone ask him?"

"Rocky did. All he could get out of him was a request to see his attorney. Even when he used a little, um, persuasion."

Desperation crossed Jack's face. "We've got to find her. She could be hurt." He turned to his mother, who was hugging herself as if the spot where she stood were twenty degrees colder than the rest of the room. "Mother, I have to go."

"I'll stay with her," Janet interrupted, stepping forward and putting an arm around Elizabeth's shoulder. "The rest of you go look for Libby. She's probably just hiding somewhere, like you told her to."

"Yeah." Jack didn't sound convinced. "But where?"

They started by checking her bedroom. When Jack saw the open bathroom window he grew hopeful, but after leaning out to reach a branch, his expression turned grim.

"I don't think she could have made it."

"Well, there's no body down there," Richard said, looking at the empty patio below. Reassuring, if not terribly sensitive.

"She's agile, she might have made it," Ellie told Jack. "Besides, I don't think Banner had enough time to tie her up and hide her."

"It doesn't take much time to shoot someone." When no one had an argument for that, he said, "I'll search the grounds. You two start up here. Call her name, and look *everywhere*."

Ellie called Libby, but working on the theory that she could be tied and gagged, or worse, she tore the rooms apart. In seven bedrooms and six baths she found an amazing number of chests, closets, and crawl spaces, but no Libby. Thirty minutes later, they decided she had either gone safely out the window, or Banner had taken her someplace else.

When they met Jack downstairs, he was covered with scratches and dirt. Ellie knew before he shook his head that he'd had no luck.

"Do you think she could have run to a neighbor's house?" she asked.

"Not likely. By now she'd have heard me calling outside or seen our cars out front and come back. I think she stayed here." Not a hopeful thought, since she hadn't appeared on her own.

They searched with renewed determination, Jack on the main floor, Ellie and Richard on the lower level. The rooms were larger with fewer places to hide, and it wasn't long before Ellie decided Libby hadn't gone downstairs. Jack joined them and repeated their efforts until he came back to his starting point and kicked the pool table in frustration.

"Damn it, where is she? Maybe I should go to the police station and have a private chat with Banner." He scowled at nothing as he said it, and she realized he was serious. "Ben's pretty rigid about the law, but he might look the other way while Banner has an accidental run-in with my fists."

"I'm sure he would." She knew what Jack didn't and thought that Ben would let him thoroughly rearrange Banner's face if it meant finding Jack's daughter. He might even help.

"Then I'm going. We're just wasting time here."

"Hey, what's this?"

They looked across the room to Richard, who was fingering the oak panel next to the fireplace. "There's a crack here, like it opens."

"It does," Ellie told him. "It has a hidden mechanism on the other side that releases it, but it's too high for Libby to reach."

They watched Richard explore the panel's edges. "I didn't look in there," Jack said. "Did you?"

Ellie shook her head. "Libby'd never be able to reach the switch. It's about where Richard's hand is now, and he's over six feet tall and stretching as high as he can."

Jack watched Richard grope along the panel and mused, "Unless she stood on something . . ."

"Like what? There's nothing there but a stone wall."

Jack's brows knit thoughtfully. "Have you ever seen those walls climbers use for practice? The handholds are pieces of rock that jut out no farther than those chunks of granite."

They looked at each other for two seconds, recalling Libby's lithe athletic build. At the same moment, Richard crowed, "Aha!" and pushed against the oak panel, revealing the pitch-black doorway to the wine cellar.

Ellie followed as Jack hurried past the poker table. She didn't think Richard would grope his way into the darkness before Jack could turn on the lights, but her ex-boyfriend was evidently tired of taking second place to Jack. Before she could say, "Wait," he stepped into the black opening and yelled, "Lib—"

Richard's shout ended abruptly with a grunt and a thud.

She was beside Jack as he stopped at the dark doorway and felt for the light switch. Rows of ceiling lights flickered, then blazed between the wine racks. Three feet in front of them, Richard lay crumpled on the tile floor. Standing over him, a dazed Libby blinked and squinted against the light, a wine bottle still dangling from her hand.

"Dad!"

The bottle hit the floor, rolling with a sharp, gritty sound across the tile, as Libby threw herself at Jack. While he folded her against his chest, Ellie rushed past them and bent over Richard.

A dark patch of blood stained the side of his head, but the faint moan told her he was alive. She lifted his hair, reassured by the tiny cut and his protesting groan that the blow had been more glancing than direct.

She met Jack's gaze over the dark head buried against his shirt. His smile trembled and his eyes shone with more than their usual brightness. Ellie grinned back. She knew Libby would never utter a single word in her life more meaningful than the one he'd just heard.

Jack pried his daughter away and held her by the shoulders, eyes scanning her body. "Are you okay? Banner didn't hurt you?"

Libby shook her head. "He tried to shoot me, but he missed. And I tried to run away, but he was on the first floor watching the doors, so I had to go to the basement." Her voice was steady, but when she turned toward Richard's groaning form, Ellie could see tears on her cheeks despite the stoic Payton calm. "I thought that man was Banner."

"So you hit him," Jack said with approval.

Libby nodded. "Who is he? Is he okay?"

"He's an old friend of mine," Ellie told her. "And he'll be fine." Just awfully damn pissed off about a third lump on his head.

Jack picked up the wine bottle that had come to rest next to him. "Didn't even crack. I guess we'll have to drink it now that it's been shaken up."

"You don't drink," Libby reminded him.

"I may start making a few exceptions to that." At her disapproving look, he added, "Don't worry, I don't have a drinking problem, honey. I still owe you an explanation about that, don't I? We'd better make plans for that fancy dinner with Ellie so I can tell you the whole story."

"Can we go tonight?" She was recovering quickly from the day's horrific experience, but Ellie was getting used to Libby's emotional leaps.

Jack made a small grimace. "I might have to take care of some business with the police tonight, and I'd like to spend some time with your grandmother. I think this family has a lot to talk about."

More than you know, Ellie thought.

"How about tomorrow night?" he asked her.

"Okay."

"But we can open this tonight and toast your clever

escape." Jack turned the bottle, read the label, and laughed. "Hey, a 2000 Lafite Rothschild." He ruffled Libby's hair fondly. "Over three hundred dollars a bottle. You must be a Payton, kid. You have excellent taste."

"Ben should be here."

Elizabeth paced in front of the soaring wall of glass in the living room, so distraught she had twisted her scarf into a thin rope. It obviously made Jack uncomfortable.

"Then wait for him. Whatever you want to tell me can wait until tomorrow."

"No." Elizabeth stopped and faced her son. "It's waited too long already. Ben wanted me to tell you years ago, and I wouldn't. And now Ellie has figured it out"—Jack looked at Ellie, confused—"and Banner almost did, or maybe he did and that's why he hated you." She paused, her expression regretful and the fingernails of her clasped hands digging into the pale, soft skin.

"Mother, what in the hell—" He glanced at Libby sitting beside him on the couch. "What in the heck are you talking about?"

"I'm talking about your father."

Jack straightened and darted another glance at Ellie before addressing his mother. "Ellie said you'd mentioned him during Libby's riding lesson. She said . . . she said you loved him."

"Yes, I do." The change in tense was not lost on Jack. "I loved him when we met at college, and I still love him. I've never loved anyone else."

"You still love . . ." Jack's puzzled expression gradually turned to amazement as he figured it out, and Elizabeth's confirmation was hardly necessary.

"Ben Thatcher is your father."

She stood still, her clasped hands digging into each other, and watched while her son absorbed her confession.

Jack's eyes bore into his mother's and his brow developed a deep crease. He began, "How . . . ," then changed to "Why . . . ," before slumping back and staring wordlessly. "Ben," he finally stated.

"Yes, Ben." Her voice was soft but no one had a problem hearing her. She had their rapt attention. "We met at a party when I was at Wellesley. We fell in love quickly, so quickly I could hardly believe what was happening to me. He wanted to get married, but I kept putting him off."

"Why?"

"Because—" She squeezed her eyes shut. "This sounds so stupid now, but it was because he was Jewish."

Jack's mouth dropped open. "That's it? For God's sake, Mother, you of all people . . ."

"I know, it sounds ridiculous, but my father would have disapproved."

Jack's face turned dark. "So what? Grandfather was an ignorant, hateful bigot."

She sighed. "Yes, he was. And if I married Ben, he would have disowned me. I had a choice between raising my family in wealth and privilege, or on a military base with the man I loved. I made the wrong choice. When I learned I was pregnant, I didn't tell Ben. By the time he got out of the service and decided to try to convince me to marry him again, I had already married Leonard Westfield and had another son."

Jack dropped the issue of marriage. "Why didn't you ever tell me?"

Elizabeth fidgeted again. "I didn't want to appear to love one of my sons more than the other. And I did, Jack. I couldn't help it, but you were more special to me because you were Ben's child, and I never loved Leonard. I couldn't let Leonard and Banner know that. So I never told you, or them. I tried so hard not to play favorites that I was harder on you than I was on Banner." She hesitated, then said, "I'm so sorry, Jack."

"It doesn't matter," he said, brushing it aside and getting to the important part. "Did Ben know?"

She smiled. "Oh, yes. He could do the math, see how old you were and count the months and years since I'd left. Besides, I'd named you after both of us."

"John Michael?" Jack said his name aloud, confused.

"You have our middle names. Benjamin John Thatcher and Elizabeth Michelle Payton."

Libby giggled. "We have the same middle name."

Jack looked at his daughter, his face gradually relaxing into a smile. "Cool," he told her, making her giggle again.

Libby looked eagerly at her grandmother. "I like Ben. Do you think I could call him Grandpa Ben?"

Elizabeth caught her breath sharply and her eyes grew suddenly moist. "I think he'd like that," she said.

Jack turned a speculative look on his mother. "After all these years I think I'll stick with calling him Ben." He shook his head and smiled again, a gentle smile that seemed to touch something deep inside Elizabeth.

"I wish I'd known about twenty years ago, when he was giving me such a hard time for being a major screwup. I couldn't understand why the police chief chose me to pick on all the time. Guess that was some weird sort of favoritism, huh?"

Elizabeth couldn't hide her amusement. "Ben swore a lot during your teenage years."

"So did I." Jack looked at Libby. "Hey, let's not give the kid any bad examples. So far, I kinda like her."

Libby smiled and rammed her fist into his in some sort of knuckle-tapping bonding routine they'd developed. Ellie's throat tightened with happiness at the mutual affection on their faces.

Elizabeth must have felt it, too. "I'm sorry you missed so much with Ben. I made a mistake, and you paid for it."

"Stop apologizing, Mother," Jack told her. "I've made enough mistakes to know you have to put them behind you if you want to move forward. I think we've got a pretty good little family going here. Don't we, brat?"

Libby's mood was as playful as his. "I'm not a brat."

"No? What are you?"

"I'm a woman."

Jack clutched his chest. "Don't do that to me. I'm only thirty-five."

"Okay," she relented, as if making a major concession. "I'm a girl."

"No, you're not. You're my girl."

Knuckles rapped again.

It was a sweet moment, and Ellie felt completely closed out of it. Jack didn't notice. He could have said he had two girls, or that Libby had to be his girl because he already had a woman. He could have said something that included her in that intimate circle. It would have been the perfect opportunity to let her know he cared.

He didn't.

Chapter Sixteen

—

"It's a really bad idea."

Jack looked at his daughter's stubbornly crossed arms and recognized his own obstinate personality. She couldn't be convinced on this point.

He gave her the rational explanation. "I don't want to do it, but I don't have any choice. You'll just have to trust me on this."

"It's risky," Libby insisted. "She'll hate you."

"Only for a minute."

Libby's condescending look was as good as her grandmother's. With precocious insight, she asked, "And then she'll get over it, just like that?"

The kid had a point. Jack had never known a woman to get past a humiliating insult in the space of one minute. Possibly not in a year. And the last thing he wanted to do to Ellie was humiliate her. He just didn't see any way around it.

He fell back on experience to convince himself and Libby that this was the right thing to do. "I dated a lot of women before you came along—well, mostly after you came along, but before I knew you—and I did just fine."

Libby frowned as if he'd told a fib. "You did not."

"Yeah? How would you know?"

With all the superiority of a twelve-year-old, she said, "You're not married."

"No, I'm not. That's how I know I did everything right."

Libby shook her head at the hopeless ignorance of men.

He loved it. Arguments with his daughter were the most refreshing, honest conversations he'd ever had with a member of the opposite sex. Except for Ellie. She never hesitated to slap him with the truth, either.

Libby placed her hands on her hips, exasperated. "Look, Jack. Dad." She rushed past her verbal slip while Jack's stomach did the giddy flip he felt each time she used his new title. "Do you want to be married or not?"

"Yes. I mean—" He forced himself to be deliberately solemn as he intoned, "I do."

God, he was getting silly. He wondered if that meant he was in love, or that he was just spending too much time hanging out with a twelve-year-old.

"Well, you won't be if you screw this part up."

That seemed unlikely. "You mean this one thing is that important?"

"Oh, yes." She was so sincere he became intimidated all over again. "I've read *lots* of stories about it. It's supposed to be magical."

"Now you're scaring me," he said, only half kidding. "I don't know how to be magical."

"Don't worry. If she loves you, it'll be magical."

Damn, now he really was scared. He had no idea if Ellie loved him. One drowsy "Love ya" was not a clear indication. If incredible sex and heart-stopping kisses meant anything, she certainly liked him, although even that was going to change once he set this stupid plan in motion. She'd have to love him in order to stick around for the whole scene.

"I'm going to need all the help I can get, Libby. If she looks at you, try to give her the hopeful big-brown-eyes look. She couldn't say no to such a pretty face."

"Okay," Libby said, then grew quiet, sucking in her lower lip and biting it thoughtfully. Finally, she said, "If I ask you something, will you give me an honest answer?"

"Always."

Her hesitation underlined the importance of the question. "If you were my age, would you think I'm pretty?"

That was easy. "Yes, absolutely."

The dark eyebrows puckered together. "You're not just saying what fathers are supposed to tell their daughters?"

"Honey, I have no idea what fathers are supposed to say. But I do know how twelve-year-old boys think, and I can assure you they have already noticed how pretty you are."

"What about thirteen- or fourteen-year-old boys?"

Shit. Steven Beyer again. He was not ready for this.

"Forget it. They have dirty little minds and I'll kill the first one who comes near you."

She smiled at that. "No, you won't."

"Ha. You don't know me."

"Yes, I do. You feel guilty about your past, and you

transfer it to being overprotective of me. Except you shouldn't do that."

He narrowed his eyes at her. The kid soaked up psychology like a sponge. "I'm gonna sue that therapist of yours."

"When can I go on a date?"

"When you're twenty-one. And I'm going along."

"Fifteen."

"Ha! Can we just get me married before we work on the love life you're not even allowed to have?"

"Okay." She adopted a more serious look as she watched him put on his tie. "You know, you should have done this right the first time, instead of pretending to be engaged."

"You're right." He hadn't wanted to explain that he'd known Ellie all of five minutes when he'd made her his fiancée. "But I wasn't sure she'd say yes."

Libby looked worried. "How sure are you now?"

After what he was about to do? He sighed. "Not at all."

Ellie's hand tightened around the phone in frustration. The woman wouldn't take no for an answer.

"I'm sorry," she said for the third time. "I appreciate Mrs. Hampshire's recommendation, but we aren't ready to do new installations. We've just . . . Yes, of course he knows how." By now she was sure Rocky could do anything with alarm systems. "We could probably recommend another . . . A consultation?" She sighed, too tired to argue. "I'll have Rocky give you a call." It wasn't her problem. Rocky could decide if Red Rose Security was ready to install new systems. The business was going to be his in two days, anyway.

Scribbling Rocky's cell phone number on a slip of paper, she handed it to Mr. Peters, who was in the front entry supervising the daily floral delivery.

"If I get any more calls for Red Rose Security, please forward them to Rocky at this number."

"Yes, Miss Coggins."

She watched the delivery boy heft yesterday's flower arrangement and start toward the door, the multicolored spray as perky and fresh as when it was first delivered. A red rose poked above the other blossoms, bobbing with the boy's strides.

"Wait."

She caught up with the boy and pulled the rose from the bouquet. She smiled her thanks and sniffed the tender petals as she walked up the staircase. If she pressed it right away, it might last a few years before crumbling to dust. Long enough to help soften the pain of leaving Jack and Libby. Long enough to remind her that she *could* be a success at something when she was ready to try again, and she *could* find a man who fulfilled her every need and every desire. That last achievement might be more difficult to duplicate, but there had to be another special man out there somewhere. Didn't there?

Ellie cradled the rose, thinking that a couple of the large magazines in her dressing room might do for pressing the delicate flower until she got home. She could get a piece of waxed paper from the kitchen and—

Ten feet into her room, she stopped. She hadn't left anything on the bed, but something lay there now. Before she even reached the bed, she recognized the sexy black dress she'd tried on during her shopping trip with Elizabeth and Libby. The one that made her feel seductive and desirable. The one she couldn't afford.

"Oh, good, it's here."

She turned, speechless, to stare at Elizabeth.

"Jack told me he'd planned a special night out with you, and I thought you might like to wear something new. It's very flattering on you, Eleanor, and I'm sure it will be perfect for the restaurant he selected."

It was far from perfect. It was dead wrong. The little black dress was made for temptation and seduction, not for saying good-bye and thanks for the memories. Then there was that coronary-inducing price tag.

"Elizabeth, it's wonderful, but I really can't accept something like this. It's too much. I have a dress that I know will be appropriate."

"I'm sure you do. Let me give you some advice, Eleanor: Never settle for appropriate when you can have fabulous." Elizabeth tipped her head and gave her a meaningful look. "You might want to get used to that philosophy. I'm releasing control of Jack's trust fund, which will provide his family with more than you could ever want or imagine."

That again. "I don't want Jack's money."

"I know you don't."

Ellie lifted her eyebrows and Elizabeth smiled. "I've learned some things about you since you've been here, and what's more, I've watched you with my son. I know you didn't choose Jack for his money, Eleanor. You're in love with him."

She couldn't deny it this time. But since Jack had passed on every opportunity to say he loved her, she had to accept that for him their relationship had stalled out at friendship. He'd been completely satisfied when she'd called him a friend. Hell, he'd been satisfied to simply be the object of her desire. How could she blame him? He was rich, handsome, and charming. He could have a dozen Christinas vying for his bed without ever having to say the dreaded "L" word.

Ellie smiled weakly. "This dress is too nice for a simple dinner."

"He told me it was a special occasion."

"Yes, we're taking Libby out, but—"

Elizabeth's voice was almost a reprimand. "It's a gift, Eleanor."

A kind and generous one. Ellie swallowed hard. "Thank you," she said softly.

Elizabeth gave her hand an affectionate squeeze. "I want to see how you look in it before you leave."

Ellie nodded. This was already a difficult evening, and it would only get worse.

She should have guessed. Elizabeth was ready with the perfect necklace to complement the dress. Ellie protested that the dark blue stone pendant was too nice, which Elizabeth brushed off with, "Nonsense, it's only quartz." Never mind that the glittering stones on each side looked suspiciously like the one on her finger, and that her parents could have quit work and retired to a Palm Beach condo on just the diamonds she wore tonight. What really got to her was how nice Elizabeth was being, giving her one more thing to feel guilty about when she left.

She was pretty sure a thank-you card was not going to cover it.

At least Libby's enthusiasm cheered her up. As unobtrusive as the girl was, Ellie had missed having her in the big Westfield mansion while Libby spent the day preparing to move into her new bedroom at Jack's house.

Libby broke into a grin as Ellie descended the stairs. "Oh my God, it's THE DRESS! I love it! Doesn't she look great?"

Jack's smile was devilish. "Better than great. Good enough to eat."

Her stomach flipped at the look he gave her. "Stop that," she whispered in his ear after brushing a light kiss across his lips. "She's twelve, not two."

Even if Libby didn't catch his meaning, Ellie's body did. Anticipatory tingles and twitches begged her to seriously consider his implication. Certain parts of her seemed to be without moral scruples when it came to Jack.

It was safer to talk about how nice Libby looked in her new dress.

"You look so grown up," Ellie told her, because it was true.

"I wanted higher heels."

"Trust me, one inch is enough. I'll let you try these torture devices on later, and you'll see what I mean." Nodding toward Jack, she asked, "Did you help him choose his clothes? Because he looks pretty handsome."

"I picked the tie and the cuff links."

"Good choice."

"She made me wear the tie tack," Jack said.

"I let him choose my nail polish."

Ellie laughed. "I'm impressed. It looks like you both spent a lot of time preparing for this evening."

Jack and Libby smiled and exchanged a sly glance,

sharing some secret. Libby giggled, and Jack did a mock scowl that silenced her, but no one let Ellie in on the joke. If she weren't so happy to see them act like a team, she might have been hurt at being left out.

And she had no right to feel hurt. Everything had worked out the way they'd planned. They had exposed Banner for the criminal he was, and thanks to Elizabeth's recommendation, Jack was getting custody of Libby. He hadn't even had to marry her to do it. Falling in love had never been part of the deal. She told herself to focus on everything they'd done right, instead of the one thing she'd done wrong.

Jack held an arm out for each of them and escorted them to the Jeep. As Ellie considered the best way to lift her leg over the running board, Jack took her hand for balance and grinned. "It may not be the most elegant vehicle, but this has become my favorite part of owning it."

"Why?" she said, occupied with keeping her dress in place while ducking under the roof.

"Because he gets to look at your legs," Libby told him from the backseat. "Great, my dad's a perv."

"Your dad's normal," he told her.

"You don't want boys to look at me like that."

"That's different."

"Why?"

"Because I said so." He paused, looking startled. "I don't believe I said that. I *must* be a parent." He gave Ellie a triumphant smile.

Damn, it was going to be tough to say good-bye to this guy.

Ellie was intimidated by the restaurant. The cuisine was French and the crystal Waterford, with a different

tuxedoed waiter for each item offered—six waiters by
Ellie's count, from the menu to the dessert. Libby was
unimpressed by the food but fascinated with the story
they'd promised her of Banner's crimes and her dad's
innocence.

"That's better than a TV show," she said with appreciation.

"Depends on your point of view," Jack told her.

"What happened to the drug dealers at the cleaning
supply company?".

"The Drug Enforcement Agency will take care of
them. Ben supplied them with all the information we
had."

"Grandpa Ben," she corrected, smiling.

"Yeah." Jack shook his head as if that part hadn't
sunk in yet.

They talked about Ben while they finished eating,
as Jack recounted all the times growing up when Ben
had acted as more than a police officer. Libby listened
quietly and Ellie thought she was bored until she noticed the darting looks at Jack and the restless way she
fingered her silverware. She almost looked nervous.

Jack ignored his daughter's frequent glances until
they were down to the coffee and Libby's ice cream
sundae. Then he set down his cup, pushed it aside, and
looked a little nervous himself. Ellie waited, puzzled.
Something was going on.

Jack cleared his throat, met Ellie's eyes briefly, then
looked away. "Um, Ellie?"

She waited.

"I need the ring back."

She blinked with surprise. Did he think she'd intended to keep it?

"I know," she said, and shot a self-conscious glance at Libby. They shouldn't do this in front of her.

"I need it now."

She couldn't believe she'd heard him correctly. "Now? Here?"

"Yes, now."

She looked at the determined line of his mouth, then at Libby's pained expression. Pained, but not surprised. She knew. He'd planned this.

Anger surged through her, mixed with embarrassment. After all their tender moments, this was how he chose to end it? Fine. He'd just made it easier to say good-bye.

She tugged on the ring and slapped it down on the table hard enough to steady the shaking in her hand.

"There, take it." A lot more words wanted to come out, but they were all things Libby shouldn't hear.

He picked it up, actually looking relieved. Bastard. She should have made it harder on him. Should have let him look like the jerk he was, instead of meekly avoiding a scene. Let Libby's wide, anxious eyes see him for what he was. She should have—

What happened, did he drop the stupid thing?

"What are you doing?" she whispered harshly as he knelt beside her chair.

"Exactly what you wanted."

He held something out to her, something small and black. She recognized it. The ring box, with the ring sitting back in its place, capturing every subdued ray of light and reflecting it back in brilliant rainbow facets.

Oh, no. She realized what was happening before he said it.

"Ellie Coggins, will you marry me?"

She stared at the ring and trembled. He was making this harder than she ever imagined it could be. He wanted a mother for Libby after all, and Libby had probably agreed. The two of them had plotted this together. Didn't he realize there was more to marriage than that?

"Jack, please don't do this now," she whispered, no longer willing to embarrass him and hurt Libby.

"I have to. It's part of the script. You're the one who thought this was such a romantic scenario, remember?"

She could kick herself for that particular fabrication. "Can't we talk about it later?"

"No. I think those two couples at the next table are waiting for your answer, too. Should I repeat the question?"

Oh no, people were watching. "For God's sake, Jack—"

"It's a simple question, Ellie."

"This isn't the time or place."

"You picked it."

"I'm serious, Jack."

"So am I. I love you, Ellie, and I want you to stay with me. We both want you to."

"This is so embarrassing—" Her mind faltered, then replayed the last few sentences. "What did you say?"

"I said we both want you to stay. Libby wants you to marry us, too. Marry me, I mean."

"Please say yes, Ellie," Libby urged.

She heard Libby but couldn't take her eyes off Jack. She shook her head and repeated the question, her voice barely audible even to herself. "Before that. What did you say?"

He thought. "I said I love you and—" Her expression stopped him. "Christ, Ellie, you didn't know that? I thought you'd realize, after everything we—" He glanced at Libby. "After everything. Didn't you know?"

She shook her head. He was starting to look blurry.

"I don't have any experience at saying these things, Ellie. I love you. I love you enough to get down on my knees in front of all these people, including the Hardenburgs, who are sitting two tables behind you and are going to tell everyone my mother knows, so I'd like an answer before the whole kitchen staff gets out here, too. Will you marry me?"

She couldn't answer, not yet. There was something she needed to say first, but her throat was so tight she could only whisper.

"I love you, too."

His grin was a little lopsided and it melted her heart. "I know. I was counting on that." They smiled at each other idiotically for a few seconds until a tiny wince crossed his face. "Honey, I hate to rush you, but there's a carpet tack right under my knee, and it must be digging into that old polo injury you invented for me."

She opened her mouth. On second thought, she didn't trust her voice. She nodded.

Jack smiled but didn't move. "I don't believe the Hardenburgs heard you, Ellie. Could you repeat your answer?"

The corner of his mouth quirked. She'd get him for this.

Clearing her throat and taking a deep breath, she said clearly, "Yes, I'll marry you."

Jack grinned. While a dozen people applauded and Ellie blushed, he returned the ring to her finger and kissed her.

After giving his audience a modest bow, Jack took his chair. Ellie laughed self-consciously and blotted her eyes. "You knew about this," she accused Libby.

"I helped him practice. Didn't he do good?"

"Very good," she said, skipping the grammar lesson for now. "It's a proposal I'll never forget."

"Good, because the wedding won't be the wonderful affair you probably hoped for," he told her. "I'm sorry, but we don't have time to plan anything fancy. We need to do it next week, as soon as possible."

"Next week?"

"Right after we go to Traverse City so Libby and I can meet your parents. If you want to get married up there, I'm sure Mother and Ben will come, too. I can't take much time off work right now, because Banner's arrest is going to shake up management. They want me to take the vice presidency and reassure the investors that Westfield-Benton will survive the crisis. But more important, summer will be over soon, and our daughter would like to visit her aunt Jenny in Indiana before school starts. We have to get married first."

Our daughter. Ellie's eyes turned watery again as she smiled at Libby. An odd feeling she couldn't identify fluttered in her stomach. It felt good.

"How do you feel about Evansville, Indiana, for our honeymoon?"

She couldn't stop smiling. "Sounds great."

"Aunt Jenny said it's only a couple hours' drive to

Mammoth Cave in Kentucky," Libby enthused. "We might see the bats!"

"See? You don't get bats in some fancy place like Paris," Jack told her proudly.

"Bats are wonderful. I love bats." Anything sounded good to her now.

"Don't forget about the concert," Libby said. "We can't go until after we see the Junkyard Dogs next Saturday."

Jack nodded. "The Junkyard Dogs, then Evansville and the bats. You're a lucky woman, Ellie."

"Yes, I am."

"We should probably get home and tell my mother about our plans before Mrs. Hardenburg starts calling everyone she knows."

"And I can return this necklace. I feel a little conspicuous wearing all these diamonds."

"You're worried about the *diamonds*?"

Ellie touched the necklace, puzzled. "Shouldn't I be? Aren't they real?"

"Of course they're real. Elizabeth Payton Westfield wouldn't own a fake jewel. But if expensive gemstones make you nervous, it's probably the sapphire you should worry about."

"Sapphire?" She fingered the dark blue stone. "She said it was quartz."

"And you believed her?"

"She lied to me?"

His eyes twinkled. "I think you're still a few up on her. It's a blue sapphire, the natural kind, not man-made. Probably worth several times what the diamonds are."

Ellie blanched. "Jack, I don't know how to tell you

this, but I'm not going to make a very good Payton. I'm a simple girl with simple tastes. The jewelry is beautiful, but it's not me."

"Not even the ring?"

She looked at the ostentatious stone on her finger. "Sorry, no." She smiled. "Although it does have sentimental value."

"How about if you wear it until I give you a plain gold band? Will that be simple enough for you?"

"Perfect."

She savored the idea of being married to Jack. Seeing him every day, sleeping in his arms every night, making love whenever— She glanced at Libby. Whoops.

She couldn't bring it up until they were in the parking lot with Libby far enough ahead of them that she couldn't overhear.

"Jack, parenting is a full-time job."

"You don't think we're up to it?" He called out, "Hey, Libby, promise not to turn into a rebellious teenager until we get the hang of this parenting job."

"Okay," she yelled back.

He turned to Ellie, smiling triumphantly. "See? I fixed it."

"Yeah, you're a great problem solver, but that's not what I meant. Full-time, as in day and night."

He smiled. "Ah, I see what you're getting at. Can't wait to get me in bed again, eh?"

"Yes, I'm weak with desire over your huge ego."

"Naturally. And you're wondering how we'll have enough privacy for you to have intimate knowledge of my very big ego?"

"Get over yourself, Payton."

"Can't, I'm too pleased with myself. I just got

engaged to the woman I love. And I'm not about to keep my hands off her."

Would her heart ever stop fluttering when he said he loved her? "That's good to know. But privacy may be a difficult thing to have with an active teenager in the house."

"So it might take some thought. Don't worry, Ellie." He wiggled his eyebrows. "I can be very inventive."

"You promise?" Ellie asked with a grin.

Jack smiled down at her. "Would I lie to you?"

Fall in love

with a bestseller from Pocket Books!

FERN MICHAELS
The Delta Ladies
When one man confronts two women from his past, there's
bound to be a little trouble … and a lot of passion.

JULIE GARWOOD
Heartbreaker
A thrilling excursion into the soaring heights—
and darkest impulses—of the human heart.

LINDA HOWARD, MARIAH STEWART, JILLIAN HUNTER, GERALYN DAWSON, AND MIRANDA JARRETT
Under the Boardwalk
Experience the cool breezes and hot passion of
summer loving in this unforgettable new collection!

And look for the thrilling new Bullet Catchers Trilogy by Roxanne St. Claire!

First You Run
Then You Hide
Now You Die

Available wherever books are sold
or at www.simonsayslove.com.

Catch up with love...
Catch up with passion...
Catch up with danger....

Catch a bestseller from Pocket Books!

Delve into the past with *New York Times* bestselling author
Julia London
The Dangers of Deceiving a Viscount
Beware! A lady's secrets will always be revealed...

Barbara Delinksy
Lake News
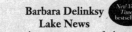
Sometimes you have to get away to find everything.

Fern Michaels
The Marriage Game
It's all fun and games—until someone falls in love.

Hester Browne
The Little Lady Agency
Why trade up if you can fix him up?

Laura Griffin
One Last Breath
Don't move. Don't breathe. Don't say a word...